LIZ *and*

NELLIE

AROUND THE WORLD IN EIGHTY DAYS

SHONNA SLAYTON

Cover design by Shonna Slayton and Jenny Adams Perinovic
Cover art © Merkushev | Dreamstime.com
Interior design by Jenny Adams Perinovic

ISBN (Print): 978-0-9974499-0-7
ISBN (E-book): 978-0-9974499-1-4

Manufactured in the United States of America

First Edition April 2016

For Mom and Dad,

Who didn't mind when I left home to explore the world

Also by Shonna Slayton

1940s
Cinderella's Dress
Cinderella's Shoes

1800s
Spindle

Foreword

A FEW YEARS ago, while conducting research for a novel set in the late 1800s, I came across the story of Nellie Bly's solo trip around the world in 1889 and was amazed. I became a bit obsessed with her story (ask my family) and dug a little deeper. Turns out, there was another woman reporter who raced against her, going in the opposite direction. Now I was doubly intrigued. What they accomplished as single women in Victorian times was simply fascinating to read. I just had to retell their tale.

This is not a story dreamed up purely out of my own head. Both young women published their experiences, and you can read their separate accounts online. In writing this novel, I preserved their actual words as much as possible, combining their public domain works to show Bly's and Bisland's alternating points of view – one going east, the other going west. Then I transformed their accounts into scenes to create a novelized version. In doing so, I had to delete (lots of flowery description) and I had to add (characters, dialogue). At the end of the novel I'll talk about some of the choices I made, and why.

As you navigate their story, take note of the chapter subheadings written in the style of Jules Verne's *Around the World in Eighty Days*, which indicate whose point of view is being expressed. Nellie Bly wrote more about her adventure, so she has more chapters than Elizabeth Bisland.

I hope you enjoy reading about these young women as much as I have.

1

Thursday, November 14, 1889

THE MORNING LIGHT GLOWS AROUND THE edges of the curtains when the maid enters and tiptoes across the bedroom toward the window. I've hardly slept a wink, and it doesn't seem right she's about to wake me up. Odd that she sneaks in so quietly. Being fond of sleep, I've never witnessed this ritual before.

She throws open the curtains with a surprising flourish and follows with a quick "Good morning, miss." She curtsies to the lump that is me on the bed, and stands patiently waiting with the breakfast tray. "Eight o'clock," she adds by way of a hint.

Despite already being fully awake, I make a show of groaning as I push myself up against the bed frame. After tucking the quilt tight up against my chest, I accept the silver tray loaded with a covered plate, a small glass of orange juice, a dainty cup of tea, and a pile of correspondence.

I scoop up the letters stacked atop the morning newspaper – replies for the five o'clock tea we are hosting tomorrow.

"Will that be all, Miss Bisland?"

"Yes, thank you." I pat the newspaper expectantly with my fingertips.

After the maid leaves, I make short work of breakfast while sorting the mail. I set aside an invitation to dinner and make a separate stack of bills. All that remains are my tea and the paper. Newspapers are a wonderful resource, despite being filled with trite, sensational writing.

I skip over Nellie Bly's latest stunt and move on to the society pages. A gentle tapping sounds at my bedroom door. *Would that girl round up some gumption and knock like she means it?*

"Come in."

The maid holds out a thick, cream colored envelope. "This just came, miss. I am to tell you it is urgent."

"Urgent?" I tip my eyebrow as I take the note and reach for my letter opener. "It's my editor at *The Cosmopolitan*. He needs me to come in as soon as possible."

My sister Molly pushes through the doorway, nudging our timid maid aside. She is already dressed in her tan wool challis. Her brown hair is swept up in a French twist, leaving her curly bangs falling over a forehead creased with concern.

"Your editor?" she asks. "But we have fittings today."

My stomach churns as I think about what the note might mean, but I turn my mouth into a smile for Molly's benefit. "I'm sure it won't take long."

I get out of bed and begin my toilet with washing my face, while Molly chooses a warm woolen dress for me. Mr. Walker has never called me in like this before. My newspaper editors did all the time, which is why I prefer working for the magazine. Of course, when I have to, I will race all over the city to write freelance features for the newspapers. My gaze lands on the stack of bills, and Molly notices.

She comes over and kisses my cheek. "Surely, as 'the most beautiful woman in Metropolitan journalism,' you are not afraid of your editor."

"Afraid? Don't be silly." *Wary.* "And it's only the writer at *The Journalist* who says that."

"They all say it," she retorts. "And you know what Mother says: Elizabeth needs to slow down so a man has a chance to get a decent look at her, or she'll never marry."

"I work with men all the time. American men aren't interested in what a woman has to say. They just want something pretty to dote over. As if I am a fancy lamp." I secure my hair with three pins.

This comment makes Molly laugh.

"Besides," I continue, "you're one to talk. You're older than I. Why aren't you getting married?"

Molly frowns at the reminder of her age but refuses to take the bait. "You wouldn't marry an editor, would you? He'd constantly be correcting you."

When I don't answer, she teases me more.

"Mr. Charles Wetmore, *esquire*, wouldn't approve of your marrying an editor. We've all noticed how he's set his cap for you."

I still don't answer, letting the heat rising up my face speak for me. The handsome Mr. Wetmore had increased his attentions toward me lately. His was one of the replies in the mail this morning: *I look forward to spending the evening together.* He had addressed the reply directly to me, not to both Molly and me as the other replies had been.

"It won't take long. I'll be back in plenty of time for our fitting." I kiss Molly on the cheek and rush off.

The offices of *The Cosmopolitan* magazine are but a few minutes walk. As soon as I step into the noisy room, every reporter stops working and watches me make my way to Mr. Walker's office. It creates an unnerving silence.

What have I done? My last article about tenement building improvements went through without comment, and the next article isn't due for another week. Yet, the secretary studies me with a bemused expression. And the men elbow each other like school children pointing out the new student.

"Mr. Walker, you wanted to see me?" I ask, settling into the chair near his desk. Mr. Walker is a handsome man, with trim black hair and matching handlebar mustache. He is also a forceful, ambitious man, intent on making a go of his newly acquired magazine. Ignoring my racing pulse, I keep my smile slight, as if I haven't a care in the world.

"Yes, Miss Bisland. You've read the Jules Verne book, have you?" He hands me a new copy of *Around the World in Eighty Days*. "Phileas Fogg and all that?"

"Of course." We had discussed the novel during one of my literary salon meetings when I lived in New Orleans.

He leans forward and stares eagerly at me. "How quick do you think a woman could go around the world?"

I examine the book cover as if it holds the answer. "I don't know. Eighty days, I suppose." I glance around. Everyone in the newsroom is watching our exchange.

"I believe you could do it in less than seventy-five."

"Me? Circumnavigate the globe?" London. Italy. Singapore. Where else did that man go? I smile, playing along with his what-if scenario. "I believe I could too."

He claps and grins, his handsome face drawing me into his excitement. "Then it's settled. How long will it take you to get a bag ready?"

"Sir?"

"You leave today."

The blood drains from my face. He is serious.

"Next spring or summer would provide better traveling conditions and give me plenty of time to map the route and make appropriate plans."

Mr. Walker is already shaking his head. "No, no. That will never do. Nellie Bly from the *New York World* left for Europe less than two hours ago aboard the steamer *Augusta Victoria*." He tosses the offending newspaper onto the desk. On the front page is a picture of Nellie Bly wearing a long black and white checkered Ulster coat and holding a small gripsack.

"This is about Nellie Bly?" My throat goes dry. "I don't wish to compete with a stunt reporter."

I stand, preparing to leave. Nellie Bly has pulled some wild schemes since moving to New York – getting committed to a mad house for one, pretending to sell a baby another. All to uncover the ill-treated of the city and sell newspapers, but mostly to sell herself. Under heaven, I don't want my name associated with hers.

Mr. Walker motions for me to sit back down. "We've done the calculations and think they have made a mistake. We can outdo them by going in the opposite direction, where the winds will be in your favor and you'll miss the January snow in the Midwest. We'll put you on the train to Chicago tonight." He circles his finger like it is the one circumnavigating the world.

"And we'll have you back here the day before Bly, even though you will have left hours after her."

"But I have fifty guests coming for tea tomorrow."

"Cancel."

"I don't have any travel clothes made up."

"Hire someone. A team!"

Silence settles as I think of my last–and most important–reason not to go. Unlike some women reporters, I am quite content writing my society articles. I relish the culture and refinement. If I do this, my name will forever be linked with that wild Bly woman – our names will be splashed across all the papers. My anonymity will be gone.

But then, consider a trip around the world! Once, when our family had money, such a trip would have been within my reach, but we lost so much during the civil war. Molly and I have talked about Europe, but with us barely making our way, we've never been serious. Could I do it? Really do it? I curl my toes in my boots, thinking back to when I first arrived in New York and the managing editor of the *Sun* advised: "My dear little girl, pack your trunk and go back home. This is no place for you."

Mr. Walker strokes his black mustache as he sizes me up. "You will be well compensated as a full-time employee."

Full-time? A reliable income. Mr. Walker is dangling a carrot that is hard to resist.

He nods towards the cluster of men, still watching. "They say you can't be packed inside of a month."

I examine the smirking group. The newest writer, a self-satisfied swarthy fellow, grins and tips his chin at me.

"They do, do they?" I lift my own chin as I focus back on Mr. Walker. "Give me the afternoon."

Mr. Walker breathes out a gust of air and leans back into his wooden desk chair. "Excellent." He reaches out to receive an itinerary from Wilson, the magazine's business manager. He studies it and frowns. "Best we can do. You are on the six o'clock train to Chicago."

"Speaking of packing, how many bags may I bring?"

Mr. Walker snaps his chair back upright. "Bly has one small gripsack. See that you find something similar."

I can't stop from lifting my eyebrows. "Oh."

There is no way I am going around the world with only one handbag, but I set my mind to pack light.

On the way home to tell my sister, I slip into the candy store below our apartment. Bad news first heard with a bag of pralines is better received than news without. Once in the apartment, the enormity of my assignment hits me, and I drop into the chair by the door.

"Liz! What is it?" Molly rushes to my side.

I hold out the candy. "I am going on a trip around the world. I leave tonight."

2

IN WHICH NELLIE BLY IS CALLED INTO HER
EDITOR'S OFFICE AND GETS WHAT SHE WANTS.

Three Days Earlier: Monday, November 11, 1889

I HELD THE NOTE IN MY HAND AS I SAT DOWN at the editor's desk. He had never summoned me with a note before, and in the evening no less. What was I to be scolded for this time? I twirled my lucky gold ring around my right thumb as I stared at him making notes on a pad. Would Cockerill hurry up and get it over with? I had plans to take Mother to *Hamlet* at the Broadway Theatre tonight.

Finally, Cockerill finished writing and looked at me. "Mr. Pulitzer wants a big story. Can you start around the world day after tomorrow?"

My heart skipped a beat. "I can start this minute," I said, jumping up and shedding all thoughts of *Hamlet*. Hadn't I proposed this scheme a year ago? Took 'em long enough to figure out it was a bang-up idea. I needed clothes, a new bag. . . and where had I filed that itinerary?

"We thought of starting you on the *City of Paris* tomorrow morning, so as to give you ample time to catch the mail train out of London. There is a chance the *Augusta Victoria*, which sails the morning afterwards, will run into rough weather, causing you to miss your connection with the mail train."

"I will take my chances on the *Augusta Victoria* and save one extra day," I said, deciding quickly. The *Augusta Victoria* had recently set a speed record crossing the Atlantic. If I were to beat Jules Verne's eighty days, that would be the ship to do it on.

"Have you a passport?"

I bit my lip. "No. Will that be a problem?"

Cockerill waved in Mr. Van Zile, the one unlucky enough to be closest to the editor's desk. "I need you to go to Washington immediately. Speak directly to the secretary of state, and get this girl a temporary passport."

───────

THE NEXT MORNING, I went to get a dress made at the William Ghormley shop on Nineteenth Street, east of Fifth Avenue. It was a more exclusive studio than I would normally patronize, but these were extraordinary circumstances, and I had to be sure of the quality.

"Mr. Ghormley, I want a dress by this evening." I spoke crisply and businesslike to the thin tailor, confident that such a task could be done.

"Very well." Without a hint of hesitation, he led me over to a sampling of materials.

I smiled as I followed. My editors always took some working over and it was nice not to have to argue for a change.

"A dress that will stand constant wear for three months," I said before he could pull out any fabrics, and to make sure he understood the quality of the work I expected despite the short notice. "I am going on a trip around the world." My last words came out breathless. It was finally hitting me.

Mr. Ghormley chose several bolts of cloth and laid them out on a small table in front of a pier glass where the light was true. He draped the samples open and studied how they looked in the tall mirror between the windows. "Around the world? And what are you trying to prove this time, Miss Bly? That the world is flat after all?"

"Ha! Not in the least, Mr. Ghormley. I'm going to beat Phileas Fogg's record and do it in only seventy-five days."

"*Around the World in Eighty Days*?" He looked up with a spark in his eye. "You think you can beat an imaginary man's record?" He returned to the fabric. "I suppose if anyone could, it would be you."

He pounded his hand on a plain blue broadcloth and a plaid camel's-hair. "What do you think of these? Strong. Durable. Fashionable. Should carry you around the world and back again."

"Excellent." I leaned on the table. "Aren't you worried for me? A young woman traveling in parts unknown without a companion?"

The decision to go alone had been an easy one. A few years before, when I traveled to Mexico, my mother had gone with me. But she didn't move fast enough for a race. I had to beat Phileas Fogg, or there wasn't any point!

Mother had not been happy to hear the news. During the intermission of Hamlet, she reached for my hand. "Pink, dear," she had said, invoking my childhood nickname, and reminding me how she used to dress me up in pink when all the other girls wore drab colors. *It's her fault I feel the need to stand out.* "This is different from your other stunts. Halfway around the world, there will be no one to rescue you should you need help."

"I am not worried, Mother. The world will meet me as I meet it."

Mr. Ghormley chuckled. "I have read your articles. I am more worried for your fellow passengers."

He put the rejected fabrics away and set about cutting out a traveling gown. Before I left Ghormley's at one o'clock, I had had my first fitting and made plans to return at five o'clock for the second.

A few more stops, and I had ordered a thick overcoat called an Ulster to take me through the winter, a lighter dress from my regular dressmaker to wear in the parts of the world where it would be summer, and lastly, a new bag to pack everything into.

That night, after Mother had gone to bed, I settled back into a chair with a deeply satisfied grin on my face. This would be my most daring adventure yet. The whole world would hear of Nellie Bly.

3

THIS IS DREADFULLY EARLY," REMARKED Fannie, one of my dearest friends. A group of us stood aboard the *Augusta Victoria*, supposedly to encourage me, but with each round of "encouragement" I was beginning to lose my nerve.

I stifled a yawn, not wanting to open up more complaints from Fannie. I had hardly slept the night before, whether from nerves or excitement I would never know. And when I did sleep, it was short-lived, as I kept waking in a start, afraid that I'd slept in and missed the boat. I forced a smile to show my friends they should not worry about me.

Jane's brows knit together and she continuously patted my hand as if we would never see each other again. "Now, you know if the ship goes down, there are life boats. It's women and children first, but make sure you get to one before they're all filled up."

"The ship won't go down," interjected Mr. Cockerill. He stood with us, repeatedly checking his watch. "Captain Albers has assured us that the voyage will not only be timely, but as smooth as he can make it."

"Never mind the ship," inserted Fannie. "What if you come down with jungle fever and there is no doctor to care for you? Like what happened to Dr. Livingstone." She gave a little laugh. "I suppose even if you are a doctor and you find yourself in desperate straits, you can't heal yourself." She blinked back tears.

I gripped Fannie's hand to stop the patting. "I'll be fine."

I dared not mention I was still getting the terrible headaches that sent me to the doctor weeks ago. "This will be like a relaxing vacation – I haven't had one in three years – and I'll come home more refreshed and invigorated than when I left."

Jane nudged my handbag, which rested at my feet on the deck along with a bouquet from Henry Jarrett, the theatrical agent. "I hope you packed something for emergencies in there."

I laughed. "One of the men at the paper tried to talk me into packing a revolver, of all things. Can you imagine me with a gun?"

My two friends exchanged a look.

"And did you?" whispered Jane.

"No! If I am in any spot of trouble, I will rely on the good nature of the local gentlemen to help me out."

Again, my two friends exchanged a look.

"What *did* you pack in there?" asked Fannie, changing the subject. "It's an awfully small bag for three months' time. I don't know how you managed it."

"Nothing but necessities. I'm not out to impress people. I'm simply going from port to port, and station to station. I won't be taking time to visit Queen Victoria, even if she asks me."

Truth was I had had a terrible time packing. In the end, my light dress didn't fit, and there was no way on earth I was going to add one more parcel to cart around.

"I've got an ink-stand, pens, pencils, and copy-paper for work. Pins, needles, and thread for *little* emergencies." I raised my eyebrows at Jane. "For clothing, I've got what I am wearing, plus a dressing gown, a tennis blazer, and slippers. Not to mention several changes of underwear, handkerchiefs, and fresh ruchings. Two traveling caps and three veils. See? I've got quite a lot. Also, my hairbrush and other toiletries. The last thing I squeezed in was my jar of cold cream."

"Yes, that is smart," agreed Fannie. "You don't want your face to chap." She pointed at my hat next. "Where did you get that?"

"My ghillie hat?" I adjusted it. "Do you like it?" I could tell by her face that she didn't.

"It's not the current style with those two brims," she said. "How do you know which is front and which is back?"

"Oh, stop. It'll keep me warm when I need to be warm and shade me from the sun the rest of the time. Jane, why the look, now?" I asked in dismay.

Jane looked stricken and was pawing through her own handbag. "You've hardly brought enough for such a long trip!" She held out some money. "Do take it and buy yourself more supplies when you dock in England. It may be your last chance."

I held back a laugh. Jane was too much in earnest.

"I'm not traveling to the moon. And I have plenty of money." I lowered my voice and showed them the chamois-skin bag around my neck. "They gave me £200 in English gold and Bank of England notes. I've also got American gold and dollars as a test to see if American money is known in distant parts of the world."

Finally, at this, my friends looked relieved. Fannie even smiled. "Keep that around your neck at all times, and for goodness' sake, quit showing people."

Then Jane wrung her hands. "But not at night. You might choke yourself with that around your neck. What will you do at night?"

A horn blast interrupted them, indicating it was time for visitors to leave. "This is it," I said, trying to sound enthusiastic.

"Keep up your courage," whispered Jane as she and Fannie hugged me tight then walked away, smiling through their tears.

Julius Chambers, the *World's* managing editor, stepped forward with the timekeeper he had brought with him from the New York Athletic Club. The men double-checked their timepiece with my gold watch I planned to keep tucked into my pocket and set to New York time.

"You're ready," he said. "Godspeed, Nellie Bly. We'll see you back here in seventy-two days." Then they were gone.

A man in uniform slipped over the side of the ship and climbed down the rope ladder into a waiting rowboat. The gentleman beside me explained that the man was the pilot and his pilot boat would lead us out of the harbor. "As soon as the pilot goes off and the captain assumes command," continued the gentleman, "then and only then our voyage begins, so now you really are started on your tour around the world."

Thursday, November 14, 1889 at 9.40.30 o'clock.

THE BREEZE PICKED up as the ship started its journey across the Atlantic. The movement was hardly noticeable at first but for the increasing distance between ship and shore. The other passengers began claiming chairs and making themselves comfortable with rugs tucked around their legs.

I am off. Shall I ever get back?

I knew the precise minute we'd left the sheltered waters for open sea – my rolling stomach was a good indicator.

"Do you get seasick?" asked a woman interested in striking up a conversation. Before I could answer, I lurched for the side of the ship and, seeing the waves all a-jumble and the undulating ship under my feet, I gave vent to my feelings. My stomach ached from heaving over the edge. As I wiped the tears from my eyes, I turned back to the concerned woman and gave her a brave nod. But the other passengers grinned back at me, amused.

"And she's going 'round the world!" said one man. I joined the laughter a little less heartily than the rest. Surely the entire trip would not be like this. Jules Verne never mentioned seasickness in his novel.

I spent the better part of the day at the rail. But I was happy to note that I wasn't the only one. When it was time for luncheon, I looked pointedly at the man who made everyone laugh at my plight and marched into the dining room. Several others attempted my bravado as well, but we all ended up leaving in a hurry.

For dinner at seven, I was invited to sit with the captain at his table in the first-class passengers' dining hall. It was a great honor and there was no way, come hell or high water, that I was going to miss it.

I arrived early and immediately noticed a small ensemble playing delightful music in the corner. The architecture and décor were after the rococo style that I love but Mother would call "gaudy." The walls were decorated with stained glass and painted panels, which I assumed were by German painters since the *Augusta Victoria* was named after the German emperor's wife. This ship was probably the most luxurious in all the world, and I wished I were feeling better to fully appreciate it. The tables were set with white china and cut crystal, and the attendants were in full dress, down to crisp white gloves. In a room like this, I could be a lady from the Renaissance.

We congregated near the table, the others having changed into their pretty evening clothes, me still in my Ghormley broadcloth. The captain, appearing very handsome in uniform, approached and made introductions. It was a noble beginning to my tour.

"I'd like you all to meet Miss Nellie Bly," said Captain Albers. "I'm sure you have heard she is attempting to break Phileas Fogg's record for traveling around the globe. The *Augusta Victoria* will set her well ahead, as there was no such ship when Verne was writing his novel." He looked pleased at his part of my adventure.

Captain Albers continued introductions in the round, but one particularly large ocean swell caught me by surprise and my stomach lurched, claiming all my focus, and I quite missed all their names. The other passengers were known to him, having made the crossing at some other time in their lives. I alone was on my maiden voyage.

"Please, take a seat here on my left," said the captain. "How are you feeling?"

I smiled bravely as I fell into the chair. "Quite well, thank you," I lied. "How long did you say the passage would take?"

Everyone laughed. I had a fleeting thought that at this rate I might be the source of amusement to people the entire world over. While I never let my youth stop me, sometimes my naiveté had come close to giving me away. A brave face and bold talk always helped. How else could I have gone undercover to find out how employment agencies take advantage of domestic servants, or sweet-talked my way through learning how a husband agency worked?

"The only way to conquer seasickness is by forcing oneself to eat," the captain instructed.

As he finished speaking, the first course appeared. It was soup. I should be able to take a spoonful or two and not have it revisit me ten minutes later. The people, whose names I had missed, began cheerily discussing the music while I suffered a conversation with my stomach. It seems it did not want soup after all. I made a good show of eating a ladylike amount before a waiter took the blessed thing away.

One of the men who had gulped down his soup kept the conversation going. "Captain, the last time I sat at your table, you told us a brilliant story about a stowaway you had found bound for America. Have you had any more mishaps on your travels?"

The captain nodded. "A hurricane last month! Our chief officer almost went overboard when the railing near the deckhouse gave way. We've got twenty feet of new railing there to prove it."

I couldn't imagine the ship tossing more than it was right now. The constant motion churned my stomach relentlessly. A young waiter who didn't know any better set down a plate of fish in front of me. Though a delicacy on any other day, today the aroma of fish while out at sea was too potent a combination for my imagination. My stomach rebelled mightily.

"Excuse me," I whispered as I dashed out of the room, pushing aside any waiter who got in my way.

This trip may not have been one of my better ideas. Almost eighty days? I could endure only ten days in that mad house and at the time it seemed forever. The cold sea air reminded me of the constant cold in that place, and my empty stomach brought back thoughts of the stale bread and rancid butter too terrible to eat.

Eighty days! Even if I went by land as much as possible, I'd still have to cross the Pacific upon my return. I leaned into my hands and let myself have a moment of pity. On the bright side, my dress was still clean.

When my hands stopped shaking, I rejoined the dinner party.

The men stood, solemnly nodding as I returned to my seat and the next course. Alas, it was not meant to be. Off I went again. Oh, the laughs they must have been having at this young girl's expense. Once I had gotten rid of everything I could get rid of, I walked along the deck, trying to reach an agreement with my insides. Dare I return to the table? It would be so easy to settle into my bunk for the night. But if I gave up now, how easy it would be for me to give up later in my journey.

"Welcome back," said the captain.

"Good job," said one of the men. "You stick to it and you'll find your sea legs yet."

Before he had yet finished his congratulations, I had run out of the room for a third time. If I were a dog, I would have been returning to the table with my tail between my legs. As it was, by the time I made a showing, the dinner was over and the rest of my party was sipping tea, quietly satisfied with their first meal onboard.

"Would you like some dessert?" asked the captain politely and with a twinkle in his eye.

"No, thank you." I replied. "But thank you for the meal. It was excellent."

4

IN WHICH A BEWILDERED ELIZABETH BISLAND
FINDS HERSELF ON A TRAIN GOING WEST
INSTEAD OF PREPARING FOR A DINNER PARTY.

A S THE TRAIN SLOWS TO A STOP AT THE Chicago station, I peer into the dark to find my contact. I'm not sure how we will find each other, since I don't know who I am looking for. But then, this whole adventure is something of the unknown and ridiculous.

Mere hours ago, I woke up as usual to a leisurely breakfast and looking forward to a regular dress fitting and preparations for a five o'clock tea. Before I can fully comprehend what I have agreed to, I am bound on a train west and to further parts unknown, and all alone!

Once Molly had gotten over the shock of me leaving, she was more than willing to make apologies for our guests and help me with other cancellations and arrangements. As I packed and repacked, she peppered me with wild ideas.

"I think you should call your trip 'Eighty Days Around the World to Find a Husband.' As I recall, Phileas Fogg found himself a wife on his trip."

"The readers of The Cosmopolitan *don't want to read about romance. They read the magazine for intellectual stimulation."*

"I'm a reader of Cosmo, and I want to read about romance."

Molly was incorrigible.

"At least find someone to compare to Mr. Wetmore so you can judge whether you'll give a 'yes' or a 'no' when he finally bends his knee."

When I left home, I smiled and shook hands and received best wishes and kisses and hugs and last minute directions. To all, I appeared an excited traveler, but I hid how deep my worries plumbed. About how important it was to make all my connections and follow the myriad of instructions as best I could. For if I make a mistake – Oh! Will I get back on track, or will I find myself lost and abandoned on the far side of the world?

With great force of character, I push these thoughts out of my mind before they overwhelm and make me quit before reaching California. Like Molly said, it's best to look at the adventure full on and with positive outlook.

At least my new hat, a fashionable glazed black sailor's, is distinctly becoming, and my new black dress fits me very well. I could not have planned it better but for bewildered Mr. Wetmore to have slipped me a big bunch of pink roses at the last minute, which complemented my traveling ensemble nicely. He is a dear man, and I suppose we shall discover which truism is correct: absence makes the heart grow fonder…or out of sight, out of mind!

If only I had had time to think about the trip ahead of time, I may not feel so lost right now, descending the train with my large Gladstone bag filled to bursting and a shawl strap slung on my shoulder. Nellie Bly is the more efficient packer, I will concede, as evidenced by a good-sized steamer trunk that will have to be carried for me, but I will be the most comfortable.

Not knowing what occasions I will be dressing for, I have packed as much variety as possible: two cloth gowns, half a dozen light bodices, and an evening silk. I wish I could have packed more of my winter and summer wardrobes, but the decision was made and I have what I have.

Wisely, I took the precaution of carrying plenty of pins and hairpins. I have had previous experience with their vicious ways and know that in critical moments they tend to play hide-and-seek. The only sure preventive is to have geologic layers of them all through the trunk, so that a shaft might be hastily sunk through one's belongings at any moment with a serene certainty of striking rich deposits of both necessities of female existence.

"Excuse me, Miss Bisland," says the conductor. "Can I help you any?"

I glance up and down the station and find no one who looks like they are looking for me. "Yes, sir. Is there another location where I can meet my party?" They are supposed to assist me making my connection onto the next train. The emptiness of the station works its way down into my toes. Hopefully this is not a sign of future missed meetings and bungled up appointments. What a beginning!

"Well now, this is usually where people meet up, but I can escort you around the station until we find who you are looking for."

We wander until the poor conductor, endlessly checking his pocket watch, must return to his main duties. He leaves me at the near-empty lunch hall where I sit all alone on a high stool at the counter and eat. Finally, I slide away into the night, feeling very homesick, very cross, and haunted by the bittersweet suspicions of the happy results of a tea-and-ham dinner.

I make it onto the correct train and, after much futile wrestling in the small space of my sleeping car, manage to change into my nightgown. Immediately, I am out for the night, only vaguely annoyed at the coffin-like smell of the compartment.

———

NORMALLY I ENJOY a leisurely morning, but when I pull up my curtains the next morning, I am delighted to see the sun about to rise. It strikes me that this daily occurrence parallels God's original command of "Let there be light!" and it happens every day without me. It is balm to my soul, and I am renewed and confident that I can continue on this journey with or without humanly help or companionship.

"Good morning," I crow later as I find an empty seat across the aisle from a gray-haired couple. They are darling and likely number one hundred or more years between them.

"Good morning, dear," says the woman. "Where are you traveling to today?"

I smile as I say, "Around the world."

The two laugh as if I were joking.

"Really, I am," I explain. "You have heard of Nellie Bly, the stunt reporter?"

"Are you she?" asks the fellow eagerly.

I shake my head vigorously. "No, but I am in a race against her. She left yesterday morning going east by ship, and I left last night going west by train."

He makes a clucking sound. "She's got a head start on you, then."

Hmm. "So who are you two?" I ask, changing the subject.

The woman looks pleased that I asked and she leans forward to confide in me. "We are on our second honeymoon. I've always wanted to see the winter orange blossoms in California, so we are on our way to Los Angeles."

The two go back to making doe-eyes at each other and I return to watching the fields outside the window. The man's discouraging comment presses heavily in my mind. I will have to find every way possible to shave off minutes, hours, and, if I can, days.

That night at Council Bluffs, Omaha, I catch just the kind of break I am hoping for.

"Miss Bisland? This way, please." A kindly fellow reaches for my bag, which I heartily hand over. He leads me across the platform toward a short train, painted all in white and with the name The Fast Mail. "Did you need to go into the station and freshen up?" he asks.

"No, I'm fine, thank you." What I want is to curl back up in a cozy bed – preferably my own at home, but a sleeper car will do.

"You are in for a treat on this train," he chatters on.

"Why is that?"

"This here is our new mail-train. We're testing it out to see how fast it can go across the continent." He smiles easily at me. "Just like you. Seems we're all in a race these days." He holds out his hand for me to shake. "Edward Dickson, General Manager."

My mood lifts immediately. In addition to the mail car, there is only one sleeper and the General Manager's private car. We are as light and fast as a train can be.

Before we get started, I am invited to look into the mail car, which is lit up by globe lamps strung overhead. Several clerks with green eye shades are busy at work sorting letters. Even they are in a race to finish their sacks and move on to the next. I feel it is a great conspiracy we are all caught up in, to move faster, faster, faster!

The pace is tremendous from the start and, as we begin the climb up the Great Divide, my hopes continue to rise alongside. Already I am settling into my role as circumnavigator of the world.

In the morning I find myself in the plains. I am the only woman aboard, and as such, content myself with watching the landscape grow more desolate and wildly drear, like the cursed site of some prehistoric Sodom sown with salt. The land is gray, covered thinly with a withered, ashen-colored plant. Settlements are few and far between.

From time to time, we pass a dwelling, a square cabin of gray unpainted boards, always tightly closed and the dwellers always absent, somewhere on business. The only distinct proof I ever see of the human habitance of these silent, lonely homes is a tiny pair of butternut trousers fluttering on the clothesline. The minute American citizen who should have occupied these trousers is invisible and I greatly fear they are his only pair.

But at night! The stars are huge and fierce, keen and scintillant as swords. The plains, though dull if you aren't looking for interesting ways to describe them, allow for a night sky like nowhere else.

Through the Bad Lands we speed, but not fast enough. Five hours away from Ogden, we are two and a half hours behind our appointed time. The General Manager takes to pacing the length of the train. Whenever he stops in our car, he fills everyone in on his race.

"I've just telegraphed an engineer by the name Downing to meet us at the next stop." He jingles the coins in his pockets as he paces. "If we don't make our time, we won't win the mail contracts." Mr. Dickson stops and grabs the seat in front of me, squeezing so his knuckles turn white. "I don't know what your race is worth to you, Miss Bisland, but mine is worth three quarters of a million."

After he storms off to the engine room, I think about what my race is worth to me. Certainly my reasons for going are different from Nellie Bly's. She likes to be the first woman to do anything. The more daring the adventure, the better.

But me? To do my duty as an employee. To help my magazine succeed. To have a little adventure of my own. To test myself, perhaps. Do I have what it takes to be a daring soul?

I smile.

I must, for here I am, though somewhat paralyzed at the thought of what will happen once I leave America.

Presently, the train arrives at the next station and a gentleman of Irish extraction climbs into the cab and remarks with jovial determination, "Howdy, folks! I'll get us to Ogden – or hell, on time." He turns to me and tips his hat before he is off.

The grade at this part of the road has a descent of ninety-three feet in a mile, and the track corkscrews through gorges and canyons with but small margin between us and destruction. To these considerations Mr. Downing is cheerfully indifferent, and pulling out the throttle, he lets the engine have her head at the rate of sixty-five miles an hour. Red sparks fly off the back wheels.

The train rocks like a ship at sea, and sleepers hold to their berths in terror, the more nervous actually succumbing to *mal de mar*. The plunge of the engine that now and then whimpers in the darkness is felt through the whole train, as one feels the fierce play of the loins of a runaway horse.

"Do you play whist?" Mr. Dickson asks me, discreetly averting his eyes from my clenched fists.

"I do," I say, forcing myself to breathe, and then join him and several others at a table. There will be no sleeping tonight, and I hope a game of cards will take my mind off my eminent death. As I recall, Phileas Fogg was known to play the game unceasingly on his trip around the world. Perhaps it was to keep his mind off these frightening fits of travel.

Not far into our game, one of the train officers joins us and stands fidgeting at the General Manager's elbow.

"Yes, what is it?" Mr. Dickson asks, not looking up from his hand.

"I don't like the sound of the engine, sir. I think we should slow 'er down before she blows." He whispers loud enough for everyone to hear. "Or we'll jump the tracks."

I am in full agreement with the officer and listen closely for Mr. Dickson's response.

Undisturbed, he takes the odd trick with the thirteenth trump. He looks over his shoulder at a passenger who appears to be quite afraid and says, "It is episodes such as this in American life that make us a nation of youthful gray-heads. Don't worry. Downing knows what he's doing."

"But Antelope Gap is coming up. The reverse loop?"

Looks are exchanged, and then we feel the wheels lift off the tracks on one side of the car. There is nothing to be done but hold on and pray. We land back on the tracks, and before another breath can be taken, we're wheels up on the other side.

When righted with a shudder, Mr. Dickson sends word to Downing to slow down. That word is ignored. He takes one look at me and goes to pull the brake. The train slows, but not by much.

To our enormous relief, we arrive in Ogden on time.

Mr. Downing dismounts with alacrity from his cab, saying "Ah! These night rides are prone to give a man a cold." Patting his belly, he saunters off to a pub with a swinging Venetian door, and we never see him again.

The ride takes on a seemingly leisurely pace after that. My heart no longer resides in my throat and the others seem visibly relieved as well. We take to looking out our windows for signs of life and point them out to help each other recover from our thrill ride. There are frequent jack rabbits, the occasional coyote, and now and then an arrangement of tepees.

Indians crowd about the train at every stop. The women who are carrying children allow us to view their babies in exchange for small current coin.

"May I look?" I ask a pretty mother who takes my coin and turns her papoose to me. It is a portable wooden cradle, the original Baby Bunting. The contented baby is asleep, nestled in a cozy bundle of rabbit skins – presumably those for which "papa went a-hunting" if the Mother Goose rhyme were to be believed. A sister, about six years old, clings to her mother's leg and stares at me with big, dark eyes set into her smooth skin and framed by Vandyked locks. Old women squat in the dust, huddled in blankets and fair ignore us all.

The night before reaching San Francisco, we find our first trees again at a little wayside eating station where a long row of poplars stands up stiffly in the dusk near our path. I've never been so happy as to step off that train and drink in the soft and spring-like air, pleasant with a smell as of white clover. Could this really be November? It is like the first breath from a promised land after long wandering in a country of wilderness and drought.

At fifteen minutes past nine, the nose of the ferry-boat from Oakland touches the San Francisco wharf. We have crossed the continent in four days and twenty hours – thanks to Mr. Downing – and the distance between New York and the Western metropolis is reduced by a whole day. A great achievement. There are crowds of reporters waiting in the soft rain to interview everybody: General Manager, engineer, conductor – even me.

"Miss Bisland!" calls a young man. "Ted, editor from the *Examiner*," he says by way of introduction, "and my colleague Annie Laurie. What do you think of rainy San Francisco?" He holds his hand palm up to catch the drops.

I smile at the pair of young reporters who look about my age. He is tall and too thin and eager. She is average height and chubby. Regarding the town through New York eyes, I answer, "Your buildings are shorter than those we have in New York. Only three or four stories, it looks like. But they all appear new and fresh."

"On account of the earthquakes and our relatively young city" he explains. "But we haven't had one in a while, so they've started to build taller." He points to a few of the more recent buildings that have begun to climb, Babel-like, into the dripping skies. Looking between Miss Laurie and myself, he says, "I'll leave you two to talk while I get my other interviews. Don't you go anywhere, Miss Bisland." He joins the crowd around Mr. Dickson.

"Have you felt an earthquake?" I ask Miss Laurie, expecting the earth to shift at any moment.

The girl shakes her head. "I've only been here six months," she says, "like most of us." She arches her arm toward the other reporters. "This is still a new town, new people arriving every day."

"Yes, indeed." The place seems charged with a disrespectful sort of youth.

"Are you looking forward to your trip?" the girl asks.

"Now that I've had some time to sleep on it, yes I am," I answer truthfully. "Though I do wish I'd have more time to spend during my stops. I'm especially interested in seeing Japan and China."

"What about Nellie Bly? Do you think you'll see her along the way?"

Oh, I hope not! But I can see Miss Laurie's eyes appear to light at the name of Bly. Another young stunt reporter in the making. "I doubt it. We'll likely cross paths and not even know it, like Longfellow's Gabriel and Evangeline."

Once the interviews with Mr. Dickson are over, we make our way through the oozing mud to the station where I am to learn about my ship. Mr. Dickson has taken hold of my bag like it's his own and leads the way for myself and Miss Laurie while Ted from the *Examiner* trails along like the young pup that he is.

"I'm sorry, Miss Bisland, but your ship does not leave for two days," says the young man behind the counter. "Your magazine has put you up in a hotel near here. I hope you enjoy your stay." He slides a telegram to me.

Secretly, I am relieved. I shall get a chance to take in the city after all.

Mr. Dickson sees me safely inside the Palace Hotel before saying goodbye. He assures me that the hotel, built in 1875, is the largest in the country with over eight hundred guest rooms. "Perhaps I'll see you tomorrow for lunch?" He glances at Ted.

Ted from the *Examiner* steps into the General Manager's shoes in taking over my itinerary. "A group of us is going out to the Cliff House for luncheon tomorrow. Some newspaper men

and some from the mail train. You must join me – I mean us."
He grins.

"Thank you, Mr. er…Ted. I would very much like that."
After I nod my consent, he is off, leaving me with cheery Miss
Laurie, who has a few more questions.

"Have you been a reporter long?" I ask the young thing as we
walk through the lobby and into a square enclosure laid with a
vast marble-floored court. The arcade is adorned with palms and
ferns and heavy tables where several men are tipped back in their
chairs reading their papers and smoking.

Her smile wavers. "I don't mind telling you, since you're a
reporter too. But this will be my first big story. You know, one not
about flowers or tea settings."

Oh, dear. I better have something worth saying for her.
But now that I am back on my own two feet, the madness of
the adventure is setting in again and threatening to undo me
completely. I hope I don't give her too much of a story.

5

OPENING MY EYES, I FOUND THE
STEWARDESS and a lady passenger in my cabin and
the captain standing at the door.

"We were afraid that you were dead," the captain said when
he saw that I was awake.

"I always sleep late in the morning," I said apologetically.

"In the morning!" the captain exclaimed with a laugh, which
was echoed by the others. "It's half past four in the evening."

I blinked. Even that was late for me.

"But never mind," he added consolingly. "As long as you
slept well, it will do you good. Now get up and see if you can't
eat a big dinner."

What was his fascination with food? But I braved the attempt
anyway, having something to prove to the other passengers, if not
to myself. Since I was still in my traveling dress, having collapsed
into bed not caring the night before, I quickly freshened up and
joined the captain.

He had swapped out some of his party for new passengers,
and so I was able to start afresh with learning to eat on the high
seas. The food was as delicious as I pretended it to be last night.
I was ravenous and went through every course without flinching.
The captain, watching carefully, nodded his encouragement.

After dinner, I returned to stateroom Number 60 and slept as
if I'd had a long exercise in the open air.

W ITH MANY DAYS remaining in my ocean crossing, I took up company with some of the other passengers. They were all interested in my adventure as I was interested in theirs. One day I discovered a girl traveling alone like myself.

"I hear you are traveling around the world to make a record for yourself," she said.

"Yes, I'm planning to beat Phileas Fogg's account."

"Good for you. I'm glad a girl is doing it. Men get too much press as it is." The girl tossed her Marguerite hair to emphasize her distaste.

"And where are you going?" I asked her.

"I'm meeting my parents in Germany. My father has promised to take me to the symphony and that is what I am looking forward to the most."

"Do you speak German?"

"Mm-hmm. Since I was a child." She looked furtively around before continuing. "Have you seen the man who counts his pulse after he eats?"

"No, I haven't," I whispered back.

"He does! I don't know why. He eats ever so much and then counts. I would ask him why, but then that would be the end of the mystery."

I agreed and vowed to myself I would find him out to observe his behavior before the trip was over.

"And then there is that man over there," said the girl.

I turned to the direction she indicated and watched a man talking quietly to himself as he paced the deck.

"He's counting his steps. I hope I never get so bored that I start counting my steps."

I admired the man in question, musing he could be the embodiment of Phileas Fogg, who in the novel counted his steps to the Reform club. *How many other characters from the novel might I meet on my trip?*

The girl swiveled in the opposite direction. "Oh, look! There's Homie. Have you met him?"

The "him" she was referring to was a little mop of a dog with long silky hair. I followed her and knelt homage before the beast. I never before thought about animals crossing the ocean. "What kind is it?"

"A silver Skye terrier. Don't get him worked up, now," exclaimed the owner, a genial- looking man who held to the leash while his wife looked on in earnest.

"No barking," she said to the dog. She explained to me, "We are moving to Paris and we couldn't leave little Home Sweet Home behind. So we've paid for his passage, but the captain doesn't want his guests to be disturbed."

I petted the wee thing and stood back to my feet. "Where does he stay?"

The wife frowned. "In the company of the butcher. Don't make a joke – I've heard them all." She fanned herself with a kerchief.

A mischievous-looking boy walked by at that moment, and I expected him to come pet the dog. Instead he called out, "Rats!"

At this, the dog began digging frantically at the deck, accompanied by short, crisp barks. The boy laughed and laughed. Homie's owners scooped him up and with angry looks at the boy, brought the dog inside.

Looking pleased with himself – and a little less bored – the boy continued on, whistling and staring out to sea.

I had almost forgotten the girl at my side until she touched my arm and said, "Do you want to race to the dining room? It's time to eat soon."

I didn't give her the chance to get ahead of me, but grabbed my hat and sprinted as fast as I could. We ended at a tie, both of us laughing and my lungs burning from the cold ocean air.

The girl sought my company often after this. We played shuffleboard until our hands froze and got in quite a few games on the bull-board. We both became rather adept at tossing the leather rings.

Captain Albers had me sit at his table every night. I wonder if my editor had requested he do so, as the other guests came and went.

"I think you'll find that most people around the world won't know where America is," the captain said. He'd just gotten through giving me some advice on how to conduct myself on my trip, in particular in taking care of my health.

"I'm testing out that theory by bringing along some American dollars which I'll try to use at distant ports."

The captain shook his head. "Not likely any of it will be accepted. Then there are plenty of people who think the United States is one little island, with a few houses on it."

I doubted that, but held my opinion in case my trip should prove me wrong.

Being that dinner was over, Captain Albers took out a card and drew the same number of lines as there were gentlemen at the table. He then marked one of the lines and folded it over so that none could tell which was marked. This he passed around the table and told the men to choose a line and write their initials.

Once passed back to the captain, he opened the fold. It was Mr. Bashful who was the winner.

"What shall it be tonight? Cigars or cordials?" asked the captain, with the expectation that Mr. Bashful would pay for the men's vices.

"Cordials," Mr. Bashful replied. And the captain rose to lead the men to the smoking room. I followed the women into the ladies' saloon, a plush, lavender space, for tea.

————

MY SEASICKNESS HAD disappeared, but other passengers were not so fortunate. There were several tales floating around describing the people who chose to remain secluded from the rest of us. At lunch, my friend on her way to Germany told me about the woman who had been a great sufferer from seasickness and had not undressed since leaving her home in New York.

"Why not?" I asked. Even as light as I had traveled, I had still kept up my toilet.

"I heard her say," and at this point the girl increased her pitch to repeat, "I am sure we are all going down and I am determined to go down dressed."

"Ha!" We at the table, who were feeling rather confident now that we knew today was our last day aboard ship, took great amusement at this.

"Has anyone seen Homie lately?" asked a young man across the table from me. He was eyeing his Hamburger steak rather suggestively.

A woman on his other side giggled nervously. "The butcher would never…"

The young man looked at me and winked, making a big show of examining his meat before taking a big bite.

Any further discussion ceased when a steward strode quickly to the captain's table. "Land, sir," we heard him say. We all looked at each other, frozen for two seconds before dashing outside.

I drank in that first point of bleak land with more interest than I would have bestowed on the most beautiful scenery in the world. We had not long been in sight of land until the decks began to fill with dazed-looking, wan-faced people. It was just as if we had taken on new passengers.

Dinner that evening was a very pleasant affair. Extra courses had been prepared in honor of those that were leaving at Southampton. Despite my rough beginnings, I had enjoyed my time on the *Augusta Victoria*. My fellow passengers were all so kind to me that I mourned leaving friends behind. Despite the late hour, many stayed up on deck with those of us who were waiting for the tug to take us to land.

The reality of my trip struck me afresh. Not only was I already sixteen hours behind schedule due to the poor weather, but I was about to leave the English-speaking world that I knew and move into parts unknown. How was I going to do this?

As I was thinking these thoughts, one of the gentlemen that had also dined frequently at the captain's table approached me.

"Do you have someone to meet you?"

"Yes, our London correspondent."

The man frowned. "It is almost two-thirty in the morning. Would he stay up this late to meet you? I shall most certainly leave the ship here and see you safely to London, if no one comes to meet you."

Just as I tried to protest, someone announced the tugboat had come alongside and we all rushed over to see it. As the men came on board, I tried to pick out the one who had been sent to meet me.

"Good luck on your trip around the world," said one of my fellow passengers who had stopped to shake my hand.

A tall young man overheard the remark, and turning at the foot of the stairs, looked down on me with a hesitating smile.

"Nellie Bly?" he asked.

"Yes," I replied, holding out my hand, which he gave a cordial grasp.

"Tracey Greaves. Did you enjoy your trip? Good. Is your baggage ready to be transferred?"

My self-proclaimed guardian stepped in and took the correspondent off for a little chat. Afterwards he came to me and said with the most satisfied look upon his face: "He is all right. If he had not been so, I should have gone to London with you anyway. I can rest satisfied now, for he will take care of you."

I went away with a warm feeling in my heart for that kindly man who would have sacrificed his own comfort to ensure the safety of an unprotected girl. Following my correspondent, I waved goodbye to my new friends and hurried down the perpendicular plank to the other passengers who were going to London. The tug cast off and away we drifted into the dark.

6

IN WHICH ELIZABETH BISLAND GOES TO LUNCH AND IS TAKEN ON A TOUR OF THE CHINESE DISTRICT.

THIS MORNING I FEEL A BIT OF THE STIRRING that worried me in the beginning of the trip. Several folks have come to the hotel to have a look at me, going so far as to send notices to my room to try to get me to come out. Have I made a mistake? Will my life ever be the same again?

It doesn't take long to discover the reason for my sudden fame. Annie Laurie's article is published in the morning newspaper and my face peers out at me from the front page!

While reading the article aloud, I pace the room. Miss Laurie writes that I don't "look like a very daring creature" and then goes on to describe me as the "…little woman with the gentle voice and appealing dark eyes."

Oh, and Molly will love this opinion: "It is always these delicate, high-bred women who have unheard of endurance and wonderful pluck." I shall cut it out and mail it to my sister at once.

Having posted the letter, I take refuge from the rain and go through the shops on the outer side of the arcade. I purchase two thin shirtwaists for the warmer climates, and while I am at it, pick up some silk and worsted thread for some fancywork. The first leg of my journey has taught me that I'll have long stretches of time with nothing to do, and I may as well redeem the time.

My hair has suffered in the rain, so I go back to my room, dig out a handful of hairpins, and set to work. Once satisfied that both my hair is ready and Ted has waited long enough, I stroll into the lobby.

As soon as Ted sees me, he jumps up, shuffling his hat brim around and around. "Don't you look a picture?" He grins and holds the door open for me. "How is your room?"

"Perfectly beautiful and has spoiled me for future accommodations, I am sure. If only for my noiseless water closet alone."

Ted laughs as he leads the way down the street. "My boss is meeting us at the Cliff House. I've never been myself, but I know you're going to love it. It's just a quick trip up on the P and O. Hope you don't mind getting back on a train so soon after getting off one." Ted keeps up a steady stream of conversation as we walk to the station. He is so eager I wonder when the last time he'd talked to a lady was.

The rain is soft and warm as we start out and a quiet sense of homesickness sneaks up on me. With the roses climbing around the porches of the houses and perfuming the damp city streets with their delicious garden odors, I can almost believe myself back in my native New Orleans again.

Several of the men from the mail-train are waiting at the station as well as other railway men, investors, and reporters. They are still glowing with their victory and send me welcoming smiles as someone who had joined them in their struggle.

We all agree that the Pacific and Ocean Railway lives up to its name. It crawls along the edge of the harbor shut in between the grassy, treeless hills. At times we cling perilously to the steep sides, hearing the waves dashing beneath. I tell Ted of our racing descent into Ogden under Mr. Downing's management and it makes him laugh.

There is a sudden turn at last, and before us is the Pacific Ocean! I feel a deep sense of discovery, of splendid vastness, of a rich new experience seized and dominated. I cannot take my eyes off the sight as I quote:

> ...like stout Cortez when with eagle eyes
> He star'd at the Pacific – and all his men
> Look'd at each other with a wild surmise –

Silent, upon a peak in Darien.

"You speak a pretty poem," says Ted.

"Keats. From his poem 'On First Looking into Chapman's Homer.' The part where the explorer Cortes sees the Pacific Ocean for the first time." I breathe a wistful sigh. "I rather feel a kinship to Cortes at this moment."

My delight continues when we reach the aptly named Cliff House. The building is a low, clapboard design, dazzling white in the sun and looking like an overly large oceanside cottage. It stands, nay, clings to the very western edge of the continent. The waves below make a constant crash at the rocks and I hope I won't get used to their lovely sound. Although if I had been a more nervous sort, I might be worried that we will slip into the ocean sometime during our second course.

A huge American flag flies from a tall pole in the middle of the roof and the ocean breeze keeps it in perpetual motion. I hold to Ted's arm with one hand and to my hat with the other until we enter into the spacious lobby of the Cliff House.

"We are meeting Mr. McEwan," one of the railway men says to the attendant.

While we wait, Ted flips through the guest registry. "Look here," he says. "President Hayes." He flips some more. "There's supposed to be a king, too. Here's Mark Twain."

Impressed, I looked to the name scrawled above Ted's thick finger.

"You should sign it Miss Bisland. After this trip, you'll be famous, too."

That thought makes me a little nervous. But here, in the quiet of the entryway, I can sign my name without a shaking hand.

After we turn in our coats and hats, we follow the man past a long table filled with pies, past several linen-draped tables, and over to a cozy corner upon the sea's edge. The men already seated at the table see us coming and stand. Mr. McEwan, editor of the *Examiner* smiles broadly as he reaches out to take my hand.

"Miss Bisland. A pleasure to meet you," he says and pulls out my chair. "How are you finding San Francisco?"

"It is very new, Mr. McEwan, compared to New York. And although the rain is similar, I must admit the temperature is a vast improvement."

After exchanging pleasantries with all the railway men, we examine the bill of fair.

"You must try the oysters, Miss Bisland," encourages Mr. McEwan.

I have never eaten oysters before. My eyes had skimmed over that section and landed on the broiled half-chicken. "Well, if I must. I am to fully immerse myself in the adventure, so oysters it is."

When Ted's frog legs and terrapin arrive, I avert my eyes lest I imagine them springing to life and making their getaway. I may enjoy the good things in life, but my food tastes are on the conservative side.

"How do you plan to beat Nellie Bly?" asks Mr. McEwan, finally exhausting the tales of our mail-train.

"I can only go as fast as my connections. My aim is to make those as efficiently as possible. Do you have any suggestions?"

He shakes his head. "I don't know if I want to get between two women stunt reporters." The table joins in the laugh, but I only smile.

"What else have you done?" asks Mr. McEwan as he picks up an oyster shell and slides the creature into his mouth.

"Done?" I know he means stunts, but I haven't done any. "I typically write society pieces. Literary reviews."

He exchanges a look with Ted. "Have you ever traveled abroad before?"

"This will be my first time," I say with enthusiasm to dissuade him from taking any more amusement from me. Then I lay into my oysters with a vengeance.

Mr. McEwan leans back in his chair. "The Cliff House has in interesting history. Perhaps you'd like to do a 'society' piece on it when you return."

"Possibly." I nod in encouragement, happy to shift the attention from myself.

"The original owner bought the land from a potato farmer. One day, a ship filled with lumber shipwrecked on the rocks out there, and he salvaged the wood for a bargain price and used it to build his restaurant."

I close my eyes for a moment at the mention of *shipwreck* since I am about to board my first ship tomorrow.

Ted breaks in with an excited voice, "And then another ship wrecked a few years back, but it was carrying black powder and kerosene. No one knew it, and in the middle of the night – BOOM! It blew out all the windows, wrecked the balconies. Made a huge mess."

My eyes widen. I wasn't expecting to be regaled with tales of shipwreck and explosions.

"Good thing my ship is not one carrying black powder and kerosene."

By now we have all finished eating, and I, for one, am ready for fresh air. When Mr. McEwan offers to show me around, I bound out of my chair before Ted can fully stand and pull it out for me.

I step onto a balcony that overhangs the water where we watch the sunset. Here, I'm face to face with the ocean, the cold air tossing a challenge my way. Tomorrow afternoon this water will be my temporary passage. A barking comes from three great crags standing out of the ocean two hundred yards away. I've been hearing it faintly all throughout the meal, but now the sound travels unimpeded. Seals!

"Seal Rocks," says Ted, following my gaze.

Seal Rocks are covered with grumbling, barking sea lions. The playful creatures sit on a clump of rocks, catching the last of the day's sun. The younger ones dive and frolic in the waves, barking their joy. To me they look like fat pigs from this distance.

"They are noisy, aren't they?" I ask.

"They're the city's pets protected by law," says Ted.

Mr. McEwan points at the rocks. "If you'd like to try a stunt, Miss Bisland, we could attach a tightrope cable for you. The last to walk it was eighteen-year-old Rosa Celeste, who beat the gentleman who did it the year before her. He only went one way, but she went there and back."

"No thank you. I'll just enjoy the sunset." Unlike other women, I have nothing to prove. At the last moment, the sun flames out gloriously. It reddens the heavens and gilds a rippling road for me across the watery world I will soon sail.

"Look at that," says Mr. McEwan. "Red sky at night is a sailor's delight. It's a sign of promise."

Mr. McEwan escorts us back to the hotel by way of cable car. The city has spent millions grading the hills, but you can't tell it by the ground's astonishing steepness.

"Are you brave, Miss Bisland?" asks Ted. "Care to sit at the open front? Nothing like the thrill of plunging down and stopping short when a passenger wants off."

"I suppose the experience would prepare my stomach for riding the ocean waves on my way to Japan, but, I'll wait for the real thing, thank you."

Looking somewhat disappointed, Ted settles in beside me at a respectable distance from the front. "Fine, but I have another proposition for you that'll be harder for you to pass up. I'm working on a story about China Town, and a detective has agreed to show me around tonight. Interested?"

"Of course, I am." It'll be a preview of my journey, a chance to learn what awaits me.

Several others are intrigued as well, so we continue on past our hotel.

Ted introduces us to his detective friend, a surprisingly young detective with sharp eyes and chin, who seems eager to show us what he knows of the Chinese district. And although Ted is a nice enough fellow for sharing newspaper stories, I am glad to have an officer of the law with us when I see where we are going.

"I reckon there are 30,000 Chinese living here in San Francisco," the detective says. "The immigrants here don't melt into society as in other places. They've taken over part of the city and converted it to a Chinese town. You'll see how they still dress, eat, and act like Chinese."

Chinese lanterns hang in front of doors that have Chinese signs, and above these, frail balconies are strung about the windows where jars of chrysanthemums droop their ragged blossoms over the sill. The air is thick with Oriental odors. Street stalls expose for-sale vegetables and fruits unknown to us, and the tiny shops with their Chinese furnishings and inscriptions sell wares which no American seeks.

"What is that odor?" I finally ask the detective. It is so strong a smell that I fear my stomach will start in early on developing seasickness.

He sniffs the air as if parsing out the smells for me. "That is the unfortunate combination of the bitter fumes of opium and the smoke of incense sticks."

"I've never smelt anything like it before."

"Miss, I'm sure before your trip is over you will encounter it again."

We wander in the streets the better part of the evening. The detective delights in taking us into places where most tourists never see. I am beginning to get an inkling as to why my family and friends are worried about me traveling the world on my own. But I'm not on my own, I am with a detective and the people around us are very aware of that.

A loud warning note sounds from somewhere near us, and in an instant the street swarms with men passing casually by with their hands under their blouses.

"Looks like they know I'm here," says the detective with a chuckle. "Follow me." He turns into a low room with a double nail-studded door. Two benches and a table covered with a strip of matting are the only furniture. The owner sits, calmly smoking a cigarette and looking deep in contemplation.

The detective turns back to us. "Ten seconds ago, this room and fifty others were packed shoulder-to-shoulder with men playing illegal fan tan. That one note emptied them all."

My knees weaken, and I look at the detective, wondering why he brought me here, and how I am going to survive the night. Is this his way of preparing me for the Eastern parts of my trip?

"What is fan tan?" someone asks.

"A gambling game using buttons."

For the rest of the night my hand does not stray from Ted's elbow, and by the grin on his face, I wonder if this is his intent in introducing me to the detective.

We leave this place and go up some stairs to a dingy Joss-house, a Chinese folk temple, where more incense sticks burn before a trinity of calm-eyed idols – the God of the Somber Heavens, The God of the Southern Seas, and the God of Happy Wealth – and stroll through the rooms of a restaurant beautiful with carvings and silk hangings, Kakemono scrolls, and marble and ebony furniture.

At eleven at night this transplanted city of Cathay is still alive, the streets crowded with a moving stream of black blouses. Everyone is cheerful, chattering, and wide awake. The shops stand open, and workmen continue their labors as if it were still high noon.

The detective turns down into a basement, and we walk into a little black room, seven by ten. A wheezy gas jet flares about the heads of several gold workers. In front of each, on the work bench at which they sit, is a small bowl of coconut oil in which smolder faintly a handful of thin white racines. The flame from these, with a blowpipe, softens and fuses the metals in which they work.

Ted nudges me and points to a basket filled with bracelets. Their work is marked with ingeniously varied chisel marks.

"I would love to pick one out for you, but…" he shrugs. "The salary of a reporter."

"There's one more place I'd like to show you, Miss Bisland. Are you up for it?" asks the detective.

I eye the Joss sticks stuck in a little earthenware bowl of sand and the tiny corkscrews of smoke rising into the air. The detective has yet to stop any crimes or make any arrests, so I am hopeful the night will end well, but I am unwilling to stay up into the wee hours of the night just to see. "Yes, one more place and then I should be getting back to the hotel."

"You've probably never seen anything like this before. Stick close."

I cling to Ted's arm even tighter, and his grin grows deeper. He is enjoying my discomfort too much. We plunge through a narrow door and grope along a low, torturous passage.

We descend into a cellar by rickety, greasy stairs, thread more back corridors, where, in little branching rooms, somnolent bundles lie motionless on shelves – sodden with poppy fumes, past greasy hot kitchens and cackling cooks, with hissing midnight meals in preparation – and emerge at last into a crowded apartment where men with hideous masks and flaming dresses – like medieval devils in a mystery play – stand idly about waiting for a cue near the stage.

The detective turns for my reaction. He obviously has enjoyed giving me this backstage tour of China Town. "This is the Dom Quai Yuen. The Elegant Flower-House. We are standing in the green-room and wings. They've been performing since four in the afternoon."

I nod, looking around, and though feeling out of place, am quite ignored. Around us they quickly change costume, stiff with gold needlework. Faces are painted and huge beards added. "When does the play end?"

"At midnight. They are performing the classic dramas of China."

We follow the detective to the edge of the stage. He motions for us to come further, and we sit on the stage! From here we can see how crowded the auditorium is. The actors walk around us as they go on and off the stage.

The heat is frightful. I fan myself with my gloves and hope that I don't faint.

The detective notices me wilting and pushes himself up off the stage. "There you go, Miss Bisland. I hope we have given you a send-off to remember." He reaches out a hand to help me up, and Ted quickly reaches for my other hand.

"I feel as if I have already left the United States," I tell them honestly. And I do feel better prepared for what is ahead when I won't have an American detective as my guide.

That night I fall into bed and don't even dream, I am so tired. Since my ship does not leave until the afternoon, I have every intention of sleeping in during my last day on American soil. Because if I don't, I might realize what a mistake I am about to make and change my mind and run straight back to New York.

IN WHICH ELIZABETH BISLAND SAYS GOODBYE TO
AMERICA AND RECEIVES A WELCOMED GIFT.

ONE OF MY FAVORITE DREAMS HAS ALWAYS been the day upon which I should set out on my travels abroad. However, I had always pictured leaving from the Cunard pier, going east. I would stand on the deck of the Cunarder, waving adieu to my unfortunate home-staying friends, with a tasteful mingling of regret and exultation. So it is a matter of active regret that by leaving America from the other side of the continent, this long-dreamed of incident would be forever robbed of the salt of novelty.

My reality is I stand aboard the White Star steamship *Oceanic* of the Occidental and Oriental line, set to cast off at three o'clock Thursday afternoon of November the twenty-first. Mr. Walker tried to bribe the captain into leaving sooner, but he is sticking to his schedule, with the promise of making the journey as fast as he can. Since the ship is powered by both sail and steam, I am confident no matter the weather, we will make good time.

Along with the first class passengers, we have four hundred Chinese in steerage. They run to and fro with queer-colored parcels of strange shapes, keeping up a cheerful chatter. I'm told most of them are going home to settle down upon money made from the "foreign devils," and whatever happens, they can laugh. As they pass, I recognize the odor from last night – opium and incense.

This afternoon I am surprised, not knowing anyone in this part of the world, that I have a gathering come to bid me Godspeed.

"I could not have had a more enchanting visit, gentlemen," I say as a farewell to my new friends at the *Examiner*.

Mr. McEwan shakes my hand. "Good luck. I hope you enjoy your adventure and this ship gets you there ahead of schedule."

"I plan to make eyes at the engineer," I say, only half-joking.

Ted takes off his hat. "If you're ever in these parts again, Miss Bisland, look me up. I'd love to hear firsthand of your time around the world."

I promise him I will. I also give a wary smile and a little wave to a delegation of those martyrs to curiosity who have afflicted me these two days. I'd never seen the like of their urgent messages sent to my hotel room until I arrived at my stateroom this morning to find it crowded with a bevy of young girls wanting a look at me.

My emotions as I stand on the deck are much less mingled and romantic than I planned they should be. I quickly write one last letter to my editor. The note is sealed, addressed, and sent back via the pilot boat. Then the gong sounds, warning all visitors it is time to go ashore. My smile begins to falter, and I wonder if I should go stand on the other side of the boat, looking out over the water, when someone hands up to me from the wharf a great nosegay of white chrysanthemums and roses.

"For me?"

There is a card attached:

"Best Wishes – J.M. Prather" and "New Orleans" is penciled in the corner.

Searching the crowd, I see a hat lifted from a handsome gray head, and two kind dark Southern eyes give me a smile of such friendliness and good-will that it warms my heart. A greeting from my own people.

My smile restored, I wave back at him, thankful for this unknown gentleman taking the trouble to bid me a silent, fragrant farewell, the most delicate and charming impulse of Southern chivalry.

The last wooden link with the shore is withdrawn. There is a fluttering storm of handkerchiefs – a brief space of water in the beautiful bay – and then we pass away to the west through the Gates of Gold.

Slowly, America sinks out of sight, leaving me with a vision of green hills in level sunshine. Even that vanishes at last, and we plunge forward lonely on the heaving, dusky plain. I shiver as the wind picks up.

The paper prayers that the Chinese passengers cast overboard to ensure a safe voyage are caught and whipped sharply away, like autumn leaves falling in the November night. I wonder what Molly is doing right now. *Likely fast asleep with no comprehension of her dearest sister being buffeted upon the sea.*

I watch the waves until the sky grows too dark and my stomach too queasy. It was suggested to me that to avoid seasickness I stay above deck, near the front of the ship, looking forward to my destiny. It does not seem to be working. The top-gallant sails are set to catch the rising evening wind, and I go below to prepare for my first night at sea.

Watch out Nellie Bly. I'm truly on my way now.

THERE WAS NO PLACE FOR US TO WAIT comfortably on the little boat, so we were all standing on deck, shivering in the damp, chilly air, and looking in the gray fog like uneasy spirits while the mail and baggage filled the only cabin, lighted by a lamp with a smoked globe.

"Mr. and Mrs. Jules Verne have sent a special letter asking that if possible you will stop to see them," the London correspondent said as we were on our way to the wharf.

A thrill raced through my mind, and for a moment I couldn't answer. Of course I had dreamed the possibility of meeting the French author on my journey, but never imagined he might learn of my adventure or want to meet me! But if I stopped now, Phileas Fogg would win. What a disappointment to come within a few extra miles of one another. And it was just the sort of things my readers would want to hear about.

"Oh, how I should like to see them," I finally managed to say. "Isn't it hard to be forced to decline such a treat?" My heart ached as I said it.

"If you are willing to go without sleep and rest for two nights, I think it can be done," he said like he didn't care one way or the other.

Dare I hope? "Safely? Without making me miss any connections? If so, don't think about sleep or rest. I can catch up on those necessities later."

"It depends on our getting a train out of here tonight. All the regular trains until morning have left, and unless they decide to run a special mail train for the delayed mails, we will have to stay here all night and that will not give us time to see Verne. We shall see when we land what they will decide to do."

Oh, to be given hope, and then have the possibility of it snatched away again. I hoped the mail we were carrying was enough to tip the scale and make them send on a special train.

The dreary, dilapidated wharf was a fit landing place for our antique boat. I silently followed the correspondent into a large empty shed, where a few men with sleep in their eyes and disheveled uniforms were stationed behind some long, low tables.

"Where are your keys?" Mr. Greaves asked as he sat my solitary bag down before one of these weary looking inspectors.

"It was too full to lock," I answered simply.

"Will you swear that you have no tobacco or tea?" the customs inspector asked my escort lazily.

"Don't swear," I said to him; then, turning to the inspector, I added: "It's my bag."

He smiled and, putting a chalk mark upon the bag, freed us.

"Declare your tobacco and tea or tip the man," I said teasingly to the passenger who stood with poor, shaking Homie under one arm, searching frantically through his pockets for his keys.

"I've fixed him," he answered with an expressive wink.

I was glad I had traveled so light, but, seeing Homie, I briefly thought how fun it would be to have a pet about to keep me company.

Passing through the custom house, we were told they had decided to attach a passenger coach to the special mail train so that we might all go to London without delay. A porter took my bag, and another man in uniform drew forth an enormous key and unlocked the door in the side of the car instead of the end, as in America.

I climbed up the uncomfortably long step and then stubbed my toe on a projectile on the floor before tumbling into my seat. No one said anything, and I pretended it didn't happen.

My escort gave an order to the porter before turning his attention back on me. "Please get comfortable. I'm going to see about our tickets."

While Mr. Greaves was gone, I took a survey of an English railway compartment. My little square was like a hotel omnibus, minus the horses, and was about as comfortable. Two red leather seats ran across the car. I carefully lifted the rug that covered the thing I had fallen over, curious to see what could be so necessary to an English railway carriage as to occupy such a prominent position. It was a bar of iron. No sooner had I dropped the rug in place when the door opened and a porter, catching the iron at one end, pulled it out, replacing it with another like it in shape and size.

"Put your feet on the foot warmer, miss," he said, and I mechanically did as he advised.

The chill was beginning to come off my toes when Mr. Greaves returned, followed by a porter carrying a large basket, which he put in our carriage. I was about to point out the heating rod but stopped myself when he automatically rested his feet on it.

The guard came and took our tickets. Then he pasted a slip of paper on the window, which backwards looked like "etavirP." He went out and locked the door.

"How should we get out if the train ran the track?" I asked, not half-liking the idea of being locked in a box like an animal in a freight train.

"Trains never run off the track in England," was the quiet, satisfied answer.

"Too slow for that," I said teasingly.

Without cracking a smile, he reached for the basket. "Do you want something to eat?"

In an equally quiet and dignified manner I answered, "Yes, thank you," and spread a newspaper across our laps for a tablecloth. We put in our time eating and chatting about my journey until the train reached London.

As no train was expected at that hour, Waterloo Station was almost deserted. It was some time after we stopped before the guard released us.

"Goodbye!" shouted several of my fellow passengers as we parted ways for the last time. "Best wishes on your journey!" And then I was shuffled into a four-wheeled cab, facing a young Englishman who had come to meet us.

"Good morning," he said.

I looked dubiously out the window. If it was daylight, I should not have known it. A gray, misty fog hung like a ghostly pall over the city. But I've always liked fog. It lends such a soft, beautifying light to things that otherwise in the broad glare of day would be rude and commonplace.

"How are these streets compared with those of New York?" he asked.

I looked out over the peaceful scene softly illuminated by gas lamps through the mist. "They are not bad," I said with a patronizing air, thinking shamefacedly of the dreadful streets of New York, although determined to hear no word against them. One can call one's own sister ugly, but don't let a stranger do it! However, if he'd asked me about the train car, I could heartily recommend the comfort of the American model over the English. The English railway carriages were wretchedly heated. One's feet will be burning on the foot-warmer while one's back will be freezing in the cold air above.

We drove first to the London office of *The New York World*. Along the way, the chipper Englishman pointed out Westminster Abbey, and the Houses of Parliament and the Thames, across which we drove. A great many foreigners have taken views in the same rapid way of America, and afterwards gone home and written books about America, Americans, and Americanisms. I will not attempt to do the same.

"Welcome, Miss Bly. Here are your cables." The secretary handed me a stack of envelopes. After opening the first one, I waved it at my correspondent. "I need to go to the American Legation to get a passport."

Off we went.

Mr. McCormick, Secretary of the Legation, came into the room immediately after our arrival, and, bless the man, offered us coffee.

"Miss Bly, welcome, welcome," he said, shaking my hand. "Congratulations on making it thus far on your trip. Please have a seat." He turned to my correspondent. "And you, sir, please wait over there for a moment. I need to ask Miss Bly an important question."

I twisted my gloves in nervousness, wondering what information he would need. He got right down to it.

'There is one question all women dread to answer, and, as very few will give a truthful reply, I will ask you to swear to the rest first and fill in the other question afterwards, unless you have no hesitancy in telling me your age."

My age? That's what the fuss was about?

"Oh, certainly, I will tell you my age, swear to it, too, and I am not afraid. Mr. Greaves may come out of the corner." I laughed. "Twenty-two," I lied. In actuality, I was twenty-five.

"What is the color of your eyes?"

"Green."

It was only a few seconds until we were whirling through the streets of London again. This time we went to the office of the Peninsular and Oriental Steamship Company, where I bought tickets that would cover at least half my journey. A few moments again and we were driving rapidly to the Charing Cross station. I was so cold I was shaking, and I wished English cabs came with heated pokers.

My correspondent went for tickets, and I went for food. It was still early, so I ordered us the only item on the bill of fair that was ready. Ham, eggs, and coffee. It was delicious.

An announcement went out, and my correspondent looked at my half-finished breakfast. "That's us. We have to go."

I took one last gulp of coffee, hoping it was enough to save me from a growing headache before running down the platform to catch the train.

Mr. Greaves tried to keep me awake by pointing out the charming farm houses and meadows, but it didn't matter. I was out until the train stopped.

"We change for the boat here," he said, catching up our bags and rugs, which he hauled to a porter. A little walk down to the pier brought us to the place where a boat was waiting. "It will be warmer in the cabin beneath," Mr. Greaves suggested.

I shook my head and wrapped my arms around my middle, wondering how quickly my body might have forgotten the motion of the waves. "I prefer the fresh air."

"I prefer the bar. I'll be back to introduce you to France. Do you know any French?"

I did not.

"I will translate." And with that, he left me alone at the rail and joined the other men seeking the bar. I tried not to be irritated, considering I was the one who chose to stay out in the cold.

My nose froze by the time we anchored at Boulogne, France. I took my mind off my chill by thinking about my detour. Soon I would be meeting Jules Verne, the inspiration for my most daring stunt. Just what did he think of my little adventure?

At the end of the desolate pier, where boats anchor and where trains start, was a small dingy restaurant. While a little English sailor, who always dropped his h's and never forgot his "sir," took charge of our bags and went to secure accommodations for us in the outgoing train, we followed the other passengers into the restaurant to get something warm to eat.

All around us people were speaking French, and I wondered what I would have done if I had been alone as I had expected. We took our places at the table, and Mr. Greaves began to order in French.

The waiter looked at him blankly.

"Maybe you should order in English," I joked. Perhaps my correspondent didn't know French as well as he thought he did.

The waiter glanced at me in relief. "Yes, please. I'm still learning French."

BACK ON A train, locked in again, my thoughts wandered to the plight of the young English girl and why she needed a chaperone. It would make any American woman shudder with all her boasted self-reliance, to think of sending her daughter alone on a trip, even of a few hours' duration where there was every possibility that during those hours she would be locked in a compartment with a stranger.

I glanced up at the Frenchman sitting opposite me to see if he noticed that I had just stepped on his foot while trying to find some room on the foot-warmer we all shared. He glared at me over the top of his newspaper.

Small wonder the American girl is fearless. She has not been used to so-called *private* compartments in English railway carriages, but to large crowds, and every individual that helps to swell that crowd is to her, a protector. When mothers teach their daughters that there is safety in numbers, and that numbers are the body-guard that shield all woman-kind, then chaperones will be a thing of the past, and women will be nobler and better.

As I was pondering over this subject, the train pulled into a station and stopped.

My escort looked out the window. "We're here. Amiens."

But the door was still locked. We waited and waited. Finally, Mr. Greaves stuck his head out the window and shouted for the guard to come let us out. For my next stunt, I should learn to be a locksmith.

I patted my hair to make sure it was in place. There was nothing I could do if my face was travel-stained. Had I been on an American train, I should have been able to make my toilet en route, so that when I stepped off at Amiens and faced the famous novelist and his charming wife, I would have been as trim and tidy as I would have had I been receiving them in my own home.

Mr. Greaves nudged me. "Quit fussing, here they come."

$\mathcal{9}$

IN WHICH NELLIE BLY ASKS TO SEE M. VERNE'S
STUDY AND HE DOES HER A GREAT KINDNESS.

JULES VERNE'S BRIGHT EYES BEAMED ON ME
with interest and kindliness. His snow-white hair, rather
long and heavy, was standing up in artistic disorder around
his hat, and his full beard, rivaling his hair in snowiness,
hid the lower part of his face. His wife was a short, plump figure
wrapped in a sealskin jacket with her hands tucked snuggly into
a muff. On her white head was a small black velvet bonnet. And
though we did not speak the same language, she greeted me with
the cordiality of a cherished friend.

They had brought their own translator with them, a young
man about my age, a Mr. Robert Sherard, who was also a Paris
journalist.

After introductions, M. Verne led the way to the carriages.
Mme. Verne walked closely by my side, glancing occasionally at
me with a smile, which said in the language of the eye, "I am glad
to greet you, and I regret we cannot speak together."

M. Verne gracefully helped his wife and me into a coupé, while
he entered a carriage with the two other gentlemen. Without a
translator, we were left to our own devices. Her knowledge of the
English language consisted of "No," and my French vocabulary
consisted of "Oui."

It was early evening as we drove through the streets of
Amiens and I got a flying glimpse of bright shops, a pretty park,
and numerous nurse maids pushing baby carriages about. Mme.
Verne pointed out sights along the way, and I smiled at her a lot.

She was a charming woman, and even in this awkward position, she made everything go most gracefully.

Our carriages stopped before a high, stone wall, over the top of which were the peaked outlines of the house. M. Verne hurried up to where we were waiting on a wide, smooth pavement and opened a door in the wall.

Stepping in, I found myself in a small, smoothly paved courtyard, the wall making two sides and the house forming the square. A large, black shaggy dog came bounding forward to greet us. He jumped up against me, his soft eyes overflowing with affection. I tried to gently pet him back down to the ground, but he was exuberant and determined to knock me to his level.

"Follet!" M. Verne called. "Arrête! Assieds-toi." The dog, with a pathetic droop of his tail, received a petting from its master then went off to think it out alone.

Mme. Verne motioned for us to follow her up a flight of marble steps and across the tiled floor of a beautiful little conservatory. We ended up in a large sitting-room that was dusky with the early shade of a wintry evening. Mme. Verne with her own hand touched a match to the pile of dry wood that lay in the wide open fireplace.

Meanwhile, M. Verne urged us to remove our outer wrappings. Before this was done, a bright fire was crackling in the grate, throwing a soft, warm light over the dark room.

Mme. Verne took my elbow and led me to a brocaded silk chair close by the mantel, and when I was seated, she took the chair opposite. Cheered by the warmth, I looked quietly on the scene before me. Though I would have loved to bring out pen and paper to record all I saw, both for my readers and for myself, I concentrated on memorizing all the details that I could.

The room was large, and the hangings and paintings and soft velvet rug, which left only a border of polished hard wood, were richly dark. On the mantel towering about Mme. Verne's head were some fine pieces of statuary in bronze, and a nearby table held several tall silver candlesticks.

A fine white Angora cat came rubbing up against my knee, then seeing its charming mistress on the opposite side, padded over to her and boldly crawled up in her lap as if assured of a cordial welcome.

Next to me in this semi-circle sat Mr. Sherard, then M. Verne, and Mr. Greaves. M. Verne sat forward on the edge of the chair and spoke quickly and with energetic hand motions while Mr. Sherard translated.

"Has M. Verne ever been to America?" I asked.

"Yes, once," translated Mr. Sherard in an attractive, lazy voice quite opposite to M. Verne's short, rapid speech. "For a few days only, during which time I saw Niagara. I have always longed to return, but the state of my health prevents me from taking any long journeys. I try to keep a knowledge of everything that is going on in America and greatly appreciate the hundreds of letters I receive yearly from Americans who read my books."

Mme. Verne methodically stroked the cat with a dainty, white hand, while her luminous black eyes moved alternately between her husband and me. I wondered what she was thinking of us. Her husband who dreamt up an adventure and the young single woman mad enough to attempt it!

"How did you get the idea for your novel, *Around the World in Eighty Days*?" I asked. I knew my readers would want to know the answer, and so did I.

"I got it from a newspaper," he replied.

As a newspaper woman, I was pleased with his answer.

"I took up a copy of *Le Siécle* one morning and found in it a discussion and some calculations showing that the journey around the world might be done in eighty days. The idea pleased me, and while thinking it over, it struck me that in their calculations they had not called into account the difference in the meridians. I thought what a denouement such a thing would make in a novel, so I went to work to write one. Had it not been for the denouement, I don't think that I should ever have written the book."

"Yes, a clever ending."

"What is your line of travel?" he asked.

Happy that I could speak directly to M. Verne without the translator, I answered with my list of destinations which I had memorized. "From New York to London, then Calais, Brindisi,

Port Said, Ismailia, Suez, Aden, Colombo, Penang, Singapore, Hong Kong, Yokohama, San Francisco, New York."

He frowned. "Why do you not go to Bombay as my hero Phileas Fogg did?"

I felt myself blushing. "Because I am more anxious to save time than a young widow!"

He laughed. "You may save a young widower before you return."

At this, and with the translator's attractive voice added on, I know I turned a deeper shade of red. But I tried to smile with a look of superior knowledge, as women, fancy free, always will at such insinuations.

M. Verne spoke to his wife, and Mr. Sherard translated: "It really is not to be believed that this little girl is going all alone around the world. Why, she looks a mere child."

Before my indignation could build to full swell, Mme. intervened in gentle tones, translated next: "Yes, but she is just built for work of that sort. She is trim, energetic, and strong. I believe, Jules, that she will make your heroes look foolish. She will beat your record. I am so sure of that that I will wager with you if you like." The lady looked at me approvingly and melted my heart. If only all women could be as encouraging as she.

M. Verne looked slightly taken aback, but she had changed his opinion. "I would not like to risk my money, because I feel sure – now that I have seen the young lady – that she has the character to do it."

I looked at my watch on my wrist and saw that my time was getting short. There was only one train that I could take from here to Calais, and if I missed it, I might just as well return to New York by the way I came, for the loss of that train meant one week's delay.

"If M. Verne would not consider it impertinent, I should like to see his study before I go," I said at last. I had read so many descriptions of the studies of famous authors and have dwelt with something akin to envy (our space is so limited and expensive in New York) that I should like to see one.

He said he was only too happy to show it to me, and even as my request was translated, Mme. Verne sprang to her feet and lighted one of the tall wax candles.

She started with the quick, springy step of a girl to lead the way. M. Verne, who walks with a slight limp, the result of a wound, followed, and we brought up the rear. We went through the conservatory to a small room up through which was a spiral staircase. Mme. Verne paused at every curve to light the gas.

Up at the top of the house and along a hall that corresponded in shape to the conservatory below, M. Verne continued, with Mme. Verne stopping to light the gas in the hall. He opened a door that led off the hall, and I followed after him.

I had expected, judging from the rest of the house, that M. Verne's study would be a room of ample proportions and richly furnished. But when I stood in M. Verne's study, I was speechless with surprise. He opened a latticed window, the only window in the room, and Mme. Verne, hurrying in after us, lighted the gas jet that was fastened above a low mantel.

The room was very small; even my own little den at home was almost as large. It was also very modest and bare. Before the window was a flat-topped desk. The usual litter that accompanies and fills the desk of most literary persons was conspicuously absent. On the desk was a neat little pile of white paper, one bottle of ink, and one penholder.

"This is part of the new novel I am working on," he said scooping up the stack of paper and handing it to me. "It's about the North Pole."

I eagerly accepted the manuscript, noting the neat penmanship. I was more impressed than ever with the extreme tidiness of this French author. In several places he had most effectually blotted out something he had written, but there was no interlining, which gave me the idea that M. Verne always improved his work by taking out superfluous things and never by adding.

The only other piece of furniture was a broad, low couch in the corner, and here in this room with these meager surroundings, Jules Verne had written the books that had brought him everlasting fame: *A Journey to the Center of the Earth, Twenty*

Thousand Leagues Under the Sea, A Floating City, The Mysterious Island, and of course, the whole reason I was here in the first place, *Around the World in Eighty Days.*

Leading off the study was an enormous library. The large room was completely lined with cases from ceiling to floor, and these glass-doored cases were packed with handsomely- bound books which must cost a fortune.

While we were examining the wealth of literature that was there before us, M. Verne got an idea. Taking up a candle and asking us to follow, he went out into the hall. Stopping before a large map that hung there, holding up with one hand the candle, he pointed out to us several blue marks.

Before his words were translated to me, I understood that on this map he had, with a blue pencil, traced out the course of his hero, Phileas Fogg, before he started him in fiction to travel around the world in eighty days. With a pencil he marked on the map, as we grouped about him, the places where my line of travel differed from that of Phileas Fogg.

"How wonderful," I murmured. This pleased me more than anything else. To think Jules Verne was plotting my trip on his map. It gave me courage to know that the author has drawn it down and thus, creatively at least, has made it so.

Down in the room where we had been before, we found wine and biscuits on the little table, and M. Jules Verne explained that, contrary to his regular rules, he intended to take a glass of wine, that we might have the pleasure of drinking together to the success of my strange undertaking.

We clinked our glasses and they wished me Godspeed.

"If you do it in seventy-nine days, I shall applaud with both hands," Jules Verne said, and then I knew he doubted the possibility of my doing it in seventy-five, as I had promised.

In compliment to me, he endeavored to speak to me in English, and did succeed in saying, as his glass tipped mine, something close to: "Good luck, Nellie Bly."

10

THE PACIFIC OCEAN IS A FOAMING FLOOD of emerald that roars past my porthole, making a dull green twilight within. I see only this and the slats of the upper berth as I lie paralyzed with seasickness.

There are six of these slats. Of this I am unwaveringly sure – though I am not usually accurate about figures – because I counted them several thousand times.

Every plank in the ship creaks and groans and shrieks without once pausing to take breath. I lie on my berth watching my most treasured possessions toboggan around the room.

What are the fleeting things of this world to one whose suffering death must soon put a period? My last will and testament is already made, which is comforting. But I hate the idea of burial at sea. It is such an unnecessarily tragic end to this ridiculous wild-goose chase.

11

IN WHICH NELLIE BLY SAYS GOODBYE
TO HER CORRESPONDENT AND WISHES
TO BE ATTACKED BY BANDITS.

THE DRIVER HAD BEEN TOLD TO MAKE THE
BEST speed back to the station, but here we were
rolling along without concern. I stared anxiously out the
window at the slowly passing scenery, faintly lit by the gas lights.

"I feel as if we are out for a Sunday stroll," I complained to my
correspondent – and continued to complain until Mr. Greaves
finally said something to the unhurried coachman, who picked
up the pace. We reached the station in plenty of time before the
train, and I ignored the pointed looks Mr. Greaves gave me. I was
too tired to try to please everyone.

Apparently, the train which was to carry us to Calais was the
pride of France. It was called the Club train and was similar to
the new vestibule trains in America, which meant you could walk
comfortably from car to car without risking life and limb trying
to cross an open platform while soot rained down from above.

When Mr. Greaves went to check on the time (or get a breath
away from me), I turned to the closest gentleman and asked,
"Why is it called a Club train?" I was uncomfortable with the
idea of traveling with some men's club even though I was going
a short distance.

He shook his head and cleared his throat. "I don't know," he
finally answered in English. "But it is the finest equipped train in
Europe."

After we boarded, I noticed the car in which we sat contained
some women, which put me at ease, but it was liberally filled with

male passengers. Shortly after we left Amiens, a porter made an announcement I was eager to hear.

"Dinner is being served in the dining car."

Everybody filed forward into a front car. There must have been two dining cars because despite the seating arranged around tables, there was enough room for us all. After we had our cheese and salad, we returned to our drawing room car, where we were served with coffee, the men having the privilege of smoking along with it.

My correspondent raised his eyebrows, wondering my opinion, since I had shown him my low thoughts about English trains.

"I am pleased," I gave him. "This is an improvement over our own system and quite worthy of adoption."

There. I would leave him with an impression of my gracious nature.

At Calais, we found I had two hours and more to spend in waiting. The train I intended to take for Brindisi, Italy was a weekly mail train that ran to accommodate the mails and not the passengers. It starts from London at eight o'clock Friday evening of each week. The rule is that the person desiring to travel on it must buy their tickets twenty-four hours in advance of the time of its departure. The mail and passengers are carried across the channel, and the train leaves Calais at 1:30 in the morning.

"Well, let's take a look around," I said to Mr. Greaves, not wanting to spend the time staring at my shoes. His duty to me was over as soon as he placed me on that train, and I wondered if he was as eager to be rid of me as I was of him. If I were to travel the world as a lone single woman, I needed to lose my tiresome escort.

We walked along the near-empty pier and looked at the lighthouse rising thin and white out of the water.

A heavily bearded man, one of the few people awake at this hour, noticed us looking at his building and opened a conversation. "This is one of the most perfect in the world," he boasted in excellent English. "It can throw its light farther away than any other."

Indeed, the revolving light threw out long rays that seemed so little above our heads, but lit up the sky.

"Do the people of Calais ever see the moon or stars?" I mused.

He merely laughed, and we moved on.

We waited in a restaurant until the announcement came that the boat from England had arrived. The be-bundled and be-baggaged passengers came ashore and boarded the train, which was waiting alongside.

One thousand bags of mail were quickly transferred to the train, and then I bade my correspondent goodbye at last. I sped away from Calais, alone once again.

There was but one passenger coach on this train, a Pullman Palace sleeping car with accommodation for twenty-two passengers, one reserved for the guard. When I entered my stateroom at the extreme end of the car, I found it occupied by a pretty English girl with the rosiest cheeks and the greatest wealth of golden-brown hair I ever saw.

"Oh, hello," she said in her smart English accent.

I smiled back to be friendly, but was so tired I hoped she wouldn't be expecting to stay up late getting to know one another.

"I'm Rose. My father and I are going to Egypt for the rest of winter and the spring time. He is an invalid and feels better when we get out of the damp weather. And what about you?" she asked as she began to arrange her bed to her liking.

"Going to Brindisi," I answered shortly. I didn't want to open the Pandora's Box of my entire trip. Perhaps at the proper time in the morning we could go over it all. Thankfully, she seemed to sense my mood and doused the light.

When I woke to the gentle rocking of the train, the room was empty. Hopefully the girl hadn't run to the porter wondering if I were dead like they teased me on the *Augusta*. Truly, didn't anyone else enjoy a good sleeping-in? Hoping I wasn't the last one to wake, I left so the porter could make up our stateroom.

I was surprised at the strange appearance of the interior of the car. All the head and foot boards were left in place, with the bed portions tucked away to allow for day seating. This gave the impression that the coach was divided into a series of small boxes.

As I walked down the car looking into these "boxes," I found them all occupied by unsocial-looking men. Some of them were drinking, some playing cards, and all were smoking until the air was stifling.

When I reached the middle of the car, my little English roommate, who was sitting with her father, saw me.

"Miss Bly!" she moved over. "Please, sit with us."

She introduced me to her father, a cultured, broad-minded man, who, it turned out, had a wonderful sense of humor.

"You must be the one who is going around the world," he started out.

"I tried to tell him you were only going to Italy," the girl broke in.

"Last night, that was as far as I could think," I said, which made them laugh.

"You did sleep in quite a long time," she said, wide-eyed, but with a smile.

"I am determined, in an undertaking such as this, to get as much sleep as I can and as much food as I can, when I can."

The father nodded at my wisdom. "We have some time to spend now," he said. "Would you tell us about your adventure thus far?" At this, he broke off into a racking cough that shook his thin frame as though he had the ague.

Once he had caught a breath, I determined to entertain them with my travels across the sea. When another racking cough hit, I stared determinately at any smoking man who would meet my eye. I never object to cigar smoke when there is some little ventilation, but when it gets so thick that one feels as if it is molasses instead of air that one is inhaling, then I mildly protest.

I wondered what would happen in America, the land of boasted freedom, if a car was thus filled with smoke. But then I concluded it was due to freedom that we do not suffer from such things. Women travelers in America command as much consideration as men.

"Father," the little English-girl said in a clear, musical voice, "the vicar sent you his prayer book just before our departure, and I put it in your bag." She took out a rather bulky book and hugged it to her chest.

"Did you pick out the largest one you could find?"

Her expression formed into a hard, determined light.

"My daughter is very thoughtful," he said to me, then, turning to her, he added with a smile in his eye, "Please take the first opportunity to return the prayer book to the vicar, and tell him, with my compliments, that he might have saved himself that trouble; that I was grieved to deprive him of his book for so long."

The young girl's face settled into a look that spoke disapproval of her father's words and a determination not to return the prayer book.

Their discussion was interrupted when the conductor, or the "guard," as they called him, served our mid-day meal. The father explained that the train picked up food while stopped for coal or water, but that in the evening a dining car would be attached to the train for us.

"Won't that be nice?" I commented, remembering my meal in the dining car coming out of Amiens.

He shook his head. "It's not the thing for women to eat in a public car with men. You two will be served in your state room."

That seemed hardly fair, but I supposed if I waited for a fully-equipped passenger train to take me where I needed to go, I would never beat Phileas Fogg. This was a minor inconvenience, though it did nothing to improve my opinion of this portion of my trip.

In the course of the afternoon, we passed some high and picturesque mountains covered with a white frost, though I might have seen more of France if the car windows had been clean. From their appearance, I judged that they had never been washed. One would think that with the extra insulation of dirt, the cold couldn't get in, but I found that, even wearing my Ulster and wrapped in a rug, I was none too warm.

My little roommate helped me pass the time trying to implant the seeds of her faith in my mind, and I listened, thinking from her words that if she was not the original Catherine Eslmere, she at least could not be more like that interesting character.

In everything else, she was the sweetest, most gentle girl I ever met, but her religion was of the hard, uncompromising kind that condemns everything, forgives nothing, and swears the heathen is forever damned because he was not born to know the religion of her belief.

About eight o'clock in the morning, we reached Modena. The baggage was examined there, and all the passengers were notified in advance to be prepared to get out and unlock the boxes that belonged to them.

"Miss Bly, are you certain you have no more than your handbag?" the conductor asked me for the third time.

"Yes, quite certain. I packed it myself." I needed to keep track how many men were flabbergasted with my lack of luggage on this trip. Was it really that hard to believe a woman could travel with less than a complete suite of bags?

"If any boxes are found unlocked, with no owner to open them, they will be detained by custom inspectors." He gave me a serious look.

"I can show them my handbag. It is quite unlocked."

He waved his hands to indicate no need. "No one will bother to inspect your handbag."

Half an hour later, we were in Italy.

I was anxiously waiting to see that balmy, sunny land, but though I pressed my face close to the frosty window pane, bleak night denied me even one glimpse of sunny Italy and its dusky people. I went to bed early.

It was so very cold that I could not keep warm out of bed, and I cannot say that I got much warmer in bed. The berths were provided with only one blanket each. It was as bad an economy as at the madhouse, where the patients were refused warm clothing to save expenses, and only given one blanket. Were it not for my newspaper articles exposing the horrors, those women would still be teeth-chattering, sitting on those cold chairs all the day long.

I piled all my clothing on the berth and spent half the night lying awake.

"The passengers last week were more fortunate than us on this stretch," I complained in the dark to my little roommate.

"The ones who were attacked by bandits?" she exclaimed. "How could you say such a thing?"

"If they felt the scarcity of blankets as we do, they at least had some excitement to make their blood circulate."

She laughed, and that was the last I heard from her until morning.

When I got awake, I hastily threw up the window shade and eagerly looked out. I fell back in surprise, wondering, if for once in my life I had made a mistake and woken up early.

I could not see any more than I had the night before on account of a heavy gray fog that completely hid everything more than a yard away.

Looking at my watch, I found that it was ten o'clock, so I dressed with some haste, determined to find the guard and demand an explanation of him. At this rate, I would go around the world and yet see nothing of it!

"It is a most extraordinary thing," he said to me, "I never saw such a fog in Italy before."

All day I traveled through Italy – "sunny Italy" along the Adriatic Sea. The fog still hung a heavy cloud over the earth, and only once did I get a glimpse of the land I had heard so much about. It was evening, just at the hour of sunset, when we stopped at some station.

I went out on the platform, and the fog seemed to lift for an instant. On one side was a beautiful beach. Its bay was dotted with boats bearing oddly-shaped sails of red, yellow, green, which somehow looked to me like mammoth butterflies dipping, dipping about in search of honey. Most of the sails were red, and as the sun kissed them with renewed warmth, the sails looked as if they were composed of brilliant fire.

I sighed contentedly. Now *that* was what I was expecting of Italy.

A high rugged mountain was on the other side of the train, and I became dizzy looking up at the white buildings perched on the perpendicular side. The road that went in a winding line up the hill had been built with a stone wall on the oceanside; as adventurous as I was, I would not care to travel up it.

To top off everything, we arrived at Brindisi two hours late.

12

IN WHICH NELLIE BLY BECOMES IN
DANGER OF MISSING HER SHIP.

WHEN THE TRAIN STOPPED IN BRINDISI, our car was surrounded with men wanting to carry us as well as our baggage to the boats. Their making no mention of hotels led me to wonder if people always passed through Brindisi without stopping. All these men spoke English very well, but the guard intervened and corralled the women together.

"I will get one omnibus and escort the two English women, the invalid man and his daughter, and Miss Bly to their boats," he said. "I will see to it that you are not charged more than the right fare."

We drove first to the boat bound for Alexandria. My roommate hugged me goodbye, and her father wished me luck. Then we drove to the boat that the rest of us expected to sail on. It was an English vessel, part of the Peninsular and Oriental Steam Navigation Company, the P. & O line, which traversed boldly through the British Empire.

I alighted from the omnibus and followed my sleepy companions up the gangplank. As seemed to be my lot in these travels, my transfer took place at one in the morning. I earnestly hoped everyone would be in bed as I dreaded meeting English people with their much-talked of prejudices. I was anxious what they would do to an American onboard.

The crowds of men on the deck dispelled my fond hope. I think every man on board was up waiting to see the new passengers. They must have felt but ill-paid for their loss of sleep, for besides the men who came on board, there were only the two large English women and my own plain, uninteresting self.

As the women were among their own people, I waited for them to take the lead. But after we had stood at the foot of the stairs for some time, being gazed at by the men, and no one came forward to attend to our wants, which were few and simple, I realized these women were more helpless than I, and I gently spoke up.

"Is this the usual manner of receiving passengers on English boats?"

They quietly answered back, "It is strange, very strange. A steward or someone should come to our assistance."

At last a man came down below, and as he looked connected with the boat, I stopped him. "Excuse me, would it be expecting too much to ask if we might have a steward to show us to our cabins?"

"There should be some about," he answered. "STEWART! STEWART!" he called with an unusual enunciation, making me wonder if the steward really was called Stewart.

Even this brought no one to us, and as he went off in one direction to find one, I set out in the other, followed by the guard from the train, who had become quite concerned. Another man directed us to the purser's office, the first door to the left.

Sitting in the office was the purser and a man I supposed to be the doctor. I gave my ticket and a letter I had been given at the P. & O. office in London to the purser. This letter requested that the commanders and pursers of all the P. & O. boats on which I traveled should give me all the care and attention it was in their power to bestow.

His lip twitched as he took it. Then after a leisurely reading of the letter, he very carelessly turned around and told me the number of my cabin.

I paused. "May a steward show me the way?"

He made a grimace. "There does not seem to be any about at this hour. The cabin is on the port side." He impolitely turned his back and busied himself with some papers on his desk.

The train guard who still stood by my side said, "I'll help you find the cabin."

After a little search, we did find it. I opened the door and stepped in, and the sight that met my eyes both amused and dismayed me. Band-boxes, boots, handbags, and gowns littered the floor, and the upper berth was also filled with clothes. Two bushy heads stuck out of the two lower berths, and two high pitched voices exclaimed simultaneously with a vexed intonation. "Oh!"

I echoed their "Oh!" in a slightly different tone and backed out.

I returned to the purser with my patience at its limits. My watch told me it was going on to two o'clock in the morning, and I still wanted to send out a cable before the ship left.

"I cannot sleep in an upper berth, even if it were not being used as a storage closet. And I will not occupy a room with two other women." My fears of being ill-treated were coming true, though I had expected the officers to show some restraint.

He looked over the letter again, as if to see how much weight he should give it, then referred me to another cabin.

"And these came for you, care of the *Victoria*." He handed me some cables, which I eagerly accepted.

This time a steward made his appearance, and he took on the part of an escort.

I found a pretty girl in that cabin, who lifted her head anxiously, and then gave me a friendly smile when I entered. I put my bag down and returned to the guard who was waiting to take me to the cable office.

I stopped to ask the purser if I had time to make the trip. The two women who had traveled with me from Calais had by this time found their way to his office. He looked around them and answered, "If you hurry."

As I walked away, I heard one of the women say, "We left home in such a rush, we left our purses and tickets lying on the table in the sitting room!" Oh dear. One more reason I had to be thankful for packing only one bag.

The guard took me down the gangplank and along several dark streets. At last, coming to a building where a door stood open, he stopped and I followed him in. The room in which we stood was perfectly bare and lighted by a lamp whose chimney was badly smoked. The only things in the room were two stationary desks. On the one lay a piece of blank paper before an ancient ink well and a much-used pen.

Dismayed, I said, "Everyone's gone for the night. Looks like I'll have to wait until the next port."

"Not at all. Write your message. I'll ring for the operator. They're used to it." He pulled at a knob near a small closed window, much like a postage stamp window. The bell made quite a clatter.

I wrote my message:

I reached Brindisi this morning on time after an uneventful trip across the Continent. The railway journey was tedious and tiresome, but I received no end of courtesy from the railway officials, who had been apprised of my coming. In a few hours I will be on the bosom of the Mediterranean. I am quite well though somewhat fatigued. I send –

The window opened with a clink, and a head appeared at the opening.

"Tell him I'm almost ready."

– kind greetings to all friends in the United States.
Nellie Bly.

The guard spoke in Italian, but, hearing me speak English, the operator answered directly. "Where do you want to send the cable?"

"New York."

"Where is that?" he asked, gathering some books.

I tried to keep the surprise out of my voice when I answered. "On the east coast of America." I hadn't expected knowledge of America to drop off the earth so soon on my trip.

He flipped through his books – looking, he explained, for the line by which he could send the message – and then for how much it would cost.

The whole thing was so new and amusing to me that I forgot all about the departure of the boat until we had finished the business and stepped outside.

A whistle blew long and warningly. I looked at the guard; the guard looked at me. It was too dark to see each other, but I know our faces were the picture of dismay. My heart stopped beating, and I thought with emotions akin to horror that my boat was gone – and with it my limited wardrobe.

13

IN WHICH ELIZABETH BISLAND EMERGES ON
DECK AND MEETS HER FELLOW PASSENGERS.

I T IS MY FIFTH DAY ABOARD, AND THE BOILING
pot of the sea has finally subsided. I begin to take beef tea and
resolve to live.

Before venturing on deck, I write a letter to my sister and tell
her of my misery. If I survive this trip around the world, she will
have some persuading to do to get me on another sea voyage. We
had always talked of taking a leisurely tour of our favorite literary
sites in England. Perhaps I could endure the seasickness better if
I have Molly to commiserate.

After slipping the letter into my handbag, I venture out to
make peace with the sun and the waves.

Other women are also beginning to straggle back to life on
deck – pale, wan, and with neglected hair tied up in lace scarves.
They lie in steamer chairs swathed in rugs, and are indifferent
about their appearance and to the charms of conversation. I have
no trouble joining them while my senses slowly return, and I find
an empty chair to claim as my own.

There is something comforting about being wrapped up tight
in a rug, face upturned to the redeeming warmth of the sun.
I hold out hope that tonight I will be able to sit at table with
the captain as he has expressed concern over me. The sea air is
surprisingly refreshing, and soon I am revived and looking for
someone to talk me out of my boredom.

The typical American girl is with us – greyhound-waisted,
with tiny feet, clad with tailor-made neatness. As she appears

to be traveling alone, I move my chair beside her to strike up a conversation.

"You are the reporter," she says, putting down her camera when I approach.

"I don't work for a newspaper. I write for *The Cosmopolitan*." To most people there is no difference, but I like to make the point anyway.

"But you are in a race around the world? Against Nellie Bly?"

I nod.

"And are you in the lead?"

I laugh at her eagerness for gossip. "I suppose I won't know until I land home again." I place my hand over my stomach. "And for the last few days I haven't cared one bit."

She nods. "I had a touch of seasickness myself." She holds up her camera. "Do you know how to work one of these? I want to have it all decided before we reach land. I'm to visit the American Minister to Japan."

I eye the box she has on her lap. "No. I've only been on the portrait side of a camera."

"May I practice on you?"

She looks so in earnest that I agree.

"Stand over there by the rigging. I think the sun will be just right, don't you?"

She spends several minutes adjusting a string, checking her notes, and finally, presses a button at the side.

"Is this your first time above deck?" she asks as she twists the key at the top of the box. "I arose from the dead yesterday and have been enjoying myself ever since." She points to the water. "Go see how the color has changed since we left dock."

My legs, still weak after all the lying down, carry me tentatively towards the rail where I look out over a vast liquid field. Sapphires would be pale and cold beside this sea – palpitating with wave shadows deep as violets, yet not purple, and with no touch of any color to mar its perfect hue. It is a beautiful but lonely view.

When I return to the amateur photographer, several other young women have gathered around her. I am introduced to a group of missionaries. It seems we have a full cargo of them – mostly young women, and on this occasion, all Presbyterians.

"Is there much missionary work in Japan?" I ask.

"Oh, yes," answers a young doctor, who has just taken her degree. She wears "reform" clothes, the hem of her skirt falling above her ankles, and I would guess she has a pair of bloomers in her trunk for healthy cycling. She has a strong, well-cut face, from which her heavy hair is brushed smoothly back.

"How long will you be there?"

She smiles with the look of someone eager to save both souls and bodies. "Ten years."

Ten years! That is a long commitment for one so young. But she has the confidence of someone likely to consider the physical welfare of her patients of more importance than the acceptance of her creed. Her future is simple and pleasant to guess at.

I am less sure of the handsome, slim girl of twenty with deep-set gray eyes, and delicate pointed fingers. In a spasm of romantic exaltation of which young women of her age are subject, she has condemned herself to a decade of lonely exile in a remote Japanese town. She smiles at me, and I smile back.

When the missionaries leave, I voice my concerns to the amateur photographer. "Her eyes are earnest, but her dimples belie she is sacrificing her best young years."

The photographer shrugs her indifference.

After a moment of reflection, I add with a laugh, "One can only hope for some modern-day Cymon to come rescue this Christian Iphigenia from her Oriental altar before the knife of distaste and ennui murder her youth and charm."

The photographer makes a show of scanning the horizon, her face in all seriousness. "There is no sign of his warship. If he is to steal her away, he best make haste."

We are both quiet as we stare out at the solitary sea. In all these many thousand miles we never see a sail or any shore. There is no sea life about us, save of the sword-winged birds that follow us from San Francisco without any sign of fatigue.

A T DINNER I join the captain at his table. He introduces me to the sturdy folk who have been with him from the start, mostly gentlemen with business ventures which cause them to cross the ocean.

"First time on a ship, is it?" asks the gentleman to my left. He is an Englishman who has made his fortune in China and since retired. Now he is bringing a new-made wife out, by way of America, to see the East, where he had lived so long.

I nod, taking a deep breath of the fresh dinner roll placed at my spot and wait for my turn with the butter. "But am happy to report that the worst of it is over, and am thrilled to be joining you all here tonight to eat real food once again."

At this he chuckles and elbows his wife, an angular English girl. She automatically smiles as one does in polite company. "The food onboard the *Oceanic* is legendary," she begins. "The poached salmon we ate last night was even better than its reputation." She goes on for a time describing all that I have missed.

"If tonight's meal is half as good, I shall be pleased," I consent.

"Wait until you taste the food in China," said the Englishman. "Ah, I miss it so. I've not had decent rice or my favorite sweet and sour pork dish…." He brings his fingers up to his lips as if tasting. "My mouth waters at the thought of that sauce." A waiter sets a plate of Beef Wellington in front of him, and he returns from his reminiscing.

My stomach grumbles at the rich smells.

"I suppose by the end of it, you'll have eaten your way around the world," the Englishman continues. "I admit I'm jealous. If I were a younger man, I would be tempted to change my plans and follow you."

As the husband and I talk, I watch the wife's reactions. She has all the makings of a British matron, one who knits gray stockings and keeps herself carefully aloof from acquaintances that might be detrimental in the future. I decide she is unsure of me and my global pursuits.

Also at our table is a couple from Georgia, Mr. and Mrs. White, who have lived twenty years in Los Angeles, but have lost nothing of their old-fashioned Georgia ways and looks and still speak with a soft Southern drawl.

"And you think going west will be faster than if you had started out east?" asks the husband. "Seems to me you are going backward."

"My editor insists the timetables in this direction are in my favor." I lean forward conspiratorially and, with an eye on the captain engrossed in discussion with the other half of the table, whisper, "And he has offered the captain a bonus should he break any speed records taking me to Japan."

This revelation achieves much laughter and knowing looks that insider information provides. I dare not tell them the amount. It would astonish them too much.

After dinner, the Englishman suggests I follow him. "I know just who you can talk with to add some color to your articles."

He leads his wife and me to the stairs going down to steerage. "Many of the Chinese are merchants who have a merchant's pass, which enables them to return to America when their business across the water is finished. But some are going home to die. See that man right there?" He points to a young fellow, leaning against the wall where he can catch the best of the salt breezes. "He is but a mere twenty-six years old. He lies there all day."

The fellow's hands are crossed, and his eyes half open. His hands and face are the color of old wax, as impassive as if indeed they were cut from some such substance.

The Englishman touches his hand in comfort as we walk past. "It is common among the emigrants to America to fall sick with a consumption and to struggle back in this way to die at home."

I look down at the man as I pass. He seems afraid to breathe or move, lest he should waste the failing oil or snuff out the dying flame ere he reaches his yearned-for-home – the Flowery Kingdom – the Celestial Empire! I feel like I should say something to him since we were just talking about him in his hearing, but I can't think of what, so I smile in what I hope is a comforting look.

We keep up our search until we end up on the after-deck where fan-tan rages all day long. Oh, what I would give to hear my detective friend blow his whistle and see the gamblers scramble. When a less dangerous amusement is desired, they also play an intricate game of chess or dominoes.

The Englishman introduces me to an old gentleman with an iron-gray pigtail and wearing a lurid pair of brocaded trousers.

"This here is Tam. A genuine 'Forty-niner.' Tell her what you told me."

The old gentleman takes on a bemused expression. "I came to California during the gold fever. I was rich in those early days," he explains in fluent and profane American. "Fan-tan, poker, euchre, and horse races have taken almost all of it."

After seeing the Chinese Quarter, I understand what this man's life might have been like – staying up all hours of the night gambling and taking in the late-night theater.

He grins. "But now I am going home to die in China. It costs less to cross waters alive than in pine box."

14

IN WHICH NELLIE BLY MAKES A FAST DASH FOR HER SHIP AND HAS A LITTLE TROUBLE AT HER FIRST TIFFIN.

C AN YOU RUN?" ASKED THE GUARD IN A husky voice.

"Yes!"

He took close grasp of my hand, and we started down the dark street with a speed that should have startled a deer – down the dark streets, past astonished watchmen and late pedestrians, until a sudden bend brought us in full view of my ship still in port.

The boat for Alexandria, Egypt had gone, but not mine. I was saved.

F INALLY, I WAS able to tumble into bed and fall right to sleep. However, I had not been asleep long, it seemed to me, until I waked to find myself standing upright beside my berth, water dripping off my traveling dress.

"Oh!" I sputtered, glancing at my drenched self.

Above me came the sounds of vigorous scrubbing on the deck, and before I could piece everything together, I was drenched again with scrub water as it came pouring into my open porthole. I fumbled to let the heavy window down and, since I was so exhausted, went back to bed, dripping wet.

I had not been asleep many moments until I heard a voice call: "Miss, will you have your tea now?"

I opened my eyes and saw a steward standing at the door, awaiting a reply.

"No, thank you," I mumbled.

"None for me, either," said the English girl on the other side of my cabin.

And then I was off to sleep again.

"Miss, will you have your bath now?" a voice broke in on my slumbers shortly afterwards.

I looked up in disgust at a little white-capped woman who was bending over me. I was tempted to say I had just had my bath, a shower-bath, but thought better of it before speaking.

"In a few minutes," I managed to get out – and then I was back asleep.

"Well, you are a lazy girl! You'll miss your bath and breakfast if you don't get up this instant," was my third greeting.

My surprise at the familiarity of the remark got the better of my sleepiness. *Well, by all that is wonderful, where am I? Am I in school again that a woman dare assume such a tone to me?*

I answered stiffly, "I generally get up when I feel so inclined."

My roommate was missing, but I felt like sleeping and I decided to sleep; whether it pleased the stewardess or not, it mattered little to me.

The steward was the next one to put in an appearance.

"Miss, this ship is inspected every day, and I must have this cabin made up before they come," he said complainingly. "The captain will be here presently."

There was nothing to do but to get up, which I did. I found my way to the bathroom, but soon saw that it was impossible for me to turn on the water, as I did not understand the mechanism of the faucet.

"Excuse me," I asked a steward, "where is the stewardess?"

"The stewardess is taking a rest and cannot be disturbed."

I threw up my hands, startling the poor boy. The irony was beyond me.

After dressing, I wandered up on the next deck and found the dining hall. A young man was putting out silverware on a round table.

"I'm sorry, miss. Breakfast was over long ago." He looked up enough to give me a sympathetic look.

Tired and hungry, I went out on deck for my very first glimpse of the lazy-looking passengers in their summer garments. They lounged about in comfortable positions, or slowly promenaded the deck, which was sheltered from the heat of the sun by a long stretch of awnings.

My gaze passed over them to the smooth, velvety looking water of the Mediterranean, the bluest I had ever seen, softly gurgling against the side of the ship, and I drank in the balmy air, soft as a rose leaf, and just as sweet, air such as one dreams about but seldom finds.

Standing there alone among strange people, on strange waters, I thought…how sweet life is. Perhaps now will be the start of my vacation-like stunt and I can catch my breath. It has been so long since I've properly relaxed.

"Miss Bly! Nellie Bly!" called my cabin mate from one of the steamer chairs. "Come join us." The "us" were several young ladies with bright faces, happy to have left cold, wet weather behind.

I gave her a hearty wave and eyed the throngs on deck lounging on their chairs. The guard had bought one for me at Brindisi and sent it on before our departure. I had no idea where it was. "I need to find my steamer chair."

She hefted her long white skirt to the side and jumped up. "I'll help."

There were over three hundred passengers on the ship, and I suppose they averaged a chair apiece. We worked our way through about two hundred before I asked where the deck-stewards were.

"There aren't any on this ship. I presume the quarter-master has charge of the decks, but we are expected to look after our own chairs and rugs, and if we don't, it is useless to inquire for them if they disappear."

I could tell my cabin mate was losing enthusiasm. "Why don't you go back to your friends? I'll look a few more places."

"If you're sure. Well, all right," she readily agreed, and I continued my search.

"Miss?" An Englishman with a touch of silver at his temples stopped me. "Are you looking for the young girl and her father?"

When I gave him a confused look, he continued, "You and I were on the same trip from Calais on the India express. I noticed you on the train."

"Oh, no. They have gone on to Egypt. I'm traveling alone."

His eyes widened. "No escort?"

The bugle blew for luncheon, potentially rescuing me from a lecture on my folly.

"Would you go with me to tiffin?" he asked, before further explaining.

"Tiffin?"

"Ships traveling in Eastern seas always go by the Indian title 'tiffin' for luncheon." He held out his arm.

As I had gone without breakfast, I was only too anxious to go at the first opportunity and latched onto his invitation and his arm.

The dining hall was on the second deck. It was a small room nicely decorated with tropical foliage plants and looked quite cozy and pretty, but it was never intended to accommodate a ship carrying more than seventy-five first-class passengers.

The headwaiter, who stood at the door, stared at us blankly as we went in. I hesitated, naturally thinking that he would show us to some table.

"Should we ask him where to sit?" I whispered.

The gentleman raised his eyebrows questioningly at the waiter.

"Sit anywhere," he said. So we sat down at the nearest empty table.

We had just been served our first course, a French onion soup, when four women ranging from twenty-four to thirty-five came in, all wearing oversized hats to match their stylish tea dresses. With indignant snorts of surprise, they seated themselves at the same table. They were followed by a short, fat woman with a sweeping walk and air of satisfied assurance. She eyed us in a supercilious way before turning to the others with an air of injured dignity.

The Englishman smiled politely at them all and greeted them with an unaware "Good afternoon."

I simply smiled and ate my soup and hoped they would leave us alone.

Next to the table arrived two men, and as there were only places for seven at the table, the young man squeezed onto the lounge with the girls, but the elderly man went out.

Then we were made to suffer.

"I do hate people coming to our table," said the older woman. She snapped her napkin before placing it on her abundant lap.

"Too bad papa was robbed of his place," said the young woman who sat at my left.

The other girl piped up in support, "Yes, it's a shame people have to be crowded from their own table."

I frowned my disapproval at the lot of them before turning to my Englishman friend. "So, you have made this trip before?"

"Several times. I've lived in India twenty years as part of the Civil Service in Calcutta." He went on to tell me the ins and outs of his job, oblivious to the brewing storm of protest at the table.

The young woman beside me was not content to confine her rudeness to her tongue, so she repeatedly reached across my plate, brushing my food with the lace at the edge of her sleeves without one word of apology.

I was never so glad to see a meal ended. I felt terribly that I had only half listened to the gentleman's interesting stories as I was trying to make it obvious that I was ignoring the rude lot at the table.

All afternoon I fussed about their behavior. I had been expecting some hatred due to my being an American, but was surprised they had treated their fellow Englishman the same way, unless it was because he was with me. But then I saw this same group misbehaving on deck and realized I was not insulted because I was an American, but because the people were simply ill-bred.

When dinner came, we found that we were debarred from the dining room. Passengers who got on at London were given the preference, and as there were not accommodations for all, the passengers who boarded the ship at Brindisi had to wait for second dinner.

It was nine o'clock when the dining room was cleared that night, and the Brindisi passengers were allowed to take their places at the table. Everything was brought to us as it was left from the first dinner – cold soup, the remnants of fish, cut up bits of beef and fowl – all down the miserable course until at last came cold coffee!

At first we all looked at one another in shock. Then it started.

"This is an outrage!"

"Where is the captain? He must hear of our ill treatment."

"The captain won't do anything," said a distinguished gentleman to my right. "It is likely he ordered it. Have any of you had opportunity to observe the man? Uncouth. Lacking in manners." Nods went round. We all had a story about the captain.

When we made inquiries, we were told that only at dinner were the places reserved, but that at breakfast and tiffin, first there were first served. I knew I would never make it early to breakfast, so the next day I went in to early tiffin. As I was leaving the dining room, I ran into the two women who traveled with me on the India Express to Brindisi.

The elder was leaving in tears. "I am a grandmother, and this is the sixth trip I have made to Australia, and I was never treated so insultingly in my life."

"What happened?" I asked, feeling somewhat protective of my fellow passengers.

The younger answered, "We went in early, so that we could get the good food, instead of the leftovers. We went to sit at a table that was empty but for a young man who sat at the head. He said, 'You can't sit there. I've reserved those places for some of my friends.'"

She paused to allow me time to be offended on their behalf. She continued, "There was another table close by, so we moved. But after we sat down, some late-comers requested we get up and give the places to them!"

"That is terrible," I agreed. "My experience was much better today than yesterday. Perhaps it will get better as we all get used to each other." That is what I said, but what I was thinking was how unaccommodating the English were.

NOTWITHSTANDING ALL ANNOYING trifles, it was a very happy life we spent in those pleasant waters. The decks were filled all the day, and when the lights were put out at night the passengers reluctantly went to their cabins.

The passengers formed two striking contrasts. There were some of the most refined and lovely people on board, and there were some of the most ill-bred and uncouth. Most of the women, whose acquaintance I formed, were very desirous of knowing all about American women, and frequently expressed their admiration for the free American woman, many going so far as to envy me, while admiring my unfettered happiness. Two clever Scotch women I met were traveling around the world, but taking two years at it. One Irishwoman, with a laugh that rivaled her face in sweetness, was traveling alone to Australia.

In the daytime, the men played cricket and quoits. Sometimes in the evenings, we had singing, and other times we went to the second-class deck and listened to better music given by second-class passengers. When there were no chairs, we would all sit down on the deck and greatly enjoy ourselves.

There was one little girl with a pale, slender face, who was a great favorite with us all, though none of us ever spoke to her. She sang in a sweet, pathetic voice a little melody about "Who'll buy my silver herrings?" until, I know, if she had tried to sell any, we should all have bought. The best we could do was to join her in the refrain, which we did most heartily.

Better than all to me, it was to sit in a dark corner on deck, above where the sailors had their food, and listen to the sounds of a tom-tom and a weird musical chanting that always accompanied their evening meal.

The sailors were Lascars. They were the most untidy looking lot I ever saw, and doubtless, if I could have seen as well as heard them at their evening meal, it would have lost its charm. Over a pair of white muslin drawers, they wore long muslin slips very like in shape to the old-time nightshirt. This was tied about the waist with a colored handkerchief, and on their heads they wore gaily-colored turbans, which were really nothing but a crown of straw with a scarf-shaped piece of bright cloth, often six feet in length, wound about the head. Their brown feet were always bare. They chant, as all sailors do, when hoisting sails, but otherwise were a grim, surly-looking set, climbing about over the ship like a pack of monkeys.

After we had been out several days, a young woman came to me on my way to tiffin with an unsealed cable.

"Are you Nellie Bly?"

"Yes."

"The purser gave this cable to some of the passengers yesterday, as he did not know who you were. We've been passing it amongst ourselves until it has found you."

I bit back my harsh words for the purser and thanked the woman. Didn't know who I was? He had to remember the woman who kept storming into his office in Italy. He did it for spite. Sending my cable through the ship as the latest gossip. I waited for the woman to leave before I read it.

Fortunately, it was from my editor and was only a note to tell me the newspaper had started a contest to see who could guess my exact time around the world. The prize was a first-class trip to Europe. Apparently, I'm a hit back home, no matter what the purser thinks.

———

A T TIFFIN, MY Englishman between bites of fruit salad, said, "People think you are an eccentric American heiress, traveling about with a hair brush and a bank book."

"Ha!" I laughed. "That explains some of the attention I am receiving. Everyone is after my money."

The gentleman across the table said, "I have always killed the desire to marry because I don't expect to find a woman who can travel without innumerable trunks and bundles."

I had noticed that he dressed exquisitely and changed his apparel at least three times a day. I could not resist a comment. "Mr. Gregory, how many trunks do you carry with you?"

"Nineteen."

"Nineteen! Are you afraid she would out do you?"

My Englishman laughed, but Mr. Gregory did not.

Leaving tiffin, I walked out on deck and was joined by a young man who seemed to be waiting for me. After several starts and stops, he spoke his mind. "You are the kind of a girl I like."

"Oh? And what kind is that?"

"You like to travel. So do I. Thing is, I'm the second son, so my brother will get both the money and the title. I figure if I were to find a wife who would settle £1,000 a year, we could get on nicely."

To my surprise, he looked earnest, like I would jump at the chance not only to be his traveling companion, but to pay for the privilege. "Is your older brother single?" I asked with a smile.

15

IN WHICH ELIZABETH BISLAND PASSES THE TIME PLAYING QUOITS – AND ALL THE WHILE GOES STEADILY WESTWARD, DRIVEN BY WIND AND STEAM.

THE WEEK IS NEARLY DONE BEFORE THE whole ship's company is assembled at table, and we begin to take note of our fellow-voyagers in this water caravansary. I realize my seasickness could have been worse now that I see all these new faces emerging more drained and delicate than mine had been.

My decision to not overly-limit my packing was wise. Changing dress for dinner provides a break in the monotony of the day, and with my silk I fit in with the fashion of the women invited to the captain's table.

Captain Kempson is proud of his ship as he only received his first commission as captain in June. He is eager to speak of all aspects of the ship and crew as they have just set a Yokohama-San Francisco record of 13 days, 14 hours, 6 minutes, and in turn we are all swept up in his excitement. Me especially.

"Congratulations. I hope you can set another record on this voyage," I say boldly, thinking of my adversary and wondering how fast she has managed to travel thus far.

Captain Kempson smiles, for he knows what I am about. "The *Oceanic* was built in 1870. The first in the White Star line and was a jewel in her day before being chartered to the Occidental & Oriental Steamship Company for the run between San Francisco and China."

A jewel, yes, but not freshly polished like the *Augusta Victoria* on which Nellie Bly began her trip. The experienced passengers have told me – outside of the captain's hearing – that other ships have since surpassed the *Oceanic* in luxury. Not knowing anything of life aboard these other ships, I am pleased the White Star company was progressive enough nineteen years ago to install electric call buttons in our first-class staterooms as well as convenient water taps instead of water jugs.

"Three sister ships were built shortly after: the *Atlantic*, *Baltic*, and *Republic*," says the captain.

The woman to my right, Mrs. Baxter, a widow traveling with the Whites, says, "Clever, but the company will run out of names if they insist on ending their ships in –ic."

"Well, I dunno," says in a gentleman across from the captain. He tips his water glass in the woman's direction. "Celtic, Adriatic, Olympic. There's three more, right there. Hardly any trouble at all."

"Germanic!" announces the businessman from Pittsburgh.

"Nomadic...er, Teutonic," says the Brit. Smiles spread as we realize it is a new game.

"Majestic," I add before someone else can take it.

The table settles into thoughtful silence as we eye each other while our main course is served, mouthwatering Filets mignons.

"Slavic," says Mrs. White, pleased she herself has thought of a name.

"Gigantic," says the Brit, complete with hand motions, and we laugh.

"Titanic," says the businessman. "It's more refined." Nods all around. That seems to settle the game, and we lapse into silence as we eat.

"You have a sampling of the world in your crew, Captain," comments the businessman.

The captain reflects for a minute before counting off on his fingers: "Norwegians, Russians, English, French, Japanese, Americans, Germans, Hungarians, and even one Manx-man – our chief-engineer. You will know him from the 'out of country' flavor given to his speech. He says it is quite common for someone from the Isle of Man."

"What island is that?" asks Mrs. White.

"Between England and Scotland."

I agree with the captain as I have heard the Manx-man speak. He could be one of Scottish novelist William Black's old Highland lairds.

"Your crew is international, but all your sailors are Chinese," notes the businessman.

"Yes, Chinese are popular with commanders. They are obedient. They don't strike at the worst possible times. And they are under the control of a boatswain, one of their countrymen. He hires them and pays them their wages, and the owners reckon with him alone."

"Is that profitable for him?" asks the businessman.

"My boatswain is a person of consequence and wealth. He owns much real estate in San Francisco."

The poverty I saw in China Town conflicts with the captain's talk of wealth. Perhaps the wealth of the boatswain, a man with a keen, shrewd face and an air of unquestioned authority, is sufficient proof that the Chinese – as the white Jack Tar – is the victim of fraud and oppression.

"Captain," I ask, "are you like the merchant Antonio in Shakespeare's *Merchant of Venice,* voyaging to the East for cargoes of tea, silk, and spices?"

He nods. "I bring out Chinese returning home; passengers for the East, like yourself; flour; Connecticut clocks; hats; shoes; and other such select assortments of Yankee notions.

"On the return trip home, we bring hundreds of bales of raw silk which must be rushed across the continent immediately upon arrival. In fact, these goods have left the ship and are on their way across the country to the eastern mills before the passengers have even landed."

"What would one of those bales be worth?" asks the businessman.

"Seven hundred apiece. The usual cargo is from 1200 to 1300 bales." The captain pauses, presumably to let us work out the calculations. "In June the tea trade begins. The whole of the Formosa crop, some six million tons, comes to us since the English will not drink the Oolong."

The Brit weighs in, "Of course we don't want it. Too light, perfumed. We prefer something coarser. Stronger."

"Spices, pepper, and tapioca come from Singapore. Also, an extract called gambier is transported in great quantities for coloring American beer. Thousands of bales of gunnysacks from Calcutta for American wheat, and, hemp and jute from Manila."

This information written down is not romantic enough for Molly, but to watch the captain's bright eyes sparkle as he speaks, one can know it is romantic for the captain!

"And you," the businessman turns his keen eye on me. "Aren't you the one traveling around the world?"

"Nellie Bly?" pipes up Mrs. White, suddenly interested in me.

"No, I am not Nellie Bly," is all I answer.

"I've heard she has a terrible temper," she whispers loud enough for the table to hear. "I can tell you're not her. If you were, you would have ordered us all around to your liking by now. She is unscrupulous, the way she hides who she is from everyone, then goes and tells secret conversations!"

I suppress my smile as I wonder what secrets, if any, this woman holds. "I'm sure she is not as dramatic as you make her out to be." Admittedly, my protest is not strong.

Mrs. White leans around me to get a better angle at the captain. "Really, you should be glad she is not Nellie Bly or she'd have spoilt all the fun we had at table tonight."

"Thank you for your warning, ma'am. I shall take care if I ever meet her."

WITH MILES AND miles of open sea to go, we must find amusement amongst ourselves. I take to my fancywork in the women's salon and meet a kindred spirit named Madge. She is traveling with her uncle but is at an age where she is straining for independence, and so she has made it a habit to join me at every possible moment. I do not mind, nor does the uncle. We talk of poems and books and how eager we are to see land, especially if it is Japan.

She will have a month's time in the Celestial land to fall in love with the son of her mother's best friend from childhood (or so the mother and the best friend hope). I will have only a few days, but then again, my traveling purpose is not to fall in love.

"I shall like to continue on with you around the world," she tells me one day as we are playing quoits. The sun has warmed the air, and we are taking advantage of the deck games. It is her turn to throw a rope hoop at the target.

"The company would be nice, but I don't believe your parents would allow it."

"No, they would not," she agrees, looking forlorn. "But until we part, I can pretend otherwise."

I toss my hoop, and it lands wildly off target. "But this young man might be the perfect one for you. Handsome and witty and caring? Give him a chance before you run away from him."

She pouts. A pretty thing she is and likely to catch the eye of said boy. She will not think of me for long after I am gone.

"But you're not married, and you are older than I," she points out as evidence that she should become a world traveler. Now I understand why Molly gets irritated when I tease her this same way.

"It is not because I do not want to be married or that I've never had a suitor." I pause to consider my words more thoughtfully. "I want the right one, and I think he will be worth waiting for."

Charles Wetmore's thoughtful face comes to mind. He appeared wounded when he handed me the roses and I rushed away from him to catch the train. He said he would cancel all his appointments and join me as my chaperone, but I wouldn't let him. Not because I didn't want his company, but because I didn't want him as a chaperone.

"Handsome and witty and caring, you say?" She considers this. "I suppose if those are his primary characteristics, he may be hard to resist."

After our game on deck, we walk by a man we have seen several times, always deeply engrossed in a book. We raise our eyebrows at each other in familiarity and curiosity as we pass and he ignores us.

He is a grave, mysterious-eyed person, who has not spoken to anyone during the voyage. He usually has his dark, smooth, mask-like face hidden behind a French novel. It is rumored he is the Japanese poet Kachi, returning from travels in America, where he has been arranging for translations of his works into English. Though I am not particularly shy, I cannot bring myself to speak with him directly and confirm the matter.

We settle in the salon again with our fancy work, barely noticing the ship's rise and fall, as we now consider ourselves seasoned travelers.

"What do you think Nellie Bly is doing right now?" Madge asks as she threads her needle.

I puff out a breath. When I am busy playing games or at meals, I am sufficiently distracted as to my purpose for travel. But when I am alone, the absurdity of my adventure comes back to mind and I wonder. Has she fallen behind schedule, or have the winds been in her favor? Has anyone been able to reach her yet, and tell her that she is not alone in her race? I doubt she will be pleased to find out.

"I don't know," I relent. "I suppose she is also on a ship, maybe in the Mediterranean or the Red Sea."

"Do you know each other?"

"No. Well. I know *of* her, which is different from knowing her. But I doubt she knows me by name since we travel in different circles. Though now that I am doing a stunt, I wish I kept my pen name."

"You have a pen name?" she asks, eager at learning about my secret identity.

"When I was first published, I went under the name B.L.R. Dane." I pause to tie off my stitch, and then continue. "Nellie Bly is not *her* real name, either. It comes from a song. I don't know her real name."

"Then why are you traveling under your real name if it isn't the thing to do?"

"I thought I had a respectable editorial position at *The Cosmopolitan.* I'm known there as Elisabeth Bisland. Never did I imagine they would launch me around the world with only a few hours' notice."

"Oh, look! There are the missionaries again. I don't know how they can stand to leave home for so long."

The young ladies are tucked into the corner, whispering amongst themselves.

"I fear not all of them are cut out for the business they have signed up for." As I say this, I am looking at the pretty one who has probably left a bevy of suitors at home. "But with enough faith perhaps they can move mountains."

16

IN WHICH NELLIE BLY EXPERIENCES THE
SUEZ CANAL AND ASSISTS A JUGGLER.

IT WAS IN THE AFTERNOON WHEN THE *VICTORIA* anchored at Port Said. We were all on deck eagerly watching for the first sight of land, and though that sight showed us a wide, sandy beach, and some uninteresting two-storied white houses with arcade fronts, still it did not lessen our desire to go ashore.

The most urgent reason for our going to land was the fact that this was a coaling port for the *Victoria*, and having to stay on board a ship during the coaling operation is an event much worse than death.

Before the boat anchored, the men armed themselves with canes.

"What are those for?" I asked innocently.

"To keep off the beggars," they said, and pointed out that the women carried parasols for the same purpose.

"I have an extra," said one of the Scottish women, looking concerned for me.

I shook my head, having an idea, probably a wrong one, that a stick beats more ugliness into a person than it ever beats out.

Hardly had the anchor dropped when the ship was surrounded by a fleet of small boats, steered by half-clad Arabs, fighting, grabbing, pulling, yelling in their mad haste to be first.

When the ladder was lowered, numbers of them caught it and clung to it as if it meant life or death to them, and here they clung until the captain was compelled to order some sailors to beat the Arabs off, which they did with long poles, before the passengers dared venture forth. This dreadful exhibition made me feel that probably there was some justification in arming one's self with a club.

Our party was about the first to go down the ladder to the boats. It had been our desire and intention to go ashore together, but when we stepped into the first boat, some were caught by rival boatmen and literally dragged across to other boats.

"Wait! They are with us," I called out.

The men in the party used their sticks quite vigorously, all to no avail. The conduct of the Arabs justified this harsh course of treatment; still, I was sorry to see it administered so freely and lavishly. And yet they stubbornly persisted even while cringing under the blows.

"Go on," waved one of the men from the other boat. "We'll meet up on shore."

So we ordered the Arabs to pull away. Midway between the *Victoria* and the shore, the boatmen stopped.

"You must pay now," they demanded in very plain and forcible English.

"Miss Bly, we are completely at their mercy," whispered one of the women, digging in her meager purse.

I could tell she was used to her husband paying.

"They will not land us either way until we pay what they ask." Her voice choked.

"Half our party is on the other boat with the money. We will pay you at the shore," I tried to reason with them.

"No. Many years with English and their sticks. If we land before he pay –" He mimes a beating.

We pay.

Walking up the beach, sinking ankle-deep in the sand at every step, we came to the main street. Almost instantly, we were surrounded by Arab boys who besought us to take a ride on the burros that stood patiently beside them. There were burros of all colors, sizes and shapes, and the boys would cry out, most beseechingly, "Here's Gladstone! Take a ride; see Gladstone with two beautiful black eyes."

If one happened to be of a different political belief and objected to riding the former British prime minister, a choice could be made of almost any well-known, if not popular name. There were Mrs. Maybricks, after the American woman convicted of murdering her much older British husband; Mary Andersons, after the actress; Lillie Langtrys, after the singer and actress, and all the prominent men of the time.

I knew all about burros, having spent that time in Mexico, but they proved to be quite a novelty to many of the passengers, almost all of whom were anxious to take a ride before returning to the boat. So, as many as could find animals to ride mounted and went flying through that quaint, sleeping town, yelling with laughter, bouncing like rubber balls on their saddles, while half-naked Arab boys goaded the burros on by short, urgent hisses, and by prodding them from behind with a sharp stick.

After seeing about fifty of our passengers started off in this happy manner, a smaller number of us went to a gambling house. In short time we were deep in the sport of placing our English gold on colors and numbers and waiting anxiously for the wheel to go 'round to see the money at last swept in by the man at the table. I do not think that any one of us knew anything about the game, but we recklessly put our money on the table and laughed to see it taken in by the man who gave the turn to the wheel.

The longer we remained at this gambling house, the less money we had to spend in the shops. I went ashore with the determination not to buy anything, as I was very anxious not to increase my baggage. I withstood the tempting laces which were offered at wonderfully low prices, the quaint Egyptian curios, and managed to content myself by buying a sun hat, as everybody else did; and a pugaree, a long scarf used to wind about the hat and drape down, thus also protecting my neck, which is customary in the East.

Having bought a hat and seen all I cared to of the shops, I went strolling about with some friends, feasting my eyes on what were to me peculiarities of a peculiar people.

Old houses with carved-wood fronts that would have been worth a fortune in America were occupied by tenants that were unmistakably poor. The natives were apparently so accustomed to strangers that we attracted very little, if any, attention except from those who hoped to gain something from our visit.

Unmolested, we went about finding no occasion to use sticks on the natives. A great number of beggars who, true to their trade, whined forth, with outstretched hands, their plaintive appeals, but they were not so intrusive or bothersome that they necessitated our giving them the cane instead of alms.

While standing looking after a train of camels that had just come in loaded with firewood, I saw some Egyptian women. They were small in stature and shapelessly clad in black. Over their faces, beginning just below the eyes, they wore black veils that fell almost to their knees. As if fearing that the veil alone would not destroy all semblance of features, they wear a thing that spans the face between the hair and the veil down the line of their noses. In some cases, this appears to be of gold, and in others, it is composed of some black material.

In comparison, down at the beach we came upon a group of naked men clustered about an alligator that they had caught. It was securely fastened in some knotted rope, the end of which was held by some half dozen black fellows. What a contrast to see the overly-covered women compared to the underwhelmingly-covered men.

Darkness came on us very suddenly and sent us rushing off for our ship. This time we found the boatman would not permit us even to enter their boats until we paid them to take us across to the *Victoria*.

"But that is double what you charged to bring us to land," said one of the men.

"It is the law. Price doubles after sunset." Again, we were at their mercy.

The coaling was just finishing when we reached the ship, but the sight we caught of the coal barges, lighted by some sputtering, dripping stuff, held in iron cages on the end of long poles, that showed the hurrying naked people rushing with sacks of coal up a steep gangplank, between the barges and the ship, was one long to be remembered.

The next morning, I got up earlier than usual so anxious was I to see the famous Suez Canal. Rushing up on deck, I saw we were passing through what looked like an enormous ditch, enclosed on either side with high sand banks, and we seemed to be hardly moving.

Mr. Gregory, one of the fellows I'd often eaten tiffin with, was already up and keeping watch. "Why are we going so slowly?" I asked him while I fanned myself with a paper, trying to get up my own breeze.

He rested his elbows on the rail and answered in his light British accent. "By law, a ship must not travel through the canal at a speed exceeding five knots an hour. A rapid passage would make a strong current that would wash in the sand banks." He splayed his hands. "When first completed the surface of the canal was three hundred and twenty-five feet wide, but the constant washing in of the banks has reduced it to only one hundred and ninety-five feet."

The hours through the canal were tedious and stifling. Mr. Gregory tried to make it more interesting by telling us its history. Started in 1859, the canal took ten years to build, claiming the lives of 100,000 laborers. He says the trip through can be made from twenty to twenty-four hours. I'm hoping for twenty.

About noon of our first day in the canal we anchored in the bay fronting Ismailia. Here passengers were taken on, which gave us time to see the Khedive's palace, which is built a little way back from the beach in the heart of a beautiful green forest.

Continuing the journey through the canal, we saw little else of interest. The signal stations were the only green spots that met the eye, but they were proof of what could be done, even in this sandy desert by the expenditure of time and energy.

The one thing that enlivened this trip was the appearance of naked Arabs, who would occasionally run along the banks of the canal, crying in pitiful tones, "bahkshish." This we understood meant money, which many of the kind-hearted passengers would throw to them, but the beggars never seemed to find it, and would keep on after us, still crying, "bahkshish" until they were exhausted.

We passed several ships in the canal. Generally, the passengers would call to the passengers on the other ships, but the conversation was confined mainly to inquiries as to what kind of a voyage had been theirs. We saw at one place in the canal, a lot of Arabs, both men and women, at work. Among them were a number of camels that were employed in carrying stone with which the laborers were endeavoring to strengthen the banks.

In the night an electric light was hung from the front and by moving it from side to side, we were able to continue on our way. Before the introduction of electric headlights, the vessels were tied up in the canal overnight because of the great danger of running into the sandbanks.

Near the end of the canal, we came across several Arab encampments. First we would notice a small dull red fire, and between that fire and us we could see the outlines of people and resting camels. At one encampment we heard music, but at the others we saw the people either working over the fire, as if preparing their evening meal, or in sitting positions crouching about it in company with their camels.

Shortly after this, we dropped anchor in the Bay of Suez. Hardly had we done so when the ship was surrounded by a number of small sailboats that, in the semi-darkness, with their white sails before the breeze, reminded me of moths flocking to a light, both from their white, winged-like appearance, and the rapid way in which numbers of them floated down on us.

These sail boats were filled with men with native fruits, photographs, and odd shells to sell. They all came on board, and among them were a number of jugglers. The passengers took very little interest in the venders, but all had a desire to see what was to be offered by the jugglers.

There was one among them, a black man, who wore little else than a sash, a turban and a baggy pocket, in the lining of which he carried two lizards and a small rabbit. He was very anxious to show us his tricks and to get the money for them. He refused, however, to do anything with the rabbit and lizards until after he had shown us what he could do with a handkerchief and some bangles.

"You. Miss," he said, waving me to come forward.

While I was stepping toward him, he shook a handkerchief as if to show us that it contained nothing. He handed it to me and then showed us a small brass bangle. He took the handkerchief back and pretended to put the bangle into it; he then placed the handkerchief in my hand. "Hold tightly," he said.

I did so, feeling the presence of the bangle very plainly. He blew on it and, jerking the handkerchief loose from my grasp, shook it. Much to the amazement of the crowd, the bangle was gone.

Some of the passengers in the meantime stole the juggler's rabbit, and one of the lizards had quietly taken itself off to some secluded spot.

"Rabbit? Rabbit?" He asked the crowd. He was very much concerned about the loss of them and refused to perform any more tricks until they were restored to his keeping.

At last one young man took the rabbit from his pocket and returned it to the juggler, much to his gratification. The lizard was not to be found, and as it was time for the ship to sail, the juggler was forced to return to his boat.

After he had gone, several people came up to me to ask about the handkerchief trick.

"How did he do it?"

"Did he take the bangle away before he gave it to you? Could you feel it?"

"When did it disappear?"

"That was an old and very uninteresting trick," I said. "He had one bangle sewn in the handkerchief, and the other bangle, the one he showed everyone, he slipped out of sight when you were all looking at me. Of course, by holding the handkerchief, I was holding the bangle, but when he jerked the handkerchief from me and shook it, the bangle wouldn't fall to the floor. He carefully kept the side to which the bangle was attached turned towards himself so it looked that by his magic, he had made the bangle disappear."

One of the men who listened to this explanation became very indignant. "Well, now. If you knew positively how this trick had been done, why didn't you expose the man?" he said in a huff.

Feeling equally huffy, I retorted, "I wanted to see the juggler get his money."

The Englishman gave me a frown and went off to fume elsewhere.

The next morning when we arose, we were out of sight of land and well out on the Red Sea. The weather now was very hot, but still some of the passengers did their best to make things lively on board.

One evening a number of young men gave a minstrel show. They displayed both energy and perseverance in preparing for it as well as in the execution of it. One end of the deck was set aside for the show. A stage was put up and the whole corner was enclosed by awnings, and the customary green curtain hung in place during service, as drop curtain between acts, as well appearing before and after the performance.

A few of those who could sing, or imagined they could, were persuaded to exercise their vocal organs. At other times, many of us went to the deck reserved for the second-class passengers and enjoyed the concerts given by them. When there were no chairs for us on this deck, we would sit on the floor, and we all acknowledged that the first-class passengers could not furnish music that was any better.

The days were spent mainly on deck lounging about in easy chairs. I found that no one enjoyed as much comfort as I did. I had changed my heavy waist for my silk bodice, and I felt cool and comfortable and lazily happy.

When dinner hour approached, we would see a few rush off to dress for dinner and later they would appear in full dress, low bodice and long train, much to the amusement of that class of passengers who maintained that it was decidedly not the thing to appear in full dress on an ocean steamer.

The evening dress, made of white linen, in which the young men in the East generally made their appearance at dinner, impressed me as being not only comfortable and appropriate, but decidedly becoming and elegant.

As a topic of interest we had the lizard which was left behind by the juggler. It was found in a quiet corner of the deck by the quarter-master the morning following our stop at Suez. A sympathizing young man took charge of it and endeavored to feed it, but after living in sullen quietness for a few days, it ceased to breathe, and its death was solemnly announced to the passengers.

The nights were so warm while on the Red Sea that the men left their cabins and spent their nights on deck. It is usually customary for the women to sleep on deck, one side of which, at such times, is reserved exclusively for them. During this trip none of the women had the courage to set the example, so the men had the decks to themselves.

Sleeping down below was all the more reason why women arising early would go on the decks before the sun began to boil in search of a refreshing spot where they could get a breath of cool air. At this hour the men were usually to be seen promenading about in their pajamas, but I heard no objections raised until, much to the dismay of the women, the captain announced that the decks belonged to the men until after eight o'clock in the morning, and that the women were expected to remain below until after that hour.

Just before we came to Aden, we passed in the sea a number of high brown mountains. They are known as the Twelve Apostles. Shortly after this, we came in sight of Aden. It looked to us like a large, bare mountain of wonderful height, but even by the aid of glasses we were unable to tell that it was inhabited.

Shortly after eleven o'clock in the morning, we anchored in the bay. Our boat was soon surrounded by a number of small boats, which brought to us men who had things to sell, and the wonderful divers of the East.

The passengers had been warned by the officers on board not to go ashore at Aden because of the intense heat. So the women spent their time bargaining with the merchants who came to the ship to sell ostrich feathers and feather boas. The men helped them to close with the sellers always to the sellers' advantage, much as they might congratulate themselves to the contrary.

I, in company with a few of the more reckless ones, decided to brave the heat and go ashore and see what Aden had to offer.

17

IN WHICH ELIZABETH BISLAND PREPARES TO VISIT "ELFLAND."

A T LAST THERE COMES THE DAY WHEN WE rise in the morning and the sailors, pointing to the horizon, say, "That is Japan."

We eagerly gather at the rail to see this wondrous land, crying with cheerful excitement. "Yes! Yes!" We are all so ready for something new to look at. Madge and I link arms at the rail as we strain our eyes across the monotonous sea and sky, but still see nothing with our unpracticed sight.

"There it is, dear Elizabeth," Madge says, holding her hat so it doesn't blow off into the sea. "Only just beyond our sight. But soon, very soon we will not only see it but set our feet upon its soil."

At a sniffle to my left, I turn and see the young missionary doctor staring straight ahead, tears falling unhindered down her cheeks. All the missionaries are full of emotion at arriving at the scene of their labors to save immortal souls.

A delicate gray cloud grows up along the edge of the water and slowly a vast cone-like cumulus, a lofty rosy cloud, takes shape and form: Fujiyama . . . the divine mountain!

None of us can leave the rail. We stand and watch as if hypnotized by the volcano, watching it grow and grow. Having seen it, one no longer marvels that it dominates the Japanese imagination; that every fan, screen, and jar, every piece of lacquer and porcelain, bears somewhere its majestic, its exquisite outline.

For more than two hundred years, the "Mother of Fire" has been clad in snows and has made no sign. Traces of terrible ancient rages lie along her ravaged sides; but her passions are all stilled, peace and purity crown her.

"And it came to pass that on the morning of the 8th day of December we rose up and perceived that we had come unto Fanland," I say in the quiet awe.

"To the Islands of Porcelain," adds Madge.

We make our way up the long bay to Yokohama. The town has been in existence only since 1859 when Japan opened a few ports to foreign trade, but in these thirty years already it is a place of size and importance; for what the Japanese did, they did thoroughly: They jettied the harbor, built ample wharves, and bade their own people confine themselves to the inner town across the canal, and not encroach upon the Europeans.

Captain Kempson has steered us in sixteen days from the coast of America to where a mountain of pink pearl rises out of the sea; and when the gray clouds about its base resolve themselves into land, we find they are the green hills of fairyland!

There is no turning back, now. My feet are about to alight onto foreign soil for the first time. I have left the forty-two states behind and will not see them again for weeks and weeks. Although, based on the rate we've been adding states – four in this month alone – my country might expand without me.

The queerest craft come to meet us in the bay – light-winged junks with gray and russet sails. They spread their great butterfly wings and skim along without fear, going far afield for the fishing. So carelessly and crazily built are they, that were the sea to give them a playful slap she would crush them in an instant to kindling-wood.

Many large ships lie at anchor in the harbor – American men-of-war, English, French, and German merchant vessels, and a few neat Japanese coasters. A cloud of sampans descends upon us as we anchor – craft as crazy as the junks.

"Look," I point out to Madge. "Those boatmen are the vanguard of elves from Elfland!" Indeed, they were small, lithe creatures with good-looking countenances, and with thick, shining black locks, through which is twisted a blue fillet.

They wear a dark blue cotton kimono, which is worn by both sexes. For the most part it reminds me of a costume like that worn in England in the time of Henry II – cloth hose to the waist, a short jerkin, and loose sleeveless coat reaching to the hips.

There are boys of ten or twelve in some of the boats with the men – quaint little brats with varying patterns shaved on the tops of their heads, working with the enthusiastic vigor known only to the small boy of all countries.

Seeing the boats coming, Mrs. Baxter begins organizing our launch party. She has been here before and doesn't need time to soak in the new and fascinating sights. Within minutes she has us organized and sends Mr. White off to secure our steam-launch.

"Why don't we take one of these sampans?" I say, hoping to steer them to the elfish ferrymen and a fitting start to our entering this dreamland.

Madge catches my eye and nods enthusiastically.

But Mrs. White shakes her head and points at the pile of luggage the missionaries are piling up. "The sampans are not practical. Do not worry; you young girls will see more exotic sights than these."

18

IN WHICH NELLIE BLY GOES TO A CAMEL MARKET AND IS NOT IMPRESSED.

HIRING A LARGE BOAT, I WENT ASHORE with a half dozen acquaintances who felt they could risk the sun. The man in charge of the boat that carried us to land was a small black fellow with the thinnest legs I ever saw. Somehow they reminded me of smoked herrings, they were so black, flat, and dried-looking. He was very energetic, notwithstanding his lack of weight.

Around his neck and over his bare breast were twined strings of beads, black and gold and silver. Around his waist was a highly colored sash, and on his arms and ankles were heavy bracelets, while his fingers and toes seemed to be trying to outdo one another in the way of rings. His hair was yellow which, added to his very light dress of jewelry and sash, gave him rather a strange look.

The four oarsmen were black fellows, thin of limb, but possessed of much strength and tireless good humor. They have the finest white teeth of any mortals, and I commented such.

Grinning, the man in charge procured a stick, three or four inches in length. One end was scraped free of the bark to reveal a soft, fibrous wood. He proceeded to rub and polish his teeth until they were perfect in their whiteness.

Some of the boatmen had their black wool pasted down and hidden under a coating of lime. I couldn't help but stare in curiosity until the first man explained.

"They are bleaching their hair," he said. "We cover the head with lime and let it set for several days. The hot sun and the water bleach the hair yellow or red."

"Do the women do this too?"

He shook his head. "It does not look good on the women. Only the men."

He spoke English quite well, and to my rather impertinent question as to what number constituted his family, told me that he had three wives and eleven children, which number, he added piously, by the grace of the power of his faith, he hoped to increase.

While we were talking, our men were vigorously pulling to the time of a rousing song, one line of which was sung by one man, the others joining in the refrain at the end. Their voices were not unpleasant, and the air had a monotonous rhythm that was very fascinating.

We landed at a well-built pier and walked up the finely-cut, white-stone steps from the boat to the land. Instantly we were surrounded by half-clad black people, all of whom, after the manner of hack-drivers at railway stations, were clamoring for our favor.

They were not all drivers, however. Mingling with the drivers were merchants with jewelry, ostrich plumes and boas to sell, runners for hotels, beggars, cripples and guides.

This conglomeration besought us to listen to every individual one of them until a native policeman, in the Queen's uniform, came forward and pushed the fellows back with his hands, sometimes hastening their retreat with his boot.

A large board occupied a prominent position on the pier. On it was marked the prices that should be paid drivers, boatmen, and like people. It was, indeed, a praiseworthy thoughtfulness, for it prevented tourists being robbed. Even in this land there was more precaution taken to protect helpless and ignorant strangers than in New York City where the usual custom of night hack-men is to demand exorbitant prices, and if they are not forthcoming, to pull off their coats and fight for it.

Perched on the side of this bleak, bare mountain is a majestic white building, reached by a fine road cut in the stone that forms the mountain. It is a club house, erected for the benefit of the English soldiers who are stationed on this barren spot. In the harbor lay an English man-of-war, and near a point where the land was most level, numbers of white tents were pitched for soldiers.

From the highest peak of the black, rocky mountain floated the English flag. As I traveled on and realized more than ever before how the English have stolen almost all, if not all, desirable seaports, I felt an increased respect for the level-headedness of the English government, and I cease to marvel at the pride with which Englishmen view their flag floating in so many different climes and over so many different nationalities.

Near the pier were shops run by Parsees. A hotel, post office and telegraph office were located in the same place. The town of Aden is five miles distant. We hired a carriage and started at a good pace, on a wide, smooth road that took us along the beach for a way, passing low rows of houses; passed a large graveyard, liberally filled, which looked like the rest of that stony point, bleak, black and bare, the graves often being shaped by cobblestones.

The roads at Aden are a marvel of beauty. They are wide and as smooth as hardwood, and as they twist and wind in pleasing curves up the mountain, they are made secure by a high, smooth wall against mishap. Otherwise their steepness might result in giving tourists a serious roll down a rough mountainside.

A number of women walked proudly along, their brown, bare feet stepping lightly on the smooth road. They had long purple-black hair, which was always adorned with a long, stiff feather, dyed of brilliant red, green, purple, and like striking shades.

They wore no other ornament than the colored feather, which lent them an air of pride, when seen beside the much-bejeweled people of that quaint town. Many of the women, who seemed very poor indeed, were lavishly dressed in jewelry. They did not wear much else, it is true, but in a place as hot as Aden, jewelry must be as much as anyone would care to wear.

To me the sight of these perfect, bronze-like women, with a graceful drapery of thin silk wound about the waist, falling to the knees, and a corner taken up the back and brought across the bust, was most bewitching. On their bare, perfectly modeled arms were heavy bracelets around the wrist and muscle, most times joined by chains.

Bracelets were also worn about the ankles, and their fingers and toes were laden with rings. Sometimes large rings were suspended from the nose, and the ears were almost always outlined with hoop rings that reached from the inmost edge of the lobe to the top of the ear joining the head. So closely were these rings placed that, at a distance, the ear had the appearance of being rimmed in gold.

A more pleasing style of nose ornament was a large gold ornament set in the nostril and fastened there as screw rings fasten in the ear. Still, if that nose ornamentation was more pleasing than the other, the ear adornment that accompanied it was disgusting. The lobe of the ear was split from the ear and pulled down to such length that it usually rested on the shoulder. The enormous loop of flesh was partially filled with large gold knobs.

At the top of the hill, we came to a beautiful, majestic, stone double gate, the entrance to the English fort and also spanning the road that leads to the town. Sentinels were pacing to and fro, but we drove past them without stopping or being stopped, through a strange, narrow cut in the mountain that towered at the sides a hundred feet above the road bed. Both these narrow, perpendicular sides are strongly fortified. It needs but one glance at Aden, which is in itself a natural fort, to strengthen the assertion that Aden is the strongest gate to India.

The moment we emerged from that narrow cut, we got a view of the white town of Aden, nestling in the very heart of what seems to be an extinct volcano. We were driven rapidly down the road, catching glimpses of gaudily-attired mounted policemen, water-carriers from the bay, with their well-filled goat-skins flung across their backs, camels loaded with cut stone, and black people of every description.

When we drove into the town, which is composed of low adobe houses, our carriage was surrounded with beggars. We got out and walked through an unpaved street, looking at the dirty, uninviting shops. Very often we were urged to buy, but more frequently the natives stared at us with quiet curiosity.

On spotting a bundle of the tooth sticks, I plunked down my penny for a dozen, though I am unable to state where they get their tree branches as I failed to see one living thing growing at Aden.

In the heart of the town, we found the camel market, but beyond a number of camels standing, lying, and kneeling about, the sight was nothing extraordinary. Nearby was a goat market, but business seemed dull in both places.

When we started to return to the ship, little naked children ran after us for miles, touching their foreheads humbly and crying for money. They all knew enough English to be able to ask us for charity.

Upon reaching the pier, we found our driver had forgotten all the English he knew when we started out. He wanted one price for the carriage, and we wanted to pay another.

"The price is listed on the board. We will pay no more," stated the gentleman who was trying to give him our money.

The driver refused to take it and blocked our path.

After several tense moments, I spotted a native policeman in the crowd. "Over here!" I called out to him.

The gentlemen explained our situation. The policeman, with a nod at us and a scowl at the driver, took the right change from us, handed it to the driver, and gave him, in addition, a lusty kick for his dishonesty.

When we returned to the ship, we found sellers of ostrich eggs and plumes, shells, fruit, spears of sword-fish, and such things. In the water, on one side of the boat, were numbers of men, Somali boys, they called them, who were giving an exhibition of wonderful diving and swimming.

They would actually sit in the water looking like bronze statues, as the sun rested on their wet, black skins. They sat in a row, and turning their faces up towards the deck, would yell methodically, one after the other, down the entire line: "Oh! Yo! Ho!"

It sounded very like a chorus of bull-frogs and was very amusing. After finishing this strange music, they would give us a duet, half crying, persuasively, in a sing-song style: "Have a dive! Have a dive! Have a dive!"

The other half, meanwhile, would put their hands before their widely opened mouths, yelling through their rapidly moving fingers with such energy that we gladly threw over silver to see them dive and stop the din.

The moment the silver flashed over the water, all the bronze figures would disappear like flying fish, and, looking down, we would see a few ripples on the surface of the blue water–nothing more.

After a time that seemed dangerously long to us, they would bob up through the water again. We could see them coming before they finally appeared on the surface, and one among the number would have the silver between his teeth, which would be most liberally displayed in a broad smile of satisfaction.

Some of these divers were children not more than eight years old, and they ranged from that up to any age. Many of them had their hair bleached. As they were completely naked, excepting a small cloth twisted about the loins, they found it necessary to make a purse out of their cheeks, which they did with as much ease as a cow stows away grass to chew at her leisure.

They never get out of the way of a boat. They merely sink and come up in the same spot when the boat passes. The bay at Aden is filled with sharks, but they never touch these black men, so they tell me, and the safety with which they spend their lives in the water proves the truth of the assertion. They claim that a shark will not attack a black man, and after I had caught the odor of the grease with which these men anoint their bodies, I did not blame the sharks.

After a seven-hour stay at Aden, we left for Colombo, being followed a long ways out from land by the divers. One little boy went out with us on the ship, and when he left us he merely took a plunge from the upper deck into the sea and went happily back towards Aden, on his side, waving a farewell to us with his free hand.

That night I tried my new tooth sticks. The wood wears into a soft pulp, and I found them the most efficient as well as pleasant toothbrush I had ever tried. I felt a regret that some enterprising firm had not thought of importing this useful bit of timber to replace the tooth-destroying brush used in America.

The passengers endeavored to make the time pass pleasantly between Aden and Colombo. The young women had some tableaux vivants one evening, and they were really very fine posing as living pictures. In one they wished to represent the different countries. They asked me to represent America, but I refused, and then they asked me to tell them what the American flag looked like! They wanted to represent one as nearly as possible and to raise it to drape the young woman who was to represent America.

Another evening, we had a lantern slide exhibition that was very enjoyable. During the exhibition, the Queen's picture was thrown on the white sheet, and evoked warmer applause than anything else that evening.

The loyalty of the English to their Queen on all occasions, and at all times, had won my admiration. Though born and bred a staunch American, with the belief that a man is what he makes of himself, not what he was born, still I could not help admiring the undying respect the English have for their royal family.

We never had an evening's amusement that did not end by everybody rising to their feet and singing "God Save the Queen." I could not help but think how devoted that woman, for she is only a woman after all, should be to the interests of such faithful subjects.

19

IN WHICH ELIZABETH BISLAND TAKES A LATE-NIGHT JINRICKSHA RIDE TO SEE NATIVE JAPAN.

MORE MEDIEVAL FOLK IN BLUE STAND about on the stone pier and welcome us with friendly smiles. Not to be outdone by Mrs. Baxter, Mrs. White assumes full command of our party and before we can decide for ourselves, she tucks us all into jinrickshas, and we are on our way to the hotel.

"They can go as fast as five miles an hour!" she shouts back from her vehicle, which has taken the lead.

The jinricksha is exactly the vehicle in which one would expect to ride in this land of fairy children – large perambulators that hold one person comfortably; but instead of being trundled from behind by a white-capped nursemaid, one of the Henry II gentlemen, who wears straw sandals and an enormous blue mushroom hat on his head, ensconces himself between the little shafts in front and prances noiselessly away with it.

Our way lies along the Bund, a broad, handsome street on the waterfront, with a fringe of slim pine trees strange of outline as are those one is familiar with upon Japanese fans.

Other jinrickshas are scampering about. Tonsured doll-babies in flowered gowns, such as one buys at home in the Oriental shops, are walking about here alive and flying queer-shaped kites, with a sort of calm unconscious elfishness befitting dwellers in fairyland.

Two little Japanese ladies with pink cheeks, and black hair clasped with jade pins, toddle by on wooden pattens that clack pleasantly on the pavement. Their kimonos are of brightly colored crepe, and their sashes tied behind like bright-tinted wings. Every one – even the funny little gendarme who stands outside of his sentry-box like a toy soldier – gives us back smile for smile.

All my fears of travel slip away, being replaced with awe and wonder and thrill of adventure. If all my visits to distant lands are as pleasant as this, I shall have the most wonderful time of my life.

The Grand Hotel is at the upper end of the Bund, which lies along the waterfront of Yokohama Bay. I'm surprised at how western the hotel looks. If Madge had blindfolded me and led me to the hotel, I would not have known I was in a country other than America. That is until another specimen of the Moyen-âge – this one in his stocking feet – arrives. He shows us into our beautiful rooms facing the water. Rooms with steam-heat and electric bells!

We congregate back in the dining room where we hungrily pour over the bill of fare. To my relief, everything is English, but to my disappointment, so is the food. My purpose in travel, aside from going faster than Nellie Bly, is to experience different cultures, including the local fare.

Mrs. Baxter holds up her menu to begin her lesson: "It is all numbered, dears. Simply tell the waiter the number you want and he will bring it to you. They speak no English a'tall. None whatsoever." She and Mrs. White shake their heads at one another as if disappointed that everyone is not fluent in English.

"But they must speak some English," I remark casually, "if they know their numbers." Madge and I exchange looks and stifle our smiles.

Number one is the soup. Two is a fish dish. I skip ahead to the desserts at the bottom and see tea and coffee listed, each with their own numbers, lumped in with numbers for apple pie and lady fingers. My stomach will not know it has left America.

After we order, I have Mr. White's full attention. "Miss Bisland," he says. "Are you familiar with the work of Rudyard Kipling? *The Jungle Book*?"

"Yes, I am."

"Did you know that he spent part of his Honeymoon in this very hotel? Why, perhaps he and his bride dined at this very table." Mr. White tapped his finger on said table for emphasis.

"I had no idea. I will enjoy my stay here infinitely more now that I know," I say in all seriousness, and Mr. White smiles, quite pleased with himself for adding to the conversation.

And while he has the floor, he continues: "If you ladies want to tour the city, I recommend chartering 'rickshas. They will only charge you seventy-five cents for the whole day. When the day is done, they will not be winded at all and will be just as charming as they were at the start. Remarkable." Having done his duty at conversation, Mr. White digs into his food and keeps silent for the remainder of the meal.

After dinner, Madge and I escape to the veranda to drink in the last of the sights on our first day in Japan. The darkness closes down swiftly, but charming things are still to be seen. The air is crisp and keen; happy cries and clinking pattens tinkle in melodious confusion from the street.

Crimped pink and white paper-lanterns swing from the shafts of the 'rickshas, and they flit by in the dark like fireflies. A broad yellow moon rises up from the other side of the water and turns the bay to wrinkled gold, against which the ships and junks show delicately black, as if drawn with a pen; and a few clear black lines of cloud are etched across the moon's path.

Madge nudges my shoulder, and I see a man dressed in the uniform of the American Navy. He is staring out across the water until Madge's nudging draws his eyes toward us, and he smiles.

"Good evening," he says, his voice a deep baritone.

I blush in response, thinking of my sister's advice to me to succumb to a bit of romance while I am gone, and am glad the night is dark.

"Hello," says Madge. "We are newly arrived today. Are there any sights you recommend to us?"

"Several," he says and joins us at the rail. "Lieutenant McDonald." He tips his hat at us. "I've been stationed here for two years. I think I know my way around the place."

"Places more Japanese than this?" I ask waving my hand back to the Grand Hotel.

"You are in the European side of town. Commander Perry may have broken their isolationist policies and let the outside in, but in practice, they like to keep us separate. I could escort you to the native side of town. Shall we meet up again tomorrow morning?"

Madge frowns. "Is there nothing we could see tonight? Miss Bisland is only staying for two days. I want her to get an eyeful of Japan."

And before I can stop her, she gives the reason why.

"She's in a race with Nellie Bly around the world!"

"Is she now?" He turns his full attention on me, but this time I do not blush. I have judged him too old for me.

"Hmm," I confirm, reticent for people to know what I am doing. Perhaps I'm tired of answering the same questions and expect I'll be answering them all the way around the world. I'd rather people see me as a simple traveler, not knowing from whence I came or where I am going.

"Then I suppose I can find some place to take you tonight." He motions for us to step off the veranda.

When the rest of our party sees us getting ready to leave, they come scurrying along after us, eager for any excitement Lieutenant McDonald can offer. He leads us into the flowery hotel court, where we find our 'rickshas standing in a row in the moonlight, each with one of the pretty lanterns swinging. Once settled, we flit away behind our sandaled steeds, only the whir of our wheels and our calls and laughter sound through the city's quiet, moon-washed ways.

Here in the European town the houses of two stories of stone stand flush with the narrow asphalt-paved street. A tiny footpath runs under the shadow of their tiled caves; but as these are paved with little cobblestones, and the roadway is smooth and clean as a table, no one by any chance ever walks in the footpaths.

Occasionally we meet a figure enveloped in dark, shapeless drapery, or a grave, bland Chinese merchant goes by on his soundless cork soles, but this is the business quarter, and people have gone to their homes on the Bund, or upon the Bluff, where consuls and foreigners of importance reside.

We skim around corners with a shrill ki-yi! of warning; debouch into a great square upon which churches and public buildings face; cross a broad canal where acres of sampans are huddled for the night, and find on the other side Shichiu, the native town.

I give a hearty wave to Madge as we cross over from the land we are familiar with to the one we've been pining to see. Hancho-dori lies before us, the wide main thoroughfare from which spring hundreds of narrow branches, all swarming with a frolicsome, chattering crowd tinkling about in pattens, their multitudinous tapping making a vibrant musical undertone to the sound of the many voices. I don't know where to look first; I don't want to miss a thing.

The houses, delicate little match-boxes of thin, unpainted wood, fifteen or twenty feet high and divided into two stories, crowd close together and lean upon the street. The fronts of these houses – indeed, the greater part of the walls all around, are sashes of many tiny panes glazed with white, semi-transparent paper, through which the inner light shines as from a lantern. The shop fronts are mere curtains of bamboo, rolled up during business hours, and let down when the shop is closed for the night.

Business is not nearly over yet. The Japanese are as little inclined to early bed as the Chinese in San Francisco, it seems, and the tide of trade runs strong. From all the eaves swing soft bubbles of tinted light – lanterns of many shapes and sizes. The shops are lit and busy, and contain every need, from crabs to curios.

Here and there cluster flocks of light, portable booths, each also with a swaying lantern, where steaming tea is sold in thimble-cups; where sake may be drunk hot and hot, poured from long-necked porcelain bottles, or trays of queer, toothsome-looking sweetmeats are to be had for coins of infinitesimal value.

Along the street lie heaps of fresh vegetables – making pretty bouquets of color, all clean and ready for the pot – or fruits of many sorts massed with skill and beauty; little red oranges in bamboo nets, set about with their own green leaves; plums, pomaloes, and fruits whose names we do not know. Everything, everywhere, is radiantly clean, dainty, and inviting.

"Where are we going, Lieutenant?" asks Madge.

"The theatre – a humbler sort. It won't be what you are used to. The stage and auditorium are on a level, and both merely platforms. The acrobats do their feats for a few cents." He ends his sentence as we arrive.

The theatre is just as he has said. A group of tumblers on the stage are going through some supple contortions to the sound of a shrill little pipe and a blattering wooden drum, playing out of time with one another.

A little gallery to one side is reserved for the moon-eyed babies with whimsically shaved heads; but they come down occasionally and rollick about as they wish, quite unreproved.

"They are never harsh with children," the Lieutenant explains, "and in return the children display a courteous tolerance of the foibles of their elders."

The whole front of the theatre, a curtain of matting, is rolled up at intervals and, when the feat in progress is at its most thrilling climax, is let fall. This artful proceeding stimulates the interest of the passers-by to such poignancy that they succumb in platoons to the pangs of curiosity, and so crowd the little platform that we depart hastily.

Madge and I are eager to move on to the next wonder, but we have to pull Mr. Mayer, whom we have dubbed the German Gentleman, along.

More moon and lanterns, more laughter and flutter, more clacking of sandals, and then a Japanese Madame Tussaud's, with pleasing little horrors in wax at the entrance as earnest of more of the same cheerful entertainment within.

Here is better music that, during a naïve pantomime of Japanese ghosts, plays a "lonesome tune" in a soft minor key. This does not hold us long either, for Lieutenant McDonald calls us. "Let's keep going. Farther up the street is a larger and more fashionable playhouse. I want to show you the best talent of Nippon."

At the box-office are piles of flat sticks, six inches long and two wide, painted with numbers in Japanese characters.

"What are these for?" asks the amateur photographer who has joined us, but left her camera behind.

"Shoe checks."

The girl gapes her mouth open, looking from her own dainty leather boots with endless buttons to the many sandals hanging on rows of pegs by the door. "Must we take our shoes off?"

"It is custom," remarks Mr. White. "In every house in Japan, one enters in stocking-feet."

"Do not worry, miss," assures Lieutenant McDonald. "As foreigners, you will be allowed to retain your shoes."

I am glad the girl asked because I don't want to take off my shoes, either. None of us women do.

The interior is large and lofty. The common folk occupy the level floor of the pit, marked into squares, where family parties sit on small wadded rugs, and are quite at home, bringing their little charcoal braziers to warm their fingers, furnish lights for their tiny pipes, and keep the teapot steaming.

The galleries on two sides are divided into matting-lined boxes, one of which they furnish with chairs, seeing that we display small skill in sitting on our heels.

We enter during an entr'acte; and a bright crepe curtain sways lightly in the draught. The men in the pit are smoking or curled up in their rugs snatching a nap, while the women drink tea and gossip, and the children romp all over the house.

High up from latticed boxes on either side of the stage comes the sound of the samisen and other stringed instruments that make a soft, plaintive, and pleasing music.

"The play has been going on for three weeks and is to end tonight," says Lieutenant McDonald.

A gong sounds, the children are recalled, the men wake, and the curtain being pulled aside shows the front of a Japanese house.

Two maids appear from a side door and wait respectfully on their hands and knees for the entrance of their mistress, played by a man very skillfully painted and gorgeously arrayed, but somewhat too masculine to satisfactorily represent the babyish roundness of the real thing.

We rely on the actions of the characters to surmise the plot, and I get swept up in the costumes and expressions of the actors. I should like to see how it all turns out, but the countenance of

Mr. Mayer is growing wan, and Mr. White, who has no chair, is becoming distinctly cross, and so we go home.

The shops are shut by this time, and we see some curious little domestic episodes shadowed on the paper window-sashes when householders thoughtlessly pass between them and the lamp. The European town is flooded with a high tide of moonlight, and we are, it seems, the only ones awake, sweeping in a long, swift line through the streets in our silent fairy carriages with the rosy lantern swinging.

I N MY JOURNAL that night I write:

Sailing so long due west, we had at last reached the East. The real East, not east of anywhere, but the East . . . the birthplace of Man, and of his Religions . . . of Poetry and Porcelains, of Tradition, and of Architecture. And I who had come to it from the country of common-sense, of steam-ploughs and newspaper enterprise, bowed my head reverently in the portal of this great Temple of the World, awed by its mysterious age and vastness.

My heart within me is stirred, and I am led to great recklessness in the use of capital letters.

IN WHICH NELLIE BLY MAKES A PURCHASE
AND ACCIDENTALLY RELAXES.

ABOUT NINE O'CLOCK IN THE MORNING, WE anchored in the bay at Colombo, Ceylon. The island, with its abundance of green trees, was very restful and pleasing to our eyes after the spell of heat we had passed through on the ocean coming from Aden.

We had already made preparations to go ashore, and as we came slowly into the small harbor among the beautiful ships lying at anchor, we all stood impatiently on deck waiting for the first opportunity to desert the ship.

Mr. Gregory offered to be my escort during our jaunt on land. He said that he would give me a novel experience, and also show me a small boat that traveled faster than a steam launch, which the other passengers were taking to shore. Since he was a traveler of vast experience, having averaged a yearly tour of the world for several years, and knows the eastern countries as he knows his home, I looked forward to the adventure.

Still, when I saw the boat in which he intended to take, I rather doubted his judgment. The boat was a crudely constructed thing, probably five feet in length, balanced by a log the length of the boat and fastened out by two curved poles, probably three feet from the side. Two seats in the middle of the boat faced one another, shaded by a bit of coffee sack that had to be removed for passengers to get in. These boats were called outriggers by tourists, but catamarans by the people of Ceylon.

"You look nervous," said Mr. Gregory.

I simply raised my eyebrows, doing my best to maintain the unflappable nature of my fictional rival, Phileas Fogg. No queer form of travel ever got him down.

"Don't be. Catamarans are used by the native fisherman. They are so seaworthy and secure against capsizing that no case of an accident has ever been reported."

Two men sat at either end of this peculiar boat with one paddle each and with only slight exertion sent the boat cutting through the water. In a few moments we had distanced the steam launch and had accommodations engaged at the hotel before the launch had landed its passengers.

The Grand Oriental was a fine, large hotel, with tiled arcades, corridors airy and comfortable, furnished with easy chairs and small marble topped tables which stood close enough to the broad armrests for one to sip the cooling lime squashes or the exquisite native tea, or eat of the delicious fruit while resting in an attitude of ease and laziness.

Most of the jewelry bought and sold in Colombo is sold in the corridor of this hotel. Merchants bring their wares with them and tourists find it pleasanter than visiting the shops.

In this lovely promenade the men smoked, consumed gallons of whiskey and soda and perused the newspapers, while the women read their novels or bargained with the pretty little copper-colored women who came to sell dainty handmade lace, or with the clever, high-turbaned merchants who would snap open little velvet boxes and expose, to the admiring gaze of the charmed tourists, the most bewildering gems.

There were deeply-dark emeralds, fire-lit diamonds, exquisite pearls, rubies like pure drops of blood, the lucky cat's-eye with its moving line, and all set in such beautiful shapes that tempt all alike.

No woman who lands at Colombo ever leaves until she adds several rings to her jewel box, and these rings are so well known that the moment a traveler sees one, no difference in what part of the globe, he says to the wearer, inquiringly: "Been to Colombo, eh?"

Mr. Gregory helped me pick out a ring and bargained a good price for it.

For the first time since leaving America, I saw American money. It is very popular in Colombo and commands a high price – as jewelry! The diamond merchants like to put a ring through American twenty-dollar gold pieces and hang them on their watch chains for ornaments.

"The richer the merchant, the more American gold dangles from his chain." said Mr. Gregory.

I saw some men with as many as twenty pieces on one chain.

"Shall we go to tiffin?" he asked as I admired my new ring now firmly on my finger.

He led the way into the dining hall, pleasant in its coolness, interesting in its peculiarities. It matched the other parts of the hotel with its picturesque stateliness. The small tables were daintily set and richly decorated daily with the native flowers of Colombo, rich in color, exquisite in form, but void of perfume.

From the ceiling were suspended embroidered punkas, long strips of cloth fastened to bamboo poles that were suspended within a short distance of the tables. They were kept in motion by a rope pulley, worked by a man or boy, sending a lazy, cooling air through the building.

Singalese waiters were employed, and were interesting to the Westerner. They were small of stature and fine of feature, some of them having very attractive, clean-cut faces, light bronze in color. They wore white linen apron-like skirts and white jackets. Noiselessly they moved over the smooth tile floor, in their bare, brown feet.

It was some time before I could tell a Singalese man from a Singalese woman. It is not difficult to distinguish the different sexes after one knows that the Singalese men wear a tortoise shell comb comb, which was as distinct a feature of their dress as men's trousers in America. Singalese women would not think of donning this little comb any more than a sensitive American woman would think of wearing men's apparel.

I ordered some real curry, the famous native dish of India. I had been unable to eat it on the *Victoria*, but those who knew said it was a most delicious dish when prepared rightly, and so I tested it on shore.

First a divided dish containing shrimps and boiled rice was placed before me. I put two spoonfuls of rice on my plate, and on it put one spoonful of shrimps; there was also chicken and beef for the meat part of the curry, but I took shrimps only.

Then was handed me a much divided plate containing different preserved fruits and other things hot with pepper. At Mr. Gregory's instruction, I partook of three of this variety and put it on top of what had been placed first on my plate.

Last came little dried pieces of stuff that we heard before we saw, its odor was so loud and unmistakable. They called it Bombay duck. It is nothing more or less than a small fish, which is split open, and after being thoroughly dried, is used with the curry. One can learn to eat it.

After all this was on the plate it was thoroughly mixed, making a mess very unsightly, but very palatable, as I found.

"I have a story that is told of the Bombay duck," said Mr. Gregory once everyone had tried it. "The Shah of Persia was notified that some high official in India intended to send him a lot of very fine Bombay duck. The Shah was very much pleased and, in anticipation of their arrival, had some expensive ponds built to put the Bombay ducks in!"

We all smiled in anticipation of the punch line, now that we knew about Bombay duck.

"Imagine his consternation when he received these ill-smelling, dried fish!"

We clapped in appreciation, and Mr. Gregory nodded modestly at our praise. We continued in our delicious meal, Mr. Gregory entertaining us with stories he had heard on his travels.

After tiffin we drove along the smoothest, most perfectly made roads I ever saw. They seemed to be made of red asphalt, and I was told that they were constructed by convicts. We ended up at Mount Lavania, the castle-like building glistening in the sunlight when we had entered the harbor. It was a fine hotel situated on an eminence overlooking the sea, and was a favorite resort during the hot seasons. It was surrounded by a smooth green lawn and faced the blue sea, whence it gets a refreshing breeze all the year through.

Later, after dinner, everybody at the Grand Oriental Hotel went out for a drive, the women, and many of the men going bareheaded. Driving through the town, down the wide streets, past beautiful homes set well back in tropical gardens, to the Galle Face drive that runs along the beach just out of reach of the waves that broke on the sandy banks with a more musical roar than I ever heard water produce before.

The road lay very close to the water's edge, and by the soft rays of the moon its red surface was turned to silver, the deep blue of the sea was black, and the foamy breakers were snow drifts. In the soft, pure light we would see silent couples strolling along arm and arm, apparently so near the breakers that I felt apprehensive lest one, stronger than the others, should catch them unawares and wash them out to that unknown land where we all travel to rest.

Lounging on the benches that face the sea were occasional soldiers in the Queen's uniform, whom I looked at anxiously, unable to tell whether their attitude of weariness bespoke a rest from labor or hungry homesickness.

Mr. Gregory pointed out a native standing waist deep fishing in the roaring breakers. "Many of the fish bite more freely after night."

That may be true, but how easily the fisherman might be washed away, and no one would be the wiser until his absence was noticed by his friends.

Where the Galle Face drive merged into another road, stood the Galle Face Hotel surrounded by a forest of palm trees. Several of us went out on the stone-floored and stone-pillared veranda to lounge on long-bottomed, easy chairs. From our perch we could see through the forest of tall palms where the ocean kisses the sandy beach. And while listening to the music of the wave, the deep, mellow roar, I let my mind drift–drift out on dreams that bring what life has failed to give; soothing pictures of the imagination that blot out for a moment the stern disappointment of reality.

I don't know why I was feeling so melancholy in such a lovely place. Mother might say I was homesick. She would have loved to lounge here with me, feeling the cooling breeze on her face. She had had a hard life and wouldn't this be nice for her?

Why was life so hard? Why did one have to scrap for everything? My father dying and leaving my mother near penniless while the courts divided his estate amongst the adult children from his first marriage was cruel enough. With little ones still underfoot, Mother must not have been thinking straight when she married the tyrant who became my drunken stepfather. He nearly broke Mother before she got away. I was glad as a teenager to testify in court against him. If we'd had the money I would have gone on to become a teacher. But then, I certainly wouldn't be sitting halfway around the world in a lounge contemplating deeper meanings. Which life would have been better?

By my own strivings I had made it in the newspaper business, and I was prouder than proud of that. My editor didn't confine me to the society pages but gave me the freedom to come up with my own ideas.

Still, there was something missing.

I was restless. Even on a trip around the world, I was restless, increasingly so as I began to feel *rested*. My mind had ceased its relentless striving, racing, and I could see and appreciate the beauty around me. Yes, I still had telegrams to send off and articles to write. And write I would, about the food, the waves, the people.

I lay my head back and took a deep breath, trying to clutch back the peaceful rest of this paradise. But, when the dreams fade away, one can drown the sigh with the cooling lime squash which the noiseless, barefooted, living bronze has placed on the white armrest.

I smiled him my thank-you, then watched the jinrickshas come silently in through the gas-lit gate, the naked black runners coming to a sudden stop, letting the shafts drop so the passenger can step out.

As it turned to a sweet, dusky night, I only half heard Mr. Gregory's words as they mingled with the sound of the ocean. He was asking something about my plans after my trip, but my attention was on a couple standing close together, face bending over a face up-turned, hand clasped in hand and held closely against a manly heart, standing, two dark figures, beneath an arch of the veranda, outlined against the gate lamp.

At first, caught up in the romance of the land, I felt a pinch of longing, wondering if I would ever be the girl standing in such a pose. After several indulgent moments, my emotions expanded to allow a little sympathy for them as they were clearly wrapped in that delusion that makes life heaven or hell, that forms the foundation for every novel, play or story. They stood such until a noisy new arrival wakened her from blissful oblivion, and she rushed, scarcely waiting for him to kiss the hand he held, away into the darkness.

Sighing again, I took another sip of my lime squash and turned to answer Mr. Gregory.

21

IN WHICH ELIZABETH BISLAND ALMOST MISSES
HER TRAIN, BUT SECURES A SILK DRESS.

AT BREAKFAST WE GATHER OUR NOW-familiar little traveling family and discuss our plans for a day trip into Tokyo. The rest are content to lounge at the hotel until it is time, but Madge and I go shopping.

Lieutenant McDonald, magnificent in brown cords and laced Russia-leather riding boots, offers us his pony carriage. "It will be a more comfortable ride," he insists.

But we scoff at anything less foreign than a jinricksha and set off together for Benton-dori, the fashionable shopping street of Shichiu. A nipping air blows among the rose trees in the court as we leave and I hug myself to trap any body heat from escaping. I've worn my warmest ensemble, and once we get moving, I'm sure it will be enough.

In spite of the drop in the thermometer, the spirits of the public in general appear in no way chilled. However, their bare feet in straw sandals look red and uncomfortable, and I am glad for my European style of boot that keeps my feet warm. At least the native people have added three or four more cotton-wadded kimonos to their costume, and they can tuck their chilly fingers away in their ample sleeves, and thus laugh at the passing discomfort.

We wander from shop to shop and are received with an air of affectionate friendliness everywhere. We warm our fingers at many different braziers, and might drink little thimble-cups of tea at every hospitable place of business were we so minded.

"Oh, Elizabeth, I must stop here," says Madge at a display of porcelain. To view the wares, we sit on the edge of the little platform that forms the floor of the shop.

I eye a beautiful vase painted with a delicate landscape of Fujiama. "You must have something to keep the flowers your suitor will no doubt be presenting you with day after tomorrow."

At this, Madge blushes! Her heart has given her away.

"You are looking forward to meeting Mr. Handsome-and-Witty-and-Caring after all. Don't lie to me, Madge. I've known you for endless days now, and I'll be able to tell."

She ignores me as she begins to bargain with the amiable shopkeeper seated on his own heels and within easy reach of all his goods. He speaks in Pidgin English and is pleased that Madge does not bargain much at all.

Though we have been instructed not to pay more than half that is asked, the prices are so delightfully low that we give them joyfully and without haggling. Lieutenant McDonald will not be pleased with us.

Our shopping thus reminds me of when we were kids and my siblings and I would "keep store" in the nursery. One child would "sell" one's toys for astonishing sums to wealthy playmates whose purses were bursting with scraps of torn envelopes – fiat money of arbitrary value.

The really valuable bric-à-brac is costly here as elsewhere; but many charming things in common use among the people are to be picked up for a mere trifle. Even in these trinkets I find pretty proofs of their universal love of beauty.

I am proud of all my purchases and glad that I did not unnecessarily limit my luggage, especially since we have not yet made it to the focus of our shopping excursion: the silk shops!

In the silk-shops, we find the very poetry of fabrics: crepes like milky opals, with the pale iris hues of rainbows; crepes with the faint purple and rose of clear sunset skies, embroidered with wheeling flights of white storks. The shopkeeper shows us Moon-cloths, duskily azure with silver gleams; crepes, pearl-white and rich with needlework in patterns of delicate bamboo fronds or loose-petalled chrysanthemum-blossoms.

"Fairy garments all, woven of rainbows and moonbeams!" I exclaim, overcome with their beauty.

When I think I will see nothing more beautiful, out of a sweet-smelling box comes a mass of shining stuff that the low-voiced fourteenth-century-looking shopkeeper calls by three musical syllables.

The European woman watching us with amusement translates for me: "The Garments of the Dawn."

Its threads shimmer like the crystals of dry snow, and amid its folds the whiteness blushes to rose, deepens to gold, or pales to blue, while through it here and there runs a sort of impalpable cloudiness like a morning mist.

Immediately I make up my mind. "I'll be quick," I say to Madge, who has already reminded me we have a train to catch. "Two gowns," I tell the shopkeeper. "One of this," I say, gently fingering the magical fabric. "And another in the purple. When will they be ready?" I ask, hoping I can take these reminders of fairyland with me when I leave.

Tomorrow! Tomorrow! I shall have my gowns tomorrow.

With our packages weighing us down, we run to our rooms and hastily toss our purchases onto the beds. We have lingered too long in the enchanted wardrobes, Madge and I, and are in disgrace with the others for our tardiness, which has nearly lost them the train.

Breathless, we stand before our party, making apologies for our thoughtlessness, though our smiles might give us away for the fun we have had.

"If you are to race around the world, you might consider paying attention to train schedules," rebukes Mrs. White.

Her forthrightness catches me by surprise. I suppose I haven't fully put myself into the race. I don't want to be anxious during the entire trip or I'll come home as on-edge and frantic as Nellie Bly seems to be. Yet, I best set my mind not risk missing important connections. A rebuke from my editor Mr. Walker would be ten times worse than one from haughty Mrs. White.

"Next time we may not wait for you," remarks Mrs. Baxter, turning her back to us as she marches away, her bustle swishing to emphasize her consternation.

Mr. Mayer sends us a sympathetic smile and holds out his elbows to escort us to the station. Madge and I grin at each other. We secretly feel this Gentleman from Germany is on our side.

It is a funny train, as absurdly toy-like and doll-housey as is everything else in this country. Our destinies are committed today into the hands of a sweet-mannered gentleman in a gray kimono and an American hat, who is to guide us amid the beauties of his country's capital.

Delicious little pictures run past our car windows, astonishing us with the sudden revelation of what nonsense we have heard on the ship about the conventionality of Japanese art. In truth, the world the Japanese artist has painted has been the world just as it exists in his own country. Moreover, he has in his art caught and expressed with perfect and subtle veracity its atmosphere, the soul of things about him that has so far escaped the brush of every foreign artist endeavoring to portray the outward forms of things Japanese.

The charm of all we see from our car – the Tokaido (the great imperial highway that intersects the whole empire), the queer little farmhouses and railway stations, and even the water-soaked paddy fields, reaped of their rice – lies in the exquisite, faultless cleanliness and propriety of it all. Nothing is out of place. Nothing requires allowance and forgiveness. All is beautifully posed and arranged as if sitting to have itself instantaneously photographed.

Recognizing this attitude of expectancy, the American girl with the camera takes aim and the click of her shutter is heard in the land.

When we arrive at Tokyo one hour later, we go via horse and carriage straightaway to the residence of the American minister to deliver our young photographer, for this is where she will be remaining as a guest.

Seeing the house, Madge leans over me and says to the girl, "You'll have no trouble staying here. You'll live like a princess."

The house is impressive, with a most astonishing profusion of flowery plants blooming and bourgeoning in every corner of the mansion. While we gawk, the minister's carriage drives up, accompanied with two out-runners in gorgeous native liveries of orange and blue. These out-runners accompany all folk of importance in Japan, and keep pace with the horses without fatigue. A fine, picturesque bit of medieval swagger they make.

We take our tiffin in a little latticed glove box of a teahouse, the polished daintiness of whose interior will not permit of our wearing our shoes.

What a grotesque spectacle they make – those American shoes, standing in a row just inside the entrance while we tiptoe awkwardly and shamefacedly in our stocking-feet up the stairs.

A mild diffused light shines through the paper panes, illuminating our tiny upper chamber, whose only furnishings are sweet-smelling mattings, a kakemono hanging on the wall, and a tall jar full of red-berried branches in the corner.

We are served by a moon-faced little maid in a flowered gown. She bows as she enters, bringing us copper braziers to warm our fingers and wadded rugs to sit upon, tailorwise. When I sit, I hide my feet under my skirt. All the women do likewise.

At each entry our server bows and draws in her breath. I wonder if her kimono is pulled so tightly that she has trouble breathing, or if her actions signify something in particular. In my short time here, I've observed customs of a national courtesy so thorough and far-reaching that even the domestic animals are civilly addressed as Mr. Cat and Mr. Dog.

Mr. Mayer, reading my mind, whispers, "She is showing us what a privilege it is to breathe the same air with us."

Then she serves us delicious tea, sugarless and straw-colored, in tiny cups without handles, and bowls of rice across which are laid crisp, freshly broiled eels – a delightful dish that we eat with polished black chopsticks.

Madge and I hide our smiles watching our friend, Mr. Mayer, try to spear his eel. But his methods are much more effective than poor Mrs. Baxter, who will likely lose some weight while she is in this foreign land.

After we eat, the 'rickshas race away with us quite to the other side of town – past great forts and fosses, past the Mikado's palaces and gardens, to the famous temples at Shiba.

The road is smooth and broad and overshadowed by pines. A superb gilded and lacquered gateway admits us to the temple grounds, and here the guide goes in search of a shaven-headed priest who will show us his treasures.

Immediately before us stands a lovely red temple, rich with gold and carvings and lacquered figures, and with a marble-paved veranda polished as onyx. We go to the left and climb the hill by stone steps strewn with crimson petals of the camellia blossoms.

"Our time is almost at an end," I say reluctantly to Madge.

"I know. I wish you could alter your plans and stay here to meet Mr. Handsome."

At the end of an avenue of tall gray stone lanterns stands the tomb of Ieymitsu, famed for consolidating the feudal system. Chivalry under his rule achieved its noblest development; Japanese arms were feared and respected abroad and at home; and under the sun of his kingly favor Japanese art blossomed into its supreme, consummate flower.

Our guide says, "Today the curios of his period are worth their weight in gold. Laying down a life of power, he yearned for an immortality of beauty – to be magnificent and impressive even in death; and, choosing this spot, he spent millions in glorifying his last resting-place."

"He had a nice taste in tombs," comments Mr. Mayer.

The hill is clothed in pines, and the westering sun shines slantingly through making golden shadows across the path we have come. The mild-moving air has stolen red blossoms from the glossy-leaved camellia-trees and shred them upon the hoary gray lanterns and mossy stairs. Never a monarch slept among sweeter verdure, space, and calm.

The tomb has, as have all these shrines and temples, walls of a deep rich red, which three centuries have not dimmed. Above is a broad frieze of gorgeous carving – dragons, birds, lotus, and chrysanthemums tangled in fantastic intricacies, and all lacquered and gilded with such honest pains that Time's teeth cannot gnaw through the color or his breath tarnish the gold.

We stroll away in the mild sunshine and down the flower-strewn stairway. I cannot contain my joy at the grace and gorgeousness of the myriad delicate fantasies wrought out by art to soothe the king's last sleep.

"*Et in Arcadia ego* – I, too, have been in fairyland!" I cry to Mr. White.

He raises his eyebrows in wonder or indulgence, I cannot tell. My love of quotations is not always shared by those around me.

"It's the title of a painting," I explain. "A group of simple shepherds outside an extravagant tomb. By Nicolas Poussin. It means 'even in Arcadia I am there' spoken by Death."

He nods. "Quite fitting," he says. "I have one for you: 'And as it is appointed unto men once to die, but after this the judgment.'"

"Hebrews," I answer, not to be outdone.

He simply smiles in return.

We finish off our visit at the great park of Uyeno, to see the sun go down behind Fujiyama, and to look out across the city's vast hive with its million or more of folk whose myriad lights begin to twinkle in the violet dusk before we board the railroad again to go back to our hotel, and I to continue on to the ship.

After regretful farewells to the charming Americans and Lieutenant McDonald, I exchange tired well wishes with Madge.

"You have my address?" she asks, stifling a yawn.

"Yes, of course. Besides, you know how to find me at *The Cosmopolitan*."

"I'll read all your articles, but I want to know about the things you won't write about."

I laugh. "And I want to know what you really think about Mr. Handsome."

We embrace before parting. She goes to her hotel room and I to my stateroom. And then the visit to fairyland is over. I must pass on in my swift course and be ready for new sights and friends. We have one more glimpse of Fujiyama the next morning as Japan sinks out of sight. I'm satisfied with my gowns, now tucked away in my trunk, but as I recall my earlier rebuke from Mrs. White, I vow to do better at racing.

22

EARLY NEXT MORNING, I WAS AWAKENED BY a Singalese waiter placing tea and toast on a small table. He was outlined by a dim light that crept in through the open glass door, which led to the balcony. He drew the table up close to my curtained bed and quietly left.

I went back to sleep but was awakened shortly by a rattling of the dishes on the table. Opening my eyes, I saw, standing on the table, quietly enjoying my toast, a crow!

"Oh!" I was about to shoo it away but changed my mind. I was not used to having toast and tea before arising, as is the custom in Ceylon, so I let the crow satisfy his appetite while I watched. When he was almost finished, he took his last bite with him and walked back through the opening in the balcony curtains and few off.

After a cool, refreshing bath, I dressed hastily and went down below. I found almost all of my friends up, some having already started out to enjoy the early morning.

"You are welcome to join us," said one of the women I recognized from the ship. "Mr. Gregory has organized a tour while the morning is cool." She adjusted her hat pin to ensure that her large white bonnet was firmly attached to her head.

With empty stomach, I joined the group. In a light wagon we again drove down Galle Face Road, and out past a lake in which men, women, children, oxen, horses, buffalo and dogs were sporting. It was a strange sight.

Off on a little green island we saw the laundry folk at work, beating, sousing and wringing the clothes, which they afterwards spread upon the grass to dry. Almost all of the roads through which we drove were perfect with their picturesque curves, and often bordered and arched with magnificent trees, many of which were burdened with beautiful brilliant blossoms.

"The breakwater," pointed out Mr. Gregory, "is a good half mile in length and is a favorite promenade for the citizens of Colombo."

Indeed, everybody seemed to be out. The white people were driving, riding, riding bicycles, or walking.

"Morning and evening you'll see gaily dressed people walking back and forth between the lighthouse and the shore. But when the stormy season comes, the sea dashes full forty feet above this promenade. After the storms are over, they have to clean off the green slime before it can be traveled with safety," said Mr. Gregory.

One of the very British women with us on the trip could not help but add loyally, "The Prince of Wales himself laid the first stone of this beautiful breakwater in 1875."

"Yes, and ten years later it was finished. It is considered one of the finest in existence," concluded Mr. Gregory.

I wanted to disagree if only for the sake of the overly-British woman, but I could not. The scene was too beautiful so I kept quiet as to not give her the satisfaction of knowing everyone agreed with her.

The next night we went to a Parsee theatre. At the entrance were groups of people, some of whom were selling fruits, and some were jinricksha men waiting to haul the people home after the performance. There was no floor in the building. The chairs were placed in rows on the ground. The house was quite well filled with native men, women and children who were deeply interested in the performance, which had begun before we reached there.

The actors were all men; Mr. Gregory had told me women never think of going on the stage in that country. The stage was not unlike any other stage, and the scenery, painted by native artists, was quite as good as is usually seen. On the left of the stage, close to the wing, was a man, sitting cross-legged on a raised platform, beating a tom-tom, a long drum beat with the hands.

The musician who presided over the tom-tom this night was dressed in a thin white material, and he wore a very large turban of the same stuff on his head. His copper-colored face was long and earnest, and he beat the tom-tom with a will that was simply amazing when one was informed that he had been constantly engaged at it since nine in the morning. If his hands did not tire, his legs did. Several times I saw him move, as if to find ease by shifting his squatting position, and every time I saw his bare feet turn up, in full view of the audience, I felt an irresistible desire to laugh.

On the right, directly opposite to the tom-tom player, was a man, whose duty it was to play a strange-looking organ. He only used one hand, the left, for playing, and with the right he held a book, which he steadily perused throughout the entire performance, reading and playing mechanically without once looking at the actors.

The actors were amusing, at least. The story of the opera was not unlike those in other countries – a tale of love and tragedy.

The lover, like all lovers, urged the girl to be his in songs that were issued through his nose for fifteen minutes at a time. The actor playing the heroine would endeavor to look shy all through this insufferably long song of nasal sound, and then "she" would take up the same refrain, and to the same tune sing back at him for the same length, and after his own style, while he would hang his head and listen. Their gestures were very few, and they usually stood in one spot on the stage. Sometimes they would embrace, but only to fall apart and sing at each other again.

We rode home from the theatre in a bullock hackery. It was a very small springless cart on two wheels with a front seat for the driver, and on the back seat, with our backs to the driver and out feet hanging over, we drove to the hotel.

The bullock is a strange, modest-looking little animal with a hump on its back and crooked horns on its head. I feared that it could not carry us all, but it traveled at a very good pace. However, not long into our trip, there was a sound of grunt, grunt, grunting that concerned me very much.

I kept peering around, checking on the health of the animal, until I found it was the driver and not the bullock that was responsible for the noise. With grunts he urged the bullock to greater speed.

The drive, along tree-roofed roads, was very quiet and lovely. The moonlight fell beautiful and soft over the land, and nothing disturbed the stillness except the sound of the sea and an occasional soldier we met staggering along towards the barracks.

Just as we turned a corner to go to the hotel, an officer rushed up, waving at our driver to stop. He caught hold of a wheel and stumbled as the hackery slowed before finally coming to a stop.

"We are under arrest!" came the translation from Mr. Gregory.

A rapid discussion ensued, with the officer pointing to the front lights. The candles in one of the lamps had burned out.

"We are driving with a dark side," Mr. Gregory explained as he hopped out to talk with the officer. He made it right and within minutes, we continued on to the hotel instead of the jail.

The next morning, I planned to pack leisurely and then board the *Oriental* for the next leg of my journey. A representative found us at breakfast and halted those plans.

"I am sorry to tell you the *Oriental* is delayed – possibly by several days." He smiled broadly.

"Exactly how many days?" I squeaked.

He shrugged. "It is hard to tell. Please, go out and make the most of your time at Colombo."

Mr. Gregory, seasoned traveler, softened the blow. "These things happen all the time. Don't worry about making connections. It only means you'll have a shorter stopover at the next port."

Thus, my companions settled into a leisurely routine established on that first full day. After breakfast, which usually leaves nothing to be desired, guests rest in the corridor of the hotel; the men who have business matters to attend to look after them and return to the hotel not later than eleven. About the hour of noon everybody takes a rest, and after luncheon they take a nap. While they sleep the hottest part of the day passes, and at four they are again ready for a drive or a walk, from which they return after sunset in time to dress for dinner. After dinner there are pleasant little rides in jinrickshas or visits to the native theaters.

No one but me seems disturbed to be delayed in Colombo. No matter how everyone assures me, I still worry. To fail so soon would be humiliating. At least let me fail close to home, stopped by a snowstorm on my way to New York!

23

HONG KONG!
I like the name of my next port. It has a fine clangorous significance, like two slow loud notes of some great brazen-lunged bell. Hong – Kong!

I have telegraphed ahead to family friends who live there to let them know of my serendipitous trip, and they have invited me to stay with them the short time my ship is in dock. My mother would have liked to have sent them a gift, but of course, there had been no time! They will have to accept me as the whirlwind that I am.

During the day the young man with the pallid waxen hands dies. He has struggled hard to keep the flame burning until he sees his own land, but the crisp breath of the Japanese coast puffs it suddenly out. A canvas screen is hung across one corner of the steerage deck, and the doctor goes back and forth from behind it. They will carry him back to his country, though he will not be glad or aware.

The steward tells me a Chinese-American benevolent group called the Six Companies has given them twelve coffins to use in the event that someone of Chinese descent dies on the trip as the Chinese do not allow burial at sea. After the ship's doctor embalms the body, he places it in one of these coffins to be stowed until we reach China. To cover the expense, Chinese sugar cubes are placed by the coffin. When one makes a donation, he may take some sugar for luck. In this way, by amounts large and small, the

Chinese people take care of their own. At Hong Kong, the man will be transported to a hospital and met by family and friends.

But the sea knows she is being defrauded of her rights – and wakes and rages. She comes in the night and beats thunderously with her great fists upon our doors. She leaps to look over our bulwarks for her hidden victim; she roars with wrath and will not be appeased. For two days we steam in the face of the northwest gale she has raised, and for three the ship plunges like a spurred horse. I wonder if these are the winds my editor was talking about, the reason he thinks the *World* editor made a mistake sending Nellie east.

At dinner the ship pitches to the right and the captain glances my way.

"I am fine," I assure him. "Bodily, at least, I am proof now against seasickness."

We are a sight to behold, all of us at table holding firmly to our plates, having had too many opportunities of late to collect our soup and entrées in our laps. I force a smile. My stomach may be healthy, but my temper has a violent attack of mal de mer. It makes me bitterly cross to go leaping and plunging about the ship, not to be able to keep my seat.

As soon as is polite, I excuse myself to the ship's library. After scouring the shelves, I retire to bed where I wedge myself in tight with pillows, and go steadily through every word the ship's library affords on the subject of Japan.

I am refreshed and cheered to find that the writer of each book fails, as signally as I shall fail, to convey any adequate idea of the fairy charms of the Land of Chrysanthemums. Shall one then paint a dragonfly with a whitewash brush?

As the boat continues to pitch and heave with abandon, I distract myself by thinking of how I will convey to Molly all the sights I have seen. She will be more interested in Madge's love story than in the description of any landscape. And of course, she will be sorry to have missed out on seeing all the lovely fabrics available in Japan. The gown I have bought for her will be a small consolation.

I spent, alas! less than two days in these fairy islands; but all ballad literature declares with great positiveness that, having spent even the briefest moment in the Land of the Fays engenders an unquenchable yearning that must some day, some hour, bring one back again – and with this I comfort my heart.

At dinner, the conversation turns to our next destination.

"The island of Hong Kong is a cluster of hills with scanty vegetation, seized by England in 1842 after a struggle with China. At that time the town was an insignificant fishing village, but the value of the site was great commercially and strategically," said Captain Kempson.

"How so?" asks the businessman.

"It is both a convenient and safe harbor for the squadron detailed to watch the Russian navy in the Pacific. Plus, the English have elevated the village into a flourishing city and made it the fourth shipping port of the world. The harbor is navigable for the largest merchant vessels and men-of-war in existence, and is perfectly sheltered and easy to access."

All of this information is interesting, but what I am most looking forward to is a visit with my friends, the Brauns whom I met briefly when I lived in New Orleans. They received my cable and responded that they will meet me at the harbor.

24

IN WHICH NELLIE BLY MAKES THE BEST OF HER DELAY AND MEETS A KINDRED SPIRIT.

AMONG THE NATIVES THAT HAUNTED THE hotel were the snake charmers. They were almost naked fellows, sometimes with ragged jackets on and sometimes turbans on their heads.

They executed a number of tricks in a very skillful manner. The most wonderful of these tricks, to me, was that of growing a tree. They would show a seed, then they would place the seed on the ground, cover it with a handful of earth, and cover this little mound with a handkerchief, which they first passed around to be examined, that we might be positive there was nothing wrong with it. Over this they would chant, and after a time the handkerchief is taken off and then up through the ground is a green sprout.

We looked at it incredulously, while the man said: "Tree no good; tree too small," and, covering it up again, he would renew his chanting. Once more he would lift the handkerchief, and we saw the sprout was larger, but still it did not please the trickster, for he repeated: "Tree no good; tree too small," and covered it up again. This was repeated until he had a tree from three to five feet in height. Then he pulled it up, showed us the seed and roots.

Although these men always asked us to "See the snake dance?" we always saw every other trick but the one that had caught us.

One morning, I exited the hotel to sightsee with my new acquaintance, Mrs. Barnes, when we were waylaid by a group of such men.

"See the snake dance?" urged one.

"Yes," I agreed. "But I will only pay to see the snake dance and for nothing else." I crossed my arms to further express my determination.

The men exchanged looks before lifting the lid of the basket and jumping back. The cobra crawled slowly out, curling itself up on the ground. The charmer began to play on a little fife, meanwhile waving a red cloth, which attracted the cobra's attention. It rose up steadily, darting angrily at the red cloth and rose higher at every motion until it seemed to stand on the tip end of its tail.

Then it saw the charmer and it darted for him.

By this time a crowd had gathered, and we all gasped, fearing for the man's life. But he cunningly caught it by the head – and with such a grip that I saw the blood gush from the snake's mouth. He worked for some time, still firmly holding the snake by the head before he could get it into the basket, the reptile meanwhile lashing the ground furiously with its tail. When at last it was covered from sight, I drew a long breath, and the charmer said to me sadly:

"Cobra no dance, cobra too young, cobra too fresh!"

I thought quite right; the cobra was too fresh!

Mrs. Barnes and I continued on to secure our jinricksha rides. It was the first time at Colombo that I ever saw one of these vehicles and it reminded me of a sulky pulled by a horse.

There are stands at different places for these men as well as carriage stands. While waiting for patrons, they let their 'rickshas rest on the shafts, and they sit in the bottom, their feet on the ground. Besides dressing in a sash, these men dress in an oil or grease, and when the day is hot and they run, one wishes they wore more clothing and less oil! The grease has an original odor that is entirely its own.

The man put his foot on the shaft when I got in, and as he raised it, ready to start, I saw my friend step into her 'ricksha. She sat down and instantly went out–the other way! The man did not have his foot on the shaft, and she overbalanced.

"Are you well?" I called over.

In good humor, she dusted herself off and climbed back in. "Yes. I've never fallen off a horse in my life, but here I am falling off 'ricksha. I will never admit it even if you do tell everyone at tiffin."

I had a shamed feeling about going around the town drawn by a man, but after I had gone a short way, I decided it was a great improvement on modern means of travel; it was so comforting to have a horse that was able to take care of itself!

With so much time available for sightseeing, we visited a great number of shops, the Buddhist college where I met the famous high priest of Ceylon, and the local newspaper offices, of which there were two, both run by two young Englishmen who were very clever and kind to strangers.

"Have you been to Kandy?" asked one.

"Never heard of it," I answered.

"You must go," encouraged the other. "It's a city in the hills of the central province to the east. The road to Kandy, in particular, is very beautiful. You'll not find a prettier jaunt in all the world. I'd go with you if I had the time, but alas, you know the paper business."

He didn't look particularly busy, sitting on the edge of his desk, hands clasped over his crossed knee, but I nodded in agreement anyway.

So, the next morning at seven o'clock, I started for Kandy with the Spanish representative, who was going to Pekin, and a jolly Irish lad named Sean Collins, who was so young-looking everyone called him The Boy. He was bound for Hong Kong, and both of them had traveled with me from Brindisi.

We drove to the station and were passed with the people through the gate to the train. English cars, and ones that leave everything to be desired, are used on this line. We got into a compartment where there was but one seat, which, luckily for us, happened to be facing the way we traveled.

Our tickets were taken at the station, and then the doors were locked and the train started. Before the start, we had entered our names in a book, which a guard brought to us with the information that we could have breakfast on the train if so desired.

As it was too early for breakfast at the hotel, we were only too glad to get an opportunity to eat. At eight o'clock the train stopped and the guard unlocked our door, telling us to go front to the dining car.

The dining car was fitted up with stationary tables which almost spanned the car, leaving a small space for people to walk along. There were more people than could be accommodated, but as the train had started, they were obliged to stand.

Several persons had told me that the breakfast served on this train was considered remarkably good. I thought, on seeing the bill of fare, they had prepared a feast for a chicken hawk.

"I hope you are hungry for chicken," I said to Sean Collins. First, there was fish dressed in vinegar and onions, followed by chicken soup, chicken aspic, grilled chicken, boned chicken, fried chicken, boiled chicken, cold chicken and chicken pie!

After we had finished our breakfast, we were compelled to remain where we were until the train arrived at some station. Then the dining car was unlocked, and we returned to the other car, being again locked in until the end of our journey.

The road winds up the mountain side and is rather pretty, but nothing wonderful in that respect. It is a tropical land, but the foliage and flowers are very ordinary. About the prettiest things to be seen are the rice beds. They are built in terraces, and when one looks down into the deep valley, seeing terrace after terrace of the softest, lightest green, one is forced to cry: "How beautiful!"

Arriving at Kandy at last, we hired a carriage and went to see the lake, the public library and the temples. In one old temple, surrounded by a moat, we saw several altars, of little consequence, and a bit of ivory, which they told us was the tooth of Buddha.

Kandy is pretty, but far from what it is claimed to be. They said it was cool, but we found it so hot that we thought with regret of Colombo. Disgusted with all we found worth seeing, we drove to Parathenia to see the great botanical garden. It well repaid us for the visit. That evening we returned to Colombo.

I was tired and hungry, and the extreme heat had given me a sick headache. On the way down, the Spanish gentlemen endeavored to keep our falling spirits up, but every word he said only helped to increase my bad temper, much to the amusement of the Irish boy. He was very polite and kind, the Spaniard, I mean, but he had an unhappy way of flatly contradicting one, that, to say the least, was exasperating. It was to me, but it only made the Irish boy laugh. When we were going down the mountain side, the Spaniard got up, and standing, put his head through the open window in the door to get a view of the country.

"We are going over," he said, with positive conviction, turning around to us. I was leaning up in a corner, trying to sleep, and the Irish boy, with his feet braced against the end of the compartment, was trying to do the same.

"We won't go over," I managed to say, while the Irish boy smiled.

"Yes, we will," the Spaniard shouted back, "Make your prayers!"

The Irish boy screamed with laughter, and I forgot my sickness as I held my sides and laughed. It was a little thing, but it is often little things that raise the loudest laughs. After that, all I needed to say to upset the dignity of the Irish boy was: "Make your prayers!"

I went to bed that night too ill to eat my dinner. The next morning, I had intended to go to the pearl market with Mrs. Barnes, but felt unequal to it. When she returned she told me that at the very end of the sale, a man bought some leftover oysters for one rupee and found in them five hundred dollars worth of pearls. I felt sorry that I had not gone.

One night, after I had been five days in Colombo, the blackboard in the hotel corridor bore the information that the *Oriental* would sail for China the following morning, at eight o'clock. I was called at five o'clock and some time afterwards left for the ship.

"Oh, Miss Bly!" called the Spanish minister, stopping my path. "We still have time. Would you go to some of the shops with me? I'd like to buy some jewelry and need a woman's opinion."

"I've been in Colombo far too long as it is," I told him. I was so nervous and anxious to be on my way that I could not wait a moment longer than was necessary to reach the boat that was to carry me to China.

148

When farewells had been said, and I was on the *Oriental*, I found my patience had given way under the long delay. The ship seemed to be deserted when I went on deck, with the exception of a handsome, elderly man, accompanied by a young blonde man in a natty white linen suit, who slowly promenaded the deck, watching out to sea while they talked. I was trying to untie my steamer chair so as to have someplace to sit when the elderly man came up and politely offered to assist me.

"When will we sail?" I asked shortly.

"As soon as the *Nepaul* comes in," the man replied. "She was to have been here at daybreak, but she hasn't been sighted yet. Waiting for the *Nepaul* has given us this five days' delay. She's a slow old boat."

"May she go to the bottom of the bay when she does get in." I said savagely. "I think it an outrage to be kept waiting five days for a tub like that."

"Colombo is a pleasant place to stay," the elderly man said with a twinkle in his eye.

"It may be, if staying there does not mean more than life to one. Really, it would afford me the most intense delight to see the *Nepaul* go the bottom of the sea."

Evidently my ill humor surprised them, and their surprise amused me, for I thought how little anyone could realize what this delay meant to me, and the mental picture of a forlorn little self creeping back to New York ten days behind time, with a shamed look on her face and afraid to hear her name spoken, made me laugh outright.

They gazed at me in astonishment, and my better nature surged up with the laugh. "And there is the *Nepaul*," I said, pointing out a line of smoke just visible above the horizon. They doubted it, but a few moments proved that I was correct.

"I am very ill-natured," I said, glancing from the kindly blue eyes of the elderly man to the laughing blue eyes of the younger man, "but I could not help it. After being delayed for five days, I was called at five o'clock because they said the ship was to sail at eight, and here it is: nine o'clock and there's no sign of the ship sailing, and I am simply famished."

As they laughed at my woes, the gong sounded for breakfast, and they took me down. The Irish lad, with his sparkling eyes and jolly laugh, was there, as was a young Englishman who had also traveled on the *Victoria* to Colombo. I knew him by sight, but as he was a sworn woman-hater, I did not dare to speak to him. There were no women on board. I was the only woman that morning, and a right jolly breakfast we had.

The captain, a most handsome man, and as polite and courteous as he was good-looking, sat at the head of the table. Officers that any ship might boast of were gathered about him. Handsome, good-natured, intelligent, polite, they were, every single one of them. I found the elderly man I had been talking to was the chief engineer, and the young man was the ship's doctor, a Welshman named Dr. Brown.

The dining hall was very artistic and pleasant, and the food was good. The ship, although much smaller than the *Victoria*, was better in every way. The cabins were more comfortable, the ship was better ventilated, the food was vastly superior, the officers were polite and good-natured, the captain was a gentleman in looks and manners, and everything was just as agreeable as it could be.

It was well on to one o'clock before the passengers transferred from the *Nepaul* to the *Oriental*. In the meantime, the ship was amply peopled with merchants from the shore, who were selling jewels and lace. How they did cheat the passengers!

At one o'clock, we finally sailed. I found it a great relief to be again on the sweet, blue sea, free from the tussle and worry and bustle for life which we are daily, hourly even, forced to gaze upon on land. Watching the hull slicing through the water, I could content myself knowing I was back in the race. My optimism had returned.

25

O N SUNDAY, DECEMBER 15TH, WE REACH Hong Kong. The sea turns to a cool profound emerald, and on the horizon the bamboo wings of the fishing and coasting junks appear. Their sails are somewhat larger and deeper of hue than those of Japan and more so resemble the fans of giant yellow and russet butterflies.

Here I leave the *Oceanic* and find I am very regretful. I have received so much kindness; but as Tennyson so aptly imagined for his mariners in his poem "The Lotos-Eaters" I, too, prefer to stay and rest on the peaceful island. After more than three weeks of travel, how delightful the thought of even three precious days on land!

Hateful is the dark blue sky,
Vaulted o'er the dark blue sea.
Death is the end of life; ah, why
Should life all labor be?

At one o'clock we are in the broad antechamber of the port, known as the Lyee-Moon, and are signaled from the lofty peak to the inhabitants of the town lying at its foot. I wonder if my friends are already at the dock waiting for me, and if they can tell this is the ship they are waiting for.

At two o'clock we drop anchor in the roadstead amid a great host of shipping of all character and nations. I record twenty-three days out from San Francisco in my journal. The White Star people had instructed Captain Kempson to make all due haste for my sake, and it is one of the swiftest voyages ever known at this season of the year, when the winds are contrary, coming to the west. We were sixteen days to Japan, where we remained thirty-six hours, and five days from Yokohama to Hong Kong.

I tuck the journal away and gaze out at the harbor. As in Japan, sampans swarm about us as soon as we are made fast to the buoy, but they are far less picturesque. Each sampan wears a bamboo hood in the stern where the owner houses his wife and rears his family.

The Chinese woman of the working class, I find, decided centuries ago the question still in its stormy infancy with us – of the divided skirt. She clothes herself in a pair of wide black trousers, a loose tunic, jade earrings and cork-soled shoes, and is ready for all the emergencies of life.

The gentleman beside me at the rail explains, "When a woman marries a sampan owner, she will but rarely set her foot on shore again. She will work, sleep, eat, bear her children, rear them, and die in that crazy little boat."

"They never leave their boats?"

"No need. There is something like twenty thousand in the water population of Hong Kong. They can get everything they need for life right here."

"I can't imagine," I say, craving to set my feet on land. I lean out over the rail, trying to see my friends in the steam launches lining up. I wonder if I will recognize them, it has been so long since we met at the Royal Street literary salon. Then I see Mrs. Bauer. Her hat is enormous, and she is waving at me. Before long, I am climbing down into their personal steam launch, and she is hugging me tight.

"It is always good to see an old friend!" she exclaims. "Is this all your luggage?"

I nod at the bags a steward is transferring for me. They are already significantly heavier after my stop in Japan. I wonder how Nellie Bly is doing with her one bag.

Mr. Bauer takes my hand and helps me board the smaller vessel. "I hear we are to show you something of domestic life in the East."

"Please," I answer. "I am eager to see how you live in this distant land."

Chairs and bearers are waiting for us on the dock – comfortable chairs of bamboo, trimmed with silver and supported by long bamboo poles. This is even more amusing than the 'rickshas. There are four men for each chair, dressed in my friend's livery – loose trousers and tunic of white cotton bordered with rose color. Their feet are bare, and their hair is gathered into Psyche knots, on the back of their heads, like the hair of the shop girls in America.

They lift the poles to their shoulders and start off in a swift swinging trot, Mr. Bauer in one chair, myself and Mrs. Bauer cozy in the other. We pass across the narrow strip of level land that lies on the water's edge.

"That is the business quarter," Mr. Bauer calls from his chair. "We live up there." He points up the broad steep ways that lead to the residence quarter.

On every wall stand rows of earthen jars full of greenery and blossom – rows on rows of them in the courtyards – more rows on both ends of every flight of steps, and on all balcony railings. Every nook and corner that will hold a jar is filled with bloom, and the rarest orchids are strewn carelessly about, industriously producing flowers, in ignorance of their own value.

We meet the most astonishing varieties of the human race. All sorts and conditions of Chinese – elegant dandies in exquisitely pale-tinted brocades; grave merchants, richly but soberly clad; neat amahs with the tiny deformed Chinese feet, sitting at the street corners, taking in sewing by the day. The street sellers hawk their wares: tea, shrimp, fruit, sweetmeats, and rice.

At the corner stands a haughty jewel-eyed prince of immense stature – straight and lithe as a palm. He wears a soldier's dress and sword and a huge scarlet turban of the most intricate convolutions. I cry out with astonishment at the sight of this superb creature.

"Is it an emperor?" I demand in breathless admiration.

"An emperor! Poof! It's only a Sikh policeman. There are hundreds about the place quite as splendid as he."

It gives me my first real impression of the power of England, who tames these mountain lions and sets them to do her police duty. It would seem incredible that the Tommy Atkins, the rosy commonplace British soldier, who comes swaggering down the street in his scarlet coat can be the weapon that tamed the fine creature in the turban.

What is the secret of colonization? Is it more beef and mutton perhaps – or more of submission to orders and power of self-discipline?

Here comes one of the conquerors of India, a kilted Highlander, swinging down the road in his plaided petticoats, with six inches of bare stalwart pink legs showing, and a fine hearty self-confidence in his mien that signifies his utter disbelief in the power of anything human to conquer him.

Mrs. Bauer squeezes my hand. "We have handsome men here, do we not?"

I lower my eyes and smile. Interesting and handsome, yes. But I am only here for a few days. Not long enough for love's sake.

We leave this stew of nations behind and mount into a broad street curved around the flank of the hill. On the upper side of it is a heavy wall, once painted a lovely light blue, and now freaked and stained a thousand charming tints by time and weather. Creepers bearing great yellow flowers trail across it; trees shadow it, and the convent's massive outlines loom from behind. Our chairs stop here but don't let us down.

"That is the Portuguese convent," says my friend. "They do a beautiful work in teaching Chinese girls the sweet decencies of life and pretty feminine arts. We live across the street."

Their house is two stories of stone surrounded by great verandas. The coolies run down a curving flight of steps and deposit us at the door. Mr. Bauer leads us into a lofty hall, terminating on a rear veranda, with a wide view of the city, buried in greenery, sloping down to the flashing emerald of the bay.

The hall is filled with more potted plants, and massive furniture of Indian ebony and marble. To the left is a great drawing room, fifty feet long and eighteen high, with a dozen windows. Here are more palms and ferns, rich European fittings, and Eastern bric-à-brac. Scattered about are photographs of Emperor Wilhelm II and all the Hohenzollerns, for my friends are Germans.

We rest awhile in the cool green gloom of this apartment and drink tea brought by a tall gentleman in silk trousers, a black satin cap, and a crisp rustling blue gown reaching nearly to his ankles.

"You must be tired," says Mrs. Bauer. "Let me show you to your room and you can settle in."

My bedchamber is another huge shadowy place, with a dressing room and bath as large as the ordinary drawing room at home.

"How beautiful," I exclaim, running my fingertips along a well-built dresser.

"The bedroom suite has been in my husband's family for years. It is old mahogany with silver fittings, brought from Germany two generations ago. This is one of my favorite rooms. Rest up tonight and we will show you Hong Kong in the morning. *Gute Nacht.*"

The room's airy, unencumbered spaces remind me of the fine old bedchambers in the plantation house in Louisiana. How I loved those old rooms at Fairfax. As I fall asleep, I picture Molly and myself wrapped in shawls on the floor that first night we'd returned home after the civil war. We'd thought the South a great deal more exciting than at grand mamma's, where we always went to bed in the regular way.

Mother had cried at how torn up the house was, but we were home. It was both familiar and foreign to us and took some getting used to. It was so strange to think of soldiers sleeping in children's rooms. Of course, Pressley was only a baby then, so he had no notion of the place, and the others weren't born yet.

My last thought before drifting off is that I need to send Molly a postcard and let her know I am with friends. She would let the rest of the family know how I am.

In the morning I am awakened by another pigtailed gentleman, who brings me my tea, prepares my bath, and arranges all things ready for my toilet. Mrs. Bauer warned me that female servants in Hong Kong are rare; and after my first surprise is over, these clean, grave male-maids seem perfectly efficient and convenable servitors.

Our meals are stately functions – adorned, of course, with profuse greenery and flowers – with fine wines and delicate food exquisitely prepared.

"What do you think of our Hong Kong so far?" asks Mrs. Bauer.

"There is so much going on, my eyes hardly knew where to look yesterday," I say before trying the *congee*, a rice porridge.

Mr. Bauer nods, looking pleased with my assessment. "The town is growing and prosperous."

"The sound of building never ends," says Mrs. Bauer, holding her head. "The buildings are made of stone, and the sound of mason's tools rings in my ears at times."

"I was amazed by all the different nationalities of people we passed in the streets," I say. "There must be work for any who want it here."

"Yes, and there is a general public amiability in the population. Although, as in all societies, there are those of the lowest class of laborers who work terribly for infinitesimal sums."

Mrs. Bauer shakes her head as of someone who sees a tragedy and doesn't know what to do about it. "You will likely see these poor folk in our travels today." She pours herself more tea. "But before we begin today's sightseeing, tell us about your trip thus far. Are you winning the race?"

"I have no idea if I am winning or losing, but I feel I am making good time." That unpleasantness out of the way, I entertain them with stories. They laugh at my description of the mad railway trip with Cyclone Bill, the nickname I learned at San Francisco for Mr. Downing. And Mrs. Bauer murmurs her approval at my description of the silk shops in Japan.

I was never in a German household before, and find here many pretty unfamiliar customs – one of them a nice fashion of repeating upon rising from the table a German phrase which expresses mutual good-will and affection, a sort of grace of friendship after meat. There is a careful sweet civility too in their intercourse with one another, very pleasant to share.

After our meal, Mr. Bauer leads us back outside where the chairs are waiting. My eyes fill once again with the sights of Hong Kong: Coolies run about at a dog-trot, bearing immense burdens swung at the two ends of a pole carried on their naked muscular shoulders. Pretty round-faced children, dressed exactly like their elders, play in the doorways and exchange smiles with the passersby.

Out of place are mountains of freshly deposited dirt dotting the harbor side of the broad water street. "What is the dirt near the harbor for?" I ask when we stop.

"The harbor is quite shallow for 200 yards. They are preparing to fill it up and give Hong Kong the benefit of this extra width of level land," explains Mr. Bauer. "They did the same thing some years ago at Kow-Loon, on the opposite side of the harbor where England owns a strip of the mainland."

"You've seen it," broke in Mrs. Bauer. "It's where the wharves are lined with *godowns*, in English you say 'warehouses.' They've also built huge dry-docks and shipyards for building and repairing ships there."

"There is much business that passes through these waters," continues Mr. Bauer. "The export trade in cotton, tea, silk, spices, and rice is enormous. Every year the place develops considerable manufacturing industries."

I examine the harbor and quickly surmise the truth.

"The strategic importance of Hong Kong is so great that four or five war ships are always in its harbor or cruise in the neighborhood, and two full regiments are kept in garrison. You may have seen the Highlanders who are here at present."

Mrs. Bauer catches my eye and smiles while her husband climbs back into his chair, unaware of our silent conversation about the Highlanders.

We come across more of these Highlanders later in the morning. They wear in this hot climate white jackets and helmets with their kilts. They are being put through a rapid and vigorous drill when we pass the parade ground, and the pipes are shrilly skirling – music to stir the heart in which runs the smallest drop of Scotch blood.

Not even the Sikh policemen stand first in my affections at this moment, as, to that wild keen sound, the solid ranks of brawny red-haired Caledonians trot by, with their petticoats fluttering about their bare knees and their bayonets set in a glittering hedge. . . . Oh, braw sight! . . . Oh, bonny lads! . . . Scotland forever!

The climate of Hong Kong at this season is of Eden. The sun is pleasantly hot at midday, and the mornings and evenings are dewily cool. Coolies do their work naked to the waist, but ordinary European garments are comfortable. Today I have stepped out in my three-quarter length sleeves with the black lace overlay, and my hem is walking length with the black lace ruffle. Mrs. Bauer thought it fetching, and I agree. When packing, I did wonder how my clothing would fit in with the ladies around the world. I have not felt under or overdressed yet.

My friends are loath that I should lose a single pleasure, and we are out all day long in this adorable weather. One of our paths lies through the green twilight of the Botanical Gardens. We pass under the lacey shadows of ferns twenty feet high, through trellises weighted with vines that blow perfumed purple trumpets, and emerge upon sunny spaces where fountains are sprinkling silver rain upon banks of crimson and orange flowers. The flaxen-haired English children play here, cared for by prim trousered Chinese amahs; and we meet pretty blue-eyed German ladies in their chairs taking this road home.

Another expedition leads to the top of Victoria Peak, whose head is two thousand feet above the water and up whose side the town climbs year by year. Our way – at an angle of forty-five degrees – is by a tram dragged up the mountain by means of an endless chain.

This tram is newly built, having only been in operation for a year and half, and my friends are very proud of this engineering marvel.

"You aren't afraid of heights, are you, Elizabeth?"

"I'm not if Mrs. Bauer isn't," I quip, looking toward the pale-faced woman and hoping the chain is strong.

She smiles only at the corners of her mouth. "Just don't look down and you'll be fine. The view is worth whatever fears one must overcome."

We board at Garden Road where a non-descript wooden station patiently watches passengers board and exit. The fare is thirty cents up and fifteen cents down, but we are coming down a different way.

A static steam engine powers the operation, and you can hear faint sounds of the beast as it builds up energy to move the tram.

The Peak is the city's summer resort and pleasuring ground. There is ten degrees difference in temperature between the summit and the town, and a summer hotel is in process of construction at the top. When completed, it will be a luxurious destination.

Handsome bungalows cling to the mountain's steep sides – built in the Italian style, of warm cream-white stone – and are named such things as The Cottage, The Bungalow, Hillcrest.

Again, I am reminded of the South, where we also name our houses. "My childhood home was called Fairfax. Did you know?" When my friends indicated they didn't, I continued. "The Confederate troops used our house during the Civil War. When we returned from New York, it was freckled with bullet holes. A canon lay abandoned in the yard behind a log barricade. Inside, the chairs and sofas were climbing, as if in clumsy panic, against the battered doors."

Mrs. Braun presses her hand over her heart. "Oh, you poor dears. I can't even imagine."

"Yes, well, it was more shocking to Mother than to us children. We thought it exciting. Naming houses is such a lovely practice. I've already picked out a name for my own house one day, and I hope it is agreeable to the architecture or I shall have to think of another. Greenway Rise. Do you like it?"

"A beautiful name. I can picture a verdant hill surrounded by a small forest of pines," says Mrs. Bauer.

"Yes, exactly," I say. "Now I only need to find such a place. It won't be in the city."

The tram stops, and we step out onto the windy hillside, holding onto our hats. The view is everything they told me it would be. From here we can see how the water winds deeply inland between the hills and flows around island mountains ringed with girdles of foam. Treeless mountains rise out of the green waters. They are broken and rugged; their naked sides show tawny as a lion's hide.

"This must be the most beautiful harbor in the world," I gasp.

"Only at Rio Janeiro and Sydney is there a harbor whose beauty compares to this," says Mrs. Bauer.

The man in charge of the windy signal station comes out and explains to us the various ways in which the town is warned of the coming of vessels, and also introduces us to an extremely low-spirited and discontented-looking lady with battered features who turns her back on us and stares in unwinking disgust out to sea.

She was once the proud and gilded figure-head of the *Princess Charlotte*, wrecked in these waters long since, and plainly resents what she looks upon as her fall in life, brought up on land to assist a low signal officer.

Our chairs have come up another way, and we are to be carried down the long winding road that sinks by slow stages to the town. During the first stage we are in full sunlight, passing under the walls of the white palace-like bungalows with smooth-shaven tennis courts where ruddy-cheeked, young Englishmen toss the balls to fair-haired English girls.

Then the road – the earth here is a thousand beautiful shades of buff and rose – winds about to the east, and we pass into the shadows. A tiny Greek church with a sparsely-populated graveyard clings to the declivity above us, and from far below comes the faint cool sound of waters foaming round the foot of the hills.

The sun has set; only the utmost heights are gilded now, and the twilight deepens on our path. We swing around the hills – in and out, and down, down, with smooth, easy motion – to the regular pad, pad, pad of the bearers' feet.

Here and there in the dusk we discern the scarlet turbans of Sikh warders, standing motionless as bronze statues. Below in the harbor the lights of the town, the ships, and the flitting sampans sparkle through the faint evening mist like multitudinous fireflies. How am I to think of racing when confronted with sights such as these?

IN WHICH NELLIE BLY UNWITTINGLY UNCOVERS ANOTHER WOMAN'S BEAUTY SECRET.

T HE FIFTH DAY OUT, A MONDAY, WE anchored at Penang, or Prince of Wales Island, one of the Straits Settlements. As the ship had such a long delay at Colombo, it was said that we would have but six hours to spend on shore. With an attentive chap named Maury as escort, I made my preparations and was ready to go the moment we anchored.

We went ashore in a sampan. The Malay oarsman rowed hand over hand, standing upright in the stern, his back turned towards us as well as the way we were going. Frequently he turned his head to see if the way was clear, plying his oars industriously all the while. Once landed he chased us to the end of the pier demanding more money, although we had paid him thirty cents, just twenty cents over and above the legal fare.

After hiring a carriage we drove to where a waterfall comes bounding down the side of a naturally verdant mountain which has been transformed, half way up, into a pleasing tropical garden. The picturesque waterfall is nothing marvelous. It only made me wonder from whence it procured its water supply, but after walking until I was much heated, and finding myself just as far from the fount, I concluded the waterfall's secret was not worth the fatigue it would cost.

On the way to the town we visited a Hindu temple. Scarcely had we entered when a number of half-clad, barefooted priests rushed frantically upon us, demanding that we remove our shoes. However, the temple being built open, its curved roof and rafters had long been utilized by birds and pigeons as a bedroom. Doubtless ages had passed over the stone floor, but I could swear nothing else had, so I refused emphatically and unconditionally to un-boot myself. I saw enough of their idols to satisfy me. One was a black god in a gown, the other was a shapeless black stone hung with garlands of flowers, the filthy stone at its base being buried 'neath a profusion of rich blossoms.

English is spoken less in Penang than in any port I visited. A native photographer, when I questioned him about it, said:

"The Malays are proud, Miss. They have a language of their own and they are too proud to speak any other."

That photographer knew how to use his English to advantage. He showed me cabinet-sized proofs for which he asked one dollar each.

"One dollar!" I exclaimed in astonishment. "That is very high for a proof."

"If miss thinks it is too much, she does not need to buy. She is the best judge of how much she can afford to spend," he replied with cool impudence.

"Why are they so expensive?" I asked, nothing daunted by his impertinence.

"I presume because Penang is so far from England," he rejoined, carelessly.

A Chinese joss-house, the first I had seen, was very interesting. The pink and white roof, curved like a canoe, was ornamented with animals of the dragon tribe, with their mouths open and their tails in the air. The straggling worshippers could be plainly seen from the streets through the arcade sides of the temple. Chinese lanterns and gilt ornaments made bright the dark interior.

"Let's go inside," I said, leading Maury through the door.

Little josses or idols, with usual rations of rice, roast pig and smoldering joss-sticks disbursing a strangely sweet perfume, were no more interesting than a dark corner in which the superstitious were trying their luck, a larger crowd of dusky people than were about the altars. In fact, the only devotee was a waxed-haired Chinese woman, with a babe tied on her back, bowing meekly and lowly before a painted, be-bangled joss.

Some priests with shaven heads and old-gold silk garments, who were in a summer-house in the garden, saw us when we were looking at the gold-fish ponds. One came forth, and, taking me by the hand, gracefully led me to where they were gathered.

They indicated their wish that we should sit with them and drink tea with them, milkless and sugarless, from child-like China cups, which they re-filled so often that I had reasons for feeling thankful the cups were so like unto play-dishes. We were unable to exchange words, but we smiled liberal smiles at one another.

Mexican silver is used almost exclusively in Penang. American silver will be accepted at the same value, but American gold is refused and paper money is looked on with contempt.

The Chinese jinricksha men in Penang, compared with those in Colombo, are like over-fed pet horses besides racers in trim. They were the plumpest Chinese I ever saw; such round fat legs and arms!

When we started back to the ship, the bay was very rough. Huge waves angrily tossed our small boat about in a way that blotted the red from Maury's cheeks and caused him to hang his head in a care-for-nothing way over the boat's side.

It was a reckless spring that landed us on the ship's ladder, the rolling of the coal barge helping to increase the swell which had threatened to engulf us. Hardly had we reached deck when the barge was ordered to cut loose; even as this was being done the ship hoisted anchor and started on its way.

Almost immediately there was a great commotion on board. About fifty ragged black men rushed frantically on deck to find that while depositing their last sacks of coal in the regions below, their barge and companions had cast off and were rapidly nearing the shore.

Then followed dire chattering, wringing of hands, pulling of locks and crying after the receding barge, all to no avail. Despite the efforts of those on it, the barge was steadily swept inland.

"They'll never get back. The tide is coming in too strong," said Maury, finally recovering some color.

The captain appeased the coolies' fears. "You can go off in the pilot's boat."

"But how? In these waves?" I asked. "This we must see." I pulled Maury with me.

They first tried to take the men off without slowing down, but after one man got a dangerous plunge bath and the sea threatened to bury the tug, the ship was forced to slow down.

Some coolies slid down a cable, their comrades grabbing and pulling them wet and frightened white on to the tug. Others went down the ladder, which lacked five feet of touching the pilot boat. Those already on board would clutch the hanging man's bare legs, he meanwhile clinging despairingly to the ladder, fearing to loosen his grasp and only doing so when the ship officers would threaten to knock him off.

The pilot, a native, was the last to go down. Then the cable was cast off and we sailed away seeing the tug, so overloaded that the men were afraid to move even to bail it out, swept back by the tide towards the place where we had last seen the land.

———

I HAVE ALWAYS confessed that I like to sleep in the morning as well as I like to stay up at night, and to have my sleep disturbed makes me as ill-natured as a bad dinner makes a man. At first, I had a cabin down below, and I found little rest owing to the close proximity of a nurse and two children whose wise parents selected a cabin on the other side of the ship. After I had been awakened several mornings at daybreak by the squabbling of the children, I cherished a grudge against the parents. They could rest in peace.

The mother made some show of being a beauty. She had a fine nose, everybody confessed that, and she had reduced her husband to such a state of servitude and subjection that she needed no maids.

The fond father of these children had a habit of coming over early in the morning to see his cherubs, before he went to his bath. I know this from hearing him tell them so. He would open their cabin door and in the loudest, coldest, most unsympathetic voice in the world, yell: Good morning. How is papa's family this morning?"

A confused conglomeration of voices sounded in reply; then he would shout: "What does baby say to papa? Tell me, baby, what does baby say to papa?"

"Papa!" would answer back the shrill treble.

"What does the moo-moo cow say, my treasure; tell papa what the moo-moo cow says?"

To this the baby would make no reply and again he would shout: "What does the moo-moo cow say, darling; tell papa what the moo-moo cow says?"

If it had been once, or twice even, I might have endured it with civilized forbearance but after it had been repeated, the very same identical word every morning for six long weary mornings, my temper gave way and when he said: "Tell papa what the moo-moo cow says?"

I shouted frantically: "For heaven's sake, baby, tell papa what the moo-moo cow says and let me go to sleep."

A heavy silence, a silence that was heavy with indignation and surprise, followed, and I went off to sleep. The fond parents did not speak to me after that. They gazed on me in disdain and when the woman got seasick, I persuaded an acquaintance of hers to go in and see her one day by telling her it was her Christian duty.

The fond mother would not allow the ship doctor to see her although her husband had to relate her ills to the doctor and in that way get him to prescribe for them. I knew there was something she wished to keep secret.

The friend, true to my counsel, knocked on the door. Hearing no voice and thinking it lost in the roar of the ocean, she opened the door. The fond mother looked up, saw, and screaming buried her face in the pillows. She was toothless and hairless!

The frightened Samaritan did not wait to see if she had a cork limb. I felt repentant afterwards and went to a deck cabin where I soon forgot the moo-moo cow and the fond parents. But the woman's fame as a beauty was irrevocably ruined on the ship.

It was so damply warm in the Straits of Malacca that for time first time during my trip I confessed myself uncomfortably hot. It was sultry and foggy and so damp that everything rusted, even the keys in one's pockets, and the mirrors were so sweaty that they ceased to reflect.

The second day out from Penang we passed beautiful green islands. There were many stories told about the straits being once infested with pirates, and I regretted to hear that they had ceased to exist, I so longed for some new experience.

We expected to reach Singapore that night. I was anxious that we should – for the sooner we got in, the sooner we should leave – and every hour lost meant so much to me.

The pilot came on at six o'clock. I waited tremblingly for his verdict. A wave of despair swept over me when I heard that we should anchor outside until morning, because it was too dangerous to try to make the port after dark.

Worse, is that the mail contract made it compulsory for the ship to stay in port twenty-four hours. Now, I was wasting precious time lying outside the gates of hope, as it were, merely because some coolies at Penang had been too slow. These wasted hours might mean loss of my ship at Hong Kong; they might mean days to my record; they might mean forfeiture of the race.

27

IN WHICH ELIZABETH BISLAND MEETS THE BUSINESSMAN WHO IS IN THE MIDST OF RESHAPING HONG KONG.

"In Xanadu did Kubla Khan
A stately pleasure dome decree –"
– Samuel Taylor Coleridge

KUBLA KHAN COMES TO TIFFIN ONE DAY – A handsome dark gentleman of forty years or so, with very white teeth and eyes like black velvet. Clad in extremely well-fitting London clothes, in his soft, slow voice he signifies that on the morrow he will take us to see the pleasure dome – not yet entirely complete. Kubla Khan was his name in Xanadu, the summer capital of the ancient Mongol ruler of course, but in Hong Kong, for the sake of convenience and brevity, he is called Catchik Chater.

Mr. Bauer and he have several business dealings, and my friend is eager to introduce me to this forward-thinking man.

"Miss Bisland, a pleasure to meet you. Ulrich tells me you are in a race around the world?"

"Yes, I am." His straightforward manner makes me want to be straightforward as well. "I left New York on November 14 and plan to make it back in less than 75 days."

"Are you a seasoned traveler? Have you been to Hong Kong previously?"

"I must confess this is my first trip of this nature, and I find Hong Kong to be lovely. The company especially so."

"I have traveled extensively myself, you know, but there is no place I've loved quite like this. The longer I stay, the more it grows into me. I am a British subject, born in India, and have a certain mixture of Greek and Armenian blood in my veins."

Naturally in Xanadu his rank and pedigree were far more complicated.

"I decided to come to Hong Kong twenty years ago, with nothing but a wooden trunk. Through hard work, I've made enough to sustain me and better the economic climate here in Hong Kong."

"He's being modest," broke in Mr. Braun. "It was he who made the long waterfront at Kow-Loon, rescuing it from the sea, and covered it with great godowns filled with merchandise of the East, and it is he who is proposing the same feat on the opposite side of the harbor."

"Yes, there is much work left to be done." He lowered his voice. "Electricity, my dear." He held out his elbow for me to take. "Come. I'll show you a little of what we've managed to accomplish in this fair land."

He took us first to see his docks and godowns, resounding with the loud clangors of trade, and then through the grassy Kow-Loon plains, by a wide red road shadowed with banana trees to this lordly pavilion set on the crest of many flowering terraces – its pale-yellow outlines cut cameo-like against the burning blue of the sky. To the right is the naked side of a hill all deep-tinted buff warmed with red, and everywhere else a sea of satin-leaved tropical foliage.

After having interested himself more or less in the banks, the shipyards, and manufactures of various sorts, he now felt prepared to erect in China a repetition of the Xanadu pleasure dome.

The centre of the pavilion is a great banqueting hall with domed roof thirty feet above the tessellated pavement. The walls are frescoed in the same deep cream color of the exterior, touched here and there with blue and rose and gold. Twenty lofty arched doors open to the veranda, from whence beyond the roses of the terrace one sees the glitter of the green waters of the harbor. At each end of the banqueting hall opens a drawing room set with mirrors and lined with divans. Beneath are tiled bathrooms, needed in this hot climate after using the tennis courts and bowling alleys.

Here Kubla Khan's guests come – come by twenties and fifties – and feast splendidly on high days and holidays and on hot star-lit tropical nights. It is like the sumptuous fancy of some splendid Roman noble, pro-consul of an Eastern province. The pavilion for the moment is in the hands of workmen, so we may not dine there; but we do dine with the Khan in his town house, eating through many courses, drinking many costly wines, and served by a phalanx of tall Celestials in rustling blue gowns.

We leave after viewing his extensive art collection. "Be sure to visit the shops before you leave. You'll see why my collection has so easily expanded."

The next day we take the Khan's advice and go to the shops to turn over costly examples of Chinese art.

We come home through the many-colored ways of the native town, steep streets that climb laboriously up and down stairs, and so narrow that there is hardly room for our chairs to pass through the multitudes who swarm there.

"They average sixteen hundred residents to the acre in this part of the town," says Mr. Braun.

The buzzing and humming of the people around us is like nothing I've ever seen before. And they all seem to be patiently and continuously busy. New York was more crowded than New Orleans, which was more crowded than our family plantation. But this! Even the children are as the flies in number and activity.

The place smells violently: of opium, of the dried ducks and fish hanging exposed for sale in the sun, of frying pork and sausages, and of the many strange-looking meals being cooked on hissing braziers in the streets and in doorways.

There is no lack of color. The shops are faced with a broad fretwork richly gilded, and the long perpendicular signs are ornamentally lettered with large black characters. Every house is lime-washed some strong tint, and the whole leaves upon the eye the color-impression one gets from Chinese porcelains – of sharp green, gold, crimson, and blue; all vigorous, definite, and mingled with grotesque tastefulness.

Despite all our attempts, I find nothing special to add to my souvenirs, save a small porcelain bowl to place on my dressing table and prove I have been here.

IN WHICH NELLIE BLY FINDS HERSELF HALFWAY
AROUND THE WORLD AND MAKES A
HASTY PURCHASE.

WHEN I CAME ON DECK NEXT MORNING, the ship lay alongside the wharf, and naked Chinese coolies carrying, two by two, baskets of coal suspended between them on a pole, were constantly traversing the gang-plank between the ship and shore, while in little boats about were peddlers with silks, photographs, fruits, laces and monkeys to sell.

Dr. Brown, the young Welshman named Bryce, and I hired a gharry, a light wagon with latticed windows and comfortable seating room for four with the driver's seat on the same level outside. They are drawn by a pretty spotted Malay pony whose speed is marvelous compared with its diminutive size.

The people here, as at other ports where I stopped, constantly chew betel nut, and when they laugh, one would suppose they had been drinking blood. The betel nut stains their teeth and mouthfuls blood-red. Many of the natives also fancy tinting their fingernails with it, as does our driver. It is a custom that takes getting used to.

We drove along a road as smooth as a ballroom floor, shaded by large trees, and made picturesque by native houses built on pins in marshy land on either side. There are no sidewalks, and blue and white paint largely predominate over other colors.

We passed several lots filled with odd round mounds with walls shaped like horse-shoes. A flat stone where the mound ends and the wall begins bears an inscription done in colored letters.

"Are those graveyards?" I ask, swiveling around for a better look. There were a great number of them, all generously filled.

"I believe they are," said Dr. Brown.

Further along, through latticed windows we got occasional glimpses of peeping Chinese women in bright gowns, Chinese babies bundled in shapeless, wadded garments, while down below through widely opened fronts we could see people pursuing their trades.

Our driver stops and points to a man getting a haircut in the open street. Apparently, a chair, a comb, a basin and a knife are all the tools a man needs to open shop, and he finds as many patrons if he sets up shop in the street as he would under shelter. From the number we see, barbering must be the principal trade.

Sitting doubled over, his head was shaven back almost to the crown, where a spot about the size of a tiny saucer was left to bear the crop of hair which forms the pigtail. When braided and finished with a silk tassel, the man's hair is "done" for the next fortnight.

We visited a most interesting museum and saw along the suburban roads the beautiful bungalows of the European citizens. People in dog-cart carriages with a driver in front and passenger facing back and wheelmen on bicycles crowded the splendid drives. Nothing is patronized more than the 'rickshas in Singapore, and while they are to be had for ten cents an hour, it is no unusual sight to see four persons piled in one jinricksha and drawn by one man.

We found the monkey cage, of course. There was besides a number of small monkeys, one enormous orangutan. It was as large as a man and was covered with long red hair.

While seeming to be very clever, he had a way of gazing off in the distance with wide, unseeing eyes, meanwhile pulling his long red hair up over his head in an aimless, insane way that was very fetching.

"Shall I give him a nut?" asked Dr. Brown.

"Oh, do!" I encouraged.

"He'd like it," added Bryce.

The doctor held up a peanut, and the orangutan stopped playing and lumbered over. But the doctor held his fingers away from the bars. "What if he takes hold of my fingers in the bargain?"

The grating was too small for the old fellow to get his hand through, but he did not intend to be cheated of his rights, so he merely stuck his lips through the gratings until they extended fully four inches.

"Ha!" I had heard of mouths, but that beat anything I ever saw, and I laughed until the old fellow actually smiled in sympathy. He got the nut.

The doctor also offered him a cigar. He did not take it, but touched it with the back of his hand, afterwards smelling his hand, and then subsided into that dreamy state, aimlessly pulling his hair up over the back of his head.

"I need to send my telegram," I said, though not really wanting to leave the place.

At the cable office, in the second story of a building, I found the agents conversant with the English language. They would accept American silver at par, but they did not care to handle our other money.

The bank and post office were open places on the ground floor with about as much comfort and style as is found in ordinary wharf warehouses. Chinese and English are employed in both places.

We had dinner at the Hotel de l'Europe, a long, low, white building set back in a wide, green lawn, with a beautiful esplanade, faced by the sea, fronting it. Upon the veranda were long white tables where a fine dinner was served by Chinese waiters.

On our return from the Governor's House, we heard a strange, weird din as of many instruments in dire confusion and discord.

"A funeral," our Malay driver announced.

"Indeed! If that is the way you have funerals here, I'll see one," I said.

So he pulled the gharry to one side, where we waited eagerly for a funeral that was heralded by a blast of trumpets.

First came a number of Chinese men with black and white satin flags which, being flourished energetically, resulted in clearing the road of vehicles and pedestrians. They were followed by musicians on Malay ponies, blowing fifes, striking cymbals, beating tom-toms, hammering gongs, and pounding long pieces of iron, with all their might and main.

Men followed carrying on long poles roast pigs and Chinese lanterns, great and small, while in their rear came banner-bearers. The men on foot wore white trousers and sandals, with blue top dress, while the pall-bearers wore black garments bound with blue braid. There were probably forty pall-bearers.

The casket, which rested on long poles suspended on the shoulders of the men, was hidden beneath a white-spotted scarlet cloth with decorations of Chinese lanterns or inflated bladders on arches above it.

The mourners followed in a long string of gharries. They were dressed in white satin from head to toe and were the happiest looking people at the funeral. We watched until the din died away in the distance when we returned to town as delighted as if we had seen a circus parade.

"I would not have missed that for anything," Dr. Brown said to me.

"You could not," I replied laughingly, "I know they got it up for our special benefit."

And so laughing and jesting about what had to us no suggestion of death, we drove back to see the temples.

We stopped at the driver's humble home on our way to the ship, and I saw there on the ground floor his pretty little Malay wife dressed in one wrapping of linen and several little brown naked babies. The wife had a large gold ring in her nose, rings on her toes and several around the rim of her ears, and gold ornaments on her ankles. At the door of their home was the most adorable monkey.

I had resisted the temptation to buy a boy at Port Said and also smothered the desire to buy a Singalese girl at Colombo, but when I saw the monkey, my will-power melted, and I began to bargain straightway for it.

"Fifty cents?" I started out, the price for the scrawny monkeys being offered off the boats at the harbor.

"Is fine monkey. Strong as a man." The driver made a muscle with his arm. "Five dollars."

"Will the monkey bite?" I asked the driver.

"He took it by the throat, holding it up for me to admire as he replied, "Monkey no bite." But he could not under the circumstances.

"Are you sure?" cautioned Dr. Brown. "You are only halfway through your journey. He might be a bother."

Bryce said nothing and barely contained a bemused expression.

The monkey made cute eyes at me and reminded me of little Homie, the Skye terrier from the first leg of my journey. He looked hearty enough to last the voyage, and wouldn't he be something to talk about back home?

"If he becomes a bother, he can join the menagerie in Central Park," I announced, the doctor's disapproval having pushed me over the edge.

We came to an agreement at three dollars, and the driver produced a cage for me to carry away my monkey. The monkey squawked angrily when the door closed, and he bounced from side to side, testing the strength of his cell. After he settled down with the swaying of the gharry, I fed him a peanut and as he reached out to take it, he scratched my finger.

"That better have been an accident," I warned him. He blinked back innocent monkey eyes at me and peeled open the nut.

"What shall you call it?" asked the doctor. "Phileas? Or Fogg? In honor of your adventure."

I shook my head. The monkey didn't look like either. "Passepartout? Fogg's servant. No, the name is too long. There is a subplot with a detective who follows Fogg, convinced he is a bank robber. His name is Fix."

The doctor made a sour face. "Do you have anyone following you around?"

"I should hope not!" I exclaimed. "I'm no bank robber."

IN WHICH ELIZABETH BISLAND LEAVES
HONG KONG THREE DAYS EARLY AND
ENJOYS SOME GOOD BRITISH FOOD.

A MESSENGER CAME TO THE DOOR FOR ME just as we were sitting down to breakfast.

"Bad news," says Mr. Braun as he joins us. "The *Preussen* has arrived, but it broke its screw as it entered the harbor."

"The ship needs a new propeller? Will it take long to fix?" I ask in dismay.

"Too long for you," he says.

"We aren't scheduled to sail for another three days. Perhaps it won't affect me at all. The *Preussen* is known for its early arrivals, so even if we are a few hours delayed, she could make it up on the trip."

Mr. Braun's lips form a line. "We better take you to the O & O office and see what they can do for you."

Mrs. Braun looks at me with sympathetic eyes, and suddenly my stomach lurches as if I were still rolling on the waves. Ever since sightseeing in Japan, I've not been able to break out of the relaxed role of tourist. But, when faced with a delay, my purpose prickles me in the stomach, waking me up to how tightly I'm scheduled.

"Eat first, then we'll decide what you should do," advises Mrs. Braun, passing me the basket of breads.

We learn that a Peninsular and Oriental steamer sails that day. I am advised to go in her as far as Ceylon. With barely time to think, I send a quick cable to the *Cosmopolitan* to let them know my change of plans.

So on the morning of the 18th of December I find myself on the deck of the slower *Thames*, surrounded by the charming friends and acquaintances of this Hong Kong episode, who have come to give me a final proof of their goodness, and wish me speed on my journey.

This boat is as polyglot as the land I have just left and swarms with queer people. The sailors are Lascars, clad in close trousers and tunics of blue cotton check and red turbans. Many of the Parsees in their purple coal-hods come aboard to bid farewell to a parting friend.

One of the Highlanders is going home, and his comrades have brought the pipes to give him a last tune. Grief and Scotch whiskey move them finally to "play a spring and dance it 'round" in spite of the heat, which brings the sweat pouring down their faces.

Sampans cluster about with pretty little Chinese dogs, bamboo steamer chairs, and canary birds for sale, driving a few final bargains.

"I can't help but mourn our three lost days, but I know you must make haste while you can," says Mrs. Braun.

"Thank you. I've enjoyed every moment and should like to repay the kindness should you visit America again."

The bell warns them all away, and I wave goodbye to my friends and to the beautiful city with the keenest regret. The fifth stage of my journey has begun under the shadow of the Union Jack.

Hong Kong vanishes in a haze of sunlight. My head swims with a glorious confusion of tropic splendors, and there is no room or capacity in it for more impressions just now. Being desperately tired – worn out with delights, I go below in search of a bed.

It is a beautiful ship, like a fine yacht in its spacious commodiousness. Here and there hang canary cages thrilling with song. Narcissus bulbs in bowls are abloom with fluttering white flowers, and everywhere are deep-colored jars full of palms and ferns.

The space assigned to me is a large, pleasant white room, from which a great square lifts up outward on the water-side, leaving me on intimate terms with the milky, jade-tinted sea. Beneath this window is a broad divan, and here, laved in tepid sea winds and soothed by rippling whispers against the ship's side, I close my eyes seeking the languorous, voluptuous sleep of the tropics.

Later, at the captain's table, I meet a charming little old lady from Boston, Mrs. Kelly. She is widowed these last ten years and has spent the last two traveling the East with her son Robert.

"You are traveling alone?" he asks, a critical edge to his voice. "A lady unchaperoned?"

"Yes," I reply curtly to end our conversation before it even begins. I am not surprised that he is unmarried.

"Have you been to Boston?" Mrs. Kelly asks me as a waiter places roast beef with Yorkshire pudding (which is not pudding as I know it!) in front of me. She doesn't seem to care I am traveling alone.

"No, ma'am, I never had the pleasure." *But I would have the pleasure of this excellent food.*

She reaches out and squeezes my hand before I can lift my fork. "You must when you get back. Visit the Common. It's the country's oldest park. Mr. Kelly and I would walk there after listening to Phillips Brooks preach." She blinks back tears. "It's too bad you will never hear him preach," she tells me. "He was a great man. The whole of Boston mourned his passing."

I am unsure if her emotions are attached to the passing of her husband or the famous preacher. I decide both as she continues throughout the main course to link the two men in conversation about Boston. Her two years of travel, if meant to help her move on, have not diminished her love for either.

"You must visit Trinity Church when you come," she continues, as if she and I have already agreed to meet up once our travels are finished. "Of course, it's not the original on account of the Great Fire of '72. But the new one is a beautiful stone church. Phillips Brooks had it built, you know. Mr. Kelly was on the building committee and helped with the fundraising."

A man on the other side of her son snaps his fingers. "Phillips Brooks. I've been trying to place the name, and I just remembered. He is the man who penned the words to *O Little Town of Bethlehem.*"

Mrs. Kelly beams. "Yes, the very same." She directs her dialogue towards the interested party, and I am free to observe the remainder of the table over a delight called Waterloo pudding (another pudding, only this one I recognize) that some quiet waiter has placed in front of me.

We are the only two women on the passenger list; so the British atmosphere has a pronounced masculine flavor, but despite even this limitation it is interesting. Noting the men around me, I can't help wondering if Mr. Wetmore had had any idea as to the makeup of British ships, if he would have insisted on traveling as my chaperone after all. Or perhaps my sister would have.

The men, from captain to cook, are fine creatures. Their physical vigor is superb – such muscles! Such crisply curled hair! Such clear ruddy skins, white teeth, and turquoise eyes. (How is that for details, Molly?) They are flat-backed and lean-loined; they carry their huge shoulders with a lordly swagger; they possess a divine faith in themselves and in England; and they have such an astonishing collection of accents.

No two of them speak alike: the burly bearded giant three places off from me at table speaks with a broad Scotch drawl; the handsome, natty fourth officer with the black eyes and shy red face who sits opposite, in white duck from head to heel, has a bit of a Yorkshire burr on the tip of his tongue; the Ceylon tea-planter talks like a New-Yorker, and there are fully a dozen variations more between his accent and that of the tall young blond, whose fashionable Eton and Oxford inflections leave one speechless with awe and admiration of their magnificent eccentricities.

Very quickly, the menu becomes of daily interest, for here I become for the first time familiar with food upon which the folk of the English novels are fed. I learn to know and appreciate the sugary Bath bun and the hearty Scotch scone.

I make the greatly-to-be-prized acquaintance of the English meat pie, including a favorite of Dickens's character Mr. Weller, the "weal and 'ammer," a veal-and-ham pie, and I recognize touching manifestations of British loyalty in the sweets christened impartially with appellations of royalty: Victoria jelly-roll, Alexandra wafers, and Beatrice tarts. Waterloo pudding is one of our favorite desserts, and other British triumphs and glories adorn the bill of fare from time to time.

If I could pass the remainder of my time around the world in this manner, I would be content. But the captain does not agree to my plan. Apparently he has a schedule to keep that does not include personally sailing me back to New York.

30

THAT EVENING WE SAILED FOR HONG KONG. The next day the sea was rough, and head winds made the run slower than we had hoped for. Towards noon almost all the passengers disappeared. Although feeling faint, I never did succumb to seasickness. However, as the roughness increased; the cook enjoyed a holiday.

The terrible swell of the sea during the Monsoon was the most beautiful thing I ever saw. I sat breathless on deck watching the bow of the ship standing upright on a wave then dash headlong down as if intending to carry us to the bottom.

"Did you know Maury is quite seasick?" asked an Englishman who had gained too much amusement from watching the man who had become my shadow.

"I'm sorry to hear it," I answered generously, though could not hide my smile.

My audience laughed. But before we could change the topic of conversation, the man himself walked unsteadily toward us, his rugs slung over his arm and his hand clutching his stomach. There were no empty chairs near me, and instead of moving on to find one, he quietly curled up on his rugs at my feet. There he lay in all his misery, gazing at me.

"You would not think that I am enjoying a vacation, but I am," he said plaintively.

I felt very cruel looking into his pale face and hearing him plead for sympathy. But as heartless as I thought it was, I could not sympathize with a seasick man.

"You don't know how nice I can look," he said pathetically. "If you would only stay over at Hong Kong for a week, you would see how handsome I can look."

"Indeed, such a phenomenon might induce me to remain there six weeks," I said coldly.

At last, the Irish boy Sean Collins told him I was engaged to the chief officer, named Sleeman, who did not approve of my talking to other men, thinking this would make him cease following me about, but it only served to increase his devotion. Finding me alone on deck one stormy evening, he sat down at my feet and, holding to the arms of my chair, began to talk in a wild way.

"Do you think life is worth living?" he asked.

"Yes, life is very sweet. The thought of death is the only thing that causes me unhappiness," I answered truthfully.

"You cannot understand it or you would feel different. I could take you in my arms and jump overboard, and before they would know it, we would be at rest," he said passionately.

"You can't tell. It might not be rest–" I began, and he broke in hotly.

"I know, I know. I can show you. I will prove it to you. Death by drowning is a peaceful slumber, a quiet drifting away."

"Is it?" I said, with a pretense of eagerness. I feared to get up, for I felt the first move might result in my burial beneath the angry sea. "You know, tell me about it. Explain it to me," I gasped, a feeling of coldness creeping over me as I realized that I was alone with what for the time was a mad man.

Just as he began to speak, I saw Chief Officer Sleeman come on deck and slowly advance towards me. I dared not call. I dared not smile, lest the mad man should notice.

I feared the chief would go away, but no, he saw me, and with a desire to tease the man who had been so devoted, he came up on tiptoe, then, clapping the poor fellow on the back, he said: "What a very pretty love scene!"

"Come," I shouted, breaking away before the startled man could understand.

The chief, still in a spirit of fun, took my hand, and we rushed down below. Once we were safely away, I explained. "He wanted to jump overboard with me! If you hadn't have come, I would have been swimming for my life right now."

"Miss Bly, how terrible. Look, there is the captain. He'll take control of the devil."

We told him, and the captain wanted to put the man in irons.

"No, I don't think he is that dangerous," I argued. Now that I was safe, it didn't seem as plausible that he truly meant me harm. "It was just a passing melancholy moment. He has been feeling seasick."

They reluctantly backed down, and I was careful afterwards not to spend one moment alone and unprotected on deck.

———

THE MONKEY PROVED a good seaman. He was especially popular with the young men on board. One day when I visited it, I found a group who had been toasting its health. (It is wonderful the amount of whiskey and soda Englishmen consume. They drink it at all times and places.)

"We've decided to call him Jocko," said one of the men.

I started over to the monkey to ask if he liked his name. "Why is he holding his head so?" I asked. Then I noticed the empty cup in front of him. Evidently thinking I was the cause of his aching head, it sprang at me, and I ran out of the room. I vowed then to not have a Jocko for a monkey!

———

THE HURRICANE DECK was a great resort for lovers, so Chief Officer Sleeman told me; and evidently he knew, for he talked a great deal about two American girls who had traveled to Egypt, I believe, on the *Thames* when he was first officer of it. He had lost their address but his heart was true, for he had lost a philopoena to one, and though he did not know her address, he bought the philopoena and put it in a bank in London where it awaits some farther knowledge of the fair young American's whereabouts.

"What is a philopoena?" asked a quiet gentleman, who was listening to us instead of reading his book.

"A game of wits," I explained. "It begins when someone finds a double nut and gives it to another, asking 'Will you eat a philopoena with me?' If you accept and eat, the game begins. The next time you meet, whoever remembers and says the word *philopoena* wins and may suggest a gift that the other is to give them."

Chief Officer Sleeman nodded. "Yes, but you can't come out and say exactly what the prize is; you must hint and the other figure it out."

The curious gentleman shook his head as if baffled. "Young people," he said, and went back to pretending to read.

The next night, we went to bed under threat of a monsoon storm. Not long after falling asleep, I awoke with a fright. The ship pitched dangerously, and water sloshed around my cabin. The angry sea had washed over the ship!

I started to climb down from my dry berth, but escape to the lower deck was impossible, as I could not tell the deck from the sea. *What was I to do?*

As I crawled back into my bunk, I thought it very possible I had spoken my last word to any mortal, that the ship would doubtless sink, and with it all, if the ship did go down, no one would be able to tell whether I could have gone around the world in seventy-five days or not.

I lay awake for hours, gripping my berth and straining my ears to listen for any alarms that might go off, calling us to the lifeboats. But could a lifeboat survive this storm? Wouldn't it be better to stay on board?

Eventually, I decided that all the worry in the world cannot change it one way or the other, so I went to sleep and slumbered soundly until the breakfast hour.

The ship was making its way laboriously through a very frisky sea when I looked out, but the deck was drained, even if it was not dry.

When I went out, Sean Collins, for whom I had developed great fondness, was stretched out languidly in a willow chair with a bottle of champagne on one armrest and a glass on the other.

"I swear, Nellie Bly, when I get to Hong Kong I'll stay there until I can return to England by land." The ship rolled with a wave, and he took a drink. "You should have seen my cabin mate last night," he said with a laugh.

The man he spoke of, a very clever Englishman, was the man who posed as a woman-hater, and naturally we enjoyed any joke at his expense. "Why? What did he do?"

"Finding our cabin filling with water, he got out of bed, put on a life preserver and bailed out the cabin with a cigarette box!"

I laughed until my sides ached at the mental picture presented to me of the little chunky Englishman in an enormous life preserver, bailing out his cabin with a tiny cigarette box. Even the box of the deadly cigarette seems to have its Christian mission to perform.

While I was wiping away the tears, the Englishman came up.

"What is so funny?" he asked.

After hearing what had amused us, he revealed: "While I was bailing out the cabin, The Boy here clung to the upper berth all the time groaning and praying. He was certain the ship would sink, and I could not persuade him to get out of the top berth to help bail. Nothing but groan and pray."

Sean answered with a laugh, "I did not want to sleep the rest of the night in wet pajamas."

Not equally amused, the Englishman fled.

Later in the day, the rolling was frightful. I was sitting on deck when all at once the ship went down at one side like a wagon in a deep rut. I was thrown in my chair clear across the deck.

A young man jumped up to catch me just as the ship went the other way in a still deeper sea-rut. It flung me back again, and I caught hold of an iron bar and clung on tight. In another moment, I would have been dashed through the skylight into the dining hall on the deck below.

As I caught the bar, the man who had rushed to my assistance turned upside down and landed on his face. I laughed as his position was so ludicrous.

He made no move to get up, so I ran to his side, still convulsed with laughter. His nose was bleeding profusely, but I was such an idiot that the sight of the blood only made the scene to me the more ridiculous.

After helping him to a chair, I ran for the doctor and from laughing could hardly tell him what I wanted. The man's nose was broken, and the doctor said he would be scarred for life.

Later at dinner, even the others laughed when I described the accident, and, although I felt a great pity for the poor fellow, hurt as he was on my behalf, still an irresistible impulse to laugh swept over me every time I endeavored to express my appreciation of his attempt to assist me.

————

THE EVENING OF December 22, we all felt an eagerness for morning and yet the eagerness was mingled with much that was sad. Knowing that early in the day we would reach Hong Kong, and while it would bring us new scenes and new acquaintances, it would take us from old friends.

"Everything is such an improvement on the *Victoria*," I said, reminiscing at dinner. "The food is good, the passengers are refined, the officers are polite, and the ship is comfortable and pleasant."

When I finished my complimentary remarks about the ship, a little bride who had been a source of interest to us looked up and said:

"Yes, everything is very nice, but the life preservers are not quite comfortable to sleep in."

Shocked amazement spread over the countenances of all the passengers, and then in one grand shout that dining room resounded with laughter.

"What is so funny?" she asked. "Ever since we left home on our bridal tour, we have been sleeping in the life preservers. Isn't that the thing to do on board a ship?"

31

WE FIRST SAW THE CITY OF HONG KONG in the early morning. Gleaming white were the castle-like homes on the tall mountain side. A beautiful bay was this magnificent basin, walled on every side by high mountains. We fired a cannon as we entered the bay, the captain saying that this was the custom of mail ships.

Hong Kong is strangely picturesque. It is a terraced city, the terraces being formed by the castle-like, arcaded buildings perched tier after tier up the mountain's verdant side. The regularity with which the houses are built in rows made me wildly fancy them a gigantic staircase.

The doctor, another gentleman, and I left the boat, and, walking to the pier's end, selected sedan chairs in which we were carried to the town. The carriers were as urgent as our hackmen around railway stations in America.

We followed the road along the shore, passing warehouses of many kinds and tall balconied buildings filled with hundreds of Chinese families, on the flat-house plan. The balconies would have lent a pleasing appearance to the houses had the inhabitants not seemed to be enjoying a washing jubilee, using the balconies for clotheslines. Garments were stretched on poles after the manner of hanging coats so they would not wrinkle, and those poles were fastened to the balconies until it looked as if every family in the street had placed their old clothing on exhibition.

Our carriers trotted steadily, snorting at the crowds of natives we met to clear the way. A series of snorts or grunts would cause a scattering of natives more frightened than a tie-walker would be at the tooting of an engine's whistle.

My only wish and desire was to get as speedily as possible to the office of the Oriental and Occidental Steamship Company to learn the earliest possible time I could leave for Japan, to continue my race against time around the world.

I had just marked off my thirty-ninth day. Only thirty-nine days since leaving New York, and I was in China. I was particularly elated, because the good ship *Oriental* not only made up the five days I had lost in Colombo, but reached Hong Kong two days before I was due. And that with the northeast monsoon against her. It was the *Oriental's* maiden trip to China, and from Colombo to Hong Kong, she had broken all previous records.

Entering the O. and O. office feeling very much elated over my good fortune, with never a doubt but that it would continue, I asked a man in the office, "Will you tell me the date of the first sailing for Japan?"

"In one moment," he said, and, going into an inner office, he brought out a man who looked at me inquiringly, and when I repeated my question, said:

"What is your name?"

"Nellie Bly," I replied in some surprise.

"Come in, come in," he said nervously.

We followed him in, and after we were seated, he said: "You are going to be beaten."

"What? I think not. I have made up my delay," I said, still surprised, wondering if the Pacific had sunk since my departure from New York, or if all the ships on that line had been destroyed.

"You are going to lose it," he said with an air of conviction.

"Lose it? I don't understand. What do you mean?" I demanded, beginning to think he was mad.

"Aren't you having a race around the world?" he asked.

"Yes, quite right. I am running a race with Time."

"Time? I don't think that's her name."

"Her! Her!!" I repeated. Poor fellow, he was quite unbalanced.

"Yes, the other woman; she is going to win. She left here three days ago."

I stared at him; I turned to the doctor; I wondered if I was awake; I concluded the man was quite mad, so I forced myself to laugh in an unconcerned manner, but I was only able to say stupidly: "The other woman?" A queasy feeling not unlike seasickness passed through me as it dawned on me that he was in earnest.

"Yes," he continued briskly. "Did you not know? The day you left New York, another woman started out to beat your time, and she's going to do it. She left here three days ago. You probably met somewhere near the Straits of Malacca. She says she has authority to pay any amount to get ships to leave in advance of their time. Her editor offered one or two thousand dollars to the O. and O. if they would have the *Oceanic* leave San Francisco two days ahead of time."

"But that is an unfair advantage!" broke in the doctor, indignant on my behalf.

"They would not do it, but they did do their best to get her here in time to catch the English mail for Ceylon. If they had not arrived long before they were due, she would have missed that boat, and so have been delayed ten days. But she caught the boat and left three days ago, and you, my dear, will be delayed here five days."

"That is rather hard, isn't it?" I said quietly, forcing a smile that was on the lips, but came from nowhere near the heart. *Why didn't anyone tell me?*

"I'm astonished you did not know anything about it," he said. "She led us to suppose that it was an arranged race."

"I do not believe my editor would arrange a race without advising me," I said stoutly. "Have you no cables or messages for me from New York?"

"Nothing," was his reply.

"Probably they do not know about her," I said more cheerfully, though still with a strong sinking feeling. All the telegrams… news about the contest, but not a word about a competitor!

"Yes, they do. She worked for the same newspaper you do until the day she started."

"I do not understand it," I said quietly, too proud to show my ignorance on a subject of vital importance to my well-doing. *Did they want me to look a fool?* "You say I cannot leave here for five days?"

"No, and I don't think you can get to New York in eighty days. She intends to do it in seventy. She has letters to steamship officials at every point, requesting them to do all they can to get her on. Have you any letters?"

"Only one, from the agent of the P. and O., requesting the captains of their boats to be good to me because I am traveling alone. That is all," I said with a little smile. I wished he would quit talking as though this other woman were mere minutes from setting foot back in New York.

"Well, it's too bad, but I think you have lost it. There is no chance for you. You will lose five days here and five in Yokohoma, and you are sure to have a slow trip across at this season."

Just then a young man, with the softest black eyes and a clear pale complexion, came into the office. The agent, Mr. Harmon, introduced him to me as Mr. Fuhrmann, the purser of the *Oceanic*, the ship on which I would eventually travel to Japan and America. The young man took my hand in a firm, strong clasp, and his soft black eyes gave me such a look of sympathy that it only needed his kind tone to cheer me into a happier state.

"I went down to the *Oriental* to meet you; Mr. Harmon thought it was better. We want to take good care of you now that you are in our charge, but, unfortunately, I missed you. I returned to the hotel, and as they knew nothing about you there, I came here, fearing that you were lost."

"I have found kind friends everywhere," I said, with a slight motion towards the doctor, who was now rendered speechless over the ill-luck that had befallen me. "I am sorry to have been so much trouble to you."

"Trouble! You are with your own people now, and we are only too happy if we can be of service," he said kindly. "You must not mind about the possibility of someone getting around the world in less time than you may do it. Whether you get in before or later, people will give you the credit of having originated the idea."

"I promised my editor that I would go around the world in seventy-five days, and if I accomplish that, I shall be satisfied," I stiffly explained. "I am not racing with anyone. I would not race. If someone else wants to do the trip in less time, that is their concern. If they take it upon themselves to race against me, it is their lookout that they succeed. I am not racing."

"You could always rent a boat as Phileas Fogg did when he missed the *Carnatic* in Hong Kong. I'm sure a typhoon won't blow up to bother you, though," said the doctor, a sly grin on his face.

"Why, Doctor! You've never let on that you've read Verne's book."

"What? Do you think I don't read?"

"Yes, but I thought you were one to stick to newspapers and medical journals."

In quick order, we arranged the transfer of my luggage and the monkey from the *Oriental* to the *Oceanic* before visiting the hotel for tiffin. Word of my arrival had spread and several invitations came my way for dinners or receptions in my honor.

The doctor acted as my spokesman and declined them all, knowing the condition of my mind at present. The remainder of the day was spent saying goodbye to my friends on the *Oriental*, after which, Mr. Fuhrmann, the purser on the *Oceanic* took me under wing to introduce me to Hong Kong.

We went one night to see *Ali Baba and the Forty Thieves* as given by the Amateur Dramatic Club of Hong Kong. It was a new version of the old story filled with local hits arranged for the club by various military personnel.

Inside, the scene was bewitching. A rustling of soft gowns, the odor of flowers, the fluttering of fans, the sounds of soft, happy whispering, a maze of lovely women in evening gowns mingling with handsome men in the regulation evening dress– what could be prettier?

If American women would only ape the English in going bonnetless to the theatres, we would forgive their little aping in other respects, and call it even.

Upon the arrival of the Governor, the band played "God Save the Queen," during which the audience stood. Happily, they made it short. The play was pleasantly presented, the actors filling their roles most creditably, especially the one taking the part of Alley Sloper.

Afterwards, the sight of handsomely-dressed women stepping into their chairs, the daintily-colored Chinese lanterns, hanging fore and aft, marking the course the carriers took in the darkness, was very oriental and affective.

It is a luxury to have a carriage, of course, but there is something even more luxurious in the thought of owning a chair and carriers.

"Mr. Fuhrmann, what does one of those cost?" I pointed to a fine chair with silver mounted poles and silk hangings.

"I figure a little more than twenty dollars. Some women keep four and eight carriers; they are so cheap. Every member of a well established household has his or her own private chair. Many men prefer a coverless willow chair with swinging step, while many women have chairs that close entirely, so they can be carried along the streets hidden from view. You'll find convenient pockets, umbrella stands, and places for parcels in the nicer chairs."

On the way back to the hotel, I marveled that at every port I touched, I found so many bachelors, men of position, means and good appearance, that I naturally began to wonder why women do not flock that way. It was all very well some years ago to say, "Go West, young man," but I would say, "Girls, go East!" There are bachelors enough and to spare!

And a most happy time do these bachelors have in the East. They are handsome, jolly and good-natured. They have their own fine homes with no one but the servants to look after them. Think of it, and let me whisper, "Girls, go East!"

The second day after my arrival, Captain Smith of the *Oceanic*, called upon me. I expected to see a hard-faced old man; so, when I went into the drawing room and a youthful, good-looking man, with the softest blue eyes that seemed to have caught a tinge of the ocean's blue on a bright day, smiled down at me, I imagine I must have looked very stupid indeed.

I looked at the smooth, youthful face, with its light-brown moustache, and I felt inclined to laugh at the long iron-gray beard my imagination had put upon the captain of the *Oceanic*. I looked at the tall, slender, shapely body, and recalled the imaginary short legs, holding upright a wide circumference under an ample waistcoat, and I laughed audibly.

The captain offered to take me out to see Happy Valley. In jinrickshas we rode by the parade and cricket grounds where some lively games were played; the city hall; and the solid, unornamented barracks, along smooth, tree-lined roads, out to where the mountains make a nest of one level, green space.

"That's where the racecourse is," said the captain. "The judges' stand is there." He pointed to an ordinary, commonplace racecourse stand. "The stands erected by private families are over there."

"Oh, I like those. Are they built of palms? They are more pleasing because they are out of the usual."

"I agree. Every year they have races in February lasting three days. Everybody stops work, rich and poor alike come to the racecourse. They race with native-bred Mongolian ponies."

Happy Valley lines the hillside. There are congregated the graveyards of all the different sects and nationalities in Hong Kong. That those of different faiths should consent to place their dead together in this lovely tropical valley is enough to give it the name of Happy Valley, if its beauty did not do as much.

In my estimation, it rivals in beauty the public gardens, and visitors use it as a park. One wanders along the walks looking at the beautiful shrubs and flowers, never heeding that they are in the valley of death, so thoroughly is it robbed of all that is horrible about graveyards.

Our tour had come to an end, and the captain was needed back on board his ship. He dropped me off at the hotel.

"You were so different to what I imagined you would be," I said as we separated, explaining why I laughed at our first meeting.

"And I cannot believe you are the right girl; you are so unlike what I had been led to believe," he said with a laugh, in a burst of confidence. "I was told that you were an old maid with a dreadful temper. Such horrible things were said about you that I was hoping you would miss our ship. I said if you did come, I supposed you would expect to sit at my table, but I would arrange so you should be placed elsewhere."

I took the joke the way the captain meant it, even though it stung to learn what people say about me. "Did your information come from a reporter trying to race me?"

"No, I did not meet her, though I heard she was aboard the *Oceanic* last November when Captain Kempson was at the helm. Rest assured we will get you back to America as fast as we can."

After saying goodbye to the captain, I stopped by the telegraph office and sent a terse note to my editor. They have done me a terrible disservice to keep me in the dark about the race. If *her* editor is willing to pay in order to speed up her trip, mine ought to be willing to apply more effort for my success. If only I could send out Jules Verne's Detective Fix and delay her!

QUEEN'S ROAD IS interesting to all visitors. In it is the Hong Kong Club, where the bachelors are to be found, the post office, and greater than all, the Chinese shops, where I spent some time, but no money.

The shops are not large, but the walls are lined with black-wood cabinets, and one feels a little thrill of pleasure at the sight of the gold, the silver, ivory carvings, exquisite fans, painted scrolls, and the odor of the lovely sandal-wood boxes, coming faintly to the visitor, creates a feeling of greed. One wants them all—everything.

The Chinese merchants cordially show their goods, or follow as one strolls around, never urging one to buy, but cunningly bringing to the front the most beautiful and expensive part of their stock.

All it took to shore up my resolve not to buy was thinking of my small bag and how much trouble I continue to have fitting in my cold-cream jar.

"Chin chin," which means "good day," "good bye," "good night," "How are you?" or anything one may take from it, is the greeting of the Chinese. They all speak mongrel English, called "pidgin" English. It is impossible to make them understand pure English; consequently, Europeans, even housekeepers, use Pidgin English when addressing the servants.

The servants are men, with the exception of the nurses, and possibly the cooks. To the uninitiated, it sounds absurd to hear men and women addressing servants and merchants in the same idiotic language with which fond parents usually cuddle their offspring.

Pidgin is applied to everything. One will hear people say: "Hab got pidgin," which means they have business to look after; or if a man is requested to do some work which he thinks is the duty of another, he will say: "No belongee boy pidgin."

While strolling about the Chinese localities, seeing shops more worthy a visit, being more truly Chinese, I came upon an eating house, from which a conglomeration of strange odors strolled out and down the road.

Built around a table in the middle of the room was a circular bench. The diners perched on this bench like chickens on a fence, sitting down with their knees drawn up until knees and chin met; they held large bowls against their chins, pushing the rice energetically with their chop-sticks into their mouths.

I also noticed professional writers stashed in nooks and recesses of prominent thoroughfares. Besides writing letters for people, they told fortunes, and their patrons never went away without having their fates foretold. If I failed in my mission to go around the world in seventy-five days, or if that woman were to beat me, perhaps I could return to Hong Kong in shame and join these writers. I was sure I could make up a fortune as well as they.

ONE DAY I went up to Victoria Peak, named in honor of the Queen. An elevated tramway was built from the town to Victoria Gap, which opened in 1887. Before that time, people were carried up in sedans.

At the Gap, we secured sedan chairs and were carried to the Hotel Craigiburn. The hotel – Oriental in style – was liberally patronized by the citizens of Hong Kong, as well as visitors. After the proprietor had shown us over the hotel and given us a dinner that could not be surpassed, we were carried to Victoria Peak.

It required three men to a chair ascending the peak. At the Umbrella Seat, merely a bench with a peaked roof, everybody stopped long enough to allow the coolies to rest, then we continued on our way, passing sightseers and nurses with children. After a while, they stopped again, and we traveled on foot to the signal station.

The view was superb. The bay, in a breastwork of mountains, lay calm and serene, dotted with hundreds of ships like tiny toys. The palatial white houses came half way up the mountainside, beginning at the edge of the glassy bay. Every house we noticed had a tennis court blasted out of the mountainside.

They said that at night the view from the peak gives one the feeling of being suspended between two heavens. Several thousand boats and sampans carried a light after dark. This, with the lights on the roads and in the houses, looked like a sky more filled with stars than the one above.

———

EARLY ONE MORNING, a gentleman who was the proud possessor of a team of ponies, the finest in Hong Kong, called at the hotel to take me for a drive. We visited two quaint and dirty temples. One was a plain little affair with a gaudy altar. The stone steps leading to it were filled with beggars of all sizes, shapes, diseases and conditions of filth.

At another temple, nearby a public laundry where the washers stood in a shallow stream slapping the clothes on flat stones, was a quaint temple hewed, cave-like, in the side of an enormous rock. A selvage of rock formed the altar, and to that humble but picturesque temple Chinese women flock to pray for sons to be born unto them that they may have someone to support them in their old age.

We whirled along through the town and onto the road edging the bay. We had a good view of the beautiful dry dock on the other side. The gentleman pointed it out to me.

"Constructed entirely of granite," he said. "It is large enough to take in the largest vessels afloat. Would you like to see it closer?"

"No, thank you. I can see it fine from here." There had to be other things more interesting left to see in Hong Kong than a dry dock!

Upon returning to the hotel I ran into Mr. Fuhrmann. "Please tell me of some interesting places I can visit. I seem to be down to dry docks and temples."

He laughed. "You need a real Simon-pure Chinese city. Ask the agent about a trip to Canton. He can tell you all the interesting sights. Make sure you are up for it, though. Some sights are not for women's sensibilities."

"Thank you. I've never been one for sensibility anyway." Besides, I knew we were trying to keep the Chinese out of America through the Chinese Exclusion Act, so I decided to see all of them I could while in their land. Pay them a farewell visit, as it were. Thus, on Christmas Eve, I started for the city of Canton.

32

IN WHICH ELIZABETH BISLAND VISITS SINGAPORE, WITNESSES AN ESCAPE ATTEMPT, AND CELEBRATES CHRISTMAS.

SUNDAY, WE ARE LOUNGING IN OUR BAMBOO chairs on the wide decks; the awning flutters lazily in the breeze; and we, swimming between two worlds of burning blue, are endeavoring to recover from the fatigues of morning service.

We sail through the blue days on a level keel. The sea does not even breathe, but it quivers. I lie half the day, warmed to the very heart and soaked through and through with color and light.

There are no pageants of sunsets. The burning ball, undimmed by any cloud, falls swiftly and is quenched in the ocean, and after an instant of violet the tide of light vanishes abruptly, like some vast conflagration blown out suddenly, and as suddenly succeeded by the constellations hanging in the vault of darkness like gleaming lamps trembling in suspension. From the deep beneath whirl up myriads of jewels, glittering with unearthly fires and trailing a broad waving path of silver along the black waters in our wake.

Every hour brings us nearer the equator, and on the morning of the twenty-third of December we sight Singapore, seventy miles only from the centre of heat. The waters of the harbor are curiously banded in broad lines of brilliant violet, green, and blue, each quite distinct and with no fusions of color.

Against the skyline everywhere are the feathery heads of palms. The vegetation is enormous, rampant, violent. It stands 'round about the place like an army with banners, ready to rush in at any breach and destroy.

I pull from the ship's library a book on Singapore so that I may learn about this distant port. Seven hundred years has this City of the Lions stood, but the never-ending battle with tropic nature's lust for disintegration has left it with no monuments of its great age, no venerable buildings to testify to its antiquity. In the twelfth century Singapore was the capital of the Malayan empire, but in 1824 the British purchased it from the sultan of Jahore, scarcely more than a heap of ruins.

Only those who travel to these Eastern ports can form any adequate conception of the ability which has directed English conquest in the Orient. When they bullied the Malayan sultan into selling Singapore, they were apparently acquiring a ruinous and unimportant territory.

Today, this port is the entrepôt of Asian commerce, a coaling station for vessels of all countries, a deep, safe harbor for England's own ships and men-of-war, and a point from which she can command both seas. The inhabitants of her Straits Settlements number considerably more than half a million, and the exports and imports are each in value something like ten million pounds yearly. The United States alone buys there every twelvemonth goods worth more than four million dollars.

As for climate, it is very hot. The tall blond, Mr. Leslie Beacham, who is grandson of one of the world-famous conquerors of the East, arrays himself in snowy silk and linen and dons a Terrai hat with a floating scarf; but even in this attire moisture sparkles on his rosy skin, and his yellow curls cling damply to his brow. He will be leaving us here, but has promised to show us the local sights before he does.

Mr. Maddock, a Ceylon tea-planter twenty years resident in the tropics, is garbed in the ordinary costume of civilization, and apparently suffers no discomfort.

Accompanied by these two and the lady from Boston, I go ashore – Mrs. Kelly in her white walking dress, and I in one of the thin shirtwaists purchased in California.

Queer little square carriages, made for the most part of Venetian blinds, wait for us, drawn by disconsolate ponies the size of sheep. Conveyance in the East is a constant source of unhappiness to me. I was deprecatory with the jinricksha men in Japan, I humbled myself before the chair-bearers of Hong Kong, and now I go and make an elaborate apology to this wretched little beast before I can reconcile it to my conscience to climb into the gharry, or let him drag me about at a gallop.

The earth beneath us is a deep red, the trees are brightly green; to the right spans a rainbow sea, and overhead a sky of burning blue. The town is every color – blinding white, azure, green, red, yellow; the houses heavy squares of lime-washed brick, mostly without windows. Interiors are gloomily cool, and more than enough of the huge fierce glare of day enters through the open door. We pass swiftly through the business part of the town, and beyond to the broad red water-road where the houses face the sea.

One is suddenly aware that the sensory nerves awake in this heat to marvelous acuteness. The eye seems to expand its iris to great size and be capable of receiving undreamed possibilities of luminosity and hue. The skin grows exquisitely sensitive to the slightest touch – the faintest movement of the air. Numberless fine undercurrents of sound reach the ear, and the sense of smell is so strong that the perfumes of fruit and flowers at a great distance are penetrating as if held in the hand. One smells everything: delicious hot scents of vegetation, the steaming of the earth, and the faint acrid odors of the many sweating bodies of workers in the sun.

The water-road is full of folk. Tall Hindus go by leading little cream-white bulls with humped necks, which drag rude carts full of merchandise or fruits – pineapples, mangoes, and coconuts. English officials spin past in dog-carts with barefooted muslin-clad grooms up behind, and wealthy unctuous Chinese merchants bowl about in 'rickshas.

Nearly all foot-passengers are half or three-quarters naked. It is an open-air museum of superb bronzes, who, when they condescend to clothe themselves at all, drape in statuesque folds about their brown limbs and bodies a few yards of white or crimson cloth, which adorns rather than conceals.

Mrs. Kelly squeezes my hand, and we both gasp for breath as there suddenly emerges from a side street what appears to be a fat old lady coming from the bath, her gray hair knotted up carelessly and a towel as her only costume.

Mr. Maddock chuckles. "You've never seen the conventional Malay business attire, have you?"

We continue to gape in wonder, though in reality there is no cause for alarm. The dignified elderly Malay merchant continues on his way, unaware of the surprise he has given us.

Everyone has long hair and wears it twisted up at the nape of the neck; this, with the absence of beards and the general indeterminateness of attire, makes it difficult to distinguish sexes.

The lower class of work people are black, shining, and polished as Indian idols. At work they wear only a breechcloth, but when evening comes, they catch up a square of creamy transparent stuff, and by a twist or two of the wrist, fold it beautifully and loosely about themselves, and with erect heads tread silently away through the dusk – slender, proud, and mysterious-eyed.

The Malays are of an exquisite bronze, gleaming in the sun like burnished gold. They have full silken inky hair, very white teeth, and dress much in draperies of dull-red cotton, which makes them objects delicious to contemplate. Mingled with all these is the ubiquitous Chinese man in a pair of short loose blue breeches, his handsome muscular body shining as satin.

We reach the hotel at last, its gloom, its cloistered arcades and great dark rooms pleasant enough as a refuge from the sun. I wonder if Nellie Bly is about the place, or if we have already crossed paths unknowingly. Do I look for her or not? I should not like to see her as I imagine what a meeting that would be!

The dining room, a great vaulted hall through the centre of the building, is level with the earth, paved with stone and without doors, opening upon the veranda through three archways. Without windows, one can scarcely distinguish anything at first entrance from the glare outside; but presently we find the place full of tables of green and growing plants, and two huge punkahs waving slowly overhead, making a cooling breeze.

We are served by Hindus in garments and turbans of white muslin, who have slender melancholy brown faces, and eyes that shine through wonderful lashes with the soft gleamings of black jewels. I can scarcely eat my tiffin for delight in the enchanting pathetic beauty, the passionate grace and sadness, of the face of the lad who brings me butter in a lordly dish, the yellow rolls laid upon banana leaves, and serves me curry with a spoon made of a big pink shell.

Everyone is in lily white from head to heel, like a bride or a debutante – white duck trousers and fatigue jacket, white helmet, and white shoes.

This is the dress of two junior officers sitting next to us with heads like canary birds, and the sappy red of English beef still in their cheeks, just out from home for their first experience of Eastern service. They are full of energy, interest, and enthusiasm; they order beer and beef and mop their hot faces from time to time, listening meanwhile with profound respect to the words of their superior officer, who condescends to tiffin with them and to give them good advice.

His dress is similar to theirs, save for the gold straps on his shoulders, but all the succulent English flesh has been burned off of him long ago, and left him lean, tawny, and dry. He quenches his thirst with a little iced brandy and soda, eats sparingly of curry and fruit, and seems not to feel the heat much.

He has no enthusiasms, he has no interests except duty and the service, and he does not think any brown or yellow person in the least pretty or pleasant. His advice to the youngsters, while valuable, is patronizing and full of disillusionment.

"Those lads look rather put out by the advice," whispers Mr. Maddock.

I startle, not aware that anyone else but me was eavesdropping, a rather shameless habit of writers. "No, in fact it falls somewhat coldly upon their youthful ardor," I reply.

Over tiffin the blond Mr. Beacham outlines his plans for us, and please call him Leslie. He is delighted to show us around in the cooler temperature of the morning, so we go off our separate ways to avoid melting on the spot.

My room is a huge dim apartment with a stone floor opening directly upon the lawn and into the dining room, and has only slight jalousies for doors; but no one peers or intrudes. The bed is an iron frame; the single hard mattress is spread with a sheet, and there are no covers at all. Even the pillow is of straw. My bathroom, a lofty flagged chamber, opens into this one, and contains a big earthenware jar which the coolies will fill for me three times a day, and into which I plunge to rid myself of the burning heat.

Temporarily cooled, I take to writing down my thoughts of Singapore thus far, followed by a lengthy letter to Molly on paper so thin I am afraid my fountain pen will scratch it to bits. I briefly contemplate including a note for Molly to send on to Mr. Wetmore but change my mind. Her teasing would be merciless. I should have copied down his address before I left.

That night I get into bed and blow out the candle. It is odd to lie in bed with no sheets, although the air is so stifling, one is not necessary. Immediately I hear what sounds like some great animal stalking about. I am cold enough now – icy, in fact. What can it be?

They tell me tigers come over from the mainland and carry off on an average one person a day. This is probably a tiger.

He could easily push open those blind doors and walk in! He is coming towards the bed with heavy stealthy rustlings. Now I wish for a sheet to draw up over me. The room is hot, utterly black and still, save for the sound of those feet and the loud banging of my heart against my ribs.

The hotel seems to be dead, so horribly silent it is. Has the tiger eaten every one else already?

The darkness is of no use; he can see all the better for that, so I will strike a match and at least perish in the light.

As the blue flame on the wick's tip broadens, I meet the gaze of a frightfully large, calm gray rat who is examining my shoes and stockings with care. He regards me with only very faint interest and goes on with his explorations through all my possessions. He climbs the dressing-table and smells critically at my hat and gloves.

This is almost as bad as the tiger, but as I have no intention of attacking this terrible beast and my notice appears to bore him, I blow out the candle and go to sleep, leaving him to continue those heavy rustlings which so alarmed me.

The next morning I meet up with my group, minus the son Mrs. Kelly has left behind because he is not interested in sightseeing today.

"Did you sleep well?" asks Mrs. Kelly. "My room was terribly hot."

I tell her about my tiger-rat, and her eyes go wide with the tale. I fear she might not sleep tonight.

Meanwhile, the men secure an open carriage with two fine bronzes in muslin and turbans on the box, and we go for a drive. Leslie takes us first to call at a great white airy stone bungalow, set on a hill where resides the chief of police, another English officer clad in white and as brown and lean as are all who have seen long service here.

He gives a command in Malay to his khitmagar, and we are served with tea in the Chinese fashion.

"You speak like a native," I comment.

He sets down his cup. "When they need an English official, they usually send me. I am quite knowledgeable of the Malay tongue and character. For example, I am sent to conduct negotiations with the sultan of Jahore, a potentate who often grows restless."

Leslie laughs. "No one who goes with him can understand what he says to the sultan. But he always comes back with the desired concessions, and so we suppose he speaks the language convincingly and with eloquence."

"In my many years here in the East, I've learned to display a great gentleness of voice and manner," says the chief of police.

"Don't let him fool you," cuts in Leslie. "Underneath all that gentleness, they can sense his iron will. The natives regard him with undisguised respect and fear."

The chief of police does not respond but sits back, squaring his shoulders, and we are all quite inclined to agree with Leslie.

From the chief of police's gates, the road turns towards the botanical gardens, a great park where wide red ways wind through shaven lawns and under enormous blossoming trees. Every plant one knows as exotic is here quite at home – the giant pads of the Victoria regia pave the moats with circles of emerald, and the lotus lifts its rose-flushed cups from glassy pools where swans float in shadow.

We leave the carriage and pace through the translucent green twilight of the orchid houses built of wire gauze, the plants needing no protection here, where for six thousand years or so the thermometer has been ranging between seventy-five and ninety-five degrees of heat. The place is full of strange unfamiliar perfumes and grotesque blossoms, ghostly white, pallidly purple, and writhen into fantasticalities of scarlet.

Our carriage waits for us in the shade of a blooming tree, and, returning, we find it sprinkled with small golden trumpets poignantly sweet.

"What a mess," says Mr. Maddock as he clears the seats.

On the way home, we pass the governor's palace with its wonderful palms and bamboos, and it is upon this road that we come suddenly upon a race of brown goddesses. We pass one alone, then two, then several more going singly along the wide road shaded by enormous trees. They are very tall, with round slender limbs. Their garments – a long scarf of thin white wrapped firmly about the hips, drawn lightly over the bosom and crossing the back from shoulder to waist – but half conceal beneath the semi-transparent drapery the fine outline of breast and hip, clear and firm as ancient statues, and warmly brown with a curious faint bloom – almost as of a grape – upon the skin.

"Who are they?" I ask Leslie.

"They are called Klings. Transplants from Pondicherry, the fragment of India still retained by France."

Mr. Maddock adds, "They are a race famous throughout India for the astonishing beauty of its women."

Mrs. Kelly dug into her sack. "I shall like a picture of one," she said.

"I'm afraid not," says Leslie, pushing closed her sack. "They will not allow themselves to be photographed."

As they go forward, lightly and fleetly, on their slim bare feet they have the proud, upstanding grace of palms, and with a strange sinuous motion make all their heavy anklets and bangles tinkle like little bells and a wave of fluent movement stir their garments from throat to heel. The ripples of their hair, drawn back from the broad brown brows and knotted in silken abundance at the nape, glitter like polished jet, and the fine, haughty, dark features lit with little points of gold – tiny studs set in the high nostrils and the upper rims of the little ears.

———

HALF-PAST FOUR! The ship is about to sail. We have wandered through the shops and museums and have returned once more to our old quarters after thanking Leslie for his hospitality.

Tiny canoes cluster about the vessel, full of beautiful shells of which one can buy a boat-load for a dollar. Other canoes hold small Malays ranging from three to seven years of age, all naked save for the merest rag of a breechcloth, all pretty as little bronze curios, and all shouting in shrill chorus for coins.

"Let's give them what they ask," I say to Mrs. Kelly.

A few shillings changed into the native currency procure a surprising number of small pieces of money, which we fling into the clear water.

"Look!" I point as the boys plunge over after these coins with little splashings like frogs, and wiggle down swiftly to the bottom, growing strange and wavering of outline and ghostly green as they sink. They are wonderfully quick to seize the glinting coin before it touches the sands below, and come up wet, shining, and showing their white teeth. We play at this game until the whistle blows, and then sail away, leaving Leslie waving his handkerchief to us from the shore.

An hour later, we are still steaming near the palm-fringed coast. There is a sudden cry and struggle forward – a naked body with manacled hands shoots outward from the ship's side and disappears in a boiling circle of foam. A Chinese prisoner, being transported to Penang, has knocked down his guards and taken to the water.

The engines are reversed and a life-buoy thrown overboard, but he does not appear. After what seems a great lapse of time, a head shows a long distance away and moves rapidly towards the shore. Evidently he has slipped his handcuffs and can swim.

A boat is lowered full of Lascars very much excited, commanded by the third officer, a ruddy young fellow – calm and dominant. They pursue the head, but it has covered more than half the distance, some two miles, between us and the shore before it is overtaken. There is some doubling back and forth, an oar is raised in menace, and the fugitive submits to be pulled into the boat.

I am standing by the gangway when he returns. He is a fine, well-built young fellow.

"What has he done?" I ask an Englishman standing nearby.

"Forgery. He is to be turned over to the native authorities against whom he has offended."

"And what will they do to him?" I wonder aloud, that he would risk drowning in handcuffs.

"Their punishments are terrible." He glances at me and appears to check his words. "Prisoners receive no food and must depend upon the memories and mercies of the charitable."

One of the Lascars holds him by the queue as he mounts the steps. He is wet and chilled and has a face of stolid despair.

They take him forward, and I see him no more.

———

IT IS CHRISTMAS Day – still very hot and not like Christmas in New York at all; and off to our right are to be seen from time to time the bold purple outlines of the coasts of Sumatra. The ship is decorated with much variegated bunting, and the servants assume an air of languid festivity; but most of us suffer from plaintive reminiscences of home and nostalgia.

"A Merry Christmas to you!" greets the captain enthusiastically to the table. He sits down and we get about the business of celebrating. We pull Christmas crackers, as in the holidays at home, and from their contents I am loaded with paste jewels and profusely provided with poetry in brief segments and of an enthusiastically amatory nature.

My poem says:
To thee, my Love, to thee –
So fain would I come to thee!

And the water's bright in a still moonlight,

As I look across the sea.

A sudden ache fills my heart. All my loved ones are across the sea. I've never spent a Christmas alone, and the feeling is so very un-Christmas like, even though celebrating the coming of the Christ child is at the center of Christmas, the feeling is not the same without family to share it.

I blink back tears and go to offer a smile to Mrs. Kelly. Tonight, she shall be my family, as are the others seated around me. Her eyes have also filled with unshed tears. I reach out and squeeze the dear lady's hand as she has so often done to mine. "What does your poem say?"

She shakes her head, like she cannot trust her voice to read it. I take the slip of paper and read aloud for the table:

In youth, we plucked full many a flower that died,

Dropped on the pathway, as we danced along;

And now, we cherish each poor leaflet dried

In pages which to that dear past belong.

The men take turns saying their poems, unaware of the quiet suffering of Mrs. Kelly's thoughts of her departed husband. But they lighten the mood as they read their love poems in dramatic fashion in the absence of their sweethearts.

There is a splendid plum-cake for dinner, with a Santa Claus atop, huddled in sugar furs despite the burning heat. The evening ends on a cheery note, but several of us retire early, ready for the day to be over and to move on to the coming of the New Year when we will be reunited with those loved ones.

33

IN WHICH NELLIE BLY VISITS A LEPER COLONY AND EATS CHRISTMAS LUNCHEON IN THE TEMPLE OF THE DEAD.

THE O. AND O. AGENT ESCORTED ME TO the ship *Powan*, on which I was to travel to Canton for the day. He gave me in charge of Captain Grogan, the *Powan's* commander, an American, who has lived for years in China. A very bashful man he was, but a most kindly, pleasant one. I never saw a fatter man, or a man so comically fattened. A wild inclination to laugh crept over me every time I caught a glimpse of his roly-poly body. Then thoughts of how sensitive I am concerning remarks about my own personal appearance, in a measure subdued my impulse to laugh.

I have always said to critics who mercilessly write about the shape of my chin, or the cut of my nose, or the size of my mouth, and such personal attributes that can no more be changed than death can be escaped: "Criticize the style of my hat or my gown, I can change them, but spare my nose, it was born on me."

Remembering this, and how nonsensical it is to blame or criticize people for what they are powerless to change, I pocketed my merriment, letting a kindly feeling of sympathy take its place.

Soon after we left, night descended. I went on deck where everything was buried in darkness. Softly and steadily the boat swam on, the only sound — and the most refreshing and restful sound in the world — was the lapping of the water.

They can talk of the companionship of men, the splendor of the sun, the softness of moonlight, the beauty of music, but give me a willow chair on a quiet deck, and the world with its worries and noise and prejudices is lost in distance. Let me rest rocked gently by the rolling sea, in a nest of velvety darkness, my only light the soft twinkling of the myriads of stars in the quiet sky above; my music, the round of the kissing waters, cooling the brain and easing the pulse; my companionship, dreaming my own dreams. Give me that, and I have happiness in its perfection.

But away with dreams. This is a work-a-day world, and I am racing Time around it. At least, that is what I tell myself and others who ask. Nothing has ever come easy for me. I've always worked hard. Harder than the others. And to find out that my own editor does not care enough to make every effort on my behalf. Ah, but I spoiled my own rest. Where are the dreams?

Before daybreak we anchored at Canton. The Chinese went ashore the moment we landed, but the other passengers remained for breakfast. While we were eating, the guide whom the captain had secured for us came on board and quietly supervised the luncheon we were to take with us.

"A Merry Christmas!" was the first thing he said to us. "My name is Ah Cum, and I will show you Canton."

We all exchanged surprised looks as the date had even slipped our minds. Without the snow and the holly and the carolers, it did not seem right that it was Christmas. I know we all appreciated the polite thoughtfulness of our Chinese guide as it was a holiday he did not personally celebrate.

He had on his feet beaded black shoes with white soles. His navy-blue trousers, or tights, more properly speaking, were tied around the ankle and fitted very tight over most of the leg. Over this he wore a blue, stiffly starched shirt-shaped garment, which reached his heels, while over this he wore a short padded and quilted silk jacket, somewhat similar to a smoking jacket.

Ah Cum had chairs ready for us. His chair was a neat arrangement in black, black silk hangings, tassels, fringe and black wood-poles finished with brass knobs. Once in it, he closed it, and was hidden from the gaze of the public.

Our plain willow chairs had ordinary covers, which, to my mind, rather interfered with sightseeing. We had three coolies to each chair. Those with us were barefooted, with tousled pigtail and navy-blue shirts and trousers, much the worse for wear both in cleanliness and quality.

Ah Cum's coolies wore white linen garments, gaily trimmed with broad bands of red cloth, looking very much like a circus clown's costume.

Ah Cum led the way, our coolies following. We were carried along dark and dirty narrow ways, in and about fish stands, whence odors drifted, until we crossed a bridge which spanned a dark and sluggish stream.

This little island, guarded at every entrance, is Shameen, or Sandy Face, the land set aside for the habitation of Europeans. An unchangeable law prohibits Celestials from crossing into this sacred precinct, because of the hatred they cherish for Europeans.

Shameen is green and picturesque, with handsome houses of Oriental design, and grand shade trees, and wide, velvety green roads, broken only by a single path, made by the bare feet of the chair-carriers.

Here, for the first time since leaving New York, I saw the stars and stripes. It was floating over the gateway to the American Consulate. It is a strange fact that the further one goes from home, the more loyal one becomes. I felt I was a long ways off from my own dear land; it was Christmas day, and I had seen many different flags since last I gazed upon our own.

The moment I saw it floating there in the soft, lazy breeze, I took off my cap and said: "That is the most beautiful flag in the world, and I am ready to whip anyone who says it isn't."

Consul Seymour received our little party with a cheery welcome. "How much time do you have? What can I show you?"

The man who has taken leadership of our little group answered. "We have a guide waiting outside for us. We only stopped a moment to pay our respects."

"Ah. Excellent. In that event, let me give you a quick tour of the consulate." He led us around the building, paying particular attention to the embroideries and carved ivories which decorated the place. He was a personable man who spoke to each of us in turn to find out what we were doing in his part of the world.

"I was an editor before I came to China with my wife and only daughter to be consul," said Mr. Seymour when he found out I was a reporter.

After leaving, we all agreed that Mr. Seymour was a most pleasant man, and a general favorite who reflected credit upon the American Consulate.

What a different picture Canton presented to Shameen. It is said there are millions of people in Canton. The streets, many of which are roughly paved with stone, seemed little over a yard in width. The shops, with their brightly colored and handsomely carved signs, were all open, as if the whole end facing the street had been blown out. As we were carried along the roads, we could see not only the usually rich and enticing wares, but the sellers and buyers.

It was here where I learned what a very clever fellow was that guide, Ah Cum.

As I was not involved in purchasing souvenirs, he delighted in offering me private commentary.

"I went to school at an American mission in Canton," he said. "But," he assured me, with great earnestness, "English was all I learned. I was not interested in the Christian religion."

Ah Cum had put his learning to good account. Besides being paid as guide, he collected a percentage from merchants for all the goods bought by tourists. Of course the tourists paid higher prices than they would otherwise, and Ah Cum saw they visited no shops where he is not paid his little fee.

In the rear of every shop is an altar, bright in color and often expensive in adornment. Near the entrance of every shop is a bookkeeper's desk. The bookkeepers all wore tortoise-shell rimmed glasses of an enormous size, which lent them a look of tremendous wisdom. I was inclined to think the glasses were a mark of office, for I never saw a man employed in clerical work without them.

As we were carried along, the men in the stores would rush out to look at me. They did not take any interest in the men with me, but gazed at me as if I was something new. They showed no sign of animosity, but the few women I met looked as curiously at me, and less kindly. I was told that Chinese women usually spat in the faces of female tourists when the opportunity offered. However, I had no trouble.

The thing that seemed to interest the people most about me were my gloves. Sometimes they would make bold enough to touch them, and they would always gaze upon them with looks of wonder.

The streets are so narrow that I thought at first I was being carried through the aisles of some great market. It is impossible to see the sky, owing to the signs and other decorations, and the compactness of the buildings. When Ah Cum told me that I was not in a market-house, but in the streets of the city of Canton, my astonishment knew no limit.

Sometimes our little train would meet another train of chairs, and then we would stop for a moment, and there would be great yelling and fussing until we had safely passed, the way being too narrow for both trains to move at once in safety.

Coolie number two of my chair was a source of great discomfort to me all the day. He had a strap spanning the poles by which he upheld his share of the chair. This band, or strap, crossed his shoulders, touching the neck just where the prominent bone is. The skin was worn white and hard-looking from the rubbing of the band; but still it worried me, and I watched all the day expecting to see it blister.

He was not an easy traveler, this coolie, there being as much difference in the gait of carriers as there is in the gait of horses. Many times he shifted the strap, much to my misery, and then he would turn and, by motions, convey to me that I was sitting more to one side than to the other.

As a result, I made such an effort to sit straight and not to move that when we alighted at the shops I would be cramped almost into a paralytic state. As the day progressed, so did a sick headache, all from thinking too much about the comfort of the carriers.

———

I WAS VERY anxious to see the execution ground, so we were carried there. We went in through a gate where a stand erected for gambling was surrounded by a crowd of filthy people. Some few idle ones left it to saunter lazily after us.

The place is very unlike what one would naturally suppose it to be. At first sight it looked like a crooked back alley in a country town. There were several rows of half dried pottery. A woman, who was molding in a shed at one side, stopped her work to gossip about us with another female who had been arranging the pottery in rows.

The place is probably seventy-five feet long by twenty-five wide at the front, and narrowing down at the other end.

"Why is the ground over there so very red?" I asked Ah Cum.

He kicked the red-colored earth with his white-soled shoe and said indifferently, "It's blood. Eleven men were beheaded here yesterday."

"Eleven? Why so many?"

"It is an ordinary thing for ten to twenty criminals to be killed together."

"How many executions take place in a year?" asked another man.

"Oh, maybe four hundred. But in 1855 over 50,000 rebels were beheaded in this narrow alley. That was a year!"

While he was talking, I noticed some roughly-fashioned wooden crosses leaned up against the high stone wall and supposed they were used in some manner for religious purposes before and during the executions. I asked Ah Cum about them.

"When women are condemned to death in China, they are bound to wooden crosses and cut to pieces."

A shiver slid down my spinal cord at his answer.

"Men are beheaded with one stroke unless they are the worst kind of criminals," he added, "then they are given the death of a woman to make it the more discreditable. They tie them to the crosses and strangle or cut them to pieces. When they are cut to bits, it is done so deftly that they are entirely dismembered and disemboweled before they are dead. Would you like to see some heads?"

I thought that Ah Cum could tell as large stories as any other guides; and who can equal a guide for highly-colored and exaggerated tales? So I said coldly: "Certainly. Bring on your heads!"

I tipped a man, as he told me, who, with the clay of the pottery on his hands, went to some barrels which stood near to the wooden crosses, put in his hand and pulled out a head!

Even I was speechless as I looked up and away until the head was safely tucked back in the barrel. In all my reporting, I'd never seen the like. It was sickening.

"The barrels are filled with lime, and as the criminals are beheaded their heads are thrown into the barrels. When the barrels become full, they empty them out and get a fresh supply," explained Ah Cum, warming up to the subject.

"How resourceful," I murmured, still dealing with the shock of seeing a head preserved in lime.

"And if a man of wealth is condemned to death, he can buy a substitute."

"Who would be willing to do that?" asked one in our party.

Ah Cum shrugged, leaving me with the opinion that Chinese are indifferent about death.

I also had a great curiosity to see the leper village, which was supposed to contain hundreds of Chinese lepers. The village consists of numbers of bamboo huts, and the lepers present a sight appalling in its squalor and filth.

"Smoke cigarettes," said Ah Cum. "It will help with the smell." He set the example by lighting one, and we all followed his lead.

The lepers were simply ghastly in their misery. There are men, women and children of all ages and conditions. The few filthy rags with which they endeavored to hide their nakedness presented no shape of any garment or any color, so dirty and ragged were they.

On the ground floors of the bamboo huts were little else than a few old rags, dried grass and things of that kind. Furniture there was none. It is useless to attempt a description of the loathsome appearance of the lepers. Many were featureless, some were blind, some had lost fingers, others a foot, some a leg, but all were equally dirty, disgusting and miserable.

"Some are able to work. They sell their vegetables in the city market," said Ah Cum, pointing out a prosperous-looking garden which is near their village.

I felt glad to know we had brought our luncheon from the ship.

"Those who can walk go to Canton to beg but must come back to sleep in their village."

What was the benefit of a leper village if the lepers are allowed to mingle with the other people?

As we left the leper city, I was conscious of an inward feeling of emptiness. I had seen such horrible things today. Human suffering on extreme levels. Yet it was Christmas day. What a contrast to the joyful celebrations going on in New York. Instead of celebrating Heaven, I had witnessed Hell.

I wondered if Mother was cooking a little meal for herself or if she had been invited to the neighbor's. Or perhaps she got up the gumption to get on the train and visit one of my brothers or sisters.

As if reading my thoughts, one of the men in the party said, "We've missed it. It is about midnight in New York." We were all quiet with reflection.

"There is a building nearby I want to show you, and then we will eat," said Ah Cum.

Once within a high wall, we came upon a pretty scene. There was a mournful sheet of water undisturbed by a breath of wind. In the background the branches of low, overhanging trees kissed the still water just where stood some long-legged storks, made so familiar to us by pictures on Chinese fans.

Ah Cum led us to a room which was shut off from the court by a large carved gate. Inside were hard wood chairs and tables. While eating, I heard chanting to the weird, plaintive sound of a tom-tom and a shrill pipe. When I had less appetite and more curiosity, I asked Ah Cum where we were, and he replied, "In the Temple of the Dead."

And in the Temple of the Dead I was eating my Christmas luncheon. But that did not interfere with the luncheon. Before we had finished, a number of Chinese crowded around the gate and looked curiously at me.

"Look, Miss Bly. They want their children to see you."

Indeed. They held up several children, well-clad, cleanly children.

Thinking to be agreeable, I went forward to shake hands with them. When I reached out, they kicked and screamed and, getting down, rushed back in great fright.

I looked at my party and shrugged. They were all a grin at the spectacle and encouraged me to try again.

Meanwhile, the children's companions succeeded in quieting them, and they were persuaded to take my hand. The ice once broken, they became so interested in me, my gloves, my bracelets and my dress, that I soon regretted my friendliness in the outset. Ah Cum set out to rescue me as he announced we were going to see the water clock.

"You must see it, Miss Bly. It is over five hundred years old."

We climbed high and dirty stone steps to the water clock. In little niches in the stone walls were small gods, before them the smoldering joss sticks. The water clock consists of four copper jars, about the size of wooden pails, placed on steps, one above the other. Each one has a spout from which comes a steady drop-drop. In the last and bottom jar is an indicator, very much like a foot rule, which rises with the water, showing the hour. On a blackboard hanging outside, they mark the time for the benefit of the town people.

"The upper jar is filled once every twenty-four hours," said Ah Cum.

"And that is all it takes?" asked one of our party.

Ah Cum nodded. "It has never run down or been repaired."

"Remarkable."

On our return to the Powan, I found some beautiful presents from Consul Seymour and the cards of a number of Europeans who had called to see me. Suffering from a sick-headache, I went to my cabin, and shortly we were on our way to Hong Kong, my visit to Canton on Christmas day being of the past.

34

IN WHICH ELIZABETH BISLAND MEETS A BENEFACTOR AND SAMPLES BETEL NUT.

PENANG. — ITS PEAKS SHOOT SHARPLY UP into the blue air two thousand feet, wrapped in a tangle of prodigious verdure to their very tops, enormous palm forests fringing all the shore. The ship anchors some distance from the docks and will remain but a few hours.

We are ferried to land in crazy sampans, the only alternative from out-rigger canoes – a narrow trough set on a round log and kept upright by a smaller floating log connected with the boat by bent poles. Only a native, a tight-rope walker or a bicyclist would trust himself to these.

The same crowd of Hindus, Malays, and Chinese. These ports are beginning to all look alike. Little girls appearing twelve or thirteen years old themselves stand about with their own children in their arms. They have been wives for a year or two. Very pretty they are, miniature women fully formed, the babies fat and brown and nearly as large as the mothers.

A gharry and another pitiful little horse take us towards the gardens and the famous waterfall. The road skirts the town and intersects lagoons, where Malay houses of coconut thatch stand upon piles like ancient lake dwellings. I am told they live over this stagnant water by preference, and apparently suffer no harm.

Farther on, where the ground rises, are the huge stone bungalows of English officials and rich Chinese merchants, the entrance to the grounds of the latter adorned with ornate doors and guarded by carved monsters, curiously colored.

We overtake a Chinese funeral winding towards the cemetery, all the mourners clad in white. The coffin, of unpainted wood, is so heavy and so large that twenty pall-bearers are required to carry it. It is a most cheerful cortège. No one seems in the least downcast or dispirited by this bereavement – death is accepted with the same stolid philosophy as are the checkered incidents of life.

The road turns and sweeps into the palm forest. Innumerable slender, silver-gray columns soar to an astonishing height – a hundred feet or more – bearing at the top a wide feathery crown where the big globes of the coconuts hang, green and gold.

A profound green twilight reigns here, with something, I know not what, of holy sadness and awe amid these silent gray aisles – delicate, lofty, still. My own heart feels heavy. Perhaps I am tired. Or homesick. Likely I am both. I feel I am missing out on parties at home and wonder what book the literary society has chosen to read next. Is Charles Wetmore attending? Has Molly gotten any of my postcards yet?

Our guide, a brown lad of ten, stands on the carriage step clinging to the door, and chatters fluently in tangled and intricate English, of which he is obviously inordinately vain.

"Everyone out. Must walk here," he says.

The garden lies between two very lofty cone-shaped peaks and is as well kept and full of tropical blossoms and verdure as are all the others we have seen.

"Miss Bisland, Miss Bisland. Look here!" The boy stops to show me tiny fronds of a sensitive-plant that shudder away from his rude little finger with a voluntary movement startling to see in a plant.

"What makes them do that?"

The boy shrugs. No one knows the answer. But the curiosity is enough to reawaken my sense of adventure and lift the melancholy. I poke at the plant and laugh when it shies away.

We hear the rushing speech of waters calling loudly in the hills, but see nothing save the mountain's garments of opulent verdure. A path zigzags sharply upward through the trees and vine labyrinth, and by this the boy leads the way with the speed and agility of a goat. We pant along in his wake, barely keeping him in sight.

"Is he trying to kill us?" questions Mrs. Kelly, dressed in an outfit meant for sunning on a deck chair. She waves her fan desperately, trying to cool her brow.

The atmosphere is a steam bath, and the moisture pours down our faces as we spring from stone to stone and corkscrew back and forth, deafened by the vociferations of the fall, but catching no glimpse of it.

"Do you want to rest here?" Robert asks. The son has decided he is bored on ship and wanted an excursion. "We can fetch you when we return."

"I'll make it," she says with surprising determination in her voice. "I've come this far."

Exhausted, gasping, streaming with perspiration, we finally emerge upon a plateau high on the peak's side and are suddenly laved in that warm wind that stirred the palm fronds.

At our feet is a wide, quivering green pool, crossed by a frail bridge; from far above leaps down to us a flood of glittering silver that dashes the emerald pool into powdery foam, races away under the bridge, and springs again with a shout into the thickets below. We lose sight of it amid the leaves, but can hear its voice as it leaps from ledge to ledge down to the valley and is silenced at last in the river.

A tiny shrine built here at the side of this first pool is tended by a thin melancholy-eyed young priest, who lives alone at this great height, his only companions the ceaseless din of the waters and the little black elephant-headed god in the shrine. He bears a spot of dried clay upon his forehead – a token of humility or submission.

"In morning he prays. Puts hand in water. Hand in dust. Hand on forehead," says our guide, miming the act of devotion. "Wash off at night."

I lay a piece of money upon the altar, and in return the priest gives me a handful of pale, perfumed pink bells that grow upon the mountainside, and are the only sacrifice offered to the little black god. He motions for me to remove my hat and decorate my hair with the flowers in the fashion in which his countrywomen wear them.

I do so, and he smiles.

Back again through the steaming woods and the palm aisles, then the ship once more, and our faces are turned towards Ceylon.

IT IS A five days' run from Penang to the island of Ceylon; the ship's company has dwindled to a handful, and time hangs heavily upon us. We are reduced, for lack of other occupations, to an undue interest in the ship's menagerie.

The fifth officer has a monkey – a surreptitious monkey, not allowed to members of the staff – and at such time as the stern seniors are on duty we amuse ourselves fearfully and secretly with his antics as we placate him with raisins.

"You should get one," he tells me. "Your friends in America would want to see it."

"Never." Imagine Molly's shock if I were to bring home a monkey!

At other times, while the powers that be look on, the Fifth and I sport ostentatiously with two gorgeous and permissible cockatoos which we find, like most things permissible, dull and uninteresting.

The consul to Bangkok – a slim, brown gentleman with a soft, languid voice and tiny feet – is carrying home a family of Siamese cats; white, with tawny legs and fierce blue eyes; uncanny beasts with tigerish ways. They live in the fo'castle in company with an impulsive Chinese puppy of slobberingly affectionate disposition; and their prowling, long-legged behavior gets upon his nerves most terribly. He is too manly a little person to hurt them, and his only refuge is an elaborate pretence of not seeing; even when they rub against his nose, he gazes abstractedly off into space and firmly refuses to be aware of their existence.

The doctor has two families of felines. One is a respectable tortoise-shell British matron, absorbed with the cares of a profuse maternity. She has five tiny kittens nestled in beside her. I kneel next to her box and tell her what a wonderful mother she is.

The doctor scoops up a kitten and hands it to me. Its legs splay wild until his claws catch onto my skirts. I can feel it quivering beneath my hand as I stroke it.

"Born last week," says the doctor with pride as if he had anything to do with it. "Now, there is another cat around her somewhere. Chibbley!" he calls. "Since the kittens, she's having fits of jealousy. If I dare to caress her without having previously washed my hands after touching the kittens, she flies into a fury, claws, spits, rages, and finally rushes up into the rigging to sulk."

I picture a pouting cat up high in the sails, pitching and rolling during a storm. "How do you get her down?"

"I grovel with a seductive bowl of dinner in my hands."

As if to prove the point, Chibbley appears and rubs against the doctor's leg, eying both me and the kitten. She is a splendid Persian lady, despite being madly jealous of the division in her owner's affections.

"Beautiful creature, isn't she?" says the doctor, stroking her with a firm hand that brings out a deep purr. "I bought her from a native on the wharves at Bombay. She was in a frightful condition. Wild with starvation and bad treatment. She had been stolen from some zenana – the inner apartments of the women. I knew it because she smelled of violet powder and had a gold thread around her neck, but I couldn't let her go back to that mistreatment. She has not, however, forgotten the ways of her mistress, and is greedy, luxurious, indolent, and bad-tempered."

WE SAIL INTO Ceylon's harbor by the light of great tropical stars, and the planet gleams of a light shining from the tall clock tower of Colombo. Already many ships lie in the narrow roadstead, and it requires the fine art of navigation to slip our boat's huge bulk into her berth between two of these and make her fast to her own particular buoy.

The pilot comes aboard just outside, and it is his firm hand that jams her nose up to within three hairs' breadth of the vessel in front, holds her there with a grip of iron, and with cautious screw-revolutions swings her into line with her heels in the very face of the Australian mail-ship – arrived a few hours earlier.

Then the entire passenger list – on deck for the last half-hour, aiding the pilot by holding its breath – sighs relievedly and joyously, and goes below in a body to recuperate on brandy and soda.

I am amazed at the skill of some men, daring enough to take on a mechanical challenge and see it through. Although in the case of Cyclone Bill Downing, I did feel my life was in his hands on several occasions instead of the Almighty's.

I linger a moment in the darkness to smell the fragrance of the night, moved by the vast flowings of a warm sweet wind. Seafarers of other days told of these perfumes of the Spice Island filling their sails far out at sea, but the coal smoke of the modern ship deadens the nostril of the modern traveler and fills his heart with naughty doubts of the veracity of the Ancient Mariner.

Nonetheless, there are in the mountain forests of Ceylon strange, treeless, lake-like expanses of aromatic lemon grass from which the winds come heavy with intoxicating scents. I fancy I can detect faint delicious savors in the air, and that night – sleeping with open portholes – I dream of perfumes.

I am up early to have the first possible view of an island so like to Paradise that I am told Adam was first banished to this place that he might not feel too sharply in the beginning his loss and the contrast.

Upon Adam's Peak – a soaring pinnacle seven thousand feet high, of which we caught a glimpse yesterday while still far at sea – stood the father of men and wept his lost Eden, for which even Ceylon might not console him; the bitter rain of this immeasurable grief trickling down the mountainside into the rocks, the rivers, the sea, and the sands, where it is found today as clear shining gems and pearls like tears.

It was upon this peak that, having clothed himself in the skins of beasts, he shred abroad to the winds the first green garments that hid his primal nakedness, and these, scattered far and wide by the breeze, sprang up in spice plants – so ambrosial a potency had even the leaves of the trees in Paradise.

In the morning light this island of jewels, of flowers, and palms look like the long-lost heavenly gardens. It floats upon smooth, lustrous waters, under a sky of pale warm violet, veiled in a dawn-mist faint and mysterious as dreams. Beyond the massive breakwater of our straitened harbor, curve the rims of white beaches frilled with foam, where palms lean over to look at themselves in a sea of green mother-of-pearl.

It is very hot. The thermometer even at this hour (it is the last day of December) registers 80°; but it is less oppressive than at Singapore, where one seemed to be breathing tepid water rather than air.

A long wharf juts out into the harbor with a customhouse at its landward end. We pause here to exchange some civilities concerning the weather, and pass on with our luggage unmolested, so soothing and plentiful a lack of curiosity have these officials in British ports.

The soil is red – bright red – the color of ground cinnabar. Not "liver-colored," as the earth seemed to the ancient Northmen, but deep-tinted as if soaked with dragon's blood, of which antiquity believed cinnabar to be made.

A broad street, fringed with grass and tulip trees, goes inland, and on either side are massive white buildings with arched and pillared arcades. The vividness of color here is astounding – brilliant, intense, like the colors of precious stones.

"Do my eyes deceive me?" questioned the lady from Boston. "Miss Bisland, can the earth be so red, the sea and sky so blue?"

"It is a miracle wrought by the luminosity of the Eastern day," I respond. "One's very flesh tingles with an ecstasy of pleasure in this giant effulgence of color, as might a musician's who should hear the vibrations of some colossal harp."

"Yes, one could feel that," she replies hesitantly.

I laugh and loop my arm through hers. She is growing used to my ebullient ways as I am to her understated ones. I can't help that language is my tool and that finding the exact word gives me a thrill.

The Grand Oriental Hotel lies to the right of this road, near the water – big and glaringly white without, cool and shadowy within. Ships from India, China, and Australia have just arrived, and the place is crowded.

The clack of many heels rings on the stone floor of the arcade, which opens upon an inner flowery court, where also look out the windows of the sleeping-rooms above, veiled by delicate transparent straw mattings – waving softly in and out in the little hot breezes, giving treacherous glimpses now and again of a pretty disheveled head and tumbled white draperies.

The arcade is full of British folk – Australians and Anglo-Indians, passing to and fro to the dining room, to the stairs, to the front entrance. Handsome, as an Anglo-Saxon crowd of the well-to-do is apt to be – tall, florid men in crisp white linen and white Indian helmets; tall, slim, well-poised girls in white muslin, with a delicious fruit-like pink in their cheeks, brought there by the heat, which curls their blond hair in damp rings about their brows and white necks. And tall, imposing British matrons, with something of the haughtiness of old Rome in their bearing – the mothers and wives of conquerors.

Our rooms are at the end of a long corridor, looking on the street. They are carpetless and uncurtained, their dim twilight being sifted from the burning glare without through green mattings hung at the windows.

Before my door sits my own particular servant, detailed to wait upon this bedroom. Similar servants are stationed along the corridor in front of their respective charges. A curious creature – of a sex not easily to be determined. Mild-browed and woman-eyed, with long, rippling black hair knotted at the back and kept smooth with a tortoise-shell band comb, the brown femininities of his face disappear at the chin in a short close-curled black beard. He is full-chested as a budding girl, but clothes himself to the waist in shirt, coat, and waistcoat, the slender male hips being wrapped in a white skirt that falls to the ankles.

He is, however, an eminently agreeable person. He not only executes orders with noiseless dispatch, but receives them with a little reverence of the slim fingers to the brow, and a look in his lustrous eyes of such sweet eagerness to serve that my heart is melted within me.

He tells me it is the sacred and beautiful hour of tiffin. The time when knowledgeable companions point out who is who and what the important people are doing.

The dining room is as white, cool, and nobly plain as a Greek temple; long and very lofty – reaching to the roof – the second story opening upon it in an arched and balustraded clerestory to let in the light. Two punkahs of gold-colored stuff wave above us. On one side we look upon the arcaded court, and through the heavy-arched veranda upon the hot gorgeousness of color outside.

Bowls of tropical flowers are set on each table, and under the salt-cellars and spoons at the corners are laid large leaves of curious lace-like pattern, freaked with splashes of red and yellow.

More of the fawn-eyed men with long hair serve us, and the assemblage gathered here for the moment is a remarkable one. Near the door sits a good-looking young man, accompanying a party of blond girls in smart frocks. It is Wordsworth's grandson, and the owner of Rydal Mount.

At the table next to him is a stern, lean soldier with a melancholy face – the Lord Chelmsford in whose African campaign the Prince Imperial was killed and the English suffered a hideous butchery, surprised by the savages.

On the other side of the room is a young man with a heavy blond countenance – Dom Leopoldo Agostino and half a dozen things more, who has just met here, in his voyage round the world in a Brazilian war-ship, the news of his grandfather Dom Pedro's dethronement and exile. The captain of the ship dares not continue the cruise in the face of peremptory cables from the new government, and the young man is suddenly marooned here, with all his luggage and attendants, under the protection of the British lion, who has always a friendly paw for *les rois en exil.*

Near us is a man with a bulging forehead and a badly-fitting frock-coat of black broadcloth – a noted mesmerist from America, with a little Texan wife fantastically gowned; she, poor soul, having a picturesque instinct, but no technique.

Beyond him is a man of middle age, with a serious countenance, lean and bold as the head of Caesar, and an air of great distinction. It is Sir William Robinson, an Irishman, a well-known composer, and a colonial governor. Beside him sits Sir Henry Wrenfordsly, a colonial chief-justice. At their table is Lady Broome, a tall, handsome woman with a noble outline of brow and head. Under the title of Lady Barker, she is the author of many well-known and delightful books on life in the Antipodes. Sir Napier Broome is also tall and handsome, and is on his way home from an Australian governorship.

"I should like to meet her," I tell our informant, hoping he *knows* her, not merely *of* her.

After tiffin, he introduces us. Mrs. Kelly has gone back to her room for a nap, and so Lady Barker and I walk together and get acquainted. I freely tell her all about my trip, so easy she is to talk to.

"What a delight you are," she says. "You would fit in nicely with our society. You know, my husband was a reporter, too. He still writes a little now and then."

"Does he? I should like to visit you in England. There are so many sites I wish to see, but won't have the least bit of time this trip."

"You must come! Rudyard would love you."

"Kipling? You are acquainted with Rudyard Kipling?"

She smiles slightly, knowing she has impressed me. "Yes, yes. There are several literary talents in our circles." She thinks a moment before continuing. "Herbert Spencer, of course, and I must introduce you to Rhoda Broughton. I think you two will hit it off splendidly."

In the arcade that faces on the street are native shops – tiny cells full of basket-work, wrought brass, laces, jewels; carvings in ivory, ebony, and tortoise-shell; India shawls and silks, Cingalese silver-work, and such small trinkets and souvenirs best calculated to lure the shy rupee from its lair in the traveler's pocket.

Most of these shops are kept by Moormen – large persons in freckled calico petticoats, heads shaven quite clean and covered with a little red basket too small for the purpose. They inspire annoying disgust and suspicion by their craven oiliness; their wares for the most part not worth a tenth of the sums asked.

Jewels are to be had at astonishing rates – cat's-eyes and moonstones being sold carelessly by the handful. The arcade is full of itinerant merchants who carry their stock of precious stones – sometimes quite valuable – tied up in a dingy rag, disposing of them by methods of barter quite unique.

Twenty times the proper value is demanded, and poignant outcries of bitter astonishment greet the unbelievably meager offer of the Sahib, who should be as father and as mother to the merchant, but who proffers him only an insult. The rag is tied up in wounded amazement half a dozen times before a compromise suggests itself.

Innocent joy dawns on the vender's countenance – chance shall settle it. Will the Sahib toss to decide whether he shall give for this beautiful cat's-eye two pounds or five?

The original sum asked having been twenty, the Sahib sees signs of relenting and consents to try the turn of the coin. The toss is fairly conducted, and whether he wins or loses, the importunate merchant appears content, as in any case he makes a profit.

A snake-charmer is squatting in the dust before the hotel, performing feats of juggling: playfully depositing an egg in one ear, and in a moment picking it, with a sweet smile of surprise, out of the other.

Tossing into the air a coconut, which obviously he has no present use for, as it remains up there out of sight for a time while he goes on with his other tricks, until we are suddenly aware of its lying beside him, and cannot recall whether it was there from the first or not.

Rubbing his egg between open, outstretched palms until they meet and the egg is rubbed away to nothing at all, and restoring it to existence by rotary movements of his palms in the opposite direction.

Simple feats that are surprising, because he is quite naked save for a turban and a loin-cloth, and has no aids to his art but the brown cotton bag in which he carries his few properties, and a small flat basket where a cobra is coiled. But his hands are marvelously deft and supple – the hands of an old race, slim, pliant, well modeled, and exquisitely dexterous.

He takes off the cover of the snake basket, the reptile within lying sullenly sluggish until a rap over the head induces him to lift himself angrily, puff out his throat, and make ready to strike. But his master is playing a low, monotonous tune on a tiny bamboo flute, with his eyes fastened upon the snake's eyes, and swaying his nude body slowly from side to side.

The serpent stirs restlessly, and flickers his wicked, thin red tongue; but the sleepy tune drones on and on, and the brown body moves to and fro – to and fro. Presently the serpent begins to wave softly, following the movements of the man's body and with his eyes fixed on the man's eyes, and so in time sinks slowly in a languid heap of relaxed folds.

The music grows fainter, fainter, dies away to a breath – a whisper – ceases. The man hangs the helpless inert serpent – drunk with the insistent low whine of the flute – about his bare neck and breast, and comes forward to beg a rupee for his pains.

We – the Lady from Boston, her son, the Ceylon tea-planter, and I – hire a guide and carriage and go for a drive. Through the town, past the tall clock tower whose flashing light showed our path last night; past the banks and the haunts of the money-changers – "shroffs" clad in crisp white buttoned with gold, and with great circles of thin gold wire in their ears and black-and-gold head-dresses on their smooth-shaven crowns. Past the beautiful sickle-shaped beach of Galle Face, and then inland along the shadowy dank roads under the heavy green vault of the multitudinous palms – coconut palms (forty millions of these, the guide says), Palmyra palms, from which the heady palm-wine is made; Kitul palms that yield sugar and sago; talipot palms, upon whose papyrus-like leaves were inscribed the sacred writings – Mahawanso – five hundred years before Christ, and preserved twenty-two centuries at Wihares; and the areca palm, that gives the nuts the natives chew with their betel leaves, turning their smiles a shocking blood-red.

We pass banyan trees with roots like huge pythons coiling through the grass, and down-dropped stems from the far-spreading branches, making dim, leafy cloisters. Breadfruit trees, monster ferns, pools full of lotus plants, and orchids growing almost as freely as weeds.

The guide, a gentlemanly person in a skirt, has the usual mane of rippling hair bound in a sleek knot at the nape. My curiosity gets the better of me again. "Will you undo your hair?" I move my hand in a circular motion to emphasize what I mean.

He grins at my request and untwists the knot. His hair falls far below his waist in silky black waves. After we all ooh and ah, he restores it in a moment by a quick turn of the wrist to its former neat compactness.

I pull out a hairpin and give it to him.

He turns it over, examining it. "What is it?"

"In America, the women use these to hold our hairstyles in place. You may have it."

"Thank you, Mem Sahib." He has never seen a hairpin, and the gift of one of mine childishly delights and amuses him. He thrusts it in and out of his hair and finally fastens it upon a string of queer charms and fetishes worn in his bosom.

From time to time along the road we come upon old women sitting upon the earth with little stores of nuts, lime, and betel leaves spread before them for the refreshment of the wayfarer. We stop at one, and our guide gets out of the carriage.

He wraps for me a bit of areca nut with a paste of wet lime in a leaf of the betel pepper and bids me chew it.

I am hesitant, but the son from Boston raises his eyebrows in challenge. "Try it. You'll always regret it if you don't. Aren't you curious as to why they like it so much?"

"Not really. Sometimes I am able to bridle my curiosity." But not this time. I take a small bite.

Instantly my mouth is full of a liquid red as blood, and tongue and lips are shriveled with a sharp aromatic astringent resembling cloves. I hasten to spit it out, but my lips are hot and acrid from the brief experiment. I check my gown to make sure it has not been stained.

Robert takes my leftovers, and he tries a small bite. He tries not to spit it out, but in the end he does.

I point at his bright red-stained mouth and laugh. "You look like a native now!"

He grins, making the effect worse.

The entire population of Ceylon is wedded to the betel habit, save the servants of Europeans who object to the unpleasant vampire red of the stained mouth and corroded teeth. It harms no more than tobacco, I'm told, and the natives prefer it even to food.

"Mem Sahib," says the guide, touching his brow with his fingers, and giving me one of those smiling glances – "you are my father and my mother. Will you that we go to the cinnamon gardens?" On the way, he feeds upon ripe mangoes that have a reddish custard-like pulp, sweetly musky in flavor.

It is a wonder I trust to eat anything he offers me now, but I do.

From among the cinnamon bushes growing without order in the white sand, and breathing faint odors in the steaming heat, starts out a lean, naked lad begging for alms. He is not to be shaken off, following in a leaping dance with flying hair and a white-toothed smile, clapping his elbows against his ribs with a noise like castanets, and rattling his bones together loudly and merrily as though a skeleton pranced after us through the dust, so that we are fain to end the exhibition of his unique powers with a few coins.

In the museum that stands in the cinnamon gardens we find Eden's serpents – the reverse side of this painted island paradise. The dull, venomous cobra in his spotted cowl; clammy, strangling folds of long pythons; twenty-foot sharks with horrid semi-circular hedges of teeth – the wolves of these pearl-sown seas – and endless stinging, biting, poisoning creatures.

Here are also the uncouthly hideous masks of the old devil dancers, great gold ornaments, splendid robes, and the ingeniously murderous weapons of this mild-mannered race, who count in their history twenty-six kings done treacherously to death.

In other rooms are the stuffed skins of beautiful birds, huge mammals, and collections of rich-colored butterflies and moths.

––––––––

A LONG ROAD among palms. Palm-thatched huts, with idle brown folk, half naked, dreaming in the heat. A door in a ruinous wall – shaven-headed priests in yellow robes – then a dim temple, with tall gods whose heads reach stiffly up to the roof.

Penetrating jasmine odors from altars heaped with stemless pink blossoms, and the Lord Buddha reclining on his elbow, drowsing in the hot semi-darkness among the stifling scents. He is forty feet long, painted a coarse vivid crimson and yellow, but his flat wooden face is fixed in the same passive, low-lidded calm that we saw upon it when he sat on his lotus among the Japanese roses, or listened in his tiny mountain shrine at Penang to loud voices of the waters.

A Nirvana peace, undisturbed by passions or pity, dreaming eternal dreams in the hot, perfumed gloom. About the walls are painted in archaic frescoes the pains and toils of his fifty incarnations of Buddhahood, through which he attained at last to this immortal peace. Vishnu and Siva are the tall gods that stand by the doorway, for to these he gives room and shares with them his altar flowers.

A swarm closes about us as we emerge, crying for alms, and not to be ignored or beaten off. They have roused themselves from their lethargy in the simmering gloom of the palm-shaded huts, and throng clamorous and insistent for the charity the Lord Buddha has enjoined, impeding our footsteps and clinging to the carriage.

Old women hold out the little soft hands of the dimpled naked babies they carry on their hip. They themselves are hideous, repulsive hags – mere wrinkled, disgusting rags of humanity, with red-stained, toothless mouths; and this at forty years.

The young women are plump and pretty, with a discontented knot in their brows, and hopeless, peevish mouths – femininity being a perplexing and bitter burden in the East. Small brown imps, naked as Adam, save for a heavy silver necklace hung about their fat, little stomachs, cling to our knees and use their fine eyes with a coquette's conscious power, smilingly seducing the coin out of our pockets.

Mrs. Kelly is powerless against them. Despite the protests of her son, she gives each a coin and we make our escape.

35

S HORTLY AFTER MY RETURN TO HONG KONG,
I sailed for Japan on the *Oceanic*, the same ship that would
take me on to San Francisco. A number of friends, who had
contributed so much towards my pleasure and comfort during
my stay in British China, came to the ship to say farewell, and
most regretfully did I take leave of them.

Captain Smith took us into his cabin, where we all touched
glasses and wished one another success, happiness and the other
good things of this earth. The last moment having come, the final
goodbye being said, we parted, and I was started on my way to
the land of the Mikado.

The monkey had been transferred for me from the *Oriental*.
Meeting the stewardess, I asked if she knew about the creature, to
which she replied dryly:

"We have met."

She showed me her arm bandaged from the wrist to the
shoulder.

"What did you do?" I asked in consternation.

"I did nothing but scream; the monkey did the rest!" She
marched away.

We spent New Year's Eve between Hong Kong and Yokohama.
The day had been so warm that we wore no wraps. In the forepart
of the evening, the passengers sat together in Social Hall talking,
telling stories and laughing at them.

I learned that the *Oceanic* had quite a history. When it was designed and launched twenty years ago by Mr. Harland of Belfast, it startled the shipping world.

"He was the first to introduce improvements for the comfort of passengers," explained a well-seasoned travel who appeared thrilled to have gathered an audience to lecture. "Improvements such as placing the saloon amid ships, away from the engine noise, and especially the racing of the screw in rough weather."

"I suppose that is only logical," I replied, letting him know I was not that impressed.

"Oh, but before that time, ships were gloomy affairs, constructed with barely a thought of the happiness of passengers. Mr. Harland, in the *Oceanic*, was the first to provide a promenade deck and to give the saloon and staterooms a light and cheerful appearance." He paused for a drink.

"In fact, the *Oceanic* was such a new departure that it aroused the jealousy of other ship companies. They condemned the ship as unseaworthy!" The gentleman shook his head and chuckled. "The outcry against the ship was so great that sailors and firemen were given extra wages to induce them to make the first trip."

We all laughed, though perhaps a bit nervously as we were right now fully trusting in her seaworthiness.

"Instead of being the great failure, the *Oceanic* proved a great success. No expense was spared to make this ship comfortable for the passengers. You must admit, the catering rivals that of a first-class hotel. Passengers are accorded every liberty, and the officers do their utmost to make their guests feel at home."

We all agreed. We had been treated very well, indeed.

"She became the greyhound of the Atlantic, afterwards being transferred to the Pacific in 1875. In the Orient the *Oceanic* is the favorite ship, and people wait for months so as to travel on her. They know she makes her voyages with speed and regularity and comfort."

He tapped his foot as if to slap congratulations on the ship. "She seems to grow younger with years."

As the man spoke, I examined the subject of our interest. I had to admit she had retained a look of positive newness.

233

"Why, just last November, she made the fastest trip on record between Yokohama and San Francisco."

I felt a ringing in my ears as the man rushed on. Last November was when that other reporter made the reverse trip: San Francisco to Yokohama. And all the while I was blissfully unaware, meandering from ship to train to ship, following the schedules like every other work-a-day passenger, and she was truly racing. Not racing against time, but taking my own idea and trying to best me. I was about to get up to walk along said promenade deck to cool my temper when the captain strode in with a diversion – an organette.

"Time for music!" he called out as he and the doctor set down the beautiful wooden box and another filled with paper music scrolls. The lecturer was quickly abandoned as we crowded around the table to hear the music.

The captain had already loaded *Fisher's Hornpipe* and started cranking the music before we had finished gathering. When that was over, he chose another from his goodly collection of polkas and folk songs. When the captain's arm got tired of the crank, the doctor would take over grinding out the music while the captain changed out the paper rolls.

During the changing of the scrolls, our lecturer filled the space with an explanation of how the air is cranked through wooden reeds to sound the notes cut into the paper. Every one of us could probably build our own; he was so thorough in the telling.

Later in the evening we went to the dining hall where the purser had punch and champagne and oysters for us, a rare treat which he had prepared in America just for this occasion.

What children we all become on board a ship. After oysters we were up to all sorts of childish tricks.

"I have a game," announced the doctor as we sat around the table. "I'm going to give each of you a word to say." He then went in rotation around the table, telling us to say sounds like: Ish! Ash! Osh!

"Now, does everyone remember their word?"

We did.

234

"On the count of three, everyone shout your word and we'll see if we can't frighten the other tables. Don't be bashful or it won't work."

As he counted with upheld fingers, he encouraged us to take a deep breath. At three fingers we all shouted! Ish! Ash! Osh!

What came from our table was one great big sneeze – the most gigantic and absurd sneeze I ever heard in my life. We laughed at the shocked expressions of the other tables. They did not find our antics equally amusing, but they tolerated us.

Afterwards a jolly man from Yokohama, whose wife was equally jolly and lively-spirited, taught us a song consisting of one line to a melody quite simple and catching.

"Sweetly sings the donkey when he goes to grass/ Sweetly sings the donkey when he goes to grass/ Ec-ho! Ec-ho! Ec-ho!"

When eight bells rang, we rose and sang "Auld Lang Syne" with glasses in hand, and on the last echo of the good old song, toasted the death of the old year and the birth of the new. We shook hands around, each wishing the other a happy New Year. The year 1889 was ended, and 1890 with its pleasures and pains began.

Shortly after, the women passengers retired. I went to sleep, lulled by the sounds of familiar Negro melodies sung by the men in the smoking-room beneath my cabin.

36

A NEW YEAR IN WHICH ELIZABETH BISLAND GETS A LETTER FROM HOME AND HAS HER HEART STOLEN AWAY.

I T IS THE LAST NIGHT OF THE OLD YEAR, and the dining hall at the hotel has been converted into a ballroom. The men, all in white, with colorful sashes about their middle, are circling languidly with pretty English girls in their arms. A high, warm wind whirls through the veranda and flutters the draperies of the lookers-on.

The woman from Texas, in a fearful and wonderful costume, that casts a slight but comprehensive glance at the modes of three centuries and muddles them all. She is tossing her powdered head and flirting shrilly with the soft-voiced governor with the Caesar face.

A ruddy old soldier with gray hair is moodily mounting guard over his three lank-elbowed partnerless daughters, whose plump and pleasing mamma is frolicking jovially about, clasped to the bosom of all Ceylon's military ornaments.

Tonight Wordsworth's grandson looks like a *Punch* magazine cartoon designed to order by the artist George du Maurier, one where the proud don't know how ridiculous they look to those around them. He is waltzing, lazily graceful, with one of the smartly-gowned blond girls. Despite his vain manner, I still wish to make his acquaintance, only that I could say I met Wordsworth's grandson! But I will never approach him on my own, to appear as one of those doting girls. What does that say about my vanity?

236

I don't stay for long with the merry-makers, but retire to my room. Though I have made many friends here, I am tired and prefer a good night's sleep to dancing all the night. I say goodnight to my attendant, still stationed outside my door. He seems never to go away, for at whatever hour I need him he is there. Even at night he does not desert his post, unrolling a rug and sleeping where he sat all day.

After completing my toilet, I lie on the bed in the dark. Faint rhythmic breathings of the music come to my chamber window. It is in moments like this that I marvel anew that I am traveling alone around the world. The quick decisions that went into such a feat!

What if Charles Wetmore meets a smartly-gowned blond girl of his own while I am gone, for surely there are parties galore to choose from in New York?

At the same time, there is something romantic about changing over to a new year when one is on an adventure such as this. It is an experience I will always look back on in awe.

The night is hot and silent – full of musky perfumes, of vague ghostly stirrings, of "old unhappy far-off things," that move one with poignant mysterious memories. At some point, I feel myself drifting away from the old year and know I will wake up in the new.

————

MORNING! – THE NEW year is coming in a beautiful green dawn. A chrysoberyl sky, translucent golden green, a misty green sea, and an ocean of feathery green plumes tossing noiselessly, as with a great silent joy, in the morning wind.

I have sprung out of bed to receive a letter – my first one from home. A few lines, scrawled on the other side of the world, that I lean from the window to read in the faint early light. How beautiful they make the new year seem.

Blessed Molly. She calculated where I would be and timed the letter perfectly. I forgive her for all the fun she is having at home without me. Whatever this coming year will contain of grief and rebuffs, at least it has begun with one good moment, and for that it is well to be grateful.

At Ceylon the Australian mail-ship *Britannia* waits for us. She is one of the enormous Peninsular and Oriental vessels built in Queen Victoria's Golden Jubilee year and is on her way home to England.

Here again farewells: to the dear little old lady from Boston and to my kind and charming friend the Ceylon tea-planter, who has placed me under an endless debt of gratitude by his many courtesies.

"Remember," says Mrs. Kelly. "Visit me in Boston, and we will walk in the Commons together."

"Yours is an offer difficult to resist," I tell her. "I'll have to wait and see what my next assignment is when I get home." I walk with the crowd to the *Britannia* and turn to give my friends one last farewell wave. We have made many memories together.

It is four o'clock in the afternoon of the 1st of January when we swing out of the harbor and direct our course towards Africa. *Africa*!

The height of luxury is achieved on these Peninsular and Oriental steamships. No steerage travel being provided for, space is not stinted to first-class passengers. Saloons, decks, and bedrooms are ample and handsome. The ship's company, Australians on their way home to England, have made themselves thoroughly at home for the six weeks' cruise.

Their rooms they have hung with photographs and drapery and bits of bric-à-brac, and on deck each one has a long bamboo lounging-chair, a little table, and a tea-service for that beautiful ceremony of five-o'clock tea – all being made possible by the fact that the sea is smooth as glass and the decks level as a drawing room floor.

A particularly friendly matron known by the name of Mrs. Detmold stops me as I am touring the ship. She is elegant with her silver hair pulled up and tucked into a straw hat banded with a navy ribbon.

"Are you alone?" she asks. "You must join me for this afternoon tea."

After I agree, she explains where I will find her. Then she adds, "I will introduce you to our favorite person on board." She smiles and her eyes dance. "You might have your heart stolen away."

"Oh?" I reply. I am not sure that I am prepared for such a happening. The lady from Boston harbored a small wish that her son would steal my heart, but it seems my heart is not so easily lost.

After learning both the layout of the vessel and the list of entertainments: three times a week, the band plays for dancing on deck; tableaux, private theatricals, and fancy balls fill the evenings, and in the afternoons the after-part of the ship is lively with games of cricket, I go to afternoon tea.

I meet Mrs. Detmold where she is holding court on deck and soon discover that the principal personage on board is not this graceful woman, nor an eligible young man as I had supposed, but a grandchild, Miss Ethel Roma Detmold, aged two and a half years, and familiarly known as Baby Detmold.

There are other infants aboard, but merely "the common or garden" baby, not to be mentioned with this blue-and-gold girl child who sparkles out upon us a morning vision in a white frock and an enigmatic smile.

"Lellow hat!" she exclaims, showing me her grandmother's bonnet.

At that simple declaration, I have joined her merry band of followers and know this portion of my trip will be delightful.

Watching her for the smallest amount of time, I learn the entire male force of the ship is her slave, and trailing about after her, humbly suing for favors she is most cautious in granting, she possessing already the secret of power over her kind in an airy, joyous indifference to anyone's attentions and services, which we therefore persist in thrusting upon her.

The cook makes a rare appearance, bringing up his pet chicken to be admired. "Would you like to hold her?" he asks. Baby Detmold watches carefully as several people attempt to meet the chicken, who forthwith flies away. Then, laughing with glee, she lunges for the chicken, which allows itself to be hauled about by one leg and then squeezed violently to her youthful bosom, and, far from protesting, looks foolishly flattered by the notice of this imperious cherub.

All women are not borne free and equal. There is some subtle force in this tiny turquoise-eyed coquette which will secure for her without effort, her life through, devotion other women may not win with endless sacrifices or oceans of tears.

———

ALWAYS ABOVE AND below us it is intensely blue, hot, and calm. Flights of film-winged fishes rise from our path and flit away like flocks of sea-sparrows. Sometimes a whale blows up a column of shining spray and leaves a green wake to show his hidden path. But nothing marks the passing of the hours save the coming and going of light.

When the azure blossom of the day dies in irised splendors, rosy clouds float up over the horizon's edge like wandering fairy islands drifting at will in a golden world – vanishing when the moon appears.

Magical white nights of ineffable stillness and purity fade into the blaze of daffodil dawns. Time goes by in lotus dreams that have no memory of a past or reckoning of a future 'til we wake suddenly and find anchor cast in the Gulf of Aden.

Red barren masses of stone, broken and jagged *"like an old lion's cheek teeth."* The land is astonishing dry, all the more startling by contrast with the fierce verdure of the lands we have last seen. Not a drop of rain has fallen here in three years, and no green thing lives in the place.

Even the tawny hills rot and fall to dust. The earth is an impalpable dun powder that no roots could grasp; the rocks are seamed, cracked, and withered to the heart, the dust and bones of a dead land.

As a coaling station and harbor from which warships may guard the entrance of the Red Sea, Aden is valuable; and therefore, like Hong Kong, Singapore, Penang, Ceylon – like everything much worth having in this part of the world – it is an English possession.

There are wharves of heavy masonry; the governor's residence, a bungalow with a large veranda protected by green shutters, standing on a little eminence some distance back from the water; and one narrow street of heavy white stone houses with flat roofs, fringing the shore.

The Detmolds hire a carriage to convey us to the Tanks – the only bit of sightseeing to be done at Aden. These Tanks are of unknown antiquity and are variously attributed to Solomon, the Queen of Sheba, the Arabs, and – as a last guess – to the Phoenicians.

Historians, when in doubt, always accuse the Phoenicians.

In this rainless region, where water falls only at intervals of years, it was necessary to collect and preserve it all, and someone built among the hills huge stone basins with capacity of hundreds of thousands of gallons. These basins are quite perfect still, though the name of the faithful builder thereof has long ago perished.

The road winds upward from the sea to a barrier of rocks, and pierces them with a black echoing pass two hundred feet high and fifteen wide, where the English fortifications lie – a place to be held by twenty men against an army. Here we find Tommy Atkins again, still clad in white linen from top to toe and still rosily swaggering.

"Miss." One especially young example tilts his hat at me as I walk past.

On the other side of the wall of hills is the town, a motley assemblage of more flat-topped stone dwellings, all lime-washed as white as snow. In the midst is a well where women in flowing drapery with tall jars draw water as if posing for Bible illustrations and a camel market in which fifty or more of the brown, ungainly beasts have been relieved of their burdens and lain down for the night – doubled into uncomfortable heaps.

The camels are a curiosity for Baby Detmold, and she squeals with delight until they answer her back with bubbling and moaning of querulous discontent. She nestles her little face into her granny's puffed sleeves, and we love her all the more.

We rattle through the silent, dusty town and find beyond it a garden where a dozen feeble trees have by constant watering been induced to grow as high as our heads, but appear discouraged and drooping and ready to give up the effort at any moment.

Behind these are the irregular bowls of masonry set in the clefts at the foot of the rocks, and stretching enormous thirsty mouths open to the arid hills and rainless sky. The tanks are terraced down the sides with steps by which the retreating water – when there is water – can be followed.

"We see only thirteen tanks today," says our guide. "Though there were many more in the past. The British have restored these ones here, hoping to use them as they were once used to gather the water and protect the town from flooding. However, their restored nature did not live up to everyone's hopes. Instead, the people here rely on the condensing-engine and the inexhaustible supply of the sea."

Night is coming on. There is a crystalline luminosity in this dry air that the vanished sun leaves faintly golden-green. Every fold and crevice of the red rock wall overflows with intense violet shadows that still are full of light.

There is no evening mistiness of vision: the little flat white town, the shore, the turbaned figures moving to and fro in the streets, the ships afloat on the glassy sea, the tawny outline of the rocks – all standing out with keen clearness through the deepening of the twilight.

So might have looked some Syrian evening of long ago, and, as if to answer the thought, there slowly lifts itself above the crest of the hills, in the green dusk, a huge white planet – the Star in the East!

The dusk has vanished when we reach the wharf for our return to the ship – "At one stride comes the dark" just as in "The Rime of the Ancient Mariner," and suddenly, in an instant, innumerable glittering hosts rush into the heavens with a wild, astonishing splendor, startling as the blare of trumpets, unimaginable myriads, unreckonable millions.

As our oars dip, the water answers with equal multitudes of wan sea-stars that whirl and wimple through the flood. Our guide suggests that we return to the Tanks again by moonlight. "You are already here," he says. "I can assure you that those who see the Tanks by night speak of their unending beauty when they return home."

Though I am unsure if our guide's desire is for us to see the Tanks by a different light, or to ensure his livelihood, I agree to go again. For he is correct on one account. I am here, and soon I will be home and will not have the chance again.

When the silver fire of a full moon, by whose light one can read and see colors, has swallowed up this glittering pageant, we go again to the Tanks – this time without Baby Detmold, who is sleeping – passing on the route a loaded train of camels lurching away to the desert through the black shadows of the pass, and, stepping beside them, lean, swarthy Arabs, draped stately in white – such a caravan as might have gone down into Egypt to buy corn from Pharaoh four thousand years ago – nothing in the interval changed in any way.

Our footsteps and our voices echo in hollow whispers from the empty Tanks and the mysterious shadows of the hills, though we walk lightly and speak softly, awed by the vast calm radiance of the African night. Other than this, it is very silent in this dead and desert spot: not a leaf to rustle, not an insect to cry – and even the sea has no speech. The world grows dreamlike and unreal in the white silence.

We should feel no surprise to come suddenly among the rocks upon a gaunt Hebrew with wild eyes, clothed in skins, and wrestling in the desert with the old unsolvable riddles of existence – a prophet whose scorching words should wither away in one terrible instant all the falsities and frivolities of our lives, leaving us gaping aghast in the awful visage of Truth.

Nor should we start to hear the thin, high voice of a wandering lad with the shadow of a crown above his brow, who should come chanting psalms of longing for green pastures and still waters.

It is a night and a place for such things as these, and I am glad I chose to bear witness.

The town, beyond which shines the silver sea, is white as pearls in the moonlight, with here and there a yellow gleam from a lamp through an open door. The population is gathered in the square playing dominoes and games of chance at little tables and drinking coffee – liquor being forbidden to these Mohammedans.

There are bearded Arabs with delicate features and grave, sad eyes, who fold their white woolen cloaks called burnouses about them with a wonderful effect of dignity, and more jovial and half-naked Negroes of every tint and race – from Zanzibar, the Sudan, Abyssinia.

The Sudanese with beardless mouths full of ivory teeth and long wool combed straight out and vividly red, made so by being plastered down for a week under a coat of lime. Egypt and England know well how these men fight; yet when I lean forward and take into my hand the little case of camel-skin hanging on the muscular black breast of one of these gigantic Africans, and ask "What is in here?" he laughs the same mellow, amiable laugh I should hear from a Negro at home on the plantation, did I show a like familiarity and interest. "Verses from the Koran."

Our way home lies through a tunnel beneath the fort. The port is fast asleep, and in the distance a man-of-war is slowly steaming out of the harbor on its way to the lower coast to over-awe the Portuguese making futile protests against English domination in the neighborhood of Delagoa Bay.

———

QUITE IN A moment it seems, it is tomorrow – our last day in the tropics – and I go up on deck before the sun has risen, into the delicious moist warmth of the equatorial morning.

A young man is lounging in one of the bamboo chairs in a negligee of India silk – drinking a tiny cup of coffee and enjoying the early freshness. No one else is visible.

I hesitate a moment, conscious of the dishevelment of locks beneath the lace scarf tied under my chin, but think better of the hesitation and remain. I may never see this again, this world, where one is really for the first time "Lord of the senses five," as Tennyson suggests – where the light of night and of day have a new meaning; where one is drenched and steeped in color and perfume; where the husk of callous dullness falls away and every sense replies to impressions with a keenness as of new-born faculties.

The young man's silky black head is ruffled too, and his yellow eyes still sleepy as he comes and leans over the rail. He is holding a little black pipe in a slim olive hand that is tipped with deep-tinted onyx-like nails, and with it he points to the first canoe putting out from shore. It is a long brown boat, very narrow, and filled with oranges heaped up in the centre. It is cutting a delicate furrow along the pearly lilac of the glass-like sea.

A faint gray mist, scarcely more than a film, lies along the shore. Above it the red rocks stand up sharply against the white sky, which the coming sun is changing to gold.

The young man turns and smiles, showing a row of white teeth through lips as red as pomegranate flowers. He is English, but takes on here certain warm tones of color like a Spaniard.

Every moment I have spent in the tropics is to me just as vivid as this. I see everything. Not a beauty, not a touch of color, escapes me. Every moment of the day means intense delight, beauty, life, and I don't regret my decision to race around the world. It is well to have thus once really lived.

Soon, the deck swarms with native merchants selling ostrich feathers, grass mats and baskets from Zanzibar, ornaments of shells, boxes of Turkish Delight, embroideries, photographs, and a three-months-old lion cub in a wooden cage.

The Bombay mail, for which we waited, has arrived, and new passengers come ashore with mountains of luggage. Among them is a man with a heavy, smooth, pink face, an overhanging upper lip and long white hair.

"Do you know who that is?" asks a man I recognize from our trip to the Tanks, a soft-spoken Mr. Goodman.

"I'm sure you will tell me."

"It is Bradlaugh, the famous atheist. He fought the whole House of Commons and forced it to admit him without taking the oath."

"And who is that with him?" I ask, testing his superior knowledge.

"His colleague, Sir William Wedderburn. He is a Scotch baronet whose heart is overflowing with vague tenderness for all mankind." He waved his hand as if dismissing the baronet. "They are returning from India. Some such congress of natives agitating for representative government. But do you know who we are really waiting for?"

"I cannot imagine."

"Why, Mr. Stanley!"

"Mr. Henry Stanley?" His was a name I recognized. A fellow American journalist made famous for finding the missionary Dr. Livingstone. "What has he been doing?"

"They say he has just arrived on the coast from the interior of Africa, and there is talk of his going home in our ship."

"I should very much like to make his acquaintance."

But we learn the government has sent down a special convoy to take him to Egypt, and we steam away without him.

Though I never had the chance to meet Mr. Stanley, I did make the acquaintance of the British atheist. Bradlaugh proves to be a jovial person, with an astounding ingenuity in misplacing h's, and an amusing little way of confiding small details concerning himself with an air of expecting you to snatch out a notebook and jot them down as one who should later make an article for one of the reviews, "Some Confidential Talks with Charles Bradlaugh, M.P."

A cold west wind meets us in the Red Sea; the passengers get out their furs, and there is no more lounging on deck – one must walk briskly or sit in the sun wrapped in rugs.

I suppose this is the way it will be from now on. I am headed home and back into winter. I wonder how cold it has been in our apartment, and if Molly has enough coal.

I wake one night missing the throbbings of the screw and find that we are going at a snail's pace in smooth water. The moon is very dim behind the clouds, and from the porthole it would appear that we are sailing across endless expanses of sand: nothing else is to be seen.

Morning shows a narrow ditch in a desert, half full of green water – so narrow and so shallow apparently that nothing would convince us our great ship could pass through save the actual proof of its doing so. The mighty Suez at last. After seeing it, I admit it does not measure up to my imagination.

At one of the wider parts made for this purpose, we pass a French troopship which dips her colors and sends a ringing cheer from the throats of the red-trousered soldiers on their way to Tonquin.

Later a dead Arab floats by in the green water, but is regarded with indifference as a common episode and merely suggestive of an imprudent quarrel overnight.

There are some sights in the East that I shall never get used to.

37

IN WHICH NELLIE BLY GOES SIGHTSEEING IN JAPAN
AND IS IMPRESSED BY ANOTHER MONKEY.

AFTER SEEING HONG KONG WITH ITS wharfs crowded with dirty boats manned by still dirtier people, and its streets packed with a filthy crowd, Yokohama has a cleaned-up Sunday appearance.

Travelers are taken from the ships, which anchor some distance out in the bay, to the land in small steam launches. From here we travel by jinricksha.

The Japanese jinricksha men were a gratifying improvement upon those I saw from Ceylon to China. They presented no sight of filthy rags, nor naked bodies, nor smell of grease. Clad in neat navy-blue garments, their little pudgy legs encased in unwrinkled tights, the upper half of their bodies in short jackets with wide flowing sleeves; their clean, good-natured faces, peeping from beneath comical mushroom-shaped hats; their blue-black, wiry locks cropped just above the nape of the neck, they offered a striking contrast to the jinricksha men of other countries.

Rain the night previous had left the streets muddy and the air cool and crisp, but the sun creeping through the mistiness of early morning fell upon us with most gratifying warmth. We wrapped our knees with rugs while the 'ricksha men started off in a lively trot, and I observed as many Japanese as I could find.

On a cold day, one would imagine the Japanese were a nation of armless people. They fold their arms up in their long, loose sleeves. The Japanese women seem to know nothing whatever of bonnets, and may they never! On rainy days they tie white scarves over their wonderful hair-dressing, but a fellow passenger leans over to tell me that at other times they waddle bareheaded, with fan and umbrella, along the streets on their wooden clogs.

Talk about French heels! The Japanese sandal is a small board elevated on two pieces of thin wood fully five inches in height. They make the people look exactly as if they were on stilts. These queer shoes are fastened to the foot by a single strap running between toes number one and two, the wearer when walking necessarily maintaining a sliding instead of an up and down movement, in order to keep the shoe on.

We are deposited at the Grand Hotel, a large building with long verandas, wide halls and airy rooms, commanding an exquisite view of the lake in front. Barring an enormous and monotonous collection of rats, the Grand would have been considered a good hotel even in America.

At tiffin I met several people who have settled into the relaxed posture of those having spent time already in the area. A middle-aged gentleman, Mr. Clark, who sat to my left, took a keen interest in developing my knowledge of Japan.

"The majority of the Europeans live on The Bluff in those low white bungalows," he said pointing vaguely in that direction. "The fashion is to have great rooms and breezy verandas built in the hearts of Oriental gardens, where one can have an unsurpassed view of the Mississippi Bay, or can play tennis or cricket, or loll in hammocks, guarded from public gaze by luxurious green hedges."

"You seem to know what you are talking about," I said.

"Yes, I have been here on business for some time. I shall be joining you on your return trip to America."

"Where do the Japanese live?" I asked as I looked passed the veranda and out onto the street where several people in English dress were strolling, being passed by others carried on the jinrickshas. "I saw several on the ride over, but not nearly as many as I expected."

"They live across the canal in Shichiu, the native town. Would you like to see?" Mr. Clark asked those of us at the table. "I can arrange a show for you as well."

We did.

So in the cool of the evening we went to a house that had been specially engaged to see the dancing, or geisha, girls. The Japanese houses were just as our guide thoroughly explained – like play houses built of a thin shingle-like board. The houses were prettily decorated in honor of the new year. The decorations were simple, but effective. Rice trimmings mixed with sea-weed, orange, lobster and ferns were hung over every door to ensure a plentiful year, while as sentinels on either side were large tubs, in which are three thick bamboo stalks, with small evergreen trees for background. Arches were formed over the streets with bamboo saplings covered with light airy foliage.

At the door of the appointed house, we saw all the wooden shoes of the household, and we were asked to take off our shoes before entering.

"Take off my shoes?" said a fashionable lady in a tone that meant it was the last thing she would agree to do.

"Is that really necessary?" chimed in a gentleman.

"It is the custom," said Mr. Clark, already standing there in his stockings and looking rather absurd.

I held my tongue, but secretly hoped the shoe-wearers would win out. Eventually, we made a compromise by putting cloth slippers over our shoes.

The second floor had been converted into one room, with nothing in it except the matting covering the floor and a Japanese screen here and there. We sat upon the floor, for chairs there are none in Japan, but the exquisite matting is padded until it is as soft as velvet.

It was laughable to see us trying to sit down, and yet more so to see us endeavor to find a posture of ease for our limbs. We were about as graceful as an elephant dancing.

A smiling woman in a black kimono set several round and square charcoal boxes containing burning charcoal before us.

"These are the only Japanese stove," explained Mr. Clark. "They don't have chimneys or fireplaces."

Afterwards she brought a tray containing a number of long-stemmed pipes–Japanese women smoke constantly–a pot of tea and several small cups.

Impatiently, I awaited the geisha girls. In the tiny maidens glided at last, clad in exquisite trailing, angel-sleeved kimonos. The girls bowed gracefully, bending down until their heads touched their knees, then kneeling before us murmured gently a greeting which sounds like "Koinbanwa" drawing in their breath with a long, hissing suction, which, we were told, is a token of great honor.

The musicians sat down on the floor and began an alarming din upon samisens, drums and gongs, singing meanwhile through their pretty noses. If the noses were not so pretty, I am sure the music would be unbearable to one who has ever heard a chest note.

The geisha girls posed with open fan in hand above their heads, ready to begin the dance. They were very short with the slenderest of slender waists. Their soft and tender eyes were made blacker by painted lashes and brows; their midnight hair, stiffened with a gummy wash, was most wonderfully dressed in large coils and ornamented with gold and silver flowers and gilt paper pompons. The younger the girl, the more elaborate was her hair.

Their kimonos, of the most exquisite material, trailed all around them, and were loosely held together at the waist with an obi-sash; their long flowing sleeves fell back, showing their dimpled arms and baby hands.

Upon their tiny feet they wore cunning white linen socks cut with a place for the great toe. I am told that when they go out they wore wooden sandals.

The Japanese were the only women I ever saw who could rouge and powder and be not repulsive, but the more charming because of it. They powdered their faces and had a way of reddening their under lip just at the tip that gave them a most tempting look. The lips looked like two luxurious cherries.

The musicians began a long chanting strain, and these bits of beauty began the dance. With a grace, simply enchanting, they twirled their little fans, swayed their dainty bodies in a hundred different poses, each one more intoxicating than the other, all the while looking so childish and shy, with an innocent smile lurking about their lips, dimpling their soft cheeks, and their black eyes twinkling with the pleasure of the dance.

After the dance, the geisha girls made friends with me, examining, with surprised delight, my dress, my bracelets, my rings, my boots – to them the most wonderful and extraordinary things – my hair, my gloves, indeed they missed very little, and they approved of all. They told me I was very sweet, and they invited me to come again. In honor of the custom of my land – the Japanese never kiss – they pressed their soft, pouting lips to mine in parting.

"How is it they know English so well?" I asked Mr. Clark as we prepared to leave, he putting his shoes back on while the rest of us removed the slippers covering our footwear.

"English is taught in the Japan schools," he said.

The next day, a Japanese reporter from Tokyo came to interview me, his newspaper having translated and published the story of my visit to Jules Verne. Carefully he read the questions which he wished to ask me. They were written at intervals on long rolls of foolscap, the space to be filled in as I answered. I thought it a ridiculous system of interviewing.

Afterward, I went with the group to Kamakura to see the great bronze god, the image of Buddha, familiarly called Diabutsu. It stands in a verdant valley at the foot of two mountains. Built in 1250 by Ono Goroyemon, a famous bronze caster, it sits Japanese style and is fifty feet in height. The face is eight feet long, the eye is four feet, and the circumference of the thumb is over three feet.

Several people lined up to have their photographs taken, and Mr. Clark, who had his Kodak, asked if we would pose for him.

"Of course! Come along," I beckoned my new friends. The only regret of my trip, and one I can never cease to deplore, was that in my hasty departure I forgot to take a camera. On every ship and at every port, I met others with cameras and envied them.

Three of us were willing and climbed up and sat comfortably on its thumb.

"I rather like this," said a man called Henry, tapping the thumb. "Wonder if I could have it for $50,000?"

"Do you have a place to display it?" asked the other climber, whose name I had already forgotten.

"I would make a place. Could you imagine it tied to the deck of the *Oceanic*? It would make quite a sight sailing into the harbor."

But we decide the image is too precious to Japan. Years ago at the feast of the god, sacrifices were made to Diabutsu. Quite frequently the hollow interior would be heated to a white heat, and hundreds of victims were cast into the seething furnace in honor of the god.

It is different now, sacrifices being not the custom, and the hollow interior is harmlessly fitted up with tiny altars and a ladder stairway by which visitors can climb up into Diabutsu's eye, and from that height view the surrounding lovely country.

We also visited a very pretty temple nearby, saw a famous fan tree and a lotus pond, and spent some time at a most delightful teahouse, where two little girls served us with tea and sweets.

"Not only do the children learn English in school," Mr. Clark explained, "but the girls are taught graceful movements, how to receive, entertain and part with visitors, how to serve tea and sweets gracefully, and the proper way to use chopsticks."

It is a pretty sight to see a lovely woman use chopsticks. At a teahouse or at an ordinary dinner, a long paper laid at one's place contains a pair of chopsticks. The sticks are usually whittled in one piece and split only half apart to prove that they have never been used. Everyone breaks the sticks apart before eating, and after the meal they are destroyed.

Needing to get some of his own business taken care of, Mr. Clark arranged for several of us to go to Tokyo with a guide for one day. Their roads there are superb.

"You have modern street cars here," I exclaim.

The guide laughs at my ignorance. "It is true that a little while ago we knew nothing of railroads, or street cars, or engines, or electric lighting. However, we are too clever to waste our wits to rediscover inventions known to other nations. We sent to other countries for men who understood the secrets of such things, and at fabulous prices and under contracts of three, five and occasionally ten years, brought them here where the cleverest of Japanese watched and learned. When the contract is up, it is no longer necessary to fill the coffers of a foreigner. The employee is released, and their own man, fully qualified for the work, steps into the position."

The more we drove, the more I realized how very progressive the Japanese people were. They clung to their religion and their modes of life, which in many ways were superior to ours, but they readily adopted any trade or habit that was an improvement upon their own.

Several men in native costume rode by on bicycles. Then our guide pointed out a Japanese woman in European dress.

"She is looking very swell, yes?"

The woman wore the bodice of a European dress, which had been cut to fit a slender, tapering waist and was likely ready-made. But since the Japanese never saw a corset and their waists are enormous, the woman was only able to fasten one button at the neck, and from that point the bodice was permitted to spread.

I cocked an eyebrow. "She is alone in her European attempts?"

"Men in some trades have adopted European attire when it is more serviceable than their native dress. However, most women who tested the European dress found it uncomfortable and inartistic and went back to their kimonos."

"Where do they keep their belongings?"

"They carry silk card cases in their long sleeves. Their sleeves are to her what a boy's pockets are to him. Her cards, money, combs, hairpins, ornaments, and rice paper are all carried in her sleeves. Her rice paper is her handkerchief."

One of the ladies leaned in and whispered in my ear. "I heard the women kept the European underwear, which they found more healthful and comfortable than nothing at all."

The best proof of the comfort of kimonos lies in the fact that the European residents have adopted them entirely for indoor wear. Only their long subjection to fashion prevents their wearing them in public.

Before starting our sightseeing, our guide led us to a silk shop, where, thanks to Ah Cum's teachings on commerce, I was sure he would earn a commission if any of us bought anything. The shopkeeper showed me how kimonos are made in three parts, each part an inch or so longer than the other, but he could not tempt me to purchase one.

Thinking I was after something finer, he displayed a kimono a Japanese woman bought for the holidays. It was a suit, gray silk crepe, with pink peach blossoms dotting it here and there. The whole was lined with the softest pink silk, and the hem, which trails, was thickly padded with a delicate perfume sachet. The underclothing was of the flimsiest white silk. The whole thing cost sixty dollars, a dollar and a half of which paid for the making. Japanese clothing is sewed with what we call a basting stitch, but it is as durable as it could be if sewed with the smallest of stitches.

We visited the Mikado's Japanese and European castles, which are enclosed by a fifty-foot stone wall and three wide moats. Moving on, the guide brought us past a forest of superb trees on our way to the great Shiba temple. At the carved gate leading to the temple were hundreds of stone and bronze lanterns, which alone were worth a fortune. On either side of the gate were gigantic carved images of ferocious aspect. They were covered with wads of chewed paper.

"The school children must make very free with the images." I said. A statue in New York would never be allowed to remain a target such as this.

The guide explained, "It is not vandalism. The Japanese believe if they chew paper and throw it at these gods and it sticks, their prayers will be answered."

"A great many prayers must have been answered," I replied, eyeing the mess.

At another gate, I saw the most disreputable-looking god. It had no nose.

"What happened to this one?" I asked the guide.

"The Japanese believe if they have a pain or ache and they rub their hands over the face of that god, and then where the pain is located, they will be cured."

I can't say whether it cured them or not, but I know they rubbed away the nose of the god.

On our way to Uyeno Park, we passed a man uttering in a plaintive melody these words: "I'll give you a bath from head to toe for two cents."

Shocked, I called over to our guide's jinricksha. "Who is that man?"

"The blind are taught massage bathing. They are the only ones allowed to do so, and thus they develop a trade with which to live."

Still, I don't know that I would like a blind man bathing me from head to toe. I wondered how much of a living he was able to make.

At Uyeno Park, where they point out a tree planted by General Grant when on his tour around the world, I saw a most amusing monkey which belonged to the very interesting menagerie.

It was very large and had a scarlet face and gray fur. It was chained to the fence, and when Henry went up and talked to him, the monkey looked very sagacious and wise. In the little crowd that gathered around, quite out of the monkey's reach, was a young Japanese man, who, in a spirit of mischief, tossed a pebble at the red-faced mystery, who turned with a grieved and inquiring air to my friend.

"Go for him," my friend Henry responded, sympathetically, to the look, and the monkey turned and with its utmost strength endeavored to free itself so it could obey the bidding.

The surprised man made his escape, and the monkey quieted down, looking expressively at the place where the young man had stood and then at Henry for approval, which he obtained.

The keeper brought out dinner for the monkey, which consisted of two large boiled sweet potatoes. Henry broke one in two and the monkey greedily ate the inside, placing the remainder with the other potato on the fence between his feet. Suddenly he looked up, and as quick as a flash, he flung with his entire force which was something terrific, the remaining potato at the head of someone in the crowd.

There was some loud screaming and a scattering, but the potato, missing all heads, went crashing with such force against a board fence that every particle of it remained sticking there in one shapeless splotch.

The young Japanese man who had tossed the pebble at the monkey, and so earned his enmity, quietly shrunk away with a whitened face. He had returned unnoticed by all except the monkey, who tried to revenge himself with the potato. I admired the monkey's cleverness so much that I would have tried to buy him if I had not already owned one.

At the end of the day, we took the train back to our hotel, pleased at all the sights we had seen, and still chuckling over the clever monkey.

My last day in Yokohama was spent at a pleasant luncheon given for me on the *Omaha*, the American war vessel lying at Yokohama. Then I went with Mr. Clark's group to the Hundred Steps, at the top of which lives a Japanese belle, Oyuchisan, who is the theme for artist and poet and the admiration of tourists. These wooden stairs provide a narrow passageway between the area reserved for Europeans and the land for the natives of Yokohama. The view at the top looks out over the canal and tiled rooftops all the way to the bay. I meant to count the steps as we went down, but then someone asked me a question and I quite lost my place. I didn't think of it again until I stood on the bridge over the canal and looked back at the way we had come.

The prettiest sight in Japan, I think, is the native streets in the afternoons. Men, women, and children turn out to play shuttle-cock and fly kites. What an enchanting sight it is to see pretty women with cherry lips, black bright eyes, ornamented, glistening hair, exquisitely graceful gowns, tidy white-stockinged feet thrust into wooden sandals, dimpled cheeks, dimpled arms, dimpled baby hands, lovely, innocent, artless, happy, playing shuttlecock in the streets of Yokohama?

Japanese children are unlike any other children I ever saw at play. They always look happy and never seem to quarrel or cry. Little Japanese girls, elevated on wooden sandals and with babies almost as large as themselves tied on their backs, play shuttle-cock with an abandon that is terrifying until one grows confident of the fact that they move with as much agility as they could if their little backs were free from nursemaid burdens.

Japanese babies are such comical little fellows. They wear such wonderfully padded clothing that they are as shapeless as a feather pillow. Others may think, as I did, that the funny little shaven spots on their heads was a queer style of ornamentation, but it is not. I am assured the spots are shaven to keep their baby heads cool.

The Japanese are not only pretty and artistic but most obliging. Mr. Clark had his Kodak, and whenever we came upon an interesting group, he was always taking snap shots. No one objected, and especially were the children pleasant about being photographed. When he placed them in position, or asked them to stand as they were, they would pose like little drum-majors until he gave them permission to move.

I ate rice and eel. I visited the curio shops, one of which is built in imitation of a Japanese house, and was charmed with the exquisite art I saw there; in short, I found nothing but what delighted the finer senses while in Japan.

If I loved and married, I would say to my mate: "Come, I know where Eden is," and like editor and poet Edwin Arnold, desert the land of my birth for Japan, the land of love–beauty–poetry–cleanliness.

IN WHICH STORMS CAUSE NELLIE DELAY
WHILE CROSSING THE PACIFIC.

I T WAS A BRIGHT SUNNY MORNING WHEN I left Yokohama. A number of new friends in launches escorted me to the *Oceanic*, and when we hoisted anchor, the steam launches blew loud blasts upon their whistles in farewell to me, and the band upon the *Omaha* played "Home, Sweet Home," "Hail Columbia," and "The Girl I Left Behind Me," in my honor. I was grateful they were excited for me, and I waved my handkerchief so long after they were out of sight that I knew my arms would be sore for days.

Everything promised well for a pleasant and rapid voyage. Anticipating this, Chief-engineer Allen ordered to be written over the engines and throughout the engine room, this date and couplet:

For Nellie Bly,

We'll win or die.

January 20, 1890.

It was their motto and was all very sweet to me.

The runs were marvelous until the third day out, and then a storm came upon us.

"Don't worry. It will only last today," everyone said at table.

But the next day found it worse, and it continued, never abating a moment; head winds, head sea, wild rolling, frightful pitching, until I fretfully waited for noon when I would slip off to the dining room to see the run, hoping that it would have gained a few miles on the day before, and always being disappointed.

And they were all so good to me. Bless them for it. If possible, they suffered more over the prospect of my failure than I did.

"If I fail, I will never return to New York," I said despondently. "I would rather go in dead and successful than alive and behind time."

"Don't talk that way," Chief Allen said, "I will do anything for you in my power. I have worked the engines as they never were worked before; I have sworn at this storm until I have no words left; I have even prayed – I haven't prayed before for years – but I prayed that this storm may pass over and that we may get you in on time."

"I know that I am not a sinner," I laughed hysterically. "Day and night my plea has been, 'Be merciful to me, a sinner,' and as the mercy has not been forthcoming, the natural conclusion is that I'm not a sinner. It's hopeless, it's hopeless!"

At last a rumor spread that there was a Jonah on board the ship. It was thought over and talked over and, much to my dismay, I was told that the sailors said monkeys were Jonahs.

"Monkeys bring bad weather to ships," said the stewardess, whose scratched arms looked healed. "As long as the monkey is on board, we will have storms." She walked ominously away, having cast her seed of doubt in my brain.

39

IN WHICH ELIZABETH BISLAND RECEIVES WORD THAT SHE WILL NOT MAKE A VITAL CONNECTION.

A DIM AND LURID SUNSET ENDS THE DAY, and when night comes, we are anchored off the town of Port Said – a wretched little place, dusty, dirty, and flaring with cheap vice – all the flotsam of four nations whirling about in an eddy of coarse pleasures.

The shopkeepers are wolfish-looking, and bargain vociferously. Almost every other door opens into a gambling and concert hall. One of these gambling places boasts an opera. At the tables stand amid the crowd two handsome young Germans – blond, but with none of the ruddy warmth of the English blond; pale and flaxen, with deep-blue eyes and haughty of manner. Not nice faces; high-bred, but cold and brutal. They are officers from Prince Henry of Prussia's ship, the *Irene*, lying now in the harbor.

In the concert hall, *Traviata* is being sung by a fourth-rate French troupe, and the audience sits about at little tables, drinking, and eating ices. I ask for something native – Turkish – to drink, and they bring me a stuff that to all the evidences of sight, taste, and smell cries out that it is a mixture of paregoric and water, and one sip contents me. We are glad to go away.

The Mediterranean is cold and not smooth, but here there comes upon one a sense of historical association. In India, nature is so tremendous she swallows up all memory of man; in Aden, one remembers only the Bible; but nearing Greece, the past takes shape and meaning, and history begins to have a new vividness and significance. Here man has been "lord of the visible earth," has dominated and adorned her. She has been but the stage and background against which he played out the tragedies and comedies of humanity.

One morning at sunrise, the stewardess taps at the door. "The first officer's compliments, miss, and will you please get up and look out of the scuttle."

I wrap myself in my kimono – treasure-trove from Japan – and thrust head and shoulders through the wide porthole. Directly before me is Candia – abrupt mountains rising sharply from the sea and crowned with snow. Among them are trailing clouds looping long scarves of mist from peak to peak, at their feet Homer's "wine-dark sea," furrowed by a thousand keels: Greek galleys, Roman triremes, fighting vessels from Carthage, merchant and battle ships from Venice, Genoa, and Turkey, the fleets of Spain, men-o'-war with the English lions at the peak, and, lastly, the world's peaceful commerce, sailing serenely over the bones and rotting hulls that lie below.

The sun comes up gloriously out of the sea, deepening it to a winy purple in its light. Suddenly the mountaintops take fire; the snow flushes softly, deepens rosily in hue, grows crimson with splendor; the sleeping mists begin to stir and heave, to lighten into gold, to float and rise into the warming blue above. Then the dressing gong clangs noisily through the ship, and the colors pale into the common day.

Next morning, we are fast to the docks at Brindisi, and but one more stage of the journey remains to be made.

––––

IT IS A vividly bright day in January 1890 – the 16th. There is a tingling crispness in the air as if it were early autumn – a slight frostiness that chills the skin, but does not penetrate the veins. Rather the deep breaths of this keen, pure sea ozone make the blood pulse with a swift, delicious warmth, like a plunge into cold water.

We are anchored at Brindisi, Italy – the ancient Brundusium of the Romans – a town more than twenty-five centuries old, but which does not by any means look its age. It does not appear particularly attractive either from the wharves, and I am more than ever certain – as I always have been certain – that I could never agree with the haughty provincial who preferred to be first in Brundusium rather than second in Rome.

Indeed, all efforts now are bent on being first out of Brundusium, as the train leaves within the hour. The *Britannia* goes on and around to Portsmouth, but the English government runs a train down through France and Italy to meet the P. and O. steamers, and thus gain five days in the arrival of the Indian and Australian mails.

This mail train carries one passenger coach for the benefit of personages from the colonies who may be in haste to reach home; and if there are not a sufficient number of these distinguished servants of the empire to fill the car, more ordinary travelers can occupy the vacant berths by cabling ahead and securing them.

I had taken this precaution at Ceylon and find there will be no difficulty in the matter, provided I can get my luggage through the customs in time. And this, dependent upon my careful packing.

Various necessary additions to my wardrobe during the voyage have enlarged the contents of my little box. I have arranged and rearranged the items several ways, and still I cannot close it, even when I lean my weight on it. Hands on hips, I frown at my predicament, doubting that Nellie Bly is having any trouble with her gripsack.

I poke my head into the hallway and catch the attention of the stewardess. "Excuse, me. Miss? Would you help me with my luggage?"

She nods, and when I give her the word, plops herself down in the most emphatic manner. With the weight of the two of us, I barely manage to close the box and secure it.

"Thank you," I say, tucking a stray hair back under my bonnet.

The whole ship is in an uproar, and it is almost impossible to get anything done. Mails and luggage are being disembarked. Many passengers are leaving for a tour through Italy before finally returning to England, fearful of the winter fogs and of the influenza raging there. Italians, with cocked hats and imperial importance of manner, are bullying everyone and getting things into a hopeless tangle.

My luggage is finally marked as passed; a porter is hired to transport it; I go off to attend to the purchase of tickets, dispatching of cables, and other minor matters, and arrive ten minutes before the advertised departure of the train.

No luggage! I fling out of the car, rush back again to the ship, and discover the missing possessions in the hands of a pig-headed Italian who insists they have not been properly examined. "Give me your keys," he demands.

"But it goes under seal and bond straight through to England!" I say in exasperation.

Still, he insists upon opening it and strewing my garments about the deck.

I hope I did not forget the dignity a gentlewoman should preserve under the most trying of circumstances, but I fancy that my tones, while low, were concentrated, and that the little American I used was "frequent and fluent and free," for the man turned pale and wavered.

I snatched up my belongings, flung them in pell-mell, jumped upon the box, snapped to the hasp, and ran off with a porter towards the train, blank despair in my heart.

Happily, Italian trains are not bound down by narrow interpretations of time-tables, and I do succeed in catching it, with the luggage and some few tattered remnants of a once-nice temper.

It is very destructive of the mental equilibrium to lose the temper so thoroughly, especially if one is out of practice, and it is fully an hour before the exceeding beauty of the country through which we are passing begins to have its soothing effect and to make me fain to forgive the Italians because of Italy!

On our right is the Adriatic, blue as lapis-lazuli and dotted with flocking sails. Here and there lie little snow-white towns along its shores, and between are the gray olive orchards that have something strangely human in their gnarled grotesqueness.

Even in flying by, one sees flashes of fantastic gargoyle-like resemblances to persons one has known caricatured in bark. It is not difficult to comprehend how people who lived among olive groves developed dryad superstitions and created legends of flying women transformed into trees.

The English government pays the Italian government a large subsidy for this train and the swift passage of the mails, but the ubiquitous person who attends to all our needs – is porter, guard, steward, cook, and brakeman in one – has his own ideas on the subject of haste and acts accordingly.

When we reach a town where he has friends, he goes out, quietly winds us up like a Waterbury watch, dismounts, and is received with affectionate enthusiasm by a little crowd on the platform. He inquires solicitously after each one's kin unto the fourth and fifth generation, gives his careful attention to all the local gossip, and retails the news he has been gathering all along the line. When he can no longer hear or tell some new thing, he remembers our existence, climbs once more upon his perch, lets us run down with a sudden whir, and we go on our way.

At mealtimes, he retires into a tiny den amidships, and from a space but little larger than a matchbox produces delightful soups and salads, excellent coffee, well-cooked game, baskets of twisted Italian bread, wine, and oranges.

At night he arranges our sleeping-berths, and I think would perform barber duties and assist with our toilets if called upon to do so. He is a fatigued and blasé personage who looks as if chronically deprived of his due allowance of sleep, and he evidently regards the traveling public as a helpless, nervous creature always in a peevishly ridiculous hurry.

We begin to climb into the mountains, and it grows very cold. Oddly-angled vineyards hang precariously to the steep sides of the heights, propped into place by dams of stone that keep the soil from sliding down hill. Queer villages are tucked into clefts, with streets that are merely narrow stairs. Now and again we flash by the bold outlines of a ruined castle crowning a crag: the site always chosen with so much discretion that one wonders not only how enemies ever got in, but how the owners themselves ever emerged – unless they fell out.

A film of snow appears here and there, and the cold intensifies. We all pull out traveling rugs and extra clothing to ward the chill. To think only a short time ago I was wearing my thinnest shirtwaist in the tropics and complaining of the heat!

Suddenly we catch a glimpse of white heights outlined against the blue.

"It's the Alps!" someone exclaims. "Mount Cenis tunnel is coming up."

A space of darkness, of thundering, clattering echoes – and then France!

Everything is quite different all at once. A fine new fortress commands the tunnel; the station is better built, larger, and in better repair than those we have seen in Italy. The customs officer, a well-set-up and good-looking Frenchman in a smart uniform, inquires politely if we have anything to declare, and when we answer in the negative, sets his heels together, gives a profound salutation, and vexes us no more.

I am delighted to use my French in its native country. The last time I spoke the language was in New Orleans. I'm glad now for the occasional French novel I've worked through to keep my vocabulary sharp.

Everywhere is an air of greater prosperity, thrift, and alertness. The train does not stop to admit of gossiping, and goes at added speed.

Telegrams have been following me along the route concerning the possibility of catching a ship at Havre. The train is rather behind time, and unless the *La Champagne* will consent to delay her departure for an hour or two, it will be useless to attempt to cover the space between Villeneuve, Paris, and Havre before tomorrow at seven.

There is hope, however, that she will wait, and Friday night, some two hours after midnight, the guard rouses me to deliver a telegram:

BE READY 4AM TO CHANGE CARS FOR PARIS.

This means leaving my box – it is under seal for London – and crossing the ocean with only a few belongings in a traveling bag. What I never considered doing starting out, I eagerly agree to now. I am almost home.

I rise and dress quietly, scribble a few notes of farewell to such of my fellow passengers as have been especially courteous, and am all ready when we halt at Villeneuve.

A young Frenchman, agent for Cook's tourist bureau in Paris, has come to meet me.

"I'm sorry, *Mademoiselle*. I have bad news for you. The ship has refused to wait."

I look at him through the haze of sleepiness. "What?" I ask. I hear the words, but I have trouble understanding them with so little rest.

"The ship," he says slowly, as if his accent has confused the words for me. "It goes without you." He mimes a ship leaving harbor.

As his meaning sinks into my mind, so does my heart descend into my feet. To have come all this way, spent so much time, only to be thwarted by a ship refusing to wait. This French ship is the fastest way home, and now my win is questionable. I want to win. Or at least be close in the losing. I collapse on a nearby bench, surprised at my passion. *Who am I?* Is this what it feels like to be Nellie Bly? Can I remain graceful these next few hours and days, and yet still strive for the finish?

It is too late – half-past four – to return to bed, so I throw myself on the couch and wait for day. A faint rime clouds the window when dawn breaks, but a breath dispels it, and outside are lovely Corot-like visions – pale, shadowy, gray – worth the lost sleep to have seen the landscapes he painted. Here and there, a thin plume of smoke curls up against the dull frosty sky from the chimney of a thatched, lime-washed cottage set amid barns and stacks.

My plans have changed again. Instead of Paris and on to the fast ship, it is on to England to catch whatever ship I can. I don't know if I can recover from this delay. There can be no more missed connections, and Nellie Bly must have a similar trial if I am to win. A snowstorm, perhaps.

40

IN WHICH A MISSING MEDICAL REPORT THREATENS QUARANTINE OF NELLIE'S SHIP.

NEXT, A MAN I DIDN'T EVEN KNOW approached me on the promenade deck. "If it would help, would you consent to the monkey being thrown overboard?"

I was speechless. A little struggle between superstition and a feeling of justice for the monkey followed.

"What do you think, Chief Allen?" I asked at dinner. "Do you think it will come to that?"

"No! Don't toss the poor creature away." He chuckled. "The monkey has just gotten outside of a hundred weight of cement and has washed it down with a quart of lamp oil, and I, for one, do not want to interfere with his happiness and digestion!"

Oh dear. That monkey was a savage little fellow, but took to most everybody but me. Once the novelty was gone, I hoped we would have bonded as he will make quite the sensation back home. There was no chance the other reporter was coming home with a monkey. No one else would be so foolish.

"Ministers are also considered Jonahs," said Chief Allen "They always bring bad weather to ships."

We had two ministers on board. So I said quietly, "If the ministers were thrown overboard, I'd say nothing about the monkey." Thus the monkey's life was saved.

Mr. Allen had a boy, Walter, who was very clever at tricks. One day Walter said he would show that he could lift a bottle merely by placing his open hand to the side of the bottle. He put everybody out of the cabin, as he said if they remained in it broke the influence.

They watched intently through the open door as he rolled up his sleeve and rubbed his arm downward, quite vigorously, as if trying to get all the blood in his hand. Catching the wrist with the other hand, as if to hold all the blood there, he placed his open hand to the side of the bottle and, much to the amazement of his audience, the bottle went up with his hand.

When urged to tell how to do the wonderful trick, he said, "It's all very easy; all you do is to rub your arm, that's just for show; then you lay hold of your wrist just as if you wanted to keep all the blood in your hand; you keep one finger free—no one notices that—and you take the neck of the bottle between the hand and the finger, and the bottle goes up with the hand. See?"

One evening, when the ship was rolling frightfully, everybody was gathered in the dining hall; an Englishman urged Walter to do some tricks, but Walter did not want to be bothered then, so he said: "Yes, sir; in a moment, sir," and went on putting the things upon the table.

He had put down the mustard pot, the salt cellar and various things, and was wiping a plate. As he went to put the plate down, the ship gave a great roll, the plate knocked against the mustard pot, and the mustard flew all over the Englishman, much to the horror of the others. Sitting up stiffly, the mustard dotting him from head to knees, he said sternly:

"Walter! What is this?"

"That, sir, is the first trick," Walter replied softly, and he glided silently and swiftly off to the regions of the cook.

But Walter was caught one day. A sailor told him that he could hide an egg on him so no one would be able to find it. Walter had his doubts, but he willingly gave the sailor a test. The egg was hidden and a man called in to find it. He searched Walter all over without once coming upon the egg.

The sailor suggested another trial to which Walter, now an interested and firm believer in the sailor's ability, gladly consented. The sailor opened Walter's shirt and placed the egg next to the skin in the region of his heart, carefully buttoning the shirt afterwards. The man was called in; he went up to Walter and hit him a resounding smack where Sullivan hit Kilrain to win the heavyweight title. He found the egg, and so did Walter! It was a gentle lesson for the boy as I doubt he will be duped like that again.

Even with low runs, our trip was bound to come to an end. One night it was announced that the next day we would be in San Francisco. I felt a feverish excitement, and many were the speculations as to whether there would be a snow blockade to hinder my trip across the Continent. A hopefulness that had not known me for many days came back when in rushed the purser, his face a snow-white, crying:

"Good Heavens! The bill of health was left behind in Yokohama."

"Well–well–what does that mean?" I demanded, fearing some misfortune, I knew not what.

"It means," he said, dropping nerveless into a chair, "that no one will be permitted to land until the next ship arrives from Japan. That will be two weeks."

41

IN WHICH ELIZABETH BISLAND TRIES TO MAKE UP FOR LOST TIME.

AS THE DAY GROWS, PEASANTS, SUCH AS those in Millet paintings, come out of the cottages and follow the road, carrying baskets of potatoes and turnips. Two legs and a pair of sabots appear under a perambulating heap of hay. A big dog drags a small cart full of milk cans, and a woman with a cap and tucked-up skirts trudges along beside, blowing on her fingers to warm them.

All this, just as did Italy, seems very familiar. I know it quite well from pictures and books. It gives one the sensation – reversed – awakened by reading a realistic novel in which all the little details of daily life are minutely and accurately reproduced.

It is ten o'clock when we reach Calais, and the Dover boat has gone, so there is time for a bath and breakfast.

The Channel is gray and stormy when we start, and a gust of rain splashes now and then upon the deck. Fat old French gentlemen spread themselves out in chaise lounges and make all necessary preparations for seasickness. The English turn up the collars of their long coats, thrust their hands in the pockets, and stride along the rolling deck. Later the sun struggles through the clouds and turns the gloom to a stormy gray-green and shifting silver – and there looms slowly through the mists the white cliffs of England.

Starting two months ago from a vast continent which the English race have made their own, where the English tongue, English laws, customs, and manners reign from sea to sea, in my whole course around the globe, I have heard that same tongue, seen the same laws and manners, found the same race.

Have had proof with my own eyes of the splendor of their empire, of their power, their wealth, of their dominance and pride, of their superb armies, their undreamable commerce, their magnificent possessions, their own unrivalled physical beauty and force – and lo! Now at last I find from a tiny island ringed with gray seas has sprung this race of kings.

It fills my soul with a passion of pride that I, too, am an Anglo-Saxon. In my veins, too, runs that virile tide that pulses through the heart of this Lord of the Earth – the blood of this clean, fair, noble English race! It is worth a journey round the world to see –

This royal throne of kings, this sceptred isle,
This earth of majesty, this seat of Mars,
This other Eden, demi-paradise;
This fortress built by nature for herself
Against infestion and the hand of war.
This happy breed of men, this little world;
This precious stone set in a silver sea;
This blessed plot of earth, this realm, this England,
This nurse, this teeming womb of royal kings,
Feared by their breed and famous by their birth,
Renownèd for their deeds so far from home,
For Christian service and true chivalry,
This land of such dear souls, this dear, dear land –
England, bound in with the triumphant sea!

– and I understand now the meaning of this trumpet-cry of love and pride from the greatest of earth's poets – Shakespeare, an Englishman.

Dover – and one sets foot at last on the mother soil. Everyone is friendly and polite as I transfer from ship to train and the blue boudoir of a first-class carriage – then English landscapes under the level rays of a setting sun.

Certain characteristics here are very reminiscent of Japan. The neatness and completeness of everything; the due allowance of trees dispersed in ornamental fashion; nature so thoroughly tamed and domesticated; the picturesque railway stations, and a certain moist softness in the air. But where everything there is light, fragile, and fantastic, here it is solid, compact, and durable.

Like the English sea, the English land swarms with phantoms – the folk of history, of romance, of poetry and fiction. They troop along the roads, prick across the fields, look over the hedges, and peer from every window.

I hear the clang of their armor, see the waving of their banners; their voices ring in the frosty winter air, their horses' hoof beats sound along the paths. Without regard to time or period, to reality or non-reality, they come in hosts to welcome me – to say, "And so you, too, have come to join us. We have waked to greet you. We are the ghosts of England's past!"

Even the folk of the contemporary fiction have not failed to be present. I see the sunk fence by the thicket where Angelina always bids Edwin an eternal farewell in the last chapter of the second volume, and they are there doing it now.

There rides Captain Cavendish in his red coat, home from the hunting field, and on his way to the handsome old country house yonder where he will squeeze Mrs. Fitzroy's fingers under the teacup he passes her and thus lay the foundation for forty-two chapters of jealously, hatred, and all uncharitableness.

"Miss? Miss?" A definite real, live, voice pierces my imagination. It is the younger of the two women in my carriage. "Ah, there you are at last. My mother was loath to interrupt your thoughts, but we are going to play a card game. Would you like to join us?"

"No. Thank you. I'm trying to see as much of England as I can." At any other time, I would have readily agreed as they looked like such accommodating ladies.

Darkness falls. A dull glare is reflected from the heavens that speaks the presence of a great gas-lit city. A myriad sparks twinkle in the distance – the "Lights o' London!"

Miles and miles and miles of houses. A huge, shadowy half-globe looming against the sky – the dome of St. Paul's. Towers and delicate spires, and lights shining through many lance-like windows – Parliament Houses, where lords and commons sit in debate. Long gleams quivering serpent-like across a wavering black flood – we have passed over the Thames, and here is Charing Cross.

"I'd like to take the North-German Lloyd steamer at Southampton tomorrow, please."

"Not possible, miss. That ship has been withdrawn and will not sail 'til late in the week. Shall I book you passage for then?"

"No! No, no, no! I must leave as soon as possible," I say, my voice having gone up an octave or two.

Clatter, hurry, and confusion – every one giving different suggestions and directions.

"Your one chance is the night mail to Holyhead and catch the *Bothnia*, which touches at Queenstown next morning." This comes from the man at the ticket booth after consulting several time tables and having his route double-checked and then rechecked by anyone with an opinion.

"And when does the night mail leave?"

"An hour and a half."

I give him a weary smile as thanks. I have not slept since two o'clock the night before, nor eaten since breakfast, and my courage is nearly at an end.

One of my fellow travelers, Mr. Goodman, who has been most kind to me all the way from Ceylon, comes to my rescue.

"Miss Bisland, allow me to help you," he says. "I dare say you look about to collapse."

I nearly cry with relief. He sends me off to the hotel to dine in company with two kind and charming fellow voyagers, Sir William Lewis and his daughter, while he arranges my difficulties.

I am far too tired and disturbed, however, to eat, and can only crumble my bread and taste my wine as my two companions keep up a stunted conversation. At half-past eight, my friend appears and carries me off to the Euston station. He has snatched his dinner, got rid of the dust of travel, and into evening clothes.

He has brought rugs and cushions that I may have some rest during the night, a little cake in case I grow hungry, and heaps of books and papers. My foot warmer is filled with hot water, and the guard is induced to give me his best care and attention.

"Adieu, Miss Bisland," says Mr. Goodman with a slight bow. "Godspeed on your journey. I hope your last stage is a swift one."

"Thank you for all your kindnesses," I say in deep earnest. Then I go away alone again, somewhat comforted by the chivalrous goodness of the traveling man to the uncared-for woman.

I fall asleep from fatigue, am shaken by horrible dreams, and start awake with a cry. The train is thundering through a wild storm. I try to read by the gaslight, but the words dance up and down the page. The guard comes now and then to see if I need anything, and deep in the night I reach Holyhead.

Gathering up my multitudinous belongings, I run through the rain and sleet to the little vessel quivering and straining at the pier. The night is a wild one, the wind in our teeth, and the journey rough and very tedious.

The cold and tempestuous day has dawned before we touch Kingstown and are hurried – wretched for lack of sleep and the means of making a fresh toilet – into the train for Dublin. The Irish capital is still unawake when I rattle across it from station to station this Sunday morning, and immediately I am off again at full speed through a land swept with flying mists and showers – a beautiful land, green even in January.

Later I see ruddy-cheeked peasants going along the roads to church – a type I am familiar with in America. I gaze contemplatively at these sturdy young men, and wonder how soon they will be New York aldermen and mayors of Chicago; how soon those rosy girls, in their queer, bunchy, provincial gowns, will be leaders of society in Washington and dressed by Worth.

I am growing frightfully hungry, having eaten nothing since yesterday morning in Calais. There is the spice cake, but with no liquid save a little brandy in a flask, I soon choke upon the cake and abandon it.

The train is behind time, owing to the late arrival of the Channel boat, and stops only for the briefest moments. At noon we reach Queenstown, having curved around a fair space of water and past the beautiful city of Cork.

The few of us who are continuing on step into the station and are greeted by an attendant with a thick accent. "The ship has not yet arrived, but will doubtless be here in a few moments." He nods his head toward the window and the stormy weather outside. "This fierce rout has delayed her. I'll send your luggage down to the tender and ye go too."

The others follow his orders, but I have other plans. "Where can I get some breakfast?" I beg.

"That you mightn't. You best wait for the signal." He looks disapproving.

"But I must or I shall faint with hunger and you'll have to pack me off with my luggage." I give him my best pleading eyes, though I am so in earnest I do not have to act.

He relents. Perhaps he heard my stomach rumble above the patter of the rain. "The Queen's Hotel is not far from the station, right out there." He points. "Hurry."

The Queen's Hotel. It sounds lovely. Already I am imagining velvet chairs, crisp linens and waiters ready to attend my every need. I dart out in the rain with visions of hot tea and a plate of eggs and ham pulling me forward. The Queen's Hotel is easy to find, a sturdy white rectangular building overlooking the water and defying the pouring rain. If only I had time, I would eat in the bandstand just beyond the trees. Such an elegant breakfast would be a fitting end to my final stop before home.

But the evil luck which has pursued me for the last two days ordains that the kitchen of this hostelry should be undergoing repairs at this particular moment, and no food is to be had.

"Nothing at all?" I ask the dutiful clerk standing in my way. "I've come from the train and haven't had a bite to eat since yesterday. It needn't be fancy. Something forgotten in a cupboard? A piece from a workman's dinner pail?" Water begins to drip off my coat and onto the carpet.

She purses her lips together as her eyes flit to the other guests of the hotel milling about. She must decide the only way to be rid of me is to find me some scraps. "I'll see what there is."

She returns with a cup of rather cold and bitter tea and a bit of dingy bread that looks as if it had been used to scrub the floor with before being presented to me as a substitute for breakfast.

"Thank you." I smile. Although I did say it needn't be fancy, I didn't expect to be taken so literally. I don't dare ask if I can take it out to the bandstand. There is a little seating area near the counter and so, there, under the clerk's watchful eye I eat and drink it all.

Back out into the rain I dash. At the station I am warned to hold myself in readiness for an instantaneous summons to the tender, for when the steamer is signaled, there is no time to waste. Hastily I make such toilet as is possible with my dressing bag aboard the tender and sit alone in the waiting room, attendant on the summons.

Hour after hour goes by, but no summons comes. I dare not move lest the call come during my absence, and so sit there hopeless, helpless, overwhelmed with hunger, lack of sleep, and fatigue.

At six o'clock, my patience is at end.

"Is there somewhere I can get some food?" I demand of the new attendant. "I've been waiting for hours, and if I was hungry before, I must be starving now."

"The signal can come at any minute, miss. If you want to risk missing it, you can go to the Queen's Hotel. 'Tis not far from the station."

"The Queen's Hotel?" I am about to tell him what I think of the Queen's Hotel when they bring the long-expected notice. The ship has been signaled, and the tender must be off.

42

IN WHICH NELLIE BLY BOARDS A PRIVATE TRAIN AND MEETS CROWDS WISHING HER WELL ON HER WAY TO NEW YORK.

I FELT FAINT. THE THOUGHT OF BEING HELD two weeks in sight of San Francisco, in sight of New York almost, and the goal for which I had been striving and powerless to move, was maddening.

"I would cut my throat, for I could not live and endure it," I said quietly. No longer checking my thoughts, I imagined the other reporter stepping foot off her ship on the east coast and beating me.

The purser pushed himself back out of the chair. "I will check again."

I followed him to the doctor's office and bit my fingernails as he meticulously searched every corner of the desk. Finally, he held up a paper in triumph. "Here it is, after all."

Later came a scare about a small-pox case on board, but it proved to be only a rumor, and early in the morning the revenue officers came aboard bringing the newspapers.

"There is a winter storm," I said in disbelief, snatching a paper from an officer. I read of the impassable snow blockade, which for a week had put a stop to all railroad traffic, and my despair knew no bounds.

"No time to worry," said the purser. "Here comes your ride."

And there was no time for farewells. While the *Oceanic* was waiting for the quarantine doctor, some men came out on a tug to take me ashore. The monkey was taken on the tug with me, and my baggage, which had increased by gifts from friends, was thrown after me.

Just as the tug steamed off the quarantine doctor called to me.

"Miss Bly! Miss Bly! I forgot to examine your tongue. You cannot land until I do."

In exasperation I stuck out my tongue.

He called out, "All right!"

The others laughed, I waved farewell, and in another moment I was parted from my good friends on the *Oceanic*.

A special train had been waiting for my arrival in readiness to start the moment I boarded it. The Deputy Collector of the port of San Francisco, the Inspector of Customs, the Quarantine Officer and the Superintendent of the O. and O. steamers sat up all the night preceding my arrival, so there should be no delay in my transfer from the *Oceanic* to the special train.

It seemed as if my greatest success was the personal interest of everyone who greeted me. They were all so kind and as anxious that I should finish the trip in time as if their personal reputations were at stake.

The first thing I wanted to know was where the other reporter was. Had she made it to New York ahead of me, or had she been delayed? The information was not in the telegrams shoved into my hands but in the mouths of the reporters waiting to interview me.

"Elizabeth Bisland missed her connection at Havre. You still have a chance." That was all I needed to know. The winds had to be in her favor and the snows against mine if she were to win now. I smiled like Elizabeth Bisland was the last person on my mind.

My train consisted of one handsome sleeping car, the San Lorenzo, and the engine, *The Queen*, was one of the fastest on the Southern Pacific. My editor came through for me.

"What time do you want to reach New York, Miss Bly?" Mr. Bissell, General Passenger Agent of the Atlantic and Pacific system, asked me.

"Not later than Saturday evening," I said, never thinking they could get me there in that time.

"Very well, we will put you there on time," he said quietly, and I rested satisfied that he would keep his word.

It did not seem long after we left Oakland Mole until we reached the great San Joaquin valley, a level green plain through which the railroad track ran for probably three hundred miles as straight as a sunbeam. The roadbed was so perfect that, though we were traveling a mile a minute, the car was as easy as if it were traveling over a bed of velvet.

At Merced, our second stop, I saw a great crowd of people dressed in their best Sunday clothes gathered about the station.

"I suppose they are out for a picnic," I remarked.

"No, they are here to see you!"

Amazed at this information, I got up, in answer to calls for me, and went out on the back platform.

A loud cheer, which almost frightened me to death, greeted my appearance, and the band began to play "By Nellie's Blue Eyes." A large tray of fruit and candy and nuts, the tribute of a dear little newsboy, was passed to me, for which I was more grateful than had it been the gift of a king.

We started on again, and the three of us on the train had nothing to do but admire the beautiful country through which we were passing as swiftly as clouds along the sky, to read, or count telegraph poles, or pamper and pet the monkey.

I felt little inclination to do anything but to sit quietly and rest, bodily and mentally. There was nothing left for me to do now. I could hurry nothing, I could change nothing; I could only sit and wait until the train landed me at the end of my journey.

I enjoyed the rapid motion of the train so much that I dreaded to think of the end. At Fresno, the next station, the town turned out to do me honor, and I was the happy recipient of exquisite fruits, wines and flowers, all the product of Fresno County, California.

The men who spoke to me were interested in my sunburnt nose, the delays I had experienced, the number of miles I had traveled. The women wanted to examine my one dress in which I had traveled around, the cloak and cap I had worn, were anxious to know what was in the bag, and all about the monkey.

While we were doing some fine running the first day, I heard the whistle blow wildly, and then I felt the train strike something. Brakes were put on, and we went out to see what had occurred.

It was hailing just then, and we saw two men coming up the track. The conductor came back to tell us that we had struck a handcar, and pointed to a piece of twisted iron and a bit of splintered board – all that remained of it – laying alongside. When the men came up, one remarked, with a mingled expression of wonder and disgust upon his face:

"Well, you ARE running like h–!"

"Thank you; I am glad to hear it," I said, and then we all laughed.

"Fellas, meet Nellie Bly."

Their eyes opened in recognition, and they shook my hand.

"Were you hurt?" I asked.

"No, no. We're fine," they assured me. Good humor being restored all around, we said goodbye, the engineer pulled the lever, and we were off again.

One place, where a large crowd greeted me, a man on the limits of it yelled:

"Did you ride on an elephant, Nellie?" and when I said I had not, he dropped his head and went away. Perhaps he was expecting my trip around the world to mimic the novel exactly.

At another place, the policemen fought to keep the crowd back; everybody was wanting to shake hands with me, but at last one officer was shoved aside, and the other, seeing the fate of his comrade, turned to me, saying: "I guess I'll give up and take a shake," and while reaching for my hand was swept on with the crowd.

I leaned over the platform and shook hands with both hands at every station, and when the train pulled out, crowds would run after, grabbing for my hands as long as they could. My arms began to ache, but I did not mind the ache if by such little acts I could give pleasure to my own people, whom I was so glad to be among once more.

The Americans turned out to do honor to an American girl who was to be the first to make a record of a flying trip around the world, and I rejoiced with them that it was an American girl who was doing it.

"Come out here, and we'll elect you governor," a Kansas man said, and I believe they would have done it, if the splendid welcomes they gave me are any criterion.

Telegrams addressed merely to "Nellie Bly, Nellie Bly's Train" came from all parts of the country filled with words of cheer and praise at all hours of the day and night.

I could not mention one place that was kinder than another. Over ten thousand people greeted me at Topeka. The mayor of Dodge City presented me on behalf of the citizens with resolutions of praise. I was very anxious to go to Kansas City, but we only went to the station outside of the limits, in order to save thirty minutes. At Hutchinson a large crowd and the Ringgold Cornet Band greeted me, and at another place the mayor assured me that the band had been brought down, but they forgot to play. They merely shouted like the rest, forgetting in the excitement all about their music.

I was up until four o'clock, talking first with a little newspaper girl from Kearney, Nebraska, who had traveled six hundred miles to meet and interview me, and later dictating an account of my trip to a stenographer, who was seasick from the motion of the train. I had probably slept two hours when the porter called me, saying we would soon be in Chicago.

I dressed leisurely and drank the last drop of coffee there was left on our train, for we had been liberally entertaining everybody who cared to travel any distance with us.

I was surprised on opening the door of my stateroom to see the car quite filled with good-looking men.

"Miss Bly, may I introduce the Chicago Press Club?" said Mr. Bissell.

"Where did you all come from?" I asked.

After laughing, one explained. "We came out to Joliet to escort you to our city." He shook my hand. "I'm Cornelius Gardener, the vice president. Our president sends his regrets, but he'll meet us later, if you have time to spare and visit the Club."

I looked questioningly at Mr. Bissell.

He nodded. "You have several hours before your connecting train leaves."

Before we were in Chicago, I had answered all their questions, and we joked about my sunburnt nose and discussed the merits of my one dress and the cleverness of the monkey.

"Where did you get this creature?" asked one of the men as he fed it raisins.

"Singapore. He was a gift from a raja." That impressed them.

"You should call him McGinty," suggested one of the men. "After the song." He hummed a few bars.

"I will!" I said, glad at last to have a name for the beast.

Carriages were waiting to take us to the rooms of the Press Club. I went there in a coupe with Vice President Gardener. In the beautiful rooms of the Press Club, I met the president, Stanley Waterloo, and a number of clever newspaper men. I had not been expected in Chicago until noon, and the club had arranged an informal reception for me, and when they were notified of my speedy trip and consequently earlier arrival, it was too late to notify the members.

Instead, I was escorted to Kinsley's, where the club had a breakfast prepared, and then they took me to visit the Chicago Board of Trade.

When we went in, the pandemonium, which seems to reign during business hours, was at its height. My escorts took me to the gallery, and just as we got there, a man raised his arm to yell something to the roaring crowd. When he saw me, he yelled instead:

"There's Nellie Bly!"

In one instant the crowd that had been yelling like mad became so silent that a pin could have been heard fall to the floor. Every face, bright and eager, was turned up towards us, instantly every hat came off, and then a burst of applause resounded through the immense hall.

The applause was followed by cheer after cheer and cries of "Speech!" but I took off my little cap and shook my head at them, which only served to increase their cheers.

Shortly afterwards, the Press Club escorted me to the Pennsylvania Station.

"Thank you for your welcome. I have not been treated better anywhere in the world." I was unable to thank them heartily enough for the royal manner in which they had treated a little sunburnt stranger.

Now I was on a regular train which seemed to creep, so noticeable was the difference in speed. Instead of a fine sleeping car at my disposal, I had but a stateroom, and my space was so limited that floral and fruit offerings had to be left behind.

In Chicago, a cable which afforded me much pleasure reached me, having missed me at San Francisco:

M. AND MME. JULES VERNE ADDRESS THEIR SINCERE FELICITATIONS TO MISS NELLIE BLY AT THE MOMENT WHEN THAT INTREPID YOUNG LADY SETS FOOT ON THE SOIL OF AMERICA.

The train was rather poorly appointed, and it was necessary for us to get off for our meals. When we stopped at Logansport for dinner, I, being the last in the car, was the last to get off. When I reached the platform, a young man, whom I never saw before or since, sprang upon the other platform, and waving his hat, shouted:

"Hurrah for Nellie Bly!"

Despite all the attention paid to me thus far, I blushed. Even though I had garnered some notoriety in New York with my stunts, I'd never been singled out like this before, and it took some getting used to.

The crowd clapped hands and cheered, and after making way for me to pass to the dining room, pressed forward and cheered again, crowding to the windows at last to watch me eat. When I sat down, several dishes were put before me bearing the inscription, "Success, Nellie Bly."

It was after dark when we reached Columbus, where the depot was packed with men and women waiting for me. A delegation of railroad men waited upon me and presented me with beautiful flowers and candy, as did a number of private people.

I did not go to bed until after we had passed Pittsburgh and only got up in the morning in time to greet the thousands of good people who welcomed me at Harrisburg, where the Harrisburg Wheelman's Club sent a floral offering in remembrance of my being a wheelman. A number of Philadelphia newspaper men joined me here, and at Lancaster I received an enthusiastic reception.

"What are you going to do next?" asked a young man from the *Philadelphia Inquirer.* I had anticipated the question to come at some point, but here, now, I wasn't quite ready for it. A brief thought of lying on a chair in Colombo flittered through my mind, and I suppressed a sigh. "I plan to go back to work again. You know I must do something for a living," came the expected answer. Needing to add something more Nellie-Bly-like and scandalous, I added, "And I expect to work until I fall in love and get married."

The questions quieted down after that, and I was left to wonder myself what I was really going to do next. I wasn't ready for another stunt. My round-the-world vacation had left me tired of stunt reporting. Perhaps it was Elizabeth Bisland nipping at my boots that did me in. There was always another reporter trying to get a leg up. Always clambering, always fighting for the story. Oh, to be rocking on the sea and listening to the Lascars chanting. *Wouldn't these thoughts shock them all!*

43

IN WHICH ELIZABETH BISLAND
FACES A WINTER STORM.

IT RAINS IN TORRENTS, MINGLED WITH SLEET, and the wind blows a tempest. The tender puts out from shore and is whirled about like an eggshell. The wind drives us back, and over and over again we essay the passage before we can make head against the wild weather.

It is two hours and a half later when we get alongside the ship, and I am chilled to the bone, sick and dizzy for want of food and sleep. I climb stumblingly across the narrow, slippery, plunging path that leads from one ship to the other. No sooner have I set foot on the glassy deck than the push of an impatient passenger sends me with a smashing fall into the scuppers, where I gather bruises that will last a week.

"Oh, Miss. Are you all right? Let me help you." A compassionate stewardess comes to the rescue and steadies me to my feet. "Nasty weather we've been having. Captain tells us it's the worst weather he's seen in years. Are you sure you are all right?"

I can only nod and blink back tears.

"Follow me. I'll get you settled." The dear thing takes me straight to my room and puts me to bed. I'm so overwhelmed I can barely thank her.

The weather is terrible – a season long to be remembered for the January storms of the north Atlantic. The waves toss our ship back and forth among them like a football. Even were I not too miserable to move, the plunging of the vessel would make it impossible to keep my feet.

The ship laboriously climbs a howling green mountain, pauses irresolute a moment on the crest, and then toboggans madly down the farther side, her screw out of water, and kicking both heels madly in the air to the utter dislocation of one's every tooth and joint.

Down, down she goes, as if boring for bottom, and when it is perfectly certain that she can never by any chance right herself, she comes nose up most with a jerk, shakes off the water, and attacks a new mountain, to repeat the same performance on the farther side.

Two thirds of the passengers are very seasick, and I quite as wretched and prostrate from my late painful experiences as if still subject to the malady.

It is the third or fourth day out, when I begin to take heart of grace and long to leave my stuffy little cabin. The ship is rolling frightfully still, and a sudden lurch sends the heavy jug full of water flying out of its basin into the berth, where it smashes into twenty pieces upon my face and chest and drenches me with icy water.

"Miss Bisland!"

My cabin mate hauls me from my dripping bed. She grabs a towel and shoves it at me. "You best change before you freeze."

The doors of the gangway are left open lest they freeze together, and therefore a bitter wind sweeps through the cabin.

I look for the key to my box, but can't find it. I am stabbed through and through my wet and clinging clothes by this terrible cold. My teeth are chattering, and I know I must get into dry clothing soon. "Have you seen my key?" I ask my cabin mate.

She shakes her head, eyeing me up and down. "My clothes will drown you, but my sleeping gown is dry. It's yours if you want it."

"Bless you, I do."

Thus suppressed again for another three days, it is only towards the end of the week – the storm being abated – that I am able once more to stand on my feet.

It is a most amiable and friendly little company that finally assembles in the cabin, the recent woes we have all passed through having made us sympathetic and considerate. We even get up in time a concert for the seamen's orphans, and play shuffleboard on the still uncertain deck for prizes.

But this crossing of the zone of storms has greatly delayed us, and it is late in the evening of the eleventh day when we take our pilot aboard. The morning of the twelfth day is cold, but evidently has some thought of clearing, and the sea is less rough.

I am woefully behind schedule and can only hope that Nellie Bly was blocked by snow storm or broken-down train engine. Mr. Walker was adamant that going west was the better winter route, but after the crossing I've just had, I have my doubts.

44

IN WHICH NELLIE BLY AND ELIZABETH BISLAND RETURN HOME.

Nellie Bly: Day 72, January 25, 1:25 pm

ALMOST BEFORE I KNEW IT, I WAS AT Philadelphia. My mother surprised me, boarding with my managing editor Mr. Chambers to escort me to New York.

"Oh, Pink," mother whispered.

I hugged her so tight it was a wonder I didn't squeeze the breath out of her. It was so good to see her, dressed for the occasion in her special velvet black wrap. She'd be on hand to witness my victory.

Speech-making was the order from Philadelphia on to Jersey City. I was pleased so many were out to welcome me, but I really wanted to get on with it.

The station at Jersey City was packed with thousands of people. My heart beat wildly with anticipation as I stood near the stairs, ready to step down when the train slowed and then to jump to the platform the moment the train arrived, for that made my time around the world.

The train slowed, and I took my position. Slowly, slowly. Jump!

The moment I landed on the platform, one yell went up from the people, and the cannons at the Battery and Fort Greene boomed out the news of my arrival. Immediately the timekeepers stopped their watches and announced: 72 days, 6 hours, 11 minutes, and 14 seconds. The variety of boats in the harbor sounded their whistles, and the crowd cheered even louder.

I took off my cap and wanted to yell with the crowd, not because I had gone around the world in seventy-two days, but because I was home again.

Mayor Cleveland greeted me first with a lovely basket of roses and callas. It was too loud that we couldn't speak to one another. He hushed the crowd so he could give a speech.

"The American Girl will no longer be misunderstood. She will be recognized as pushing, determined, independent, able to take care of herself wherever she may go."

It was difficult to keep my attention focused on the speech. I wanted to remember this moment. The people, happy with my accomplishment, and every last one of them come out to see me finish my trip around the world. I'm sure I've never grinned so much. I thought I'd caught sight of my good friends Fannie and Jane, but then suddenly, the mayor ended his speech, and it was my turn.

"From Jersey to Jersey is around the world. And I am in Jersey now." It wasn't the cleverest thing I could have said, but it made the crowd happy.

"Hurrah for Nellie Bly! Hurrah for Nellie Bly!"

The police encircled the mayor and me as we tried to squeeze through the crowd towards the ferry terminal. There were too many people, and we were stuck. The large officer at my elbow signaled to another fellow, and before I could protest, they had me lifted above their shoulders and marched directly to the landau. I was worried the horse might panic with all the noise, but he steadily plodded through to the ferry.

But once we were on the ferry, the people there were not content. They wanted to *see* me.

"Open – open – open the coach!"

And so the driver took the roof off. I stood and waved to the thousands on the ferry until we landed in New York. There, the scene repeated itself all the way to the *World* offices on Park Row.

"I am so glad to be home again!" I called out as I was shuffled through the doors. There was a party up in the editorial room, where I was met with cheers and flowers and piles of letters and telegrams. Mr. Cockerill showed me a basket of rare roses sent by *The Cosmopolitan*, admitting my accomplishment.

I flipped through several of the congratulatory letters, and the other reporters all returned to their desk, the novelty of my return worn off. Today I did well for my readers, but tomorrow they will start asking: What is next, Nellie Bly?

After pouring another cup of coffee, I surveyed the busy newsroom. Everyone had gone back to work. Typewriters clacking. Heads bowed over copy. Not one person looked my way. I was this morning's news and now they'd all moved on. Don't they realize what I'd done? I'd just gone round the world!

People were insatiable for a stunt. One right after the next. But my trip gave me an appreciation for the slowness of life. My headaches had all but disappeared, and life was so much more enjoyable when one's head wasn't pounding.

I would always be a writer, but that didn't mean I needed to stay a reporter. I could hang up my ghillie hat and write another novel in my series. Perhaps while I was gone, *The Mystery of Central Park* picked up in sales.

But first, I would see what I could do to capitalize off my trip. A lecture tour would allow me to go back to all those towns along the railway where the people came out to meet me. Norman Munro might be willing to compile my newspaper stories into a book, like he did for *Six Months in Mexico*. So many possibilities. My trip around the world might be my greatest accomplishment, but it wouldn't be the end of them. I did it!

———

Elizabeth Bisland: Day 76, January 30, early afternoon

A RIM OF opaque film grows on the horizon that the emigrants on the forward deck regard with eager interest and hope. The passengers stand about in furs, pinched and shivering, their noses red, but their eyes full of pleased anticipation. Any land would be dear and desirable after near a fortnight of this cold and frantic sea – but when it is one's own!

The film thickens and darkens and suddenly resolves itself into Coney Island, where, as we swiftly near the shore, the plaintive reproachful eyes of the great wooden elephant are turned upon us as if to deprecate our late coming. The Elephantine Colossus, at twelve stories high and covered in blue tin, is not the symbol most of us are looking for.

The water has smoothed itself into a bay, and a huge gray woman, holding an uplifted torch, awaits our coming; the emigrants regard her wonderingly – the symbol of liberty held aloft, and a compassionate countenance turned towards all the outer world. We are by the shores of Staten Island.

A pretty English girl who has braved the winter storms to follow her new husband to a foreign country remarks surprisedly that all this looks much like England – evidently having expected log cabins and a country town. But I have no time to be amused at her ignorance – I am saying joyously to myself: "Is this the hill, is this the kirk/ Is this mine ain countree?"

Suddenly a great flood of familiarity washes away the memory of the strange lands and people I have seen, and blots out all sense of time that has elapsed since I last saw all this.

I know how everything – the streets, the houses, the passers-by – are looking at this moment. It is as if I had turned away my head for an instant, and now looked back again. My duties, my cares, my interests, which had grown dim and shadowy in these last two months, suddenly take on sharp outlines and become alive and real once more. I feel as if I have but sailed down the bay for an hour and am now returning. I am even wearing the exact outfit I started out in.

The ship slides into dock. I can see the glad faces of my friends upon the pier. My journey is done. I have been around the world in seventy-six days. But I can tell immediately that Nellie Bly has made it back before me. There are not enough people or reporters here. It is quickly confirmed to me that my suspicions are correct when I reach the dock and Molly hugs me, bursting into tears. "She has beaten you, but you did well."

Blessed Molly.

Mr. Walker and several editors extend to me their congratulations.

"And what of the *La Champagne*?" I ask Mr. Walker. All across the Atlantic, that one question lingered. If I had made that connection, would I have gotten here sooner?

He shakes his head slightly. He looks disappointed. "You should have been on it. I was paying them to wait for you. They waited three hours extra!"

My stomach drops. "But the Cook's agent. He told me the ship couldn't wait."

"A falsehood."

"But how? Why?"

He shrugs, "It doesn't matter, anyway. *La Champagne* was delayed due to winter storms on the North Atlantic. Waves went over the decks, the riggings coated with ice, and they had to navigate around three icebergs. Captain Boyer admits that if you had been aboard, he would have pushed his ship faster and would have only had you back on Sunday afternoon, but still too late."

I'm feeling better about not being aboard *La Champagne*. "And Bly got back…?"

"Sunday morning."

I purse my lips and nod. Four and a half days before me. "Well, I had a good trip. I am fairly bursting with adventures to tell our readers." It's not what Mr. Walker wants, but it is enough for me. I will never forget my trip around the world.

I look to Molly for strength as several reporters surround me. "How was your journey? How were you treated? Do you have any regrets?" They ask questions all at once.

I answer each one politely. "My journey was delightful, and I am in love with the world. The people in every country I visited were exceedingly kind and courteous toward me. My only regret was that I was not able to beat Nellie Bly's time."

With that, Molly and I make our escape in the carriage she has waiting. Again, I think: blessed Molly!

And before I know it, we are back in the apartment, adorned with bouquets of flowers from my dear, sweet friends, welcoming me home. To think, I have nowhere to go. No tickets to purchase. No sightseeing adventures planned. I should be relieved, but instead I feel disappointed.

"So, sister, how was it really?"

"Once I left the Continent and settled into my role of traveler, I quite enjoyed myself. Partly because no one knew that I was racing unless I told them, but mostly because the people were so interesting. I've always been curious about other cultures, and I got to witness them firsthand. I believe I ended well enough in my own right. I went around the world!" I grab Molly's hands and spin the two of us around the room until we collapse in a heap on the carpet. "It was the *experience* that made it worth more than winning the race for Mr. Walker."

Molly rolls over to her stomach and picks at the carpet. "Nellie Bly will be incorrigible after this."

I guffaw. Oh, I've missed Molly. "I'm glad Nellie won. It was her idea, and she should be rewarded for it." I sigh. "But where does that leave me? A sad curiosity in the eye of the public?"

Molly shakes her head. "The flavor of the month, like in the candy store below." She points out the bouquets of flowers perched on every flat surface in the room. "Before long, you can go back to being your regular self. You will no longer be notorious."

"Notorious!"

"I'm teasing you."

"If only I could hide out until everyone has forgotten. I didn't ask to become a public figure. It all happened so fast, as you recall."

"Do you regret it?"

My mind skitters over the past few months. "I don't regret seeing the world. Molly, it has changed me. However, racing around the world was ridiculous. I should never have done that."

"Did you know her real name is Elizabeth, just like yours? You two are the same."

I gasp. "We are not. Similar, in some ways. I doubt we'll ever be friends. I'm sure she doesn't want to meet me."

"No, I've heard she pretends you don't exist and were never traipsing around the world at all."

To change the subject, Molly points out an especially pretty bouquet of pink roses that match the ones I launched my journey with.

Charles Wetmore.

"He's missed you most of all," says Molly. "Almost more than me."

"You are both darlings. I missed you, too, and I have so much to tell." I walk around the room, touching a lamp here, straightening a pile of books there. "Everything's changed," I murmur. *How can I go back to my old life after having traveled the world?*

"What do you mean? Everything's the same, just as you left it."

"I'm being silly. Do I have any mail?"

Molly laughs. "Three months' worth!" She brings out a telegram. "But I think you might be asking about this?"

It's from Lady Broome. She has invited me to spend the upcoming London season with her and her husband. A detailed letter is to follow. I smile. This time I'm not limiting my luggage.

———

Author's Note

IN REWRITING THE historical account of Nellie Bly and Elizabeth Bisland racing around the world in the late 1800s, I wanted to make their story more accessible to the modern reader without taking away the women's writing styles, their point of view, or the feel of the times.

The two reporters had very different writing styles. Elizabeth Bisland was much more literary, referencing poems, novels, and even paintings. She wrote long passages of descriptions, yet little dialogue. In turning her report into a novelized form, I had to extrapolate likely scenes based on what little information she gave. I also tried to explain some of her references for the modern reader so you wouldn't have to constantly be looking items up online. Of course, you may still go do that to further deepen your understanding of her writings.

Nellie Bly's writing style fits more easily with today's readers. She wrote more directly, simply, and with an eye for entertainment. If you compare this novel with her original writings, you will see that I did not change that much, but tried to bring out a thread of continuity such as you would find in a novel.

In creating scenes, I've turned passages of description and information into dialogue. Some characters are attributed to giving information that in real life they may not have actually said. Likewise, several nameless passengers have been given names and larger roles.

In my other historical novels, I add historical spellings and hyphenations to help create mood. But in this novel, I chose to scale back by modernizing the words and conventions. By the number of exclamation points left in, you'd be surprised at how many I took out!

Regarding the times, Both Nellie Bly and Elizabeth Bisland sometimes wrote about race and ethnicity in ways that we wouldn't today. Some of these references I have deleted or changed. For example, they both refer to *Chinamen*, whereas today, we would simply say *Chinese*.

In Hong Kong I hint at Nellie Bly sending a telegram to her editor requesting help. There is no record of this happening. However, I feel such a telegram would have been consistent with Bly's character. She would have been furious at finding out that someone had taken her idea and was trying to best her with it. Since the other reporter was allowed to bribe ship's captains, she would only be leveling the playing field.

Several passages were cut. I tried to keep as much as possible, but deleting several paragraphs of literary description and underdeveloped passages served to help keep the word count down and the story moving along. Of course, if you want to read every word these women wrote, unaffected by my hand, you can search out their accounts online.

My chapters have one sentence preview descriptions as a literary nod to Jules Verne's *Around the World in Eighty Days*. It was my way of tying in the three historical works, especially since his novel was Nellie's inspiration.

The one question I haven't resolved: Did these women ever meet? I found no references to any meetings. Elizabeth Bisland mentions knowing who Nellie Bly is, but Nellie Bly never acknowledges Elizabeth. I'll leave that up to your imagination.

Acknowledgments

THIS BOOK WAS made possible by the original writings of Nellie Bly (Around the World in 72 Days) and Elizabeth Bisland (In Seven Stages: A Flying Trip Around the World). It was a joy to combine their work and create a novelized version to bring their story back to life for a new generation.

Thanks to the support of my newsletter group! All of you encourage me to keep writing. Gratitude also to my early readers Kristi Doyle, Sarah Chanis, Shawna Shade, and especially Julie Ropelewski who went above and beyond. To my street team: Sydney, Alice, Jen, Sarah, Charity, Emily K., Julianna, Emily M., and Carissa, thank you for your encouragement. To Brandi Stewart, for a final edit and your constant support. To my writing pal Kitty Bucholtz who challenges me to try new things and assured me the path to indie publishing wasn't as dark and scary as it seems.

To my family, maybe now that the book is done I'll quit talking about Liz and Nellie. Maybe. Thanks for your patience while I worked out this fun story. If I ever retrace their route, I'll take you along.

And finally my readers. It would be a much duller life if my stories stayed in my head. The introvert in me finds it nerve-wracking to imagine people reading my stories, but I'm glad you are. Please consider leaving a review to help other readers decide whether to read about the around the world adventure of Liz and Nellie.

**Sign-up for new book release information at
ShonnaSlayton.com.**

About the Author

SHONNA SLAYTON is a YA author who writes historically-based stories. She finds inspiration in reading vintage diaries written by teens, who despite using different slang, sound a lot like teenagers today. When not writing, Shonna enjoys amaretto lattes and spending time with her husband and children in Arizona. Other works include: *Cinderella's Dress* and *Cinderella's Shoes* set in the 1940s; *Spindle*, a Sleeping Beauty inspired tale set in the late 1800s.

also by Shonna Slayton